True Jacob

True Jacob

A Novel

Tom Sriver

2009

FAIR OAKS

Published by Fair Oaks Editions, Kalamazoo, Michigan 49008-2022
U.S.A.

ISBN 0615291376
ISBN 978-0-615-29137-6

The illustration on page 72 courtesy of Friends Historical Library of Swarthmore College; the illustration on page iv is Vincent van Gogh, "Starry Night," Kunsthalle Bremen (Baldin Collection, Moscow); illustrations on pages vi and 324 by George P. Lewis, in *Views of Netherlands India: Series Tosari* (Soerabaya: Kurkojian, *ca* 1910); the illustration on page 160 from Erich Scheurmann, *Samoa: Ein Bilderwerk* (Horn in Baden: Selbst-Verlag E. Scheurmann, [1926]); the illustration on p. 218 shows the Bosscha Observatory at Lembang, Java, in 1924; the illustration on page 341 shows the fireplace at the entrance to the former Macdonald Physics Building, McGill University, Montreal.

Publisher's Statement

True Jacob is a work of fiction. Names, characters, places, incidents, and circumstances, all issue from the author's imagination or have a fictitious use. Resemblance to actual persons, living or dead, to establishments, institutions, corporations, events, situations, or climates, is completely coincidental, except for the following quotation:

"Comme vous avez raison—et comme vous faites oeuvre utile—en mettant ainsi l'accent sur la nécessité pour l'historien d'intégrer consciemment son travail dans l'histoire universelle et l'histoire comparée! Rien de plus dangereux pour toute science—et pour la nôtre notamment (je prends le mot de science dans son acceptation la plus vague)—que le divorce du général et du particulier." Marc Bloch to Henri Pirenne, summer 1931, in Bryce Lyon and Mary Lyon, *The Birth of Annales History: The Letters of Lucien Febvre and Marc Bloch to Henri Pirenne (1921-1935)* (Brussels: Académie Royale de Belgique, Commission Royale d'histoire, 1991), p. 131.

For Thomas Pynchon

James the Apostle preached for harmonizing the Messiah's teachings and Hebrew practice. James was one of the first martyrs. According to tradition, his body was taken to Spain. In 835 AD a star revealed the apostle's grave to Theodomir, Bishop of Iria, who called it San Jacome Apostel of the Campus Stellae. The grave sprouted a town, Santiago de Compostela, which became such an attraction that, in Spanish, the Milky Way is known as El Camino de Santiago. German pilgrims received instructions to stay on the road until they reached the genuine Santiago, and not be distracted by closer shrines of the same name. In this way they would arrive at the True Jacob.

Contents

ACADEMIE GEBOUW. LEIDEN.

J.J. HENS

Part I

Old World

Science is the mode of cognition of the West. It is what gives us the moral authority and physical strength to dominate the world's civilizations. We are in agreement here. It does not follow, however, that Hegel must be abandoned in favor of the sense impressionists. The so-called universal facts of science are mostly something else—technology. Steam engines, airplanes, electrical motors, and machine guns are indeed universally embraced products of Western culture, but they derive from bricolage rather than from profound scientific meditation. In this it is as one of the Rossettis said, "What does it matter to me if the earth moves around the sun or the sun around the earth?" The spirituality of Western scientific thought is quite separate from its reflection in the marketplace or the factory.

Edmund Husserl to Jacob Witte, 3 April 1924, Witte papers,
Boerhaave Museum, Leiden

It is good to learn that you share my notion of technology. Machines are tools for building a new nation. It does not matter who invents something. What matters is what the thing does. And I shall use machines for the people. The Dutch did not provide widespread access to technical studies, but neither did our traditional society demand it. My teachers were clever men. They even taught me, a student of architecture, about the powers of the atom.

Soekarno to Ho Chi-Minh, 4 March 1962, Archives of State,
Bundle 57/34, Ministry of Foreign Affairs, Hanoi

1

A Letter from the Indies

Leiden is a compact, old town. The university is spread out in a number of buildings, each one on a canal. Kamerlingh-Onnes's physics institute is one of the biggest operations. There are about twenty students working on research projects, all using liquid nitrogen. I attended the low-temperature "tea," a weekly meeting where people speak about their work. Atypically, the theoretician Lorentz spoke about electron transport in metals. There was a young Russian in the audience, Ehrenfest, who is said to be Lorentz's successor. His entire body seemed to be aflame, glowing and waving this way and that. This is the spirit of physics here. After the talk we were served black tea from the Indies by a beautiful woman physics student.

Jun Ishiwara to Hantaro Nagaoka, 4 November 1912,
Physics series, A 4/12, Graduate Library of the University of Tokyo

Jacob Witte's truant fingers sorted papers into various boxes. He worked in the cool and damp of May, swaddled in a woolen gown. There was not much time. Paper flashed up to reveal a sequence of quanta, some large, others small, a synchronic archaeology of calculations, projects unrealized, professional and intimate correspondence. Several pages of tensor calculus flew across the room and settled on the floor, taking the form of bird tracks. Jacob caught the ciphers from the corner of his eye, as a cyclist might take in, for an instant, trackings on the road ahead. They escaped judgment and could be granted neither preservation nor memory. Virtual realities, from the moment of their apprehension they ceased to exist. Jacob saw his life as scores of vaguely connected sequences or strands, thick and thin, short and long, a magpie's nest of bright and faded colors. The remote past lived alongside yesterday in separate boxes.

Jacob's eyes rested for a moment on a package that had arrived the previous week. He had gone through its contents then. Now the package was wrapped once more in its layers of heavy waxed paper, a stuffed cabbage whose top leaf showed ten weeks of customs declarations and labels in Dutch, French, and English. The recent past could not be judged, he thought, merely acted upon. The great paradox of life was that, in achieving distance and equanimity, one lost the ability to act.

A thumbnail scraped the surface of the desk. Jacob stood up and walked to the window. His pocketwatch read 15h. A hopeless task. The street was quiet on each bank of the canal, as if the small university town were between terms. Shops were deserted or closed. An occasional bicycle catapulted the bowed bridge that led to his laboratory. He saw a motor launch mooring under the bridge, sail furled and mast stepped-down, a figure in a fisherman's smock at its helm. Jacob looked up toward the horizon, as he had so often over the past lustrum when puzzling over a peculiar set of data. The small cloud that had first appeared earlier in the day was now a black anvil. Much of Rotterdam, he imagined, had been incinerated. He wondered if the meteorologists at De Bilt were documenting it from their observation tower, if meteorologists were still there, if De Bilt still existed.

He heard unfamiliar steps enter the room. He did not acknowledge the figure, whom he knew by her breathing. She had never before worn lug-soled boots in his study.

"Henk is here with the boat," she said.

"Yes."

She looked at the mess around the room. "Which of them are ready to go?"

Jacob looked behind him. Were your last hours like this, he wondered, when, faced with the confusion and comedy of a lifetime, you try to make sense of it all? But in death everything remained behind. How could you possibly decide, in an afternoon, between the essential and the superfluous? His past engulfed him, as a heavy surf would thunder over a skiff sent out to bring in a drowning man. He was on the skiff, he thought. He had been through worse. He summoned up one part of his life to leave it, and then found himself abandoned to a newsreel without a narrator. He saw the stone steps in Utrecht where his wife, hurrying to catch a train, lost her balance.

"Father." The young woman with whitish-blond hair, faintly flecked in red, had spoken. Jacob stared at his desk. A dark wooden carving of Ganeça, the wise elephant deity, anchored a pile of barely sorted correspondence against the breeze. The top letter hummed, the rebab drone in a *gamelan* orchestra. The doves, as women singers invisible behind the window's proscenium, softly ridiculed the man in a heavy gown. The door downstairs slammed open with the sudden knock, the sharp concussion punctuating the story told by the *gamelan*'s narrator. A woman sang.

"Ica will help me clear everything away." Ica, the housekeeper, had complete responsibility for the house. Finally, there was not much value to the paper scattered around the room. The letters of a lifetime carried little significance, Jacob thought. He had never corresponded intensely with the professional colleagues he respected most. For the rest, even when a genuine idea or emotion was called up, it generally found an inaccurate representation. Jacob abandoned his task. The boxes hung open, their flaps gesturing in broad supplication. Unsorted papers sang from the desk.

"I'm coming," he answered and circled back to stand between his chair and desk. With his left hand he picked up his thin briefcase, packed with a summary of work-in-progress. His right hand entwined the cord that circled the package with instructions in three languages. The package and the current work would go to England with his children. He was too old, too closely tied to Leiden, and the physics institute needed him. The breeze blew back his robe, a pretense worn in defiance of what was happening to his country. With his arms at his side, each one ending in a large object, the effect was of a condor ready to take flight.

"You look like you could fly through the window," the young woman said.

"Today I'm a water bird."

Jacob turned and headed down the steeply pitched stair. The package being larger and a great deal heavier than his briefcase, he led with his right hand. The thought came, How fortunate that I picked things up in the order I did, for the staircase is a right-handed screw. On the large second-floor landing he cast a glance into the room that had been his and his wife's in their last year together. He felt her just out of sight, adjusting an earring.

Hesje Witte-Boomstra always wore earrings, even in bed. She had shared Jacob's life in physics. She began medicine in Groningen as a commuting student, living in her parents' modest apartment twenty kilometers distant. The arrangement was time-consuming and awkward, and it placed intolerable strain on her father, who was the local mayor. Hesje Boomstra decided in any event that she cared less for the practical Aristotelian compromises of medicine than for the pure Platonic forms of physics. She became tutor to the children of a Leiden merchant and began studying physics at the local university. She gravitated to the low-temperature laboratory of Willem Kamerlingh-Onnes, where students could work as paid assistants. As the laboratory's only woman, she served tea at the afternoon colloquia. There she met Jacob Witte. He finished a doctorate, issued a great ream of print on both experimental physics and Neohegelian philosophy, and found various junior teaching posts until, in 1919, he was tapped to direct the physics laboratory of the new *technische hoogeschool*, or institute of technology known as TH, at Bandung, on central Java. Hesje and their two children followed. There Hesje, who had abandoned a doctorate to start a family, became Jacob's assistant. The couple published together.

He wanted to hold a pair of earrings, but he continued around the landing and down to the entrance hall. The staircase here was wide enough to accommodate his descent with some dignity.

His son waited by the door, two suitcases in hand.

"Hi, Jaap." When he was young, Henk often addressed his father with a diminutive. As he grew up, he kept the form of address as a prelude to intimate and optimistic conversation.

"Aye-aye, Skipper," Jacob raised his briefcase to his chest in mock salute and laughed. "Nice afternoon for an ocean cruise."

"You just leave everything to me," Henk replied. Jacob followed him. The young woman in heavy boots formed the end of the procession. She wore woolen trousers and an anorak. She carried two suitcases and an overstuffed rucksack. On the cobblestone quay they faced a boomerang-shaped puddle left by the brief morning rain; the Wehrmacht had for the most part enjoyed magnificent May sunshine. Henk sloshed through the puddle in his knee-high rubber boots. Jacob tried a leap. He swung the masses in his hands in imitation of Greek jumpers portrayed on an urn in the local museum and wound up with his left foot soaked to the ankle. His academic robe absorbed a good part of the splash. The young woman watched her father, smiled, and crossed the puddle near the boomerang's tip.

Jacob had grown up as a farmer's son near 's Hertogenbosch, and he stubbornly called the eight-meter yacht a boat. He was proud of his son's interest in sailing, which had blossomed after the family returned from Java to settle in Leiden. Jacob had bought the yacht for his son three years previously, as a diversion from his architectural studies at Delft, and Henk had spent much of his time and cash on it since then. The boat had become an object of special devotion over the preceding eight months, after Henk had been rejected by the Dutch army in its general mobilization because his left leg was slightly shorter than his right one. In a previous incarnation, the boat had been converted, bizarrely, as a coastal fishing trawler. Henk stripped it to its bones, installed a reconditioned motor, and slowly rebuilt the rigging. In the summer of 1939 he had pieced together some sails and taken the yacht on runs up and down the coast. He had not yet rebuilt the cabin, so the yacht was really just a shell. The bow corner was wood, and three meters behind the mast had a wooden deck as well. Canvas covered the gap between the mast and the bow.

The family stowed their belongings under the wooden deck. Henk started the motor and cast off. He held the tiller. Jacob and the young woman arranged themselves for the two-hour's trip to the far side of a bridge where they would stop to set up the mast and prepare for open water. She wedged herself against the wooden half-deck on Henk's left. Jacob sat close to Henk's right. He made sure that he touched the large package with his dry foot.

The young woman, Joanneke Witte, shared her father's detachment about sailing. The motion did not bother her. The smell and the spray and the confinement did. Arriving in the Netherlands in 1935 after having spent her formative years on Java, Anneke was still not comfortable with the flat landscape and the sea's weather. She loved the Javan mountains and highlands, the lush tropical smells, seasons that passed gently from one into the other. Since arriving in Europe, her form of adventure was with the alpinists. There she found a reflection of the dramatic vistas that she had known, and the variation in ecology with altitude. The open fires and the star-studded heavens reminded her of Bandung. There was nothing like spending the night out with a close friend under mountain skies, she concluded. Henk found exhilaration in commanding the destiny of his vessel, but, in the view of his sister, experiencing changes in wind and waves was not sufficient reward for vigilantly monitoring them. A yacht under full sail was not unpleasant for her to contemplate, though the notion of a race had always struck her as artificial.

The peculiarly dressed family glided by the building that housed Jacob's laboratory. It was in an annex to the observatory. The astronomers rather liked him, and the birds of a feather found much to talk about together. The quarters were to have been temporary. His theoretician predecessor had kept only a small office in the experimental physics institute, and, in the years before his suicide, he had hardly ever been there. Jacob was called from Bandung in 1935 to infuse new life into the post. From his cosmic-ray research, which had garnered him a nomination for the Nobel prize, he was as much at home in theory as in experiment. He was also the foremost Dutch philosopher of science, having authored several large works on the epistemological significance of the quantum theory. The idea had been for him to set up a program in nuclear physics. Funding would depend on his ability to persuade industrialists and traders that there were practical and emotional rewards to be had from a Dutch cyclotron. Jacob knocked on doors for five years, but there was no money for his laboratory. He was determined to have his big machine, however, and late in 1939 he had returned to Java to arrange for repatriation of the laboratory's intended centerpiece, an enormous magnet that, in the 1920s, had formed part of the Poulsen generator establishing the first direct wireless contact between Bandung and the motherland. It was near Bandung, at the Bosscha astronomical observatory, that Jacob had heard from an old astronomer colleague. What the man said would transport the Netherlands to the pinnacle of physics.

Jacob boxed up the magnet and sent it on its long voyage home, but his thoughts went beyond this project. The magnet would give him a relatively large atom smasher, if he could manage to assemble everything else required to make it work, but his effort was really a sideshow compared to what the Americans were mounting. The astronomer had revealed something much more promising. Even without installing his magnet in Leiden, the Netherlands could have the world's finest nuclear physics program. Jacob placed his shoe against the package at his feet. The proof was all there.

He imagined the giant magnet, rounding the Cape of Good Hope, ballast in the hold of a latter-day Flying Dutchman. Which port of call would receive it? With the Netherlands having fallen to Germany, merchant ships would divert to friendly ports. Suppose the cargo were unloaded at Cape Town. Would anyone think to construct a cyclotron in South Africa?

The destiny of a large magnet concerned Jacob less than the

package at his feet. The report was unambiguous, although the author did not recognize its full significance. What had been discovered on Java would change the course of history. It would be up to the physicists at Cambridge to use the information wisely.

The yacht passed under a bridge and then into the shadow of the university's convocation hall. Anneke had been to an official function there once, to hear her father's inaugural address. His had been a general survey of Western physical thought, culminating in the new epistemology of Niels Bohr. Anneke, then in her last year of *gymnasium*, had heard much of it before. She thought, as the yacht emerged into the afternoon sun, that it was probably at base the same text that Jacob had begun preparing in 1922, when, after two years at Bandung, he thought that he would be named to a chair of philosophy at Leiden. But the curators had overturned the faculty's recommendation, and the government appointed a theologian to the vacancy. How odd it seemed to her that someone like her father, who had spent the best fifteen years of his professional life on Java, should have absorbed virtually nothing of the Hindu, Buddhist, Muslim, Chinese, and animist legacies there. Oriental philosophy, insofar as she had looked into it, offered just the right way of thinking about notions of complementarity and indeterminacy, insofar as she understood them.

Anneke had for as long as she could remember been interested in the mixture of cultures on Java. She spoke Low Sundanese and knew enough High Sundanese to enjoy an evening of *wayang purwa*, the traditional puppet show that, with its voices, orchestra, conventions, and spontaneity, struck her as the equal of the best Western operas. Malay, the new language promoted by nationalist students as Bahasa Indonesia, came to her naturally, for since she was a girl she had been going to events run by the student union, "Ganeça." It was, furthermore, the language of the young men who haunted the tennis courts, and she was the best tennis player in Bandung. She had thought, four years previously, that she would study Oriental philology at Leiden. On the shores of the North Sea, however, the subject became dry and abstract, the pursuit of scholar-pedants. She turned to what she thought would be closest to life, medicine. It too was a caricature of the living world, but, perhaps because physicians so irrationally resisted abandoning their art form to the formulas of chemists and the contraptions of physicists, human beings never seemed far from what she was studying. When it came time to specialize, she chose psychiatry. Most people she knew were a bit neurotic.

As her father carried his papers and his strange parcel, so Anneke took along, in her rucksack, what she thought was important. Her medical bag and microscope gave it a boxy appearance. There was no room for books or dictionaries, but she spoke English, French, and German, and she knew England to be the land of lending libraries. A few smaller items were wedged here and there in the sack. She packed it as if for a weekend outing in the mountains.

The yacht moved north. Their goal, some thirty kilometers distant, was the canal linking Amsterdam with the North Sea. Nothing had been touched here, Jacob noted, inside Fortress Holland—the northern part of the country defended by canals and troops. The dikes and locks were intact. Rotterdam was apparently an object lesson. The Germans wanted to rob the country, not raze it. It seemed a bit like a quiet holiday, except for how people moved about. The Dutch were a purposeful people, Jacob thought, a characteristic interpreted by foreigners as being dull and plodding. On the first day of the invasion, bus drivers continued their routes, stopping only for German strafing.

Henk was in his element. Two years younger than his sister, he had absorbed his father's Eurocentrism. He had no clear childhood memories of anything except Indonesia, even though he had been born in Delft, but for him, as for his parents, Bandung was just a step on the road to civilization and Holland. On vacations, and during his father's sabbatical in 1927, he had come to know his homeland, and he readily abandoned himself to it. Jacob had arranged for Henk to take courses at the TH from the time that he was fifteen. Henk liked science and especially engineering, and he did well in them. When the family returned to Leiden, Henk, at age eighteen, was more than ready for advanced work in engineering at Delft. He decided that what he loved most about Holland was its architecture, and so that was what he studied. In January he had become a licensed builder. He could build things in England, he thought, but it would not be the same.

His tongue rimmed the sandy mustache that drooped the corners of his mouth, a reassuring gesture. He had done his best to prepare for the crossing. There were two small drums of petrol, enough to carry the yacht fifty or so kilometers. A large, olive-drab can, belonging at some point to the British army, was filled with water. It was more than they would need, but Henk thought that it might provide the yacht with stability. Water was free, anyway, and Henk had been able to fill and stow the can quickly. A sack contained some cheese, a tin of biscuits, apples, and chocolate. The contents of the shed near the yacht's slip rounded out its manifest: bits of rope and sail, fittings, awls, chisels, saws, shears, wrenches, tins of paint and varnish, a warped boom. There was no reason not to take the stuff. It was Henk's contribution.

They encountered a fishing ship returning home. Jacob saw the crew cleaning its catch. The men had been out for days, he thought, for no one would have set off in the face of an invasion. There were still commercial vessels without a wireless, and it might be that some had left port before learning the awful news. The Wittes had no receiver on board. Jacob wondered what else they did not have. They were not wearing life vests. They had no binoculars. He had not taken gloves, and although the engine gave off some heat, there was no portable stove. He wanted to know if Henk had taken along flares. He pursed his lips. It would do no good to ask now. Other ships were cruising the inland waterways, but Jacob wondered, as he saw the mouth of the North Sea Canal, if his vessel alone would follow the setting sun. A number of large and small ships, tied up at docks, showed little activity. Perhaps most people would stay home.

The yacht passed under the last bridge before the sea. Henk wondered if it could be seen as a military objective. No sense in taking chances. He guided his craft along the north bank for half a kilometer before he shut down the engine and made fast to a pile rising three meters above the water.

"That wasn't too bad," he announced to his father. "Now for a bit of sailing." He stood on the half-deck and unwrapped the lines that had secured the five-meter mast, a single length of Norwegian fir. Henk had it simply rigged to carry a mainsail and jib. The mast shed its rope and Henk maneuvered to catch its base in the well. The yacht pitched on a swell and Jacob saw mast's length flashing in the afternoon sun. The varnish that Henk had been so proud to apply everywhere did not serve their best interests now.

Anneke had not moved since they entered the large canal. Her elbows rested on her lap. The muscles in her arms were tense and beginning to quiver. She knew that to be her passive reaction to an emotional situation, like watching a theatre production. She did not think that she was afraid, but her senses were heightened, as when she would get her gear in order at the bottom of a long rock face.

"Would you hold the base against the well while I edge a bit up this cliff?" She felt relieved to act on Henk's request and scrambled up to crouch on the half-deck. Henk held the thinner end of the mast and stepped from the bow to the pile. He picked his way toward the center of the yacht along a beam halfway up the pile. The mast rose above the pile's top.

"This is the first time I've seen you mountain climb," Anneke called. Henk looked not unlike several of her alpinist companions. She guessed that he had a high ape index, what she called the ratio of the distance between the fingertips of outstretched arms and straight-up height. There was grace and fluidity in his movements. He was not an insect against a wall, as some of her medical-student girlfriends had been when following their lovers up the heights; in time he could develop into a mountain animal. On a rock face, the same as in a yacht, his limp meant nothing. A swell rolled the yacht toward the pile, enabling Henk to drop the mast into its hole. He climbed down and attached the boom.

"Let's have a bite to eat, Jaap," Henk began. "We have time to kill before sundown." Jacob looked at his pocket watch. That would be an hour and a half. The trip to the sea had been quicker than anticipated.

"Yes." Usually he loved to talk with his son about deep or intense matters, but he thought now that the less said, the better it would be. The decision to leave had been taken by the entire family in anticipation of an invasion, but he and Anneke really carried Henk along. Jacob's return to Leiden made him aware of dozens of displaced Jewish scientists. Early on Jacob had landed a good position for one, but others, equally talented, scrounged temporary jobs of any kind or accepted charity. Anneke's excursions to Switzerland took her up the Rhine, and she saw the Nazi cancer consuming the nation. An enormous contrast grew between the endpoints of her journey and the frightening train ride on the middle part. On the train, unlike on the mountainside, she had no control of her destiny. Henk did not bring these feelings to the issue. He was swayed by reason. Any deep discussion now, Jacob thought, could only erode his son's confidence and conviction. Much depended on Henk's skills.

Henk opened the food sack and handed the biscuit tin to his father. He placed the wedge of Gouda on the heavy glass pane that sat, hinged, on the wooden engine housing just behind the marine compass. Henk had installed it to allow the tillerman to read maps placed beneath the glass. He had not had time to make the thing watertight. Now it served as an elegant cheeseboard. He placed his small fishing knife next to it. Then came three chunks of chocolate and three apples. The yacht pitched and an apple rolled off to disappear under the half-deck.

Jacob opened the tin, placed it next to the cheese, and then squeezed forward to retrieve a suitcase. He placed it on the half-deck, rummaged around a bit, and came up with a pair of Anneke's woolen socks. He hitched up his robe, hoisted himself on the half-deck, and proceeded to unlace his left shoe. His foot was warm, but he wanted to change. Anneke and Henk both smiled at his labor. Jacob wore high, laced-up shoes, normal enough in his youth but now an oddity.

Henk wanted a drink. He wrestled the large tank upright and opened its mouth. Then he realized that he had forgotten a cup. He looked around. Anneke had not followed.

"Lady and gentleman," Henk announced, "I hope there are no objections to drinking as our friends the elephants do."

"I have something that will help," Anneke said. She opened an outside pocket of her rucksack and presented Henk with a battered tin cup. Henk looked beyond to see candles and a box of matches in the pocket.

"What else does your rucksack hold?" he asked.

"Tools of the trade," Anneke answered guardedly.

Jacob finished lacing up his shoe. The suitcase went back under the half-deck, damp socks balled up in one of its corners. He returned to his place and started in on the cheese and biscuits.

Anneke did not feel much like eating, but thought that she should anyway. She was getting tired of the pitch and the roll. She gnawed off a corner of chocolate, and then her stomach rebelled. She excused herself and clabbered up the pile to its top. It was spattered in guano with the appearance of marbled candy. She strode to the far side, out of sight to the men below and, she thought, the other boats nearby. She dropped her trousers and pants and squatted. She was careful to use only her left hand, as she always did for private bodily functions. It was a Javan cultural practice that she had adopted as sensible and, in circumstances like these, practical.

She stood up and looked south. She detected a smudge on the horizon and wondered if it was Rotterdam's incineration. A speck in the air drew her scrutiny. The Germans had controlled the air for four days, since the invasion. A plane, or a bird? It disappeared from sight.

When she descended to the yacht she found her father and brother discussing how to repack for the crossing. It was the first extended conversation of the voyage, and it was uncharacteristic of the interlocutors. Henk proposed, and Jacob nodded ready agreement. Jacob's parcel caught Anneke's eye. Part of the wrapping was soaked.

"Father, what about your package?"

"Oh, there's a box inside."

"But the papers," Anneke assumed that the package contained papers, "they would be ruined by a leak." Jacob paused. Those papers must tell some story, Anneke thought. "Look, my rucksack can expand to take your package and your briefcase." The rucksack had a liner that, turned out, doubled its length. It was designed for use as an enormous sock in an emergency bivouac. Anneke had never opened it out of doors before. She pulled the liner up, trying to leave the contents of the rucksack undisturbed. As she pulled on the front part, a heavy, cylindrical object slid out and dropped at her feet. The object was wrapped in dark cloth.

"Just what we need, Joke," Henk laughed, "a hand cannon." He used the diminutive from the time when they were small children. Anneke had rejected it when she was eight or nine. Jacob tensed the corners of his mouth for a moment. Henk's use of the nickname was involuntary. Jacob looked at the oblong object. It was the wrong shape for a firearm, whatever Henk meant by the remark.

Anneke showed no sign of resentment about the name. "Soekarno's kris," she said. Henk smiled. Jacob raised his eyebrows.

Soekarno had been one of the most articulate of Jacob's students at the Bandung TH. His schoolteacher father, nominally a Muslim but known as a free-thinker, gave Soekarno elementary instruction in East Java and then arranged for him to study at the Dutch secondary school in Soerabaya. There he fell under the spell of Tjokroaminoto, the nationalist leader with whom he boarded. Upon receiving a diploma, Soekarno headed for the TH. He brought in tow Tjokroaminoto's fifteen-year-old daughter, the object of a *kawin gatung*, or "hung marriage"—a formal declaration of allegiance for which consummation was postponed due to, generally, the immaturity of a partner. Soekarno, at any rate, matured at the TH. He divorced his child bride to marry the wife of his Bandung landlord. His involvement with the nationalist cause deepened, and with it rose his interest in women, especially non-Javan women. He loved them and left them, all across Java and the nearby islands. One of the most highly educated Javans, his proficiency in engineering found an outlet in organizing mass resistance to Dutch rule. He was arrested in the early 1930s, and then released. The fifteenth anniversary yearbook of the TH, published in 1935 when the Wittes returned to Leiden, provided an alumni register. Soekarno's occupation and whereabouts were passed over in silence; he was serving a long prison sentence for sedition.

Anneke knew Soekarno from the tennis courts. She first became aware of him in 1925, during his final year as a student. He was a flamboyant and winning player. She was an impressionable, flaxen, blue-eyed eleven-year-old. She played with him a number of times that year. Over the next several years, Soekarno remained in Bandung. Events allowed him to forge a united front of nationalist parties. He kept up his tennis game, and Anneke became a regular, if informal, partner of his. She had more time for the sport and fewer consuming side interests. By 1929, she regularly trounced him, and all other comers. They had never talked much, and certainly not politics. One day he came to her with an elaborately wrapped package. He told her that he greatly admired her game, he greatly admired her as a person, as a woman. He said that he would probably soon be arrested for slandering the government. He offered her a token of his esteem. It was a kris in a leather sheath. Anneke apprised the situation as payment in advance for future favors. She was flattered and uncertain, but accepted the gift. There was no question of keeping it a secret from her parents. Ten days later Soekarno was taken into custody.

Anneke took the kris from its cloth casing, pulled off its sheath, and placed it next to Henk's fishing instrument on the glass tabletop. They all stared at the two different kinds of knife, the one multipurpose and practical, the other ritualistic and ornamental. Henk's was short and thin, with a slight curve to the point, a saw-toothed scaler on the spine, and a cork handle; a cheesy film reflected dully on the blade. Soekarno's gift was a representative of its genus: an undulating blade, hand-forged in the manner of Wagner's operatic smithies, anchored in a short pistol grip. The metal, built up from dozens of folds, exhibited a memory: Its hysteresis could be read from the patterns of carbon or nickel alloyed steel left by each layer. The kris was a thrusting, offensive weapon quite unsuited for the grim task of hand-to-hand combat. It lacked balance, and it left completely unprotected the hand that guided it. It was useless around a kitchen, as it was unable to scale or debone fish or cut cheese. Anneke thought that this particular piece of bygone Indonesia would have been a cheap way to win her virtue. Soekarno's kris lacked gold overlay. The handle was severely plain. The widest part of the blade bore an Arabic inscription. The giver had added the weight of his name to the iron that had been wrought and fired, folded, beaten, and annealed six generations earlier.

"What has become of our dear Soekarno?" Anneke wondered aloud.

Anneke returned the kris to its protective sheathing and held it for a moment. She had brought it as a gesture of defiance, or rather bravado. She wanted to stick it through her belt against the small of her back, as prescribed by the etiquette of Javan royalty. That would be silly, evident to no one under her anorak and uncomfortable in view of the long journey ahead. Slip it between her shin and a woolen sock, Scottish style? She settled for inserting it upright into a zippered pocket on her anorak just behind the right sleeve. Its bulk was evident but unobtrusive. She hardly felt it.

They cleared the engine housing of food and finished stowing the gear and baggage. Mostly this meant wrapping things in canvas and securing them with rope to something solid on the yacht's frame. Anneke reckoned that her rucksack was more impervious to water than Henk's canvas sheets. As she picked it up she caught her father's long gaze. He thinks I'm silly for the kris. But he is also sending something from Java to England. She felt the slight pressure of the thickly-wrapped kris against her right side and thought to fasten her rucksack where Jacob could see it. She wedged it between two starboard ribs just under the half-deck. There Henk had substituted mahagony inserts for several short courses of rotten oak planking. Anneke tied the bunched top of the rucksack's extension into an eyebolt that protruded from the higher insert.

They settled down to wait until dusk. Henk was uncomfortable at the thought of bobbing beside the pile for another hour. The wind was just right at the moment to send them clear of land in an hour. The sea was relatively calm. Insofar as he knew, the weather promised to be fair over the next day. He twisted his hands together and tongued his moustache. If we leave now we might well land in Suffolk or Essex while there was still light tomorrow. He did not have English hydrology charts. It would be dangerous to come up on an unknown coastline in the dark.

Jacob surveyed the southern sky. He saw neither smoke nor planes. No other ships had cast off. Henk's fidgeting concerned him. Henk was sharp now, a sprinter preparing to brace against his starting blocks. An hour would scrape the edge away and rock him into an aberrant state of nervous anticipation or sluggish withdrawal. He looked at Anneke, sunk into her corner and eyeing the compass as it pivoted in response to the yacht's motion. It was clear how she viewed the prospect of thirty hours on the North Sea. He closed the top of his robe and motioned to his son. The Germans might bomb everyone huddled together at the canal's mouth. It would be better to sail on the open sea.

"What do you say about casting off, Skipper? There is an appointment to keep."

Henk started the motor and nosed the yacht a hundred meters into the bight. He cut the engine. The foresheet went up, and then the mainsail. He lashed the boom to run before the land breeze that bore down from the northeast. It might take them ten kilometers out.

Jacob scanned the horizon for smoke. The sun, low in the sky, was away to the north. The south radiated immediate danger. A ship or plane from the south would have difficulty spotting the yacht in the direction of the setting sun. He wondered if Amsterdam was occupied. Would the Germans sweep south to gird the country? Low-flying fighters would lead such a maneuver, or, perhaps, fast coastal patrol boats. There was no sign of either.

He rested his eyes on Anneke. Nestled in her corner she was studying the sky. Anneke was the reflective one. Jacob remembered mornings when he would stand at the back door leading into their Delft garden, watching Anneke talk to the flowers and birds. The sound and cadence of the child's voice became for him, from that time on, nature's voice. Before the birth of his children he thought that nature resonated in the concatenated shells of Neohegelian dialectic, and that the road to truth was paved in Germanic sentences that repeated and qualified themselves. During his early years at Bandung he delivered talks in this vein because it was expected of him in his role as an ambassador of European civilization. But watching Anneke grow had removed conviction from these lessons. While he measured and pondered cosmic rays from his Bandung laboratory, he sought to keep pace, in his research, with Anneke's development. He tried to approach nature with the wonderment of a child, asking the sky the questions Anneke would ask him, probing in different directions at once, as a child probed in a garden. Although fact-gathering, the process was not Baconian; it was organic without being dialectically convoluted. His had been an interior journey. As he grew older, he felt that he floated through a mixture of big and small particles, a Brownian motion that, oddly enough, revealed a rudimentary structure.

Anneke was lost in the sky. A few dark clouds tracked by in the direction of the sail's bow. Above them, thousands of kilometers deep and almost fixed, were ranks of white feathers. A gull flew across the progress of the low clouds, craning its head toward land. She stretched her arms along the half-deck and gunwale, arms as two sides of a square, and abandoned herself to the yacht's rhythm. Forward progress stopped, and she found herself suspended, inverted, looking down on two layers of clouds. She imagined a speck just obscured by a white feather's wisp, the yacht she was on, moving through an endless sea of blue. Her eyes, emanating her father's cosmic rays, focused to resolve the invisible vessel on its voyage of discovery. The boom swung round to nudge her head. She fell directly down and gasped into her father's gaze.

"Are the heavens like a flower garden?" Jacob asked his daughter. He had seen Anneke slip away into nature and longed to know what she felt.

"I was the sky, looking down on us."

Jacob felt a tingle on the back of his neck as he took in her visionary radiance. He did not feel what she had experienced. He sensed a pale reflection of her reality, a pulsing mass of indistinct outlines and vaguely luminous color. He saw in her face a quantum atom, whose constituent elements throbbed with probable existence, where flashes of radiation emerged unpredictably. But he felt sure that her face would never transmute into another face, as an atom of uranium could. It was the same child's face he first knew.

"I imagined we were traveling to England. Father, do you think it will be hard for me to practice there?" She wanted to say, "Do you think we will arrive safely?" But she decided to transform her uncertainty into a safely hypothetical question.

"England has a long tradition of women professionals. Special university colleges are reserved for women. There are women writers and professors and fellows of the Royal Society. Yes, women have thrown themselves under the king's horse to bring attention to their cause, but I am sure you will not have to do that." Jacob stuck to generalities. He did not know much about the medical profession and nothing about medicine in England.

"I am fond of Virginia Woolf," Anneke said. "How nice it would be to meet her. Do you know, in one of her books she talks about a woman isolated by the sea, and in another a woman's husband is always off sailing on a ridiculous quest. The sea is so much more special to her than the mountains, which never make a proper appearance. They are strong and sensitive, Virginia's women, I mean. I used to think of them as models for what I wanted to become."

Jacob nodded dutifully. He did not know about Virginia Woolf or any other English wolves. The English were fond of fox hunting, and he had seen canvases of fat English lords in full cry across the countryside—*their* countryside. The Dutch aristocracy were not like that. Their extravagance allowed them to sample the vices of a dozen foreign cultures, leaving the polders and canals and towns to those they ruled. Jacob was not much of a sportsman. He would excuse himself when, in the Indies, the opportunity came up to hunt tigers on Sumatra or dragons on Komodo. What pleasure was there in mutilating a sentient creature and watching insects plunge into its blood as life ebbed away?

Did his children know how much he loved them? He told them so as often as he could, but did they know that he meant it? They would be parted for a long time, maybe longer than ever before. He depended on them so very much, but they had now grown up, and it was time for them to carry on in their own way. Anyway, England was a good place to spend a few years.

They reached the last breakwater.

"Good-bye," Jacob said. He hugged each of his children and kissed them. "Good-bye," they said. Jacob scrambled up the jetty as Henk shoved off. Jacob waved and watched as they sailed into the sun.

The sun, an orange-red disk, danced on the horizon. It projected a white shaft on the sea in the distance. The shaft broke up into sharp scintillations on the tops of waves as Henk followed it to the side of his yacht. The wind was steady, and the yacht ran smoothly. Holland disappeared astern. Henk threw his elbows back and tucked his chin to straighten out his spine and relax the place where, had he been a dolphin, his dorsal fin would have emerged. He stretched out his legs and flexed the small of his back. Would Venus be out when the sun set, he wondered? He did not know the stars—Venus, the Big Bear, and Orion being about all he could identify in the night sky. He had grown up not far from several large telescopes on a hilltop near Bandung. His father was good friends with the director of that observatory, and the two families not infrequently went on outings together. Henk found the astronomer distant, unsympathetic, and a bit looney. He stood in the wings of his father's celestial vision, but, perhaps because he took the astronomer to be the distilled essence of the high heavens, he grew shy of the stars. He was comfortable with things anchored in the ground, like buildings, or floating on the surface of the water.

Henk did not know the first thing about celestial navigation, and the matter of precisely where they would land had given him trouble whenever he contemplated the eventuality of their unorthodox emigration. An atlas revealed King's Lynn as one of the large towns closest to Holland. He was not sure why it had acquired a royal appositive instead of a regal prefix (to distinguish it from King Lynn, a cousin of King Ludd, or maybe from King Wilhelm, the German emperor who lived exiled in the Netherlands). The apostrophe ess came to rest in his memory as having an affinity with the genitive prow attached to the town where his grandparents lived, 's Hertogenbosch. King's Lynn sat on a broad bay called, simply, the Wash. Henk figured that he would raise the Wash if he headed due west by compass. But no matter if they missed it. England formed a thousand-kilometer barrier just over the horizon.

Henk's bladder signaled to void the water that he drank earlier. He fastened the tiller in place with two short lines and stood to face his native land. He raised his smock. He unbuttoned his fly and pulled out his penis. He held it in both hands and watched as it sent out a yellow-white arc, not without some side splashes. Anneke looked on with a smile. A drop in the bucket here, but with such bravado. Male alpinists would piss like that, too, standing, over a ledge or down a precipitous slope, their wastewater an insignificant arc next to the adjacent mountain cascades. Nature had made women much more sensible about these matters. Such a ridiculous gesture. On Java men pissed from a squat.

They heard the plane as it opened fire.

It had come up out of the south and dropped down to strafe the yacht. The sail obscured it to Anneke and Henk, who both faced a concave wall of white. Henk turned to face the sound over his right shoulder, his hands still guiding the tool at work. He saw a blurred mass centered on a thick line. Near where the mass joined the line, there were regular flashes of light.

When Anneke heard the guns she twisted from her corner and into the line of impact. The boom splintered behind, and she felt a sharp tug at her anorak. Glass shattered in front of her and bits of wood flew into the air from starboard. The plane passed overhead. She watched it hang in the air and grow smaller and softer, a dragonfly slowly humming between a red orb on the horizon and the darkening horizon that wrapped around the yacht's stern. Anneke was drenched cold and hot. Her heart thundered in her ears. Henk faced her, mouth open and white. His penis had shrunk to the size of a large pimple, and his hands no longer touched it. His testicles had fled up against his empty bladder. Then he fell.

The yacht lost the wind. Its progress slackened. Anneke's eyes passed to her chest and neck. They were coated in a splatter of blood. She fingered through and around the anorak. There was a large rip down the right side under the arm, exposing the blade of Soekarno's kris. She felt no pain at all. The kris had parried the bullets.

Henk slumped against the starboard ribs. Bright red blood flowed from his neck. Anneke's eyes rested on the source of the torrent. She stretched across broken glass to blot it with his sweater. A shard had made a five-centimeter incision on his neck. It was still embedded there, a fingernail of blue-green crystal against red and black. When it hit the carotid artery, blood had sprayed across the deck, the sail, and Anneke. She pulled the fragment from Henk's neck, and a new surge of bleeding began. She moved to cradle his head in her lap, a wad of sodden black framing the relaxed face. What to do? Surgery—concern about nicking an artery or being unable to return to the body what had been festooned over retractors and white linen—had directed Anneke to her superficial specialty. What could be done now, here, to someone she had lived with her entire life, whose mind was closing and whose pulse wound down, the pendulum's regulator swinging inexorably through smaller arcs, destined to stop after its weights touched ground? She thought wildly to clamp off the tube and sew it together.

She sought her medical bag in the rucksack, stepping around the engine housing, crunching shards underfoot. She pulled wildly at the sack's canvas straps. A bit of seawater washed in. She pulled harder. The sack moved half a meter and then stopped. More water ran in. Her hands sought the sack's closure. A thin line, taut, passed through a gap in the yacht's side that descended nearly to the waterline. The far end of the line still engaged a fitting solidly anchored in a mahogany plank, but the plank swung freely over the side. Anneke saw that it was the longer, top course. The shorter, second course was gone. The rucksack itself was mostly empty. A large-caliber bullet had knocked out the wooden patch. The rucksack would have gone with it over the side, but Anneke's microscope box had caught against the irregular hole. The medical bag and Jacob's package were gone, ripped out of the rucksack's extension.

Anneke was crying. She rocked her brother's head. She could not feel a pulse in his neck. Liters of blood had issued from his neck, and then printed a batik on the front and arms of Anneke's shadowed anorak. She looked at the man's face, with incipient beard, shaded from the ruby, three-quartered circle of sun behind them. She was staring down the wrong end of a telescope. Her brother and her hands grew smaller as she felt herself rising up against the low clouds, floating with them, considering this inverted, transformed *pietà* of man and woman, smelling of bilge and salt and bobbed by the slap of the sea. Her head expanded into the hallucination that she had experienced whenever, as a child, she ran a fever. She moved in front of the house in Delft, watching enormous wheels of stone roll down the street toward her, stacking first as if they were beads on an abacus but then cascading one over the other, as the atoms of a crystal sheared and pitched under pressure, issuing faster and faster from an unseen source. The mass engulfed her in perfect confusion, and then all was flat and calm.

In the darkening calm that stretched her head across the softly lit horizon, Anneke saw her father sleeping, wrapped in a heavy blanket, on the deck of a P & O steamer nearing Aden as the family traveled to Holland on holiday. She was fifteen and eager for the trip to end so that she could play tennis and go shopping and revel in the metropolis. For her father, however, the voyage was all-important. He had erected a small shed on deck, and he fiddled with the instruments inside it at all hours. A measurement made, he would run up to the bridge to ask for a precise latitude determination. He told her that he was catching cosmic rays. Anneke thought about magic bullets flashing by her eyes, streaking through clothes, entering her softness and leaving without a trace, and she wondered how her father held on to the vagabond specks no one else could see.

Her mother floated by and smiled. Anneke always pictured her as gliding, suspended just above ground. She hovered about because she was the same as the earth, alike in polarity, her feet tiny magnets dancing on an enormous pole face. Her father collected messages from the heavens, which, written in a barely known language, he labored to transform into mathematical scrawl. Her mother spoke with ordinary words and counted in guilders and cents. His decoding was all effort and exertion and silence. Hers was ease and grace and twitter. So it would be forever, the action stopped while the clockface gleamed, undimmed by rust, scale, dust, or sludge.

The Dutch earth had taken in her mother. Her brother's face scanned the night sky, a pose like her father's when he shipped about the Indies or halfway around the world. But this was no steamer. Anneke glanced around. She did not know where she was. They must return, give up this nonsense. They would take her brother to a hospital, then go home and soak in a hot bath. Ica would set out spice cake and cream and she, Anneke, rested, would attend a clinic on psychosomatic illness and Henk would pick up whatever he was doing about starting a firm and the great cyclotron would rise from the marshes outside Leiden and they would take a train to place flowers on her mother's grave.

Anneke's eyes had adapted to the dark. How? In the glow of the departed sun and the oddly luminescent sea, the jagged crown of the marine compass, still containing a bit of alcohol, rose from the engine housing. Creased by a bullet, it had ruptured. What course could she possibly hold? Her eyes were wide open, emotionless; her mouth and chin were furled in a tense frown. She grasped the dead man tighter in her arms.

"Turn around, turn around!" She grew rigid, from her neck past her thighs to her toes. In the enormous but not quite black night, a ferry had lost the way to the distant fields where the living and the dead would be judged.

2

North-Atlantic Drift

So here everything is out of joint, but people try to do what they did before. I work, mostly calculations. Food is hard to find. I am back to my weight as a student. Please look up my children in England, Cambridge maybe, give them my love, and do ask them to remember the mountain in the Indies. Heisenberg came through last week. He spoke at the institute, a theory of quantum electrodynamics. He came without invitation, but I made him welcome. He is evidently in favour, for he had an automobile and an escort, but why such resources for a theoretician? He said that Planck is still active in Berlin, speaking on quasi-religious matters to the soldiers. Trust your cyclotron is in good shape.

Jacob Witte to Arthur Holly Compton, 4 October 1941,
Compton papers, University of Chicago

Every fifteen seconds Leonard Ranov's trousers swung through a thirty-degree arc, measured relative to the corners of the room. Everything else not firmly nailed down executed a comparable roll or slide. The pull-cord for the light above the wall mirror oscillated as if it was an impossibly long-period clock pendulum. For ten seconds a chair squealed against the deck. Leonard pitched forward in his bunk, his eyes and ears puffed up as his stomach pushed to expand his diaphragm and his head touched the wall below the porthole. The chair began another ten-second riff. He pitched back and his stomach sought his toes, which came to rest against the railing at the foot of the bed. Leonard opened his eyes to a slit and watched the single vertical line in his field of vision—the pull-cord—as he see-sawed and twisted, for the ship pitched forward and back as it rolled from side to side. He swung his feet free of the top sheet and made to plant them on the floor in front of the bed. The far wall dropped below the horizon and Leonard found himself airborne. Ankle, knee, hip, elbow, and chin hit the deck, which then lofted its inert sacrifice skyward.

This was as good a way as any, Leonard thought, to brush away his nightmare. It came whenever, over the past seven years, he found himself under pressure. He was at college during examinations. A profusion of magenta azaleas and the sweetness of freshly manicured lawns and newly unfolded leaves enveloped him as he walked from his room, across the railroad tracks, to the commons. His mind jumbled the first few pages of half a dozen texts. He looked around at the children of doctors and rentiers, radiant-haired willows bent with purpose as they streamed up the incline with him, set to spill their knowledge over a sea of white paper. He drifted across their flow. He was back in his room, pouring furiously over an algebra text he had never opened before. He could not begin to understand. He had to sit for the examination later. He floated above the crowd of young women and men to bob against the commons door, and then found himself repelled, pushed back into a torrent of ignorance. He sweated, choked, and ran an aimless course around immaculate flower beds and ivy-decked stone walls. Pages of incomprehensible scrawl turned over before him. Smiling, clean, relaxed faces appeared outside the commons as he, dark and angular, wrestled with an unseen and malevolent presence to take his seat in the hall of white paper. He fled in total confusion.

Leonard's right eye focused on a shoe six inches from his nose. His present state of motion, regular if extreme, was preferable to that of the discontinuous and contradictory dream. Motion was one of the universal mysteries. He had never really understood its key concept, inertia. It was hard enough to grasp the notion of mass, a ratio of force and acceleration, much less how an oddly-shaped extension of this ratio would respond when subjected to sudden torque or impulse. To do it properly required solving simultaneous differential equations, and if the solver didn't want to plunge into the abyss of Galois theory, he had to abandon himself to the gadgets and fittings readily available on the shelf above the physicist's workbench. Well, not exactly. An outfielder loping after a fly ball intuitively solved the equations of his and the ball's motion. A reaper swinging a scythe also mastered motion. Leonard had never been able to field fly balls, much less throw them any distance. The farm implements he felt confident wielding were pitchforks and shovels. He consoled himself with the thought that Einstein had made over inertial mass into an active player on the fields of physics. The baseball really was as smart as the outfielder. In his trajectory from the bed to the floor he had remained purposeful and sentient, appearances to the contrary.

He pulled himself into a squat, his back resting against the side of the bunk. The grey light entering the porthole indicated that it could be any time between nine in the morning and three in the afternoon. Leonard wasn't sure if his head spun from his impact with the deck, from the general rocking and rolling of the ship, or from the nightmare. He pulled his shirt off the chair back, thrust his arms through the sleeves, stood up and took a step toward his trousers on the door. The trousers, infused with purpose, approached him twice as fast as they should have. The floor tilted Leonard back and away from the gravitating, two-legged apparition. The trousers accelerated through a circular arc. Leonard watched them recede and found himself propelled by the floor toward a figure standing in the doorway where his trousers had been.

"Ten after ten, Greenwich mean," the round, bespeckled face beamed, pronouncing each word with special attention to its final sound. "Chow time."

Corporal Ernest Bit was Leonard's clerk and traveling companion. Leonard had become accustomed to the corporal's

Lithuanian-Brooklyn accent, but the short man was an enigma. Ernest spoke several Eastern European languages. When the United States entered the war, he had been working in his father's trucking company after putting his studies "in the icebox," he said. Ernest promptly volunteered for the air corps because he knew that he would never fly. Now he was heading to England and Cambridge. Ernest radiated good cheer at the prospect. Leonard wondered why.

"All right," he responded glumly. "Let me get my pants on." The trousers went on over Leonard's long johns. He laced on his shoes, wrapped himself in his sheepskin-lined flight jacket emblazoned with a large white lambda and rho on its back, thrust an arm through his life vest, and set off for the head. There were chocolate bars and hard candy in the jacket pockets. Leonard was prepared for a quick break to the lifeboats.

As he shuffled down the narrow corridor, Leonard felt annoyed at his present circumstances, just above the waterline in a North Atlantic gale. His annoyance focused on Ernest. Had it not been for Ernest Bit, he thought, he would have by now been in England after a flight by way of Gander. But Ernest's ears would not allow him to fly: They filled with fluid the moment he climbed above one thousand feet. Ernest concealed his infirmity, which he knew about from driving trucks around the Catskills, from the air-corps recruiter. Ernest shared no blame, though, for what they were about to do in England. He, the same as Leonard, was assigned to look into a story of silly proportions.

Over the four years before Pearl Harbor, Leonard had come to enjoy what life threw up to him. He was teaching physics to the sons and daughters of ranchers at the University of Wyoming. He had the leisure to climb all over the Front Range and the fortitude, acquired at Swarthmore, to pursue his own program of advanced study. It was an amalgam of quantum mechanics, as conveyed by the Copenhagen theorists, and Zen meditation, as relayed by English and German commentators. He found a research interest in atmospheric radioactivity, which infused his mountain rambles with new purpose as he carried measuring instruments to the tops of Colorado's peaks. He let fly dozens of high-altitude balloons. He succeeded in publishing some of his results in the *Physical Review*. In 1940 his university awarded him a master's of science for his efforts.

Leonard enlisted with the air corps at Denver following Pearl Harbor. After some months he was a second lieutenant headed for flight school. His entire class went overseas. He was assigned first to attend radio classes, then to acquire the skills of a bombardier. His requests for immediate transfer to the action were rejected, definitively, by order of the Military Intelligence Division. While in college Leonard had gone along with something of a family tradition and joined a communist cell, and, though he had remained politically quiescent in Wyoming, the military authorities concluded that his loyalty was too uncertain to be entrusted with anything important or sensitive. By September 1942, he was spending much of his time thinking about ways to place bonehead superiors in the worst possible light. Then a pilot, he experimented with belly-flopping B-17s, so that he and his crew could vacation on the Gulf of Mexico or the Jersey shore while the landing gear was rebuilt.

He recounted this apocryphal story to friends. Arriving for a month in Oakland, he announced in the mess that he could teach anyone to fly. Next morning he found himself in charge of a chimpanzee with the words "play or fold" printed on its T-shirt. The night before he was to leave for Carlsbad, he watched the chimp, strapped into a trainer, rise off the landing field and head over San Francisco Bay before stalling out at five-hundred feet and plunging into the water.

Every now and again Leonard heard about a monster project under General Leslie Groves sucking up thousands of scientific brains. What lent credence to the rumors was that he had never met anyone in the service with a diploma in chemistry or physics who had not been assigned to classified work. He was forecasting weather in Omaha when he met one of Groves's staff, a Colonel Cratsley. A thunderstorm provided the occasion for the two to talk. One week later he was in Washington, shuffling paper for the Uranium Committee.

Leonard sat. He stared at the dull metal door, a field of olive green crossed by random scratches and the occasional expletive. He was undoubtedly the only physicist in the military with a diploma who had not been assigned to classified work. By the military's peculiar logic, then, he was the only person for a wild goose chase of no conceivable relevance to the war effort. Leonard was supposed to find out about the cosmic-ray research of a Dr Witte in Cambridge. That was all.

Leonard smiled. During his time at Laramie, he had requested reprints about high-altitude cosmic-ray measurements from Jacob Witte. In Leonard's mind, Witte was master of the extra-terrestrial messengers. A paper by Witte carried a Java dateline, early in 1940, and Leonard had read it in *Nature*. He knew that Witte had been placed in charge of providing Leiden with an experimental facility for nuclear physics. Leonard had guessed that nothing came of it because the *Nature* paper was still reporting on cosmic rays. Witte must have escaped to England. Someone in the Pentagon must have been apprised of the immense energy contained by the rays from outer space. One or another general would have written a memorandum asking to verify whether cosmic rays could be used against the Nazis. Even to an untrained eye, Leonard's mission appeared ridiculous. That was why they had assigned him to investigate.

Leonard found his way back to the cabin. He dropped jacket and vest on the deck and stared at his face in the mirror. He had not shaved or showered for two days, and he reaffirmed his decision not to undertake either operation until his world stopped swaying. Ernest had installed himself in the chair. He appeared freshly laundered. Light reflected off a thin film of soap on his cheeks.

"You look positively grey," Ernest began. "But that is because you consider your present circumstances as abnormal. Life on this tub makes you sick because you have not embraced your fate. You are holding your life in abeyance until you set foot on Albion's firm shores. Suppose, however, that this roll, pitch, and occasional yaw in a dark cavity were all you knew about the world. You would happily manage to walk a straight and steady line. And to do so, your senses would invest the external forces and torques with real existence. The fundamental laws of motion would be festooned with garish, Rococo flourishes. Nature would still appear as a perfect lady."

This was Ernest's way of starting a discussion that rambled, rough-shod, over the fields, gardens, and drawing rooms of the civilized world. His gambit began and ended with an observation involving his interlocutor. In the middle was an innocuous digression that would blossom into an outrageous proposition. Leonard saw that the topic of the morning's conversation would be the relativity of values. He had strong views on the matter.

"Nature isn't a person," Leonard protested. "It isn't a thing. It isn't controlled by a goddess stamping her foot or a gnome manipulating dials behind a console. Nature is the wide field of phenomena. All parts of it act everywhere, all the time, on all other parts. It's true that if we, born and raised in this room, tried to understand the motion of a marble rolling on the floor as a natural phenomenon, we would make the sides of our cage into sources of non-linear forces. The marble would dance to the changing configuration of the mass of the rest of the universe. But by transforming coordinate systems, the room's motion could equally become artificial. And I *know* that it will only last for four or five days."

Ernest grinned. "Your phenomenological mumbo-jumbo with its nihilist overlay misses the point. The world is not as it seems. More especially, the world has not always been as it seems now. You may think that the Copenhagen interpretation of indeterminacy is a revolutionary development in the rational reconstruction of the universe. But there is really nothing new in its rejection of the hierarchical logic popularized by French barristers. In the seventeenth century, Bohr would have been Pope Urban, insisting to Galileo that he not infer anything about reality from what he saw through his telescope. Newton, the unifier of celestial and terrestrial mechanics, was a devoutly religious man whose physics depended on biblical numerology and whose mathematics came from divine inspiration. The scientific revolution was inspired not by rational deduction and experimental proof but by Rosicrucian holism and specious observation. The point is that more can be known than can be proved."

Leonard took a deep breath. His companion would string together fragments of physics in a maddeningly incomplete fashion, but one that carried, once it was stripped down and polished, the germ of an idea that Leonard found appealing. When he was younger, Leonard spun these kinds of discourse in mock seriousness. Unhappiness resulted when the mature authors of such schemes took themselves seriously.

One year at Laramie, when he taught a course on the philosophy of physics, the class included a Romanian refugee. She lacked Ernest's command of English, as she lacked control of just about everything except her belief that she would be the next Bertrand Russell. When Leonard analyzed her papers and examinations, he found them mere tautologies or trivialities, and he flunked her. She took him before the university judiciary. At the time of his enlistment, the case remained unresolved, but it taught Leonard when to disengage from a hopeless argument.

"A man of your attainments, Ernest, needs something to eat," Leonard said.

The two wended their way down corridors and stairs to the galley. Leonard led for two reasons. First, he had a powerful torso, and he tended to handle himself better in the pitching ship than his companion, whose champagne shoulders were of no use for bracing against walls and gripping railings. Second, Leonard could find his way around the ship in the dark. Having been somewhere once, or having briefly looked over a map, he knew immediately and forever where he was. Ernest had avowed that he knew the ship as well as Leonard, but after getting lost on the first day, he silently took his place in the rear guard.

Leonard had always known where he was. His talent as an orienteer made him sought after by spelunkers, although he did not really enjoy dropping hundreds of feet through holes in the ground or going up chimneys in search of an exit. The inside of the ship bore some resemblance to a cave. The corridors and rooms were cold and damp, stalactites everywhere. Caves carried the sound of dripping water, ships the hum of engines and exhaust fans. A cave, however, was organic and primordial. One entered a soft, wet, narrow cleft. A ship's interior was artificial, hard, and geometrical. Its sense of life came from the outside, from action imparted by wind and waves. Leonard loved the feel of natural forces. He hated the prison of the ship.

Physics attracted Leonard because it promised to reveal the essence of nature's forces—the blueness of the sky, the formation of late-afternoon summer thunderheads, the inner glue holding together glass and bricks and mortar, how radio signals passed through the void. The useful part of physics seemed distinct from its deeper explanations. Notions of thermodynamics or hydraulics might make one feel easier about reviving an ancient truck or placing a venturi in a well, but the tradition of mechanical knowledge seemed grafted, and uncomfortably so, to physical theory. In America, physicists were supposed to be able to remake the world and eliminate toil and suffering. Leonard did not want to intervene in the world so much as to understand it.

Cosmic rays were his ticket to impractical, universal, and mechanically uncomplicated wisdom. While in college he had rejected the idea of serving as a cog in the vast machines being constructed by the Aryan masters of the scientific establishment— Compton, Millikan, Lawrence, Tuve, and others—to smash atoms or accelerate electrons. He recoiled at the thought of becoming a wage slave in a knowledge factory. Leonard wanted to explore the world on his own terms, constructing his own instruments and designing his own theories. Near the end of his last year in college he saw an advertisement for laboratory supervisor at Wyoming. He applied, and received the position.

Before he accepted, he talked the move over with his parents. "If it will make you happy," his mother said. "All right, all right," his stepfather said, the farm could manage without him. "Where is Wyoming?" his sister asked.

Wyoming became his standard for judgment. The people in Wyoming were unassuming and straightforward, enjoying every day as it came. There he forged an eclectic vision of life and engaged in a modest program of research. Wyoming did not react to atrocities in Asia and Europe, to battles fought by the industrial unions, or to American troops in the Philippines and the Caribbean. Berlin and Canton were as remote as Philadelphia and San Diego and Havana. What mattered was the price of cattle and the winter's supply of hay, hunting camps and barroom brawls, a weekend in Denver or two weeks at Jackson Hole. Leonard felt relaxed and in charge of his destiny.

Leonard retained his peace of mind in the army, even though there he had no control over anything. He saw it as his education in democracy. The army put him into contact with a wide spectrum of humanity, and, finally, most of the lower-ranked people he met were not unreasonable. Their resilience and humor would allow America to survive, he concluded, the promises of rural Bonapartes and the sectarian tirades of big-city socialists. But he grew weary of hayseed bunkmates. Ernest Bit appeared as a distinct change.

Leonard and Ernest emerged in the galley. They picked up trays and walked down a line of enormous serving pots and trays, the surface of whose contents generally remained parallel to the gyrating floor. One cauldron had library paste that the cook announced as chicken gumbo. Grits and bacon floated in separate lakes of grease. Stewed prunes poked their reptilian heads through a pool of swamp water, while next to them a field of powdered eggs seemed just to have been cultivated. Yellow biscuits lay heaped on a platter. Leonard took several biscuits (which he doubted he would eat), spooned out peanut butter on his plate, and filled cups with what passed for orange juice and coffee. Leonard supposed that the military started with good ingredients. That was the point of civilian rationing. But everything came out of the kitchen wrong.

Ernest loaded his tray with grits, bacon, eggs, and prunes. They found a table. Ernest arranged his plates as the four on a die and began to eat. He took a bite of the grits on the lower right, and then proceeded clockwise, sampling each item in a rhythm matching the ship's roll. "Preparation for English cuisine," he said to Leonard, and took a second pass at his breakfast. Leonard constructed a peanut-butter sandwich and bit off a chunk. He drank some orange juice. The effect was unsatisfactory. The galley evoked the smell of an elementary-school lunchroom—slightly rancid and strongly disinfectant.

"Excuse me, Ernest," he said, "I've got to get some air." He left his tray and bolted for the door. He walked down a short corridor and up three decks to a door that, he knew, opened to the outside. He zipped up his jacket, donned his life vest, and left behind the odors of metal corrosion and engine oil as he stepped into North-Atlantic February.

The ship was making its way crosswise through large swells, generally executing a simple harmonic roll but occasionally taking a hit as a whitecap crested over the bow. Sunlight diffused through a low cloud ceiling that, for the moment, neither rained nor sleeted. Leonard took a deep breath and felt better. His friend, the ocean. He liked to taste its salt, feel its wind, listen to the pounding of its waves, smell the rotting vegetation and creosote piers, see the marine life and detritus it expelled. As a boy he would walk along the New Jersey shore for miles, in every season. In winter, he found the silence and the cold congenial. He faced the ocean until his nose seemed frozen. Then he would hike back into the dunes to warm up in front of a driftwood fire. Leonard clung to a rail on his narrow gallery. The air temperature seemed around 10°F, not cold by Wyoming standards. He watched the sea, looking without success for companions in the naval convoy.

After twenty minutes Leonard left the North Atlantic winter and threaded his way back to his cabin. He stripped off his outer gear and lay back on the bunk. He had never before traveled outside the United States. In several days he would be with Witte in Cambridge. Leonard tried to imagine Witte as short, wearing a vandyke beard, tinkering with galvanometers in a laboratory. Leonard would meet him at the Cavendish Laboratory, where Thomson and Rutherford had supervised fifty years of discoveries. They would walk down the narrow streets to a college commons room for a sherry, then on to High Table with roast beef and vintage wine. Leonard would regale the dons with tales of launching balloons from American mountains.

*
*   *

The first British soil that Leonard saw was not soil at all. The convoy had been driven apart in the early days of the crossing. Leonard's transport stayed with the main current of the North-Atlantic drift, circled north of Ireland, and made for Fair Head on the North Channel. The igneous prisms of Giant's Causeway were Leonard's landfall.

The ship docked in Belfast, and the crew went on leave. While the ship rode at anchor, Leonard shaved. Then, with Ernest in tow, he had a launch deliver him to the Glasgow ferry. Fifteen hours later they sat in a second-class railway compartment halfway between Glasgow and the American B-17 base at Bassingbourn, where Leonard would report to the commanding officer before traveling on to Cambridge.

For those fifteen hours, Ernest had been lecturing him on Orangemen and Scotsmen, Irish whiskey and scotch, Macs and Mcs, Irish and Scottish civil wars, Irish and Scottish kilts, Irish and Scottish Gaelic, Irish and Scottish bank notes, George Bernard Shaw and Robert Louis Stevenson, William Rowan Hamilton and William Thompson Lord Kelvin, the *Irish Times* and the *Scotsman*. Leonard's occasional contributions and queries would set Ernest off on another comparative topic. Leonard took it in as background music to the unfolding panorama of Ireland, Scotland, and northern England. Around 10:00 p.m., Corporal Ernest Bit finally ran out of steam. He rolled his woolen coat into a pillow, stretched out across three empty seats, and bade Leonard good night.

In the dark, speeding train, during the hours before they reached their station, Leonard pondered Ernest's monologue. Ireland and Scotland, the underdeveloped and subjugated peripheries of England, sharing many characteristics and yet having distinct characters, provided arenas for English exploitation and reservoirs of talent that blossomed under English ascendency. *The finest sight a Scotsman can see* and *a modest proposal*, but the dominated, impoverished cultures produced outsiders of extraordinary intensity who transformed English civilization. Despite its class-bound rigidity, England had a genius for assimilating the clarity of an outsider's vision. It was a civilization that worked on centripetal power. The two of them, their only allegiance to England being in the language they spoke, were being sucked into the bosom of the Midlands.

We make sense of what we see by comparison, Leonard thought. Comparing like phenomena in separate settings can isolate superstructures, separating essential forces from fictitious ones, and can intimate ancestral causes. Examining one phenomenon in all its settings carries as its reward the privilege of postulating an unseen cause. Thus, Newton's orbital equations and universal gravitation, Darwin's speciation and natural selection, Planck's radiation law and the quantum of energy. This is the opposite of induction, for in comparison the subject is delineated at the outset by malice of forethought. And even barring the "each and every" restriction that, properly speaking, permits causation to be invoked, comparison still functions as a primitive integrating machine, sorting new observations into existing categories or calling old categories into question.

But all this was true, Leonard began to see, only if Aristotelian kinds were allowed, and immutable kinds were anathema to both Zen poets and Ernest Bit. Perhaps all life was a self-correcting mechanism, in which there were no roots and branches or bones and muscle (for how could a root appear without a branch, or bone without muscle?). It might be that all elementary particles were a single essence manifesting various states of energy or quality. Perhaps everything in the universe was a single electron weaving back and forth in time. Everything was an illusion.

Leonard's mind churned on illusions until the train stopped at Bassingbourn. He shook his companion awake, and the two dragged their bags into a taxi for the five-mile ride to the aerodrome. There they were led to bunks in a dilapidated out-building with a large coal stove at its center. The night air in East Anglia was damp but above freezing. The stove radiated heat. Ernest carefully undressed and brushed his teeth with water from his canteen. Leonard abandoned himself to a cot and let sleep darn his rents.

The next morning Leonard concluded that airfields were universally depressing. Airfields were located as far as reasonable from civilization. They existed on sufferance from the general staff. Their only function was to coddle and service flying machines. The engines of destruction were crowning glories of engineers, who manipulated slide rules and adding machines to hoist aloft ever more tons of aluminum, aviation fuel, nitroglycerin, and flesh. Airfields had no place for antique biplanes, standard equipment just fifteen years earlier, quite unlike how a naval facility would tolerate old dreadnoughts at anchor and use older freighters to flit through coastal waters. Airfields had no cache of old ordnance and side-arms, stockpiled at infantry posts in anticipation of a German invasion or a communist uprising. Everything was for depersonalized and technological mass destruction. Warehouses of blockbusters and incendiaries, piles of 105-mm shells. In fact, there was no general rule about whether airmen were to carry personal firearms aloft, opinion blowing hot and cold on whether an armed flyer was more likely to be shot by German troops or an unarmed flyer hacked to pieces by enraged German citizens. Tradition for airmen was measured in months; men were the final cogs in an infernal and rapidly evolving industrial nightmare. They were the last people to save civilization, the rôle planned for them by H. G. Wells.

Only a few B-17s stood on the field, and some of these were attended to. Most of the rest had gone on the daylight run, it being the privilege of the Americans to see the countryside they sought to pound into oblivion while the British unloaded their bombs under cover of night. Perhaps the squadron was already running for England.

The wind eddied dust and leaves as Leonard walked to the commanding officer's post, a tarpaper shack at the nexus of the field's electrical and telephone lines. Britain had red tile or slate roofs, Leonard thought, but the American airmen lived and worked under cheap American shingles. He opened the unpainted door and announced himself to the clerk, who looked up from his typewriter and pointed to a row of steel folding chairs.

Leonard hung up his jacket and took a chair facing a civilian in suit and tie, clutching a large map case. The civilian, a boy in his late teens, had straight blond hair, brown eyes, and a high-bridged nose. He was painfully thin, and his skin seemed almost translucently white. A door behind the clerk opened. A captain strode out, nipped at by wisps of cigar smoke. The clerk carried a file through the door and returned. Cigar smoke floated through the waiting area. A minute after the captain left, "Mr Goodaye" received a summons from the inner office.

Mr Goodaye remained inside for ten minutes. Leonard watched the expressionless clerk slowly process forms in quadruplicate, most of his time taken up with sandwiching carbons between the copies and collating the results. Exclamations, profanity, and thumping emanated through the walls of the inner office. Mr Goodaye emerged red-faced and close to tears. He donned overcoat, overshoes, and muffler, picked up his umbrella, and left without a word. "Next," came through the door clearly. Leonard walked past the clerk, who closed his eyes and raised his eyebrows.

The commanding officer, a major, was on his feet and in a stew.

"Take a seat, Lieutenant," the major said. "That goddam creep, what the hell does he know about flying planes. You know what he came here for? Do you?" Leonard shook his head. "That creep says that we should rip all the guns off our planes! He says that without guns and gunners more of the crews would come back. Lookit this, for crissake."

Leonard studied the charts on the major's desk. They came from the Operational Research Section of Bomber Command. Several of the charts dealt with statistical studies of British bombing missions over Germany. The conclusion seemed to be that guns were useless for defending bombers. The guns, their ammunition and housing, and the gunners just slowed down the plane. Maneuverability remained the key to survival, and without gun turrets the bombers would be quicker and more agile. Another chart proposed larger bailout hatches. The suggestion resulted from a detailed correlation of prisoners-of-war with their aircraft. Crew from late-model British bombers were the least likely to survive the destruction of their aircraft. The Operational Research Section concluded that it was all a function of the size of the escape hatches, the newer British-built machines having those of the smallest diameter.

While Leonard was studying the material, the major faced a window and continued talking. "I go up every week, goddammit, and my gunners have knocked out bandits, and no mamma's boy'll tell me how to come back alive. The crew's a team and the gunners are insurance. You been up over, Lieutenant?"

"Not yet," Leonard replied.

"Well, when you do, you better pray that your gunner's got a good night's sleep."

Leonard knew how close crews were. They lived and trained together. They came to trust each other. To know that gunners aft and below scanned the heavens for enemy craft was a source of comfort to the bombardier looking down his bombsight, the navigator plotting a course, the radio operator tuning in on a frequency, and the pilot monitoring his gauges. A crew would never agree to give up its defensive armament. The escape hatch did not merit being addressed. It was inconspicuous. Ream it out and paint it red with yellow stripes and fewer crews would make the effort to guide a crippled plane home.

"What do you want?" the major asked abruptly.

Leonard said that he and Ernest were to find out about the work of a physicist at Cambridge. In a few weeks he was supposed to report back to Washington. He wanted to return on a plane by way of Gander.

"Plane leaves Thursday morning on the weekly run to Iceland. Can't promise more than that. Now you tell them in Washington that we'll keep our goddam gunners, so they better keep making turrets." The interview was over.

Leonard saw himself out and went off in search of Ernest. Leonard found him in the canteen, pouring over an old Manchester *Guardian*.

"Get your things. We're off to Cambridge."

The two missionaries skipped lunch and had a jeep drive them to the station. There, waiting for the train, Leonard bought an apple and a cup of tea, and Ernest went for a toad-in-the-hole. Leonard split one of his chocolate bars with his companion.

"Relativity originates at train platforms," Ernest noted in a deliberate voice. "Einstein took trains everywhere. A passenger sitting in a train moving slowly through a station feels no different from someone sitting on the platform watching the train pass. Before the railroad, such symmetry was possible only near the shore on the stillest of lakes." He paused, and then spoke even more slowly for emphasis. "The symmetrical analogy is based on a new development in the world."

"Right," Leonard said. "Every culture has its own physics, which expresses a unique vision of the universe and humanity's place in it. We can go further, and postulate that relativity was invented in a culture with a superb system of rail transport and a special vocabulary, in German, for talking about it. It always struck me bizarre that, with only a few exceptions, English and French physicists have never known what to make of Einstein's theory. Relativity has been irrelevant to physics beyond Central Europe. Our physicists invest relativistic formulas with absolute meaning. The reception of relativity may even confirm the relativistic nature of scientific understanding. Relativity, from this point of view, is a happy accident of German grammar."

"I rather think not," said Ernest, shifting from one foot to another. "The ideas and concepts of physics really do diffuse, transfuse, suffuse, interpose, interject, flow, and careen from one culture to another without much distortion. The implicit foundations for these thoughts, though, are virtually impossible to convey across cultures and languages. Consider multi-valued logic, an intuitively satisfying notion for someone schooled in Eastern European languages, but one quite abstract for a native English speaker. Consider the extraordinary exertions of someone like Bohr to formulate an epistemology of indeterminacy, something long on the agenda in Oriental philosophy."

Leonard was intrigued that Ernest seemed to reject relativistic skepticism, which, he thought, fit Ernest's temperament.

Ernest continued. "There is a way to save the useful parts of cultural relativism without doing violence to the objective measure of the outside world." He paused for effect. "It is simply that the physical properties of the universe conform to our changing understanding of them."

"What?" said Leonard. He thought that he must have misunderstood. "Do you mean to say that, before Copernicus, the sun really did circle around the earth, that before Harvey there was no circulation of the blood, before Galileo heavier bodies actually fell faster than lighter ones, before Einstein time ran at the same rate everywhere and always?"

Ernest smiled. "You state the matter crudely, but, yes, something like what you say is what I want to look into at Cambridge. You see, the mechanization of the universe was accomplished at the expense of a de-spiritualization. Matter was separated from mind, thought from action. The foundations of the modern world, however, reach back to a time before the schism was carved in stone. The alchemical notion of substance is infused with spiritual meaning. This spiritual residue lies in many of the thorniest mathematical and physical problems. What interests me especially is the worldview of the alchemists. This may be retrieved from their language. Just now I cannot say whether it was possible, four centuries ago, to transmute lead into gold."

The train arrived. They boarded and sat facing each other in an empty compartment. Leonard studied Ernest's round, smiling face. He was more than a truck driver from Brooklyn.

"Ernest," Leonard said, "how did you learn about all these things?"

"Oh," Ernest replied, "I read here and there."

"No," Leonard continued, "I mean, how come?" In Washington, Leonard had worked with Ernest for many months, but the two had never gone into personal matters.

Ernest then relayed, matter-of-factly, his upbringing in Lithuania. Ernest's father, a prosperous merchant, sold the business and moved the family to New York in 1930. Ernest was then seventeen and burning to study at a university. He stayed behind, wandering up and down the Baltic in search of an education. He spent a semester or two in Copenhagen, Kiel, Danzig, Königsberg, and Riga. He landed a lectureship in philology at Tartu, but in 1936 he rejoined his family to supervise the garage servicing his father's fleet.

The pair arrived in Cambridge. Leonard steered toward the head of the taxi rank. They drove down Trumpington Street to

Trinity Street and the Blue Boar, a rambling structure that seemed to have enveloped neighboring territory by unpremeditated expansion. Leonard insisted on a hot soak before they looked for dinner.

Leonard's room on the third floor faced out on a back alley. There was a cast-iron double bed and space to accommodate additional cots. Leonard turned up a gas heater located on an inside wall and ran hot water in the tub. He found a clean shirt and underwear and unlaced his shoes. When the tub filled up he plunged in. It had been years since he enjoyed a bath. Here a bath admitted of no qualification, there being no provision for a showerhead either on the wall or attached to the faucet. Showers would be efficient and American; baths, wasteful of time and resources, were British.

The two American airmen walked to Market Hill and entered a restaurant. Leonard ordered what he understood: ham, potatoes, and carrots. He listened as Ernest asked for stew of something.

"Ernest," he said, "what is that stuff?"

Ernest described the dishes. He lamented that the war probably made it impossible to find the best, in his opinion, of traditional fare—cockles and beef-and-beer.

"Have you been to England before?" Leonard asked.

"Yes," Ernest replied, "during my time at Copenhagen I was able to get to Oxford for a conference on linguistics. They put me up at Corpus Christi. A lovely experience."

"After all that," Leonard asked, "how could you repair trucks in Brooklyn?"

Ernest laughed. "It was a new experience for me. Anyway, I had decided to make my home in America, and during the '30s we were lucky to make ends meet. In a way, the daily routine freed me to write and think. Evenings and weekends were my own, and the New York Public Library was only a subway ride away. I actually think that, during my time in Brooklyn, I sharpened my skills. It is all compensation, overcorrection for the absence of endowment." He quoted:

Blind Milton

Blind John Milton, how can it be,
That bereft of your vision you have us to see
In Death's hateful uprising to love's tyranny
A defense of rebellion?
The new age and its heroes in verse damned and chided,
You gave myth new forms when by inner flames guided.

Once your heart, Einstein, failed, compassion up fired
From rest where it had by sweet learning retired.
Your pump sped blood worse as you strong voice required
To flail oppression.
Law-giver in cipher for God's mystery,
You've willed your poor heart to all humanity.

Do you colorfully dream, drab-cell-bound Siqueiros,
Reflections from walls in proportions precarious
And brighter than real? How in space nefarious
Can your insight unfold?
For speaking on justice, to prison confined,
There murals with grandiose lines you refined.

"It's not quite right yet," Ernest added, "but you get the idea."

Leonard knew about Siqueiros through a Trotskyist uncle in the Bronx, and he admired *Areopagitica*, but he had never thought to connect the artist, the poet, and the physicist.

"The Mexican muralist!" Leonard exclaimed. "A lovely poem. But Einstein's not dead."

"Well," Ernest said, "it was just an exercise in rhyme, to help my English, you know."

"How did you learn about Siqueiros?"

"Oh," Ernest said, "I met him in New York. There was a possibility of his doing windows for a Lithuanian church. The congregation, of course, did not appreciate his drawings. I found them fresh and appealing. We talked, and I learned about his politics. I don't actually know if he has been in prison, but if he hasn't, he will be."

"You would make a fine teacher." Leonard offered. "Did you ever think of looking for a position in a university?"

Ernest shook his head abruptly. "There is no place for me in American higher education. Consider. Professor is a respected state title in most of Europe. But in America, it is risible, an address reserved for medicine-show hucksters and pianists in bordellos. Most American university professors do conform to the popular image: twangy preachers unable to complete even a moderate-sized work of science or scholarship, incapacitated by their lack of languages and higher mathematics. What hiring committee would be able to read, let alone judge, what I have written? And suppose the good burghers in a place like West Lafayette or Chattanooga were to hire me as a German instructor—absence of libraries would spell the end of my probe into Renaissance Hermeticism. I really did not mind working in a Brooklyn garage."

Their dinners came. Leonard had been an assistant professor at Laramie. It was true that his university did not have a research library and the faculty was undistinguished. He had enjoyed his time there, however. He was encouraged by the direct and forthright character of the people, and by their vigorous interest in life and the land. The thin air of the high plains seemed to give him a clear head and a clean conscience. He felt fresh and optimistic there, free from the class and ethnic barriers of the East. He would not much have liked to repair trucks in Brooklyn, even if the weekends were available for launching high-altitude balloons.

They returned to the hotel and agreed to meet for breakfast. In his room, Leonard scanned a slim file on Witte. Next morning he would look up Witte in the telephone directory. He tried to imagine the features of a distinguished Dutch physicist. He was excited at the prospect of visiting Witte in his college lodgings. Perhaps they would lunch together. He hoped that the food would be better than what he had just experienced. He was glad that Ernest would accompany him to the interview. As Leonard fell asleep, he thought about chasing cosmic rays across the Front Range of the Rocky Mountains.

3

By Granta's Banks

When I arrived in Leiden from Stockholm, Witte was ill. Influenza, or maybe just poor nutrition. And he was anxious to learn about his children, who had fled to England just after the fall of the Netherlands. He was working at home, calculating. We recalled Lembang before the war, where I spent six months observing Mars at its closest approach to the Earth. Good food, good music, splendid astronomy. He would come up sometimes from Bandung to look through the big telescope with me. It had two eyepieces, one for observing and one for a camera. We removed the camera and looked at the same image. He joked that he could see the canals. I thought that, from month to month, I could make out changes in shadows, perhaps indicating mountains or canyons, maybe part of a crater or volcanic cauldron. Then he walked over to me and clutched my hand. "Do you remember the volcano?" Of course I did. It smouldered not far from the observatory and occasionally clouded the skies. An odd comment from an expert on cosmic rays.

Åke Wallenquist to George Ellery Hale, 4 December 1941,
Hale papers, California Institute of Technology

British breakfast might have lost the war. Tiny links floating in grease, gluey porridge, and gritty flakes crying out for warm milk. The fare had fortified generations of Tommy and Pommy before they shoved off for foreign parts. Leonard eyed it with hostility. To his mind decent food came from the colonies. Who could live without the ingestible narcotics—coffee, tea, cocoa, sugar, vanilla, cinnamon, pepper, and spices—or the commonplace staples—peanuts, rice, potatoes, tomatoes, and bananas? Europe conquered the world to compensate for its culinary shortfall. Leonard had exotic marmalade toast with tea. He faced his colleague Corporal Bit, who had some of everything and was proceeding around each serving, a spoonful at a time.

Leonard rang Witte's home. A woman with an Eastern European accent answered the telephone. Leonard explained that he was an American who had come to learn about Dr Witte's research, and he wanted to visit as soon as possible. After asking him to hold the line for a few minutes, the woman came on to say that 10:00 that morning would be suitable. Leonard obtained directions.

Leonard and Ernest walked down to Bridge Street and gawked at the shops and old stone buildings. Then over the Cam at the spot where, in clement weather, punts and canoes could be rented. They headed downstream along Chesterton Road and away from the colleges. Leonard was astonished that he had been through the center of Cambridge and had seen nothing of university life except the books in Heffer's windows. Apparently everything of importance lay behind the towering college walls.

"Jude the Obscure," Leonard said to Ernest, "filled up with knowledge and yet permitted to see only the towers and steeples of the academy." Leonard felt detached and ambivalent toward the accomplishments of thirty or more generations of Cambridge scholars. What he valued about modern civilization—electricity, antiseptic surgery, secular public education—owed little to life at Cambridge. None of the music, the art, the literature that he loved had a base on the banks of the Cam. The place seemed to him a kind of monument to medieval masonry.

Ernest was more circumspect. "The colleges should be somewhat more exposed from the Backs," he said. "Over the centuries, learning spread out from the medieval town, and new colleges have appeared on fields and farms, like peripheral spots of radioactive scatter on a photographical plate. Maybe Dr Witte teaches in a new college."

They passed by a row of college boathouses, where the boys

could exert themselves when their juices began to flow. The road arched away from the Cam. Buildings decreased in size and splendor. Nineteenth-century villas dribbled away, along with trees and grass. Grimy shops, a milk-processing plant, a hospital, and hundreds of narrow brick row-houses took shape as they walked. These were proletarian lodgings for a vast army of gardeners, dustmen, porters, maids, servants, cooks, carpenters, glazers, plumbers, electricians, and provisioners. No college, Leonard reasoned, would be situated among these buildings.

A thin Red Persian cat crossed the street to beg for attention. Leonard reached down to scratch its ears. He loved cats, and he thought that he enjoyed a special relationship with them, even though as a boy, they had almost caused his death. He had been playing with kittens in the feed room, and one climbed up where the bags of grain were stacked in ranks and files. The kitten then dropped down the hole where the corners of four stacks sagged together, as if the Grand Canyon were placed where Utah, Colorado, New Mexico, and Arizona met. Leonard scrambled up and plunged, headfirst, after the kitten, which had in the meantime disappeared out the bottom of the stacks. Leonard was not strong enough to push himself out, and the hole was too narrow for him to bring his feet to the ground. He remained there, he thought for hours, crying for help, until he was rescued by his father, who had just happened by. The experience intensified his admiration for cats.

The presence of cats seemed to Leonard a strong sign of civilization. Cats had native grace and intelligence. They were clean and compact. Any society that sustained cats had protein to spare, for if cats were to remain domestic they had to be offered regular meals. Either that, or lots of mice.

Wherever he went, Leonard noted cats he saw. In Sandy Creek most were shorthaired tabbies, grey or orange. In the suburbs of Philadelphia he first saw large numbers of dark longhairs, and these predominated in Wyoming, too. In Cambridge, the cats were mostly spotted, with medium-length hair. Cats followed humankind everywhere, but for the most part, as Darwin had cleverly observed, they resisted being bred into lines. Varieties of cat—the Siamese, Burmese, Birman, Korat, Abyssinian, Manx, Himalayan, and Van—were distinguished by secondary characteristics. Leonard wondered why the feline genotype became geographically specific, why certain colors and markings seemed to appear in distinct environments. Domestic cats seemed to have differentiated just in the way that the races of humankind diverged. Ten generations of cat occurred in the span of a single human generation. Perhaps the colors of cats could be used to trace the diffusion of civilization.

Leonard and Ernest came to Witte's address. It was a rowhouse on the end of a block. The Red Persian cat was sitting on the step. Next to the door was a brass plaque for "Dr. J. Witte, M.D." Leonard rang the bell. The door opened to a slight, blue-eyed woman with thin, short-cut, whitish-blond hair. The cat darted in.

"Residence of Dr Witte," the woman said. "May I help you?"

Leonard recognized the voice on the telephone. He presented themselves as Lieutenant Ranov and Corporal Bit, and apologized for being a half-hour early. The woman faded behind the opening door and then showed them into the combination living room and dining room that took up most of the ground floor.

"Please sit down, gentlemen," the woman pointed to a worn plush sofa with its back to the front window. "Let me take your coats." Leonard handed over his flight jacket and Ernest his woolen trench coat. They sat next to each other on the sofa and looked over the surroundings.

The room was about a dozen feet wide and thirty feet long. The walls and ceiling were tan plaster framed in dark wood. The floor was dark oak covered by several large, worn Oriental carpets. On their right was an arch leading to the front vestibule and, ten feet inside, a narrow staircase leading to the second floor. At the far end of the room was a paneled door, propped half open to reveal the kitchen and pantry. Centered against the far wall was a dark wooden dining table with three unmatched ladder-back chairs. The cat crouched on the side of the table nearest the kitchen door and surveyed the intruders. The dining section had apparently once been separated from the parlor by a sliding door, for, two-thirds of the way down the room, two short wings emerged at right angles from the walls. In the parlor, along the left, out-side wall, was a ceramic fireplace fitted with a gas heater. It burned a barely visible, blue flame.

On the outer wall was a large glass-front bookcase, filled with variously sized treatises in half a dozen languages. Next to it stood the torso of a female medical dummy. Against one of the protruding wings was a music stand and cello case, while on its corresponding half rested an ice axe, rucksack, and lug-soled boots. The wings were partially hidden by two armchairs, each covered by a printed cotton throw. An English pastoral scene hung over the mantle. Magazines appeared in what might have been studied disarray, except for a layer of grime.

A second woman appeared in the arch by the foyer. "I trust Nadia has made you comfortable. I am Dr Joanneke Witte. I'm afraid I don't carry out any research." Leonard and Ernest rose to their feet and shook her extended hand. She was dressed in trou-sers, a woolen jacket, and house slippers.

"Glad to make your acquaintance," Leonard said. "We've come from America to learn about the latest research of Dr Jacob Witte. I've admired his work on cosmic rays for many years."

"I am, you see, only a medical doctor at the local hospital," Anneke Witte said. "I really can't tell you much about my father's work."

"Might we speak with him?" Leonard asked.

Anneke smiled. "Maybe if you go to Leiden, if as I hope he still lives." Nadia hovered at the kitchen door.

"Excuse me for a moment," Anneke said, and disappeared into the kitchen. Nadia reëmerged and asked if the guests would like tea. They mumbled, Thank you, Yes. Leonard, felt the call of nature from the morning's breakfast. Nadia motioned him toward the kitchen. Leonard walked through the door, stopping just long enough to stroke the cat behind its ears. The kitchen seemed brighter than the dining room, as it had both a window and a door opening through the outer wall. Leonard found it at once familiar and foreign. The fixtures and appliances—a gas refrigerator, a wringer-washer, a sink—seemed too small. The utensils were archaic: an enormous meat cleaver, heavy crockery mixing bowls, whisks, grates, and items he could not figure out a use for. Food was scattered about in various states of preparation and preservation.

Nadia pointed to a door at the back of the kitchen. Indoor plumbing had apparently come to the house as an afterthought, for, by the slope of the roof, the bathroom began life as a winterized shed. The bathtub, lodged directly under the slope, suggested a difficult maneuver for entry and exit. It was possible to stand in front of the loo, however, and Leonard peed in the manner prescribed for men throughout the Western world. He washed his hands in cold water and returned to the parlor, glancing in the kitchen at Nadia, who was occupied with a tea tray. What he had seen of the house suggested a marriage of fussiness and cavalier disarray.

Ernest was up and studying the objects in the parlor when Leonard returned. Anneke entered at the same time with a cardboard box.

"Lieutenant," she said, "Here is all that remains from my father's briefcase. Do you read Dutch?" Leonard took the box that she offered and realized, for the first time, that she was speaking to him in clear and nearly idiomatic English.

"I don't think so, at least not well," Leonard replied weakly, looking at Ernest. "We'll manage. But does anything else survive? Notebooks, correspondence files?"

"Perhaps in Leiden," Anneke said. She shrugged her shoulders and left the room.

Nadia arrived with tea and biscuits, placing them on a butler's table in front of the sofa. Leonard ignored what she had prepared and opened the box on his lap. Most of the fifty-odd pages seemed to be the draft of a paper. Parts had been typed, but there were many changes inserted by hand. The sheets were wrinkled, as if they had survived a downpour. On a number of the sheets the corrections, added by pen, had washed away. Dutch cognates with German suggested to Leonard that the manuscript concerned nuclear physics. Leonard looked up and saw Anneke standing behind the butler's table, teacup in hand.

"Was it worth coming all the way from America, Mr Ranov?" she asked.

"I don't know," Leonard said. He placed the box on the couch, next to Ernest, who held the purring cat on his lap and a teacup in his hands. He picked up a biscuit and took a bite. "Might I ask how only this material is left?"

Anneke's cheeks sagged slightly, carrying the corners of her eyes down with them. The effect was to make her seem at once weary and younger, as her crow's feet smoothed away.

"We left Holland when the Queen went to England and we learned about the destruction of Rotterdam," she began. "My father and I hated the Nazis, and after Norway and Denmark fell, we concluded that the Dutch army could not possibly resist an invasion. We were right. The Dutch lasted five days.

"We sailed for England in my brother's yacht. Although we had talked about the possibility of the voyage for weeks, I suppose that we were not really well-prepared for it. Oh, we had some petrol and enough food and water, but we lacked marine charts. My father would not leave. At dusk on the first day we were strafed. My brother bled to death in my arms. Our compass was smashed, and so was the engine. The bullets opened a hole in the yacht's side. I kept warm by exercising. On the third night I was taken in tow by a ship out of the Wash.

Anneke scrutinized Leonard's insignias. "Are you a pilot?"

"Sometimes," Leonard said. "But I am trained to be part of

a bomber crew."

"It will do nothing to win the war," Anneke snapped. "Rotterdam did nothing to break the Dutch spirit, the heavy air attacks on London did not destroy British morale or production. Massive and largely indiscriminate terror does not by itself achieve results. Terror produces an intense counterreaction. The Terror did not secure the aims of the French Revolution; it subverted them, and the revolution failed. Bonaparte's much heralded social and cultural reforms came to nothing, when they did not actually infect noble institutions: Napoleonic Holland would certainly have been better off without its Frenchified Quislings. This war may be won, eventually, but it will depend on ordinary people, not on technology or fancy speeches. Like the English, you Americans think brute force can solve any problem."

Leonard watched Anneke. Her face, basically pleasing, now glowed. She cut his stare by looking out the window to the street and brushing a displaced lock toward the barrette at the back of her neck.

"Nothing matters," she said. "It all comes to nothing. What is the use of trying to prove things? It is simply accidental whether the strivings of a life bear fruit. Friends and family live or die, and we have no control over it. I see women die at the hospital. I cannot explain why. I cannot stop it. The boys go up in their mechanical insects to fight the war of Churchill and his generals—corpulent, anemic gentlemen who never worried much about their next meal. Boys die heroes, their families grieve, the generals tally up the figures, and it is all for nothing."

"Once," Leonard said, "I believed in a world without war."

Anneke turned and left the room. While Ernest stroked the cat and leafed through a book that had been lying on an end table, Leonard studied the box of papers more carefully. There was a long report referring frequently to correspondence from a Dr Létoile. Leonard picked up a second name, G. C. Ratansi, which seemed more familiar. Leonard wrote these in a small notebook.

After five minutes with his material, Leonard concluded that

Witte's work had nothing to do with cosmic rays, at least so far as he could determine, but it did concern a major discovery, in Witte's words. There were three parts to the pages in the box. First was a description of the land around a town on Java called Lembang, with special attention to a nearby volcano. Second came description and calibration of two Geiger counters. Third was an analysis of a number of radioactive sources, all alpha, beta, gamma, and neutron emitters. Leonard had not known that Witte was interested in radioactivity. Perhaps the material was for a joint paper with Létoile, whoever he was.

Anneke, composed and distant, came back into the parlor and asked if she could bring the guests more tea. Leonard declined and decided to press the matter one more time.

"Is there anything that might shed light on these notes?" he asked.

"I think not," Anneke said flatly. "What you hold is what I carried away from Holland in his briefcase. There was a tin box that he brought for the trip, but it disappeared overboard when the yacht was attacked."

"Did you see what was in the box?"

"No," Anneke said. "I do know that the box came from Java several weeks before we left, and its arrival was anxiously awaited. It came from a colleague. Father was using it to write up a report. He was excited. He painted a brilliant future for physics in Holland. He was always like that, an enthusiast anxious to see around the next hill. What difference does it make now, Lieutenant?"

Leonard believed that scientific discoveries did matter in human affairs, although he ran into trouble whenever he came down to listing positive contributions. The problem was that technology and medicine stole the show. Antisepsis, the internal combustion engine, and the electric light were the products of either autodidact mechanics or scientifically naïve medicos. Even wireless broadcasting, the crowning glory of Maxwellian electrodynamics, developed within a tradition of technological ingenuity.

Scientific discoveries remained a matter for the intellect, their partisans to be vilified or lionized depending on reigning ideologies. What difference, finally, did the Copernican worldview make in the lives of ordinary people? That's how Sherlock Holmes admonished Dr Watson—heliocentrism had no practical advantages. How could students, let alone the celebrated man-in-the-street, honestly be urged to spend years of their life in an attempt to understand relativity and quantum theory?

Witte may well have discovered something important. A new particle, Leonard wondered, a new decay series? He had not realized that Witte's activity extended beyond cosmic rays, but here it was. Did the box contain photographic plates? Did the Dutch have a cloud chamber on Java? What was Witte's interest in the East Indies? Why was the army bothering about it all?

Anneke placed her hands on her hips, a Javan gesture of defiance lost on Leonard. "You Americans. Foreigners produce the artifacts of genius, and you spend millions to install them in your alabaster marketplaces and museums. You process tens of thousands of children through hundreds of finishing schools, where pygmies on stilts teach them to bow down before graven European images. Let no one dispute any of the silly little ideas a pygmy produces. Your mean-tempered, narrow-minded Professor Millikan made sure that my father did not win a Nobel prize after my father disproved his so-called theories of cosmic rays. For all your bluster, it took the Japanese to persuade you to act against the Germans. Your government acted as stupidly in the matter as mine." Nadia came up behind her and softly held her arm.

Ernest spoke up. "That is a handsome kris on the mantle. May I inspect the blade?" Anneke nodded slightly. Ernest placed the cat on the couch and walked to the fireplace. He unsheathed the kris. The blade had a lateral twist and a long gouge running the length of one side. He stood with it above the coffee table.

"The kris suits its owner exactly," Ernest observed. "It is in all respects a substitute for the person, invested with the right to take a wife and father a child. But it has a spirit of its own. It can talk, fly, or swim like a snake. Its spirit and power feed on blood. It makes the wearer invincible. This blade has been used in battle."

"The kris drank my brother's blood," Anneke said, her eyes opening wider when she heard Ernest's accented delivery. "It turned a German bullet and probably saved my life. And that is only part of the power it has absorbed." She looked at Ernest. "You have not said much, Corporal. Are you also a scientist?"

"No, *madame*," Ernest answered. "I am merely a clerk who has come to Cambridge to read about iatrochemistry and Paracelsus."

"Paracelsus is a hero to the physicians," Anneke said. "I studied his work in medical ethics at Leiden. He struck me, however, as being quite infused with mysticism and fantasy. His chemistry depended more on faith than on measurement."

"Precisely," Ernest said quickly. "Modern science is not what people think it is. In its formative period, science was merely an adjunct to a dozen forms of magic and spiritual enlightenment. Paracelsus, Kepler, Newton, and Leibniz were both less and more than modern scientists."

"Yes," Anneke continued. "In my last year at medical school, at my professor's recommendation I read a small book in English on Paracelsus. What you say was, I think, the point of the book." She smiled. "I even remember the author. His name almost rhymed with the subject. Bitivilius."

"My book," Ernest said. Leonard, who had been stroking the cat, looked up in astonishment. "Actually, it was my doctoral thesis, which never managed to appear in German or Lithuanian. When I arrived in New York, I translated it as an exercise in improving my English."

"So," Anneke said in German, "a philologist. Dr Bitivilius. So knowledgeable about magic. What other secrets, I wonder, do you hide? It doesn't matter." Anneke crossed her left arm to hold Nadia's hand, still in place on her right arm.

"There is always more to know than can be demonstrated or easily explained," Ernest answered in German. Leonard, who spoke passable German, took in every word. Ernest then said something which Leonard thought could not possibly be German. Nadia reddened, looked down at the floor, and answered in a short phrase.

"Well," Anneke said in English, "it has been a pleasure to make your acquaintance. I hope that your stay in Cambridge will be useful."

Leonard stood up and thanked her for her coöperation. Nadia fetched their coats and showed them out while Anneke remained on her feet in the parlor. The cat, with a front paw extended over the seat cushion, watched through half-opened eyes.

They walked toward the Cam. Leonard wondered what there was to report about Witte and his research. A few water-stained sheets of manuscript, a few names. Corporal Bit was a more interesting discovery.

"Ernest,there is much about you I do not know."

"No doubt, no doubt."

"How did you know about the dagger on the mantle?" Leonard asked.

"The kris is a capital example of the fruitful intersection of science and imagination," Ernest answered. "The technology of forging the blade is quite involved. The best blades are, in fact, a form of carbon or nickel steel derived from meteoric iron. They are drawn and quenched scores of times. A complicated protocol determines how they may be worn, and in Javan folklore and drama the kris becomes a man's alter ego. I had read about them, of course, but this was the first time that I have held one."

"What did you say to the other woman in the house?"

"Oh, just that I hoped she liked staying in Cambridge. She's Czech, you know. There were a number of Czech novels in the parlor. It's been a while since I tried Czech. Ten minutes of reading put me back into it."

Two refugees from the Nazis, Leonard thought, living in the

genteel poverty that might be socially acceptable to a Cambridge academic. Probably neither had a college affiliation. What an imposing and hostile figure Witte's daughter cut. So much contempt, even hatred, toward the world. How should her remarks be interpreted? He wondered how Nadia had come to England. By way of Denmark? Switzerland? Holland? Portugal? The daughter spoke fluent English, but Nadia's speech was heavily accented and hesitant. Did she learn Danish or Dutch before fleeing again? Or perhaps she was simply shy and retiring. How did she wind up in Cambridge? There were bonds of affection between the two women. What was the *ménage*? But, then, it was none of his business.

"Do you think that her reporting is reliable?" Leonard asked Ernest. "I mean, what she said about the loss of the rest of her father's papers." If the material was so important, why didn't Witte take better care of it?

"As far as it goes, yes," Ernest said. "She is a woman with intense internal conflict. I think that she is hostile toward Europe in general, toward rationalism and efficiency. Even in Holland she must have felt adrift. She must find the Javan way of thinking more congenial. The kris is very important to her. A lovely and valuable object."

They reached Chesterton Road and turned toward the center of Cambridge. Leonard saw other uniformed figures walking across Jesus Green on the opposite bank of the Cam. Two British soldiers. A naval officer. A bevy of nurses. Cambridge had been integrated and democratized at just the time that learning ground to a halt. The best brains had been plucked and set down in one or another warehouse to propose arcane strategies and design the instruments of war. Leonard was sure that these thinkers merely proposed, while the warlords and their capitalist bosses disposed. Remaining to drink themselves into a stupor at High Table and amuse themselves with the boys were the superannuated, the crippled, and the incompetent.

"I want to see the library," Ernest said. "Care to come along?"

Leonard followed Ernest's lead down the country lane that was Queen's Road. People on bicycles passed in both directions. How odd that bicycles had never found a firm place in American culture. Neither had English gardens, evident in winter hibernation on either side of the road. These were the Backs, which the colleges had turned into private pleasure haunts. Ernest stopped and consulted a small map.

"There," he pointed. "The university library, America's contribution to this community, rises behind this college. We go this way."

They walked through an open quadrangle toward the gothic-inspired castle that Rockefeller had built for Cambridge's books. This, Leonard thought, might well have been lifted from an American campus. They went through the massive doors and faced an impassive guard.

"I think we must disrobe first and apply for temporary access," Ernest said. Reëmerging from the cloakroom, they presented themselves to the guard, who indicated that they had to see the registrar. After a minute a man with a thick black beard emerged from a door on the left of the entrance hall. He was clutching a slip of paper.

"That's our cue," Ernest said.

Ernest knocked on the door and the two men entered when asked to. Before them was a flabby man sitting in front of a large, bound register. They filled out application forms and, after ten minutes, found their way to the catalogue room. Ernest was smiling broadly, looking around in delight. Leonard imagined spirits emerging from the library's books to reconstitute giant robed presences, and he shrank from their judgment. Ernest pulled him into the outside hall.

"I want to spend the rest of the day in the manuscript room," Ernest confided. "Now cheer up," he insisted, "there's still work to do here." Leonard knit his brows in a query. "Sure," Ernest continued. "Why don't you look up your man Witte in the catalogue here and then ask around at the local physics laboratory about him."

"Yes," Leonard said. "Why not?"

Ernest looked at Leonard intently. "We won't be seeing much of each other from now on."

"You mean, you return later by boat?"

"No," Ernest said, "I'm staying on here, at least for the coming months."

"What?"

Ernest continued. "Coming as your superfluous aide-de-camp was really not the main purpose of my trip. You see, now that the B-17s are gearing up to hammer Germany, the air corps needs someone to compose its propaganda leaflets in Eastern European languages. That's me. Or, that's what they told me in Washington I'd become. I believe that the job is related to a new British-American policy of support for sabotage in the Baltic. I'll be billeted somewhere in Cambridge, near books, dictionaries, and the odd Slavic linguist. I imagine that once or twice a week I'll deliver my work to Bassingbourn or perhaps to London. And for the rest, I may lose myself in the library."

How like the military, Leonard thought. He was simply Ernest's cover, although he could only guess why Ernest needed one. His aide had in effect been seconded to Cambridge as a don. Ernest's universal and synthetic vision seemed ideally suited to the resources of a place like Cambridge. He was aggressively intellectual without being in the least resentful about what fate prepared for him. Leonard imagined his never leaving Cambridge.

Leonard thought to express an appreciation of Ernest's view of the world and even his companionship. But he sensed that it would not mean much to Ernest. "If I don't see you at the airfield," Leonard said, "take care, Professor." Ernest set off down a long corridor.

Leonard surveyed the catalogue room. There was no need to look for Witte's name here. He already knew enough about the man and his research. Leonard was intrigued, however, by the name frequently mentioned in Witte's notes, Létoile. In his days as a physicist, he seldom had occasion to refer to the French literature. If Létoile were French he would surely have written manuals that might be entered in the catalogue. The unexpected answer came after a minute of thumbing through a drawer of index cards. Leonard found that J. Létoile, the only entry with that surname, was the author of six monographs published beginning in 1928 by the astronomical observatory at Lembang in the Dutch East Indies. The monographs, in English, concerned surveys of double stars.

This would be the right man, Leonard thought, for Witte to have conferred with on Java. Despite his French name, Létoile seemed to be a permanent fixture at the Dutch observatory there. How odd, though, that Witte would have discussed radioactivity with an observational astronomer. Witte's successor at the institute of technology on Java would surely have known more about such matters. Leonard regretted now that he had not asked Joanneke Witte about her time on Java, and whether she knew about the astronomer Létoile.

Leonard slowly exited from the Rockefeller cathedral. He had plenty of time to catch a train to Bassingbourn, and he did not feel hungry. Ernest had provided a second suggestion. Leonard pulled up his collar against the early February damp and walked off toward the center of Cambridge in search of the Cavendish Laboratory.

At Queen's Road he found himself in front of a well-worn path that led directly toward the river. He followed it through a garden that, he thought, should have kept a small crew busy for much of the growing season. Now the garden was a monument to idleness, that of the economic system permitting such excesses in wartime and that of the self-indulgent college wardens directing the diggers, planters, and mowers. Leonard crossed the Cam, here appearing as a narrow and murky stream. On the other side there were more gardens, stone walls, and various palisades. He threaded his way through sunless alleys and soon found himself on Trinity Street. He studied Trinity's enormous wooden gate, which he thought able to withstand anything less than a tank assault. A large tabby cat curled up on the cobblestones by the open door which was cut into the gate. Leonard took this as a good omen. He went through the door and asked a watchman for directions to the Cavendish. The Cavendish Professor, after all, was a fixture of Trinity.

He saw that the central court at Trinity was an immaculate green. To the right was the chapel, frequented by physicists from Newton to Rayleigh to Rutherford. Before turning to the Cavendish, just a ten-minute walk away, Leonard decided to look closer at the storied house of God. He went up to the door and pushed, not expecting it to give way. It did. Here was a Protestant church open to casual inspection.

The entrance hall featured many centuries of memorial plaques on the uneven stone walls and floors. The names and offices of benefactors, martyrs, and illuminati bore mute witness through the ages. Leonard had never been inside a Catholic church and only several times inside a provincial American Protestant one. His experience with regular religious services came from weekly Collection at Swarthmore, an obligatory gathering in a stripped-down, neo-Gothic assembly hall which was addressed by one or another sage. To him the Trinity chapel dripped with overpowering and unnecessary ornament, curlicues and gilded fairies that could only intervene between the worshiper and his God. He passed into the nave with its rows of hard oak pews and soft knee stools, the convoluted altar, the stained-glass windows, and the vaulted roof—everything, he thought, designed to impress the assembly that the path to spiritual salvation lay through obedience to the temporal lords who endowed the structure. He could not begin to imagine sitting through a service in the place.

Leonard left the chapel and walked out the Trinity gate on his way to the Cavendish. Ornamentation and ceremonial function, he concluded, were central features of English life. These things reminded the ruling class of their prerogatives and the working class of their duties. The deprivations and horrors of war took form within the constraints of ceremony.

He passed by haberdasheries and pharmacies. Life seemed oblivious of the war. He jogged left off King's Parade and arrived at the beginning of Free School Lane, a grimy, cobblestone alley. He reached the stone arch that the Trinity watchman had indicated as the entrance to the Cavendish, a building with all the appearances of an American college dormitory.

Just through the arch he saw a young man carrying a hacksaw and a piece of tubing. Leonard introduced himself and asked to speak with the director or his secretary about nuclear physics. The man—tall, blond, and slightly stooped—said, "Follow me," and threaded his way through doors, stairs, and passages. The interior seemed to Leonard like a slum: cracked and stained plaster, creaking pine floors, grey windowpanes, an intaglio of ancient pipes and electrical wires apparently strung at random. He passed by vacant and filthy laboratory rooms. The young man knocked on a door and entered when acknowledged.

"Dr Plum, sir," he said, "you have an American visitor."

"Well, have the man come in," Alasdair Plum said. When Leonard appeared in the doorway, Plum continued, "Throw your coat on the chair there and take a seat." He pointed to the sofa. "And then tell us what brings you to this quiet corner of the world."

Having sunk into the sofa, which lacked a good number of springs, Leonard explained that he was following up on Witte's recent research on nuclear physics and had been led to the work of G. C. Ratansi, which, he recalled, appeared in French around 1940. Leonard asked if Plum knew what Ratansi was doing, and where he might be. Plum was sixtyish, thin, and relatively short. He seemed quite enveloped in his three-piece wool suit. As Leonard spoke, Plum sucked on a pipe without taking care to light it, and his eyes rolled back into heavy lids. Leonard struggled to associate this man sitting behind an untidy desk with the last name on a string of seminal papers dealing with the neutron and radioactivity.

"Ratansi, well, yes," Plum said when Leonard had finished. "He did carry through some interesting calculations. Let's see. He did leave Paris, I think, when France fell. I think he never made it to England, or if he did, I never found out about it." There was a big sucking noise from the dead pipe. "Oh, yes, now I remember." Plum stared at Leonard. "He's in Montreal at the university there, doing war work. They've assembled quite a group, integrating several of our brightest prospects. Yes, someone visiting from McGill mentioned him in passing a year or two ago."

"Thanks," Leonard said.

"Not at all," Plum rejoined, "glad to be of help. I regret that there is not much here to show you at the moment, what with staff flying off in all directions. The military, you know, has licked the honey out of the pot." He scanned Leonard's uniform. "Odd, though, that the American staff was unable to trace Ratansi for you, but things are so confounded hierarchical in wartime. Do you expect to see him?"

Leonard took the question to mean, Did he now think that he might like to see Ratansi? It was probably not difficult to stop by Montreal on the way back to Washington, although the detour would mean cutting two or more days out of his time with his parents.

"Yes," Leonard answered, "I'd like to look him up."

"In that case," Plum continued, "let me give you a note for him." A bit of presumption, Leonard thought, in this offer, and also a bit of gallantry. Plum was old enough to remember when officers were gentlemen. Maybe in England they still were. Perhaps Plum was a friend of Ratansi's. Or perhaps Plum thought to improve his lines of scientific communication. And perhaps Plum just wanted to be helpful to a foreigner who had expressed an interest in nuclear physics. Plum wrote a few lines on a sheet of foolscap with a gold-pointed fountain pen that he pulled from a vest pocket, sealed the message in an envelope which he addressed to G. C. Ratansi in Montreal, and handed the envelope to Leonard.

Efficient, professional, and collegial.

Leonard rose to his feet and allowed Plum to show him out. As they walked, Plum described how he had come to specialize in physics during the First World War, when he was interned as a prisoner in Germany with a young graduate of Rutherford's Manchester. "It is all chance and happenstance in life," Plum concluded as they reached the arch facing the street. "What a man decides to pursue, whom to love and marry, when and where he will die, there is no control over any of it. The world no longer responds to the actions of key players, like the ghost of Hamlet's father. Little men and dwarven spirits determine our destiny. We can only act generously and honestly, don't you think, in the face of such leveling mediocrity."

Leonard thanked the Cavendish physicist again and set off toward the center of Cambridge. It was 1:30. He wanted to sit quietly and plan his next moves. He ducked into a pub, claimed a table, and found himself nursing a pint of bitter.

Leonard quickly sensed that he was not at High Table, or even at middle table. No tutors or scholars frequented this place. The room was close and sour-smelling, its wooden floor slick with libation and disinfectant. A mouse wriggled along the bar's footrail. A handful of people talked, smoked, and drank. The men and two women were short and thick, their clothes hanging for the most part in shapeless folds. He understood little of their banter and dialogue. Who was to say that the flip side of collegial intercourse did not have dons and receptions, scandal and ecstasy, to mirror what Leonard knew he would never see behind the walls and gates?

It was not, after all, mere chance that brought him to be drinking a beer in a Cambridge pub. He had acted on the basis of decisions, and actions entailed consequences. Suppose he had not joined a communist cell in West Philadelphia, or had not gone to Wyoming, or, now, had not met Alasdair Plum. Leonard concluded that quite the most interesting experiences occurred when he followed an unconventional, if not recondite, inclination, and he was still young enough to value new experiences highly. What better way to harass the military than by investing their fool's chase with the dignity of a quest. He would knock on Ratansi's door.

Leonard returned to the Blue Boar. The innkeeper had already charged him for a second night's lodging. He paid without complaining. Waiting for the train to Bassingbourn, and then from the train carriage looking out, he absorbed English sensations. He had expected, he realized, a grandeur and elegance that was for the most part absent, at least from his brief encounters. British understatement appeared in forthrightness, as if people always and everywhere sought to project the sum total of their character. The countryside did not seem, at this time of year, to belong to an emerald isle set in a silver sea.

He was at the airfield by dinnertime. From the lights and activity he could see that B-17s spotted the runway. His plan now was to catch the first flight to Gander, then on to Montreal, and from Montreal home by train. He found the duty officer. To his surprise he heard that a Liberator would depart for Gander in an hour. Leonard had not thought that Liberators regularly made the North Atlantic run. He made sure that he was on as supercargo. He would find a connection to Montreal later, in Newfoundland. He walked off into the night, searching for the giant bird in whose belly he would sleep for the night and then awake to walk on the New World near where Leif, Erik's son, claimed it for the first transatlantic civilization nearly a thousand years earlier.

Part II

New World

I've spent the evening with a book by an Austrian physicist. The world, he says, is filled with images. We may imagine a deeper reality behind the images, but all truth derives basically from the superficial images. I don't know how you could work out any laboratory idea if you followed this notion. But the man is right about one thing. Old ideas are crumbling quickly. There are, dearest Mary, great forces locked inside what used to be called the immutable building-blocks of nature—atoms. They break up and change themselves from one chemical type to another. There is enough energy inside a gram of radium to power a city like Montreal—or to turn it to ash.

Ernest Rutherford to Mary Newton Rutherford, 5 February 1905,
Rutherford papers, McGill University Archives, Montreal

Daddy dear, Santa Fe is just lovely. The car is holding up. We are staying in an apartment with the mountains on two sides and the high plains on the south. The adobe structures take on light in marvelous ways. People really do wear heavy silver and turquoise–rings, buckles, necklaces–and ponchos. It is so unlike anything back East. We see the scientists and their families wandering the streets. They are dressed in what you would call "weeds." Some of them are very young, I think, at least they act like children, waving their arms and shouting for no apparent reason. Maybe it is compensation for the tedious nature of their top secret work. Or maybe scientists are like that. I saw Niels Bohr, I'm sure it was he. How can indeterminacy win the war?

May Sarton to George Sarton, 3 June 1945, Sarton papers,
Houghton Library, Harvard University

4

A Frozen Heat

Correspondents say that things are not going well in the Netherlands. The Nazis are robbing it blind. Physics is in eclipse–all the laboratory equipment has been confiscated. I've heard from two colleagues now about Witte in Leiden. He is alive, but his health is deteriorating. He is working on a theory of short-range nuclear forces, I think. Somehow it's related to cosmic rays. But he talked most earnestly with both men about a volcano on Java. Nostalgia for the absolute. When he was dying, my uncle gripped my arm, the arm of a six-year-old boy, and told me about his arrival on Ellis Island. People so much want the significant parts of their life to continue in other minds. Is that why we write?

I. I. Rabi to J. Robert Oppenheimer, 25 December 1941.
Oppenheimer papers, Institute for Advanced Study, Princeton

A wave cemented Leonard Ranov's shins into the sand as it rose to his armpits and then receded. The undertow drew enough wet sand from around his legs to allow him to scramble higher on the dune. He plunged his arms through a crust of dry sand and kicked steps into the concave erosion left by the wave. He gained two feet in height. A rhizome of beach grass, dislodged by the action of the last wave, blew his way. He grabbed it with his right hand and pulled. It held firm, higher up. It cut into his palm. Salt and sand brought fire to the wound. Leonard pulled harder. He heard another wave thunder behind him. Water softly buoyed him up. Somewhere above a voice was shouting.

Leonard awoke to see a figure in black leather, oxygen mask

turned aside, bending over to him, "Lieutenant, we set down in Montreal in fifteen minutes. You might want to clean up this mess." The bombardier was shaking Leonard's shoulder as he lay on the floor of the plane, wrapped in his parachute. A line coiled tight around his right hand. He had slept since leaving Gander.

He disentangled hand and feet and sat up against a strut. He could feel the plane descending. It was the first ocean nightmare that he could remember since he was a boy. There was anxiety in crossing the ocean, and anticipation about returning home to the ocean's shores in New Jersey. He had read that ocean dreams carried sexual meaning. He thought back to the Witte woman's peculiar *ménage*. Ernest Bit was right. More could be known than could be proved.

The interior of the Liberator glowed from the illumination of the radio and the instrument board in the cockpit. There was enough light for Leonard to stuff the parachute back into its pack. He stood up, stretched, and made his way toward the nose. He poked his head through the partition.

"Hi, guys," he addressed the two men in charge of the flight. "Nice trip."

> *Beautiful dreamer, wake unto me,*
> *Gremlins and cross-winds have troubled your sleep,*
> *Under the stars we shall fly round the globe,*
> *Beautiful dreamer, your fortune's been told.*

A suggestion of dawn appeared out the port windows. Leonard was not tired so much as hungry. He stood watching the pilot guide the bomber into its landing approach. Then he went aft and strapped himself in. In his experience, landing was the worst part of flying. When taking off you could have confidence in the machine and the men who serviced it. The ground crew *saw* you disappear into the fuselage, start the engines and taxi down the runway. The machine had been activated by living, breathing human beings. Landing was quite the reverse. A tiny sputtering speck of painted metal would grow to superhuman proportions and then stop. With luck it would disgorge the usual number of flyers. It was harder to achieve rapport with the ground when landing. Small slip-ups led to embarrassment or disaster.

The bomber bounced four times before settling on the runway. The pilot cut the engines and strode back past the bomb bay to open the rear hatch.

"Now for the ladies," he laughed, "if I don't freeze my arse on the way in." Then followed a disquisition on the pleasures to be found in the wide-open city of Montreal. His voice trailed off as he disappeared through the floor. Leonard pulled his gear to the hole in the floor and dropped it through. He felt the wind whip up into the cabin. He secured the strap of his helmet and lowered himself to Canadian ashphalt, they called it.

A low ceiling had obscured the city from the air. The runway featured the usual landing flares and floodlights, hangars and ramshackle wooden offices. It was freezing cold. Patches of grey ice blazed with reflected light. Leonard could see a snowplow idling near a maintenance shed. No fun servicing an airstrip in this climate.

Leonard shouldered his duffle bag and dangled his parachute as he loped to check in with the duty officer. He dropped off the parachute for refolding and proceeded to a Canadian sergeant, who handed him a shore-leave pass. He found his way to the American officers' mess. There he showered, shaved, and changed into a clean uniform. When he finished it was 7:30, and a dim light suffused the unfinished, frame barracks. He wanted a real breakfast before he looked up Ratansi at McGill. He put on his overalls and boots and called for a taxi. Within five minutes he was winding around streetcars on the way to Montreal's center on the south slope of the mountain. He told the driver to drop him off at a place for an unpretentious, civilized meal.

"Yes sir, the Desire Café," the cabbie said. "Decent food, right off the Main." He spoke with the up and down cadence of

French-Canadian English, which Leonard had never heard before.

"All right," Leonard said, "Just so long as it's not far from
McGill."

"Not too far. Are you American?"

"Yeah," Leonard nodded, "That's what they tell me."

"Me too," the cabbie added, and glanced back in the rear-
view mirror. "I am born in Massachusetts, but my father moved
back here when the mill closed." Leonard saw that his driver
was a boy, perhaps sixteen years old, with light brown hair and
pale blue eyes.

Leonard leaned forward. "I was born in New Jersey." On
the front seat he saw a violin case and under it some sheet music.

"I want to go to Atlantic City to play on the Boardwalk," the
boy touched his violin.

They drove down a boulevard flanked on both sides by three-
storey row-houses. Each had curved, iron-railed stairs leading to
the second storey. Spanish ornament, Leonard thought. This is
the forest primeval.

"My old school." The boy pointed to a long stone structure
with a mansard tin roof, a stripped-down interpretation of middle
nineteenth-century French design. It was near a church and had
a large cross over the entrance. "The priests wanted me to study
Latin, but I thought it was no use. Maybe I will go back to an
English school and learn something." Several blocks along they
passed another building where children were congregating. It
had a cross over the door. Leonard wondered if the English
schools were also run by clerics. His experience with Catholic
institutions, limited to novels and movies, brought nothing encouraging to mind.

The city seemed to him a shabbier, exotic version of Philadelphia. The streets and sidewalks reflected the flat grey sky.
People picked their way through ice-encrusted snowdrifts to trol-
ley stops or shops. Color appeared in the mittens and scarves of
schoolchildren and the primitive, garish, English billboards, which

exhorted the populace to abandon themselves to American soft drinks or harsh Canadian tobacco.

The cab turned off the boulevard and headed up Mount Royal Avenue toward the mountain. It would be a hill in Wyoming, Leonard thought, but in the East all things are exaggerated. The cab pulled up in front of Desire's. Leonard handed over a Canadian ten-dollar bill. The cabbie snapped it, clucked and shook his head, and darted into the café for change. Leonard wished the boy luck. He spied an empty booth and sat facing the entrance, the duffle on his left. To his right, the mountain's white mass remained visible through rime on the picture window.

By delivering his fare to the Main, the immigrant receiving area occupied largely by Jews, the violinist cabbie had sized things up correctly. Leonard felt at ease. He heard accented English and Yiddish. He could be on New York's East Side, he thought, minus the action and the intensity. Leonard shed his jacket and unzipped his overalls. He gave an order of poached eggs and bagels to the waiter, a boy with protruding eyes and a black pompadour. He nursed a coffee and glanced around. The place radiated an unpretentious honesty that he found encouraging. Two middle-aged businessmen discussed their children's summers. A university student in tie and three-piece suit hunched over a book with fine print. A news vendor arrived to join two older men at a table near the door. A bear of a man entered carrying a large box of milk and butter, which he handed over the counter to the cook. The two joked familiarly. Leonard's breakfast arrived, and the waiter ambled to a counter stool and immersed himself in an open newspaper.

Leonard thought about the lives displayed before him. He could feel, but remained unable to describe, the unstudied dignity and easy flow of what he saw. These were people with a heavy past and, surely, burning desires, but there seemed a self-possession, an internal compass, that placed them outside the war and the dull, frozen climate. It was more than mere ethnicity, and completely unlike what he knew in Sandy Creek, or the big

American cities, where the immigrants—Jews, Poles, Italians—
became civic-minded and progressive. There might come a writer
to provide a caricature of this morning's experience—perhaps the
waiter would go on to McGill and reinvent his youth in a fantas-
tic novel—but how hard it would be to get the action right, to
describe a dozen people simultaneously acting out a half hour of
their lives, hands and arms moving, the punctuated equilibrium
of three or four conversations serenaded by the clatter of cutlery
and dishes and the whirl of an exhaust fan which, while evacuat-
ing smoke from the grill, did nothing about the cigars, sweat, and
wet melton of the patrons. How sad if the boy waiter would someday recast these people in a low-life comedy. Broad humor, he
thought, could be found only in the street that paralleled the mountain, St Urbain, namesake of the seventeenth-century pope who,
ridiculed by Galileo, unleashed the Inquisition on Italy's prince
of reason.

The cashier had black hair pulled back into a bun. Her lips
and fingernails were bright red. As Leonard approached she put
down her cigarette and offered a smile of perfectly regular teeth.

"So, what was it?" As she spoke in something like a Brooklyn accent she looked past Leonard to the back of the room where
the pay phone had just rung. "Wait here, darling," she said, as
she walked to answer the call. After ten seconds she returned.
Leonard described his meal. The cashier's lips fluttered silently
as she added up the bill.

Leonard learned from the cashier that it was a short walk to
McGill around the northeast slope of the mountain. He sealed
himself against the cold and stepped out. He was not a tall man,
but here he looked over most pedestrians. The duffle on his shoulder made him seem even more formidable, and he received wide
berth. People young and old moved with the concave cheeks and
downturned lips of dental prosthesis. How different from in England, where ugly teeth flashed honorably and mashed effectively.
Leonard felt as he thought a surgeon must feel, peeling back layers of tissue to reveal the throbbing core of a patient.

After several minutes Leonard left the cluttered shops and narrow sidewalks that spilled over from the Main. He walked along a broad avenue marking the northern boundary of Mount Royal. He passed a statue of George-Etienne Cartier and a deserted bandstand. He continued along to the right and the south slope of the mountain. A stadium appeared, and then, at the top of University Street, a hospital. He descended the street that he thought would surely lead him to McGill's campus. He came to a gate through which he could see a squat neoclassical façade mounted by a small, round tower. He asked the guard for the way to the Macdonald Physics Building.

"You go in, in." The man motioned vigorously toward his left.

Leonard followed instructions and found himself doubling back along one side of a horseshoe-shaped campus that opened, behind him, into a mass of Montreal's taller buildings. Across the field and to the left of a squat pimpled structure was a Grecian temple rather too tall for its width. Then, further along, two Gothic cathedrals. Three tall buildings, crenelated Victorian pastiches, formed the flank along which he walked. The first two buildings faced in toward the campus, and neither was devoted to physics. His goal would be the third crenellation, whose entrance faced to the city.

Leonard followed a shoveled and salted walk to the doors of the physics building. For a moment he took in its turrets, its dozens of chimneys, its two tiers of balustrades, its Romanesque columns and masonry of red stone. Names of the immortals appeared on cornices and above the massive, hemispherical protrusion that covered the front steps. He recognized Ohm and several others, but the physicists he admired most had not been considered suitable inspirations for immature minds; he was struck by the empty spaces waiting to be engraved. He climbed the steps, opened the massive oak portal, and found himself in a foyer. To his left were stone stairs, to his right a grand fireplace bearing on its mantel St Paul's injunction, assimilated by the founders of the

Royal Society of London, "Prove All Things." This, the Macdonald Physics Building, was the birthplace of nuclear physics.

He headed up the stairs to the main floor, where he assumed the departmental secretariat would be, still hefting his belongings on his shoulder. In contrast to its façade, the building's interior radiated practical elegance and a sense of proportions. Belonging to the last generation of physics laboratories constructed without iron, which would disturb delicate magnetical measurements, it was all bricks and masonry and hardwood beams and arches. It featured special laboratory desks mounted on stone pillars independent of other structural components. Rutherford had revolutionized physics by completely ignoring the building's provision for making detailed and delicate measurements on mechanical properties and the weak magnetic fields of the earth. Rutherford studied subatomic particles traveling with colossal velocities. He built his own apparatus, which sat, dwarfed by the building's massive beams and pillars, on ordinary tables subject to the experimenter's movements. Within thirty years the new physics had grown too large for the laboratories where it first saw light. Antiquated, dusty, creaking, the Macdonald Physics Building became the haunt of medical students learning about Newton's laws and engineering students reinventing Galileo's telescope.

Leonard found the departmental office and walked in. He announced himself to the secretary and asked to see Professor Ratansi.

"We have no one here by that name," she said looking up from her typewriter and pronouncing each word.

"I was told by Professor Plum at Cambridge that he had a position at the university here."

"You must be mistaken," the secretary continued. She stood up and crossed her hands to pull her black sweater close. The action made her seem pious and protective. "Professor Woodger is in just down the hall. He may be able to help you." Leonard thanked her and walked to knock on Woodger's door.

"Yes?" he heard. "Come in."

Herbert Arthur Woodger had come in early to speak with two metallurgical engineers about casting a bust that he had recently completed. He was bubbling with excitement at the prospect. The foundry's heat drew him, as an insect to a flame. His career as a physicist had centered around measuring the thermal properties of ice, a topic coherent with the original design of the Macdonald Physics Building and fitting with the Canadian climate; now he thought only of fire. Woodger was a student of physics at McGill during Rutherford's tenure, but instead of becoming one of Rutherford's assistants, he chose to concentrate on the skills required of a structural engineer. Before the First World War he hung around Cambridge for a few years, rubbing shoulders with British lords and the sons of colonial administrators. Having acquired the right moves and the best friends, he returned to McGill and rose to a professorship at just the time that he lost interest in studying ice floes on the St Lawrence River. His post required that he lecture to medical students. His pleasure was poetry, painting, and now sculpture.

Woodger looked up from the box that held his latest creation and saw a figure in leather and sheepskin standing beside a large duffle bag.

"How can I help you?" he mumbled.

Leonard stared at the stooped man whose torso approximated a ski slope. Woodger's eyes were red and runny. The smell of whiskey pervaded the room but none was evident.

"Can you tell me where I might find G. C. Ratansi?" Leonard asked. "Dr Plum indicated that he was in Montreal."

"Ratansi, Ratansi," Woodger shook his head. "Oh, yes, the Italian. Yes, he's here all right. Fine chap. Not much of a conversationalist. And how is dear Alasdair? It's been years since I've seen him. He's bang in the middle of it at Cambridge. Had the strangest way of hitting a tennis ball. Like this." Woodger bent his wrist and flexed his arm from the elbow.

"Is his office around here?" Leonard asked.

"Oh! No, no, he's over the hill. I mean, working on some secret war project. A whole group of them over there, at the French university. He came by last year to look around. Spoke in French, don't you know? Too bad we don't get more people passing through from England. You say you were studying there?"

"I was just visiting," Leonard said.

"Come, let me show you my heart's desire," Woodger motioned to his guest. Leonard looked into the box on Woodger's chair and saw the bust of a woman. Her face was smooth, chin, lips, and nose barely indicated, but large eyes and arching eyebrows. Hair cascaded in gently curled fettuccini from the high forehead.

"Is the lady sculpted from life?" Leonard asked.

"Quite so, quite so," Woodger replied. "I had so much trouble getting the hair to fall just right. Don't you think? Like Botticelli's Primavera she floats on high o'er hill and dale. Oh, there are some good sculptors here, like Laliberté. I do so detest the representations of dog doodle and bird's feathers which artists favor these days. You see, the real works of art are in the hall under glass."

Woodger tugged at Leonard's arm and led him into the hall by the stairs. Their progress was slowed by the duffle that Leonard dragged. "Step lively, young man. Here they are, Rutherford's machines."

Leonard had not noticed the glass cases when he came in. Now he looked at shining brass contraptions, boxes and cylinders with levers, springs, screws, coils, and baffles. Woodger continued, "In my day I saw these built, machined not by Rutherford, who had ten thumbs, but by a skilled mechanic. I don't know how they were supposed to work, but this is art the mistress of science." Leonard nodded. The instruments were indeed beautiful, much finer than the apparatus he had put together in Wyoming. It must be most satisfying to construct a beautiful instrument that resonates with harmony from the spheres. Jacob

Witte had done that.

"Well, good day, Mister, Mister...."

"Ranov," Leonard supplied.

"Ranov, and remember me to Alasdair Plum."

Leonard pulled his duffle down the stairs and sat on a stone bench facing the physicists' ceremonial fireplace. "Prove All Things," it proclaimed silently. Alasdair Plum had not actually said that Ratansi worked at McGill. He may or may not have known about what was happening on the other side of Mount Royal. If Ratansi was working on a secret war project, he would probably not want to talk about Jacob Witte and nuclear physics. Leonard had not tried to speak French since his freshman year at Swarthmore, and he knew no Italian. How would he communicate with Ratansi? But what did it matter? He could board the train for New York, write up his report, and put a colophon to it all. After a few days with his parents in Sandy Creek, he would be in Washington. This peculiar, grey, frozen city would vanish.

He scolded himself for forgetting his mission to confound the air corps and actually find out what Witte had discovered. Leonard noticed a public telephone in the hall. What did it hurt to see if Ratansi was in the directory? "Prove All Things." Two Ratansis, one of them "G. C." Leonard hesitated. He disliked speaking over the telephone. Why not appear on Ratansi's doorstep?

*
*   *

"Sit down, Signore Ratansi," the rector motioned from behind his massive desk.

Ratansi took an armchair and faced his inquisitor. Wan and drawn, with round hairy ears and black-rimmed eyes, enveloped in ecclesiastical garb, the rector looked not unlike a wooden Christ hanging behind him. The crucifix was the only decoration in the room. Suspended halfway up the eighteen-foot wall, it lent gravity to the living figure below. A tall window flanked each of the rector's sleeves. Ratansi sat toward one corner of the rector's desk. As he looked over toward the old man he was able to see, through a window, white masses and grey lines partially obscured by a light snowfall.

"Two years ago the university engaged you to teach chemistry. It provided you with a laboratory for carrying out research. Almost from the beginning we have been disturbed by your comportment. You would not open your lectures with a prayer, something we were prepared to overlook. Students have complained about your courses. They are mystified instead of being enlightened. That we attributed to your unfamiliarity with how things are done here." The rector had been speaking in Italian until the last sentence, when he switched to French.

"We think it is not a question of your ability to express yourself in the language of the country," the rector continued. "We are confounded by the doctrines that you disseminate. We begin to think that you are not one of us."

Ratansi had prepared himself for bad news when, earlier that morning, the rector's secretary had called to request his presence at 11:00. Things had not been going well over the past year. Students commented to the dean about his courses; the dean constantly grumbled that he was not spending enough time mixing chemicals in the laboratory. His scientist colleagues had been trained in Swiss, Belgian, or American Catholic universities, and his Parisian pedigree and accent provoked resentment. He had not thought it possible, however, that his colleagues would openly accuse him of doctrinal heresy.

"I teach scientific truth," Ratansi replied in French. As he spoke he looked intently past the rector's eyes and focused on a an icicle outside the window, a deliberate avoidance that he thought would inflame the old man. "Does Your Grace claim to know all nature's secrets?"

"Nature's laws are God's laws," the rector snapped. "Instruction in science is a means of educating good Christians.

These latest ideas of chemistry, all this indeterminism and relativity," he flapped a hand in the air, "these things are unproven. They issue from untutored minds and subvert Christian morality. Our students do not need the abstract speculations of some *petit juif*. They need practical instruction in the laboratory."

Ratansi ignored the slur directed against Einstein. "I am a theorist," he said. "I studied in Rome and Leipzig and Paris. I teach what the world knows to be true. It is of no consequence to me who happens to reveal the truth." Ratansi smiled. "What does Your Grace think goes on in the West Wing here? There are scores of scientists from England and France who are applying modern science to win the war. Should not our students know something about this?"

The rector's eyes narrowed. "Do you have knowledge of the secret research?"

Ratansi remained silent. He was completely frozen out of whatever went on not a hundred meters from his office.

The fall of France had found Gian Carlo Ratansi in Paris. Asthma disqualified him from military service in Italy and made it possible for him to complete his studies at the Milan Institute of Technology and then spend six months with Werner Heisenberg at Leipzig. Although he had never really known any way of life except fascism, Germany in the late 1930s frightened him. In 1938 he left for a temporary position with Joliot-Curie's group at the Collège de France in Paris. His career blossomed there. Papers of his on theoretical nuclear physics were communicated to the Academy of Sciences by Joliot. In 1939 he married a young French student and became a permanent resident, just at the time that Joliot's nuclear physics sustained draconian cuts in funding. He found a new position as a calculator in Pierre Auger's cosmic-ray laboratory at the Ecole normale. Ratansi stayed in Paris during the fall of France. He watched as Joliot's collaborators Halban and Kowarski spirited France's supply of heavy water to England via Bordeaux. He watched as Joliot went to work in his laboratory under German supervision. After two months he and his wife returned to Italy and sailed from there to Spain and on to Buenos Aires, where he had received an informal promise of a position. Wheels turned slowly in Argentina. With his money nearly gone, Ratansi telegraphed a distant cousin in Montreal and told of his imminent arrival.

Ratansi was detained for two days when he and his wife docked in Halifax. His Italian citizenship made him a candidate for internment. Reprieve came at the hands of the French *chargé d'affaires* in Ottawa, a man in Vichy's pay who believed that a policy of French neutrality would best serve his people. The civil servant saw the opportunity of planting a Vichy sympathizer in a French-speaking milieu that had been traditionally hostile to republican values. He arranged with the rector of Montreal's French university for Ratansi to teach chemistry as a visiting professor, at half a normal salary. Ratansi and his wife received resident-alien passes.

Ratansi settled in to make the best of his situation. By the end of 1942, the French university in Montreal had become temporary home to a large team of French and British scientists who had been recruited by Halban to work on a fission bomb. At first Ratansi was ecstatic at being reunited with many of his Parisian colleagues. He quickly found out that his Vichy *laissez-passer* made him suspect. He was simply a chemistry teacher without security clearance. No one at the university, in fact, had any commerce with the foreigners. Although Ratansi knew that the team was planning an atomic pile, he wanted less to be a party to their secrets than simply to discuss new ideas. But the French contingent avoided any detailed discussion of physics. Whenever he met them, conversation began and ended with Montreal winters and Parisian bistros. Auger, who had just arrived in Montreal from Fermi's group at Chicago, seemed less than eager to bring Ratansi into the secret group, even though he had arranged for another Italian émigré to France who had also worked with Fermi, Bruno Pontecorvo, to be initiated. As 1942 came to a close, Gallic eyes turned to de Gaulle's network of Free French in America and North Africa. What had saved Ratansi in 1940 damned him in 1943. His only real scientific contact came through the mail from correspondence with another European-born outsider, Leopold Infeld, in Toronto.

"The foreign savants will leave," the rector spoke again, "but our students remain. And they need to learn practical skills, like the research of Brother Hormisdas."

Ratansi's heart was pounding. For five years Brother Hormisdas had been measuring the specific gravity of maple syrup. His reports regularly appeared in the proceedings of the local society for the advancement of science. He had been vocal in his opposition to Ratansi's theoretical lectures. Ratansi took a deep breath.

"I am unfamiliar with the reception accorded Brother Hormidas's research by the world of science," he began slowly. "What he is doing may or may not be of use to the inhabitants of the countryside here. It is not clear to me that the chemistry department needs more than one professor to tap sugar maples."

The rector picked up a piece of paper from his desk. There was something else.

"We have known about your opinions regarding your colleagues for some time. You regularly slander the name of our university. Until now we have had no proof. However, one of your colleagues has sent me evidence of your malicious pen."

The rector handed the paper to Ratansi. He recognized the typed, single-spaced, German text. It was a transcript of a letter he had sent to Infeld a number of months earlier. After they had exchanged correspondence about theoretical questions, Infeld asked about the general disposition of Ratansi's university toward hiring refugee scientists. Ratansi's reply, which he read again now, was a broad and explicit indictment of higher learning at the university. Brother Hormisdas appeared as a "poor, sad, tired old man with no family or close friends," the rector as a "weak administrator lacking in scholarly credentials, who pilots his institution with one eye on the province's ecclesiastical gerontocracy." A few more unflattering vignettes rounded out the missive. The letter had passed through many hands. Infeld must have showed it to a colleague or acquaintance. Someone made a copy of the offending passage. It was worse than useless to wonder about the sequence that resulted in the betrayed confidence. He now stood accused by his own words.

"You are on notice," the rector stood up. "I would fire you this morning but for the high recommendation of Marshal Pétain's former minister in Ottawa." Ratansi quietly got up and left the rector's office. He did not excuse himself. The rector, in the middle of a sentence, fell silent in consternation and anger.

Ratansi walked up two flights and down a long corridor to his office. It was time to go home for dinner. He had left the rector's office with the evidence of his *lèse-majesté*, secure in the knowledge that copies had been circulated throughout the university's administration. He consigned the transcript to a battered leather briefcase of the kind schoolboys carried. Then he prepared to throw himself into the waiting arms of winter.

The Ratansis had arrived in Montreal in December after spending a delightful spring in Argentina. The ground was frozen and brown. People—his cousin, their landlord, the dean—had told them to buy warm clothes for the winter, but the advice, finding no anchor in the Ratansis' experience, blew aside in the face of more pressing adjustments to Canadian life. The season's first blizzard dumped two feet of snow between Christmas and New Year's. Then followed a week of minus 30° temperatures and forty mile-per-hour winds. Ratansi's ears grew red, he feared frostbitten, from the fifteen minute walk to and from his office. His shoes were quickly ruined by salt and melted snow. His wife contracted a virus. They could not afford the furs that all the natives seemed wrapped in. Beginning in the second week of January, they walked the streets smothered in oversized army greatcoats and tuques and rubber boots. The regimen kept them alive, and they continued it for a second year.

Ratansi padded out of his office to one of his building's two helical staircases and started down the left-handed spiral. There was more than a touch of Mussolini's Roman university, *La Sapienza*, in the recently completed structure of sweeping vertical planes trimmed with art-deco drollery. It was one enormous complex of six wings in the shape of two adjacent capital ees. Between the ees rose a commanding library tower, not unlike the basic design of the university library in Cambridge. Ratansi descended from the fourth floor to the base of the tower. A wide staircase under the tower led through fifteen-foot doors to the ceremonial hall and main lecture theatre. The structure sat near the summit of the north slope of Montreal's central feature, Mount Royal. Gleaming in yellow brick, the university beckoned for miles in the afternoon sun: *I am a monument to transcendental power, and those within me labor in insignificance.* From the beginning, Ratansi found the effect both familiar and unsettling.

It had begun snowing harder during Ratansi's interview with the rector. When he stepped outside and started down the hill, he found himself in a blizzard. The university's maintenance crew had not begun to clear the sidewalks. Ratansi proceeded in a slow shuffle, fearful that the inch-thick blanket of fluff would obscure a patch of ice. His briefcase flapped against the billowing skirts of his coat. He attained the great apron that stretched in front of the university's six wings. On a clear day one could see the distant Laurentian Mountains from there, but now Ratansi could barely make out his street, running parallel to the apron one hundred feet lower and two hundred feet north. From the corner of his eye Ratansi caught a figure clothed in the jet preferred by Montreal's French bourgeoisie, scurrying to the nearest protruding wing. Driving snow from the north had adhered to the man's back to create a parable in truth and falsity. The figure, half-converted by God's driving whiteness, sought the caverns of darkness where the immaculate crystal sequins would form translucent beads before being absorbed into the black heat out of which they would vaporize and return to heaven.

From the front edge of the apron, Ratansi faced a dozen

flights of capriciously angled wooden stairs. He grabbed the railing and stepped more confidently. Here there was less worry because water flowed easily through the latticework and vibrations from pedestrian traffic dislodged any ice that did form from melted snow. Squinting into the blizzard, Ratansi made out children on toboggans gliding around trees and rocks. The snow cut into his face and through his woolen gloves, but the children seemed oblivious of the cold. Their metabolism ran higher than his, Ratansi concluded, and perhaps they were fortunate possessors of silk underwear or whatever it was that anxious parents saw their children bundle up in.

Ratansi reached the street. He shuffled through a drift and scooped snow into the tops of his overshoes. By the time he got home, he knew, his oxfords would be soaking and his toes cold. He guessed that the temperature was minus 25° centigrade, but the wind made it seem colder. Several times a year, snow and cold brought a stop to all activity in Montreal. Schools and businesses closed. Mail ceased and garbage accumulated. No bread was baked, no banks were robbed. The earth in the vast cemetery that shared the north slope of the mountain with the university received no bodies. It was a time of reflection and rest.

A lone car with chains on its rear tires clattered by with a *whutta-whutta-whutta-whutta-whutta*. Ratansi listened for the classical, asymmetric, Doppler-shifted rise and fall of the sound. He heard nothing else over the continual drilling of snow against his tuque. The light, fresh snow, carpeting trees and buildings, grounds and roads, was a gigantic muffler. Ratansi thought that if God ever decided to speak to humanity, He would do so just after a Montreal blizzard, when everything was quiet and the heavens clear.

Ratansi walked on the side of the street that was wooded and owned by the university. He looked for animal tracks in the snow. This part of town, nestling against Mount Royal cemetery and park, was home to squirrels, skunks, and raccoons. A family of foxes was thought to make its home nearby. During hard winters, great snowy owls would feed on pigeons and sparrows and rats. There were stories of wolves running through the streets of nearby country towns. Ratansi shivered at the thinness of civilization's veneer in this city that satisfied European wants. Was America any different? Its industries and farms supplied material for both an eastern and a western war. To judge from the American scientific publications that he had studied, though, American learning was ponderous and unimaginative. It was as if American scientists placed the constructions of their European colleagues in a museum, under glass, and then painstakingly peeled back the layers to report their findings. There was no sense of the enterprise's spirit. Culture in America was something reserved for museums. Canada had not yet reached the stage of museums.

By the time that Ratansi crossed the street to his apartment building, he was a white apparition. He had become part of the blizzard. He entered the door and stood in the vestibule. There he shed his outer layer and shook it on the chipped terrazzo floor. His briefcase, trouser bottoms, shoes, and socks were drenched. He cradled greatcoat, tuque, and overshoes in his left hand as he climbed the stairs to the second floor where he lived. The concierge would not appreciate his trail of water. The three-storey building, one of dozens like it forming a continuous façade before the university property, was thirty years old. It housed its owner, its caretaker, and eleven paying tenants.

A misplaced lump of black and white hung over the landing rail by Ratansi's door and attracted his attention as he trudged up. It smelled of leather and wool. He rang the bell and noted that the lump was accompanied by zippered boots of the same construction. The lump resolved into a sheepskin-lined jacket and matching overalls. Evidently this was the exotic outerwear, hung out to dry, of a visitor. His wife opened the door.

"Carlo, dear," she cooed and kissed him. "You're home a bit early. And a good thing, too, with this tempest, *dio cane.*" God's hound. Odile was a child of mild, Mediterranean climates and she gasped at the cruel temperature swing from summer to winter in Montreal. Despite strenuous mental exertion, she had not yet convinced herself of the unreality of blizzards.

"What's this about?" Gian Carlo motioned to the sheepskins as he arrayed his own garments beside them.

Odile Ratansi shrugged her shoulders and guided him in. "An American has come to see you about your work." Gian Carlo and Odile Ratansi spoke Italian at home. She had learned the language from her mother, who was Niçoise. Odile was at once more and less than a Frenchwoman of Italian descent. She was born in Beirut, where her father had been posted after the First World War as a member of the French occupying army. She grew to maturity on Réunion, the tiny piece of France thrown off from Madagascar into the South Indian Ocean, where her father taught French history in a *lycée*. In her middle teens, Odile fell in love with how the regularities of the universe—the water-sculpted beaches of Réunion, the lush tropical gardens, the mountains and forests of Lebanon—found expression in folk designs on cloth and carpets. Upon finishing secondary school on Réunion, she went off to study tapestry-weaving at the Gobelin school in Paris, located, happily to her, near the Place d'Italie in the thirteenth *arrondissement*. A working-class quarter that still sprouted windmills, the streets were quiet and the rents were low. In the summer of 1939 she found a small apartment just over the one where Gian Carlo Ratansi lived.

Husband and wife entered their home. Large and modern by the standards they had known in Paris, the apartment was Odile's kingdom. A wooden loom occupied a small bedroom opposite the foyer. It was surrounded by the tools that Odile had used to bring it into existence. Piled against the wall were remnants of woolen fabric, which Odile picked apart for yarn and thread. Excepting a rickety dining-room set, a double bed, and a sofa in the back parlor, the apartment lacked conventional furnishings. Each of the rooms displayed one of her tapestries.

Gian Carlo knew that Odile rather liked receiving guests at

unusual hours. He did not mind, but he was not sure if an American would take it the right way.

"He's been waiting for an hour," Odile continued. "I've been getting him drunk on hard cider and listening to his story, in German." During their time in Montreal, Odile had picked up a great deal of Yiddish, for she preferred to buy food on the Main. She was as uncomfortable as her husband was with English.

Gian Carlo kicked off his shoes and slid into house slippers. His socks squished softly against the leather insoles. Odile preceded him into the parlor. "Lieutenant Ra-noff," she announced in what she took to be German, "Professor Dr Ratansi."

Leonard Ranov glowed from the far end of the sofa. He had downed a quart and a half of apple cider without realizing that it was eight percent alcohol. The apartment was nicer than any accommodation he had lived in. Bohemian chic. He smiled. Madame, Contessa, or Frau Professor Dr Ratansi (as he talked to her, he kept changing the form of address) shimmered before him. He imagined falling up over her short chin by her petite mouth along her diminutive nose and into her large green eyes. He salivated at her narrow waist and curvaceous bottom. He hung, fascinated, at how her brownish-red hair waved half-way down her back and around her décolleté. Now he looked over the wiry man with brown teeth who stood at the parlor door and clutched a soggy old briefcase. Leonard set his glass on the floor and struggled to his stocking feet.

"Lieutenant Leonard Ranov, United States Army Air Corps. Forgive me for arriving unheralded. I knock on your door at the suggestion of Alasdair Plum, who sends you this note." Leonard extended a damp envelope.

Ratansi accepted the envelope, dropped his briefcase, and read the note. It simply commended the bearer to him and urged him to help speed the American lieutenant's progress. Ratansi had never met Plum, but like most physicists he was familiar with his name. Especially after the events of the morning, he had difficulty accepting the situation at face value. It was a joke, and the man with oversized shoulders and a slight Yiddish accent was really the brother of their favorite butcher. It was a trap, and the man was really a German or a Soviet secret agent. Maybe he was in league with Arcand's Canadian fascists. Maybe he was a spy of the rector's. The visitor stood relaxed and smiling. Ratansi was working himself into knots.

"I understand that you may be involved in secret research," Leonard ventured, "but that's not at all why I came. I merely want to talk with you a bit about Jacob Witte."

Ratansi's jaw went slack and his mouth gaped wide, something that had happened to him once before when, while waiting for a streetcar soon after landing in Montreal, a woman standing in front of him, a total stranger, had smiled and punched him in the stomach. His face recovered.

"I've not heard from him for three years. How is he?"

"I don't know."

Silence descended over the two men. They came from dissimilar backgrounds. Each had been granted temporary passage in Canada. They spoke to each other in a language that neither had completely mastered. Each harbored misperceptions of the other. But when they came to think about a man far away, their thoughts ran parallel and a silent, sympathetic electricity flowed between them.

Odile, watching her husband from the corridor that led by a dogleg to both the front door and the dining room, sized up the situation. She reintroduced herself and asked the visitor to stay for their noon meal.

"Yes, you must, by all means," Gian Carlo echoed.

Leonard smiled and followed them into the dining room. He felt as if a great load had been lifted from his shoulders, as it in fact had been. When he left the McGill campus, he learned from the guard that Central Station was only a ten-minute walk away. It had begun to snow. Leonard decided to purchase a ticket on the overnight to New York and check his duffle in a locker before taking a taxi to Ratansi's door. As he walked to the station—under construction in the style of a Soviet shoe factory—and then, in the back of a taxi going over the top of the mountain by Côte-des-Neiges, he puzzled over his interview with Woodger. Pinpricks of lucidity, one after the other, but the whole of it quite discontinuous. And the remarkable sculpted head. Leonard concluded that Woodger would be a prime exhibit in favor of a human uncertainty principle that could no doubt also account for his having met Ratansi.

Leonard entered the dining room after Odile. The window in front of him faced an airshaft. A golden radiator stretching along its length offset the faded eggshell walls and nondescript, lace curtain. To the left, the dining room connected with a small kitchen. The wall opposite the kitchen disappeared under a tapestry, Odile's largest. She had executed it with geometrical undulations, curls, swirls, and arcs in a dozen browns, greys, and dark blues, offset occasionally by spots of brilliant green and red. Patterns projected as much as a foot from the background in textured masses that formed arteries and sinew, pumping vital fluid from one part of the mass to another. Pasta-like tendrils hung from the bottom.

An embroidered white-on-white cloth covered the table. Three places were soon set with ancient sterling, each piece gleaming white with a patina of scratches, set on linen napkins. Behind the plates of plain glass stood undistinguished wine goblets. A soup tureen steamed at kitchen end of the table. At the center, under an arrangement of dried flowers, a baguette lay next to a small block of butter. An uncorked bottle of cider stood at attention in front of the tapestry.

The Ratansis ate their main meal at noon. They rolled with the punches of the black market, available raw materials providing inspiration for the cuisine. One could generally find butter and cheese and chicken and some kind of meat or seafood. Apples, tubers, rice, and flour were plentiful and legal. Fresh fruit, vegetables and spices, smuggled in from the American South and the West Indies, cost dearly. This noon they were eating chicken soup *à la créole, fèves au lard* in the Canadian style, and a *soufflé*. There followed an apple tart.

Leonard was asked to sit facing the window, with its view of snow clinging to the bricks, glass panes, and fire escape of the apartment building not ten feet away. Gian Carlo Ratansi sat with his back to the tapestry. He grabbed the cider with a practised flourish and filled the glasses. Odile carried the tureen to fill the three waiting bowls. Leonard had never eaten in an Italian home. He waited until Gian Carlo picked up his spoon.

"I met Witte only once," Ratansi began in German after he finished his soup. "It was some time after I spent a semester in Germany studying cosmic rays with Heisenberg. I was in Paris and had what I thought was a clever idea that seemed to relate to secondary cosmic rays. Joliot-Curie suggested that I talk about it with Witte instead of subjecting myself to the deprivations and stupidities of Germany. Yes, it was the summer of 1939, several weeks after I got to know Odile. Holland seemed prosperous and reasonable. I gorged myself on chocolate and coffee. Witte and I talked for an hour every day. He was the most extraordinary physicist I have met, next to Fermi. He could move easily from the heights of theory to the nuts and bolts of machine design, from the physics of low temperatures to the heat of nuclear reactions." As soon as the words "nuclear reactions" came out, Ratansi felt that he had betrayed himself. But his guest made no remark or gesture to pick up the thread. He thought it best to continue with matters of personality.

"One evening he invited me to his home for dinner. There was an astronomer, Jan Oort I think, and a philologist. I sat next to Witte's daughter. A fey, brooding girl, quite unlike her optimistic and rational-minded father. She talked a great deal about Java and her time there. On Java, after all, is where Witte carried out his seminal research on cosmic rays."

The *soufflé* had just come into the room from the oven, and Odile deflated it with a large serving spoon. Leonard sucked in a deep breath. His pectoral muscles tightened as he leaned forward slightly to stare at his host.

"Unfortunately I know Witte only from his publications on cosmic rays," Leonard said, "and not all of them reached my small university library before I entered military service. You may be interested to know that I followed your publications, too, but Heisenberg's thoughts on cosmic rays eluded me." Leonard broke off a piece of baguette and took a bite.

Ratansi continued. "The daughter talked that evening about rambling around the countryside near the town where Witte taught. She talked all about the natives and their customs. I think she missed Java very much. She wanted to return with her father later in the year, but she thought that she would probably stay in Leiden to complete her medical training. I wonder what happened to her."

"I saw her several days ago in Cambridge," Leonard offered. "She is well."

Salad and desert came and went. The snow, and how life in the city conformed to it, occupied conversation. Gian Carlo asked his wife if they could have coffee in honor of their guest. The sounds and smell of coffee being prepared out of sight in the kitchen carried across the dining room. Gian Carlo excused himself as Odile filled three demitasses.

"Your creations are really quite lovely," Leonard said. "Have you considered selling any of them?"

"Thank you," Odile said. "I am afraid it is hopeless. There is no interest here in such things."

"Your work speaks to me," Leonard continued. "Just this morning, I met another artist who was puttering over a bust he had finished, Professor Woodger at McGill. But this is much more original." Leonard watched Odile's face as he spoke Woodger's name. He saw just a slight tightening of her lips.

Ratansi returned with a small envelope, darted into the kitchen, and emerged with a dark bottle and three liqueur glasses. "Let us drink to Witte," he said. "I hope you like Calvados." Leonard nodded unknowingly. Like an undergraduate let into the faculty club, the brandy was just refined enough to get by the door. Ratansi poured another round. He placed the envelope on the table near Leonard's elbow. "I received this letter from him early in May 1940, just before the *débâcle*." Leonard drank and opened the envelope. It was in German, but he recognized the round, even, and clear hand from the notes he had seen in Cambridge.

22 April 1940

Dear Ratansi,

Please forgive me for this overly late reply to your letter of last autumn. It arrived after I had departed for the Indies. Over the past several months, since my return, I've thought about your lines a number of times, but other responsibilities forced me to postpone my reply.

Then followed a page of calculations, apparently referring to a manuscript of Ratansi's. Leonard skipped these and came to the last paragraph.

It is certain now that Holland will become a major player in the game of nuclear physics. The large magnet should arrive from Batavia in June, and with it, by hook or by crook, we shall have a respectable cyclotron. But I can tell you that even if the magnet is lost in a storm at sea, Holland will become a nuclear power thanks to her East Indies colony. I have seen the proof with my own eyes and have verifications from Dr Létoile. The detailed report should arrive here soon. Imagine how astonished the world will be when Holland is the first to harness the atom's energies.

"I have often wondered what Witte meant," Ratansi said. He had decided to seek his visitor's confidence by returning to matters nuclear. He knew no secrets, unless the military sought to make secret the knowledge that a chain-reaction could be sustained. "I cannot understand it. Sure, there was cosmic-ray research on Java, but that is not the same thing as a large experimental facility in nuclear physics. He was not a man to chase after illusions."

Leonard handed the letter back to Ratansi. Witte had discovered something important on Java. Leonard thought again about the morning's motto carved in stone. Witte could be referring to anything about nuclear energy, from a theoretical advance to an insight into radioactive decay or cyclotron design. "To harness the atom's energies" clearly signaled generating useful power from the atomic nucleus. Perhaps it was a new kind of atom smasher, something that made cyclotrons obsolete. That would explain Witte's dismissal of the magnets, and Leonard knew about a few different ways of accelerating subatomic particles to bombard metals and transmute chemical elements by artificial radioactivity. It would not explain why Witte had sought the opinion of Létoile, according to the Cambridge card catalogue an observational astronomer of no theoretical attainments whatever. At issue was something prosaic. Java supplied Europe with raw commodities. Then it came to him: A deposit of uranium accounted for all the facts. Uranium for the Uranium Committee.

Leonard finished the second glass of Calvados, which tasted better than the first. The letter and the Calvados were leading up to something more.

"Fortune has thrown you in my path," Ratansi said. "I must not spurn her advances. I will be frank with you. I am not engaged in any war work at all. I am only teaching chemistry to the farmers' sons who want to become pharmacists. I want to apply my skills toward defeating the fascists. My misfortune is to be a citizen of Italy. Help me."

Leonard said, "Why haven't you signed up?"

Ratansi glanced down at his dessert plate. "As an enemy alien I was given the privilege of teaching at the university for half pay. Every day I die a little there. I worry about pleasing the clerics who are my superiors. I worry about my papers being revoked. My old boss Auger hesitates to bring me into his secret

research here. I've done nothing intelligent in nearly three years."
He looked up. "The Canadians arrested tens of thousands of their
countrymen with Japanese and Italian ancestors. They could ar-
rest me. Suppose I were let into the Canadian army. They would
have me peeling potatoes twenty blocks from where we sit. You
know what I can do. Get me into the American army."

What did Ratansi's wife think of all this, Leonard wondered.
Did she follow their conversation? Would she welcome her
husband's being swallowed by a behemoth, an inconscient monster, his possible reëmergence to be unheralded? Perhaps the Italian physicist wanted distance from her. Or perhaps an unseen
force drove him to seek a change.

Leonard sighed. The alcohol had begun to weary him. He
was tired of speaking German. He did not want to become en-
meshed in the Ratansis' real or imagined web of intrigue. The
meal sat heavy. He wanted to burn it off outside, in the driving
patter of a snowfall that turned the world pure and silent. "I will
do what I can," he lied. "When I see my superiors, I will ask
them to recruit you." He pushed back on his unstable chair and
heard a small sound of wood splitting apart. He continued with a
truth: "What a splendid dinner, Frau Dr Ratansi. I shall remember it always." He wanted out.

Ratansi recomposed himself in a rapid motion and said, "Let
us move into the back room, a more comfortable setting."

"Thank you," Leonard said, "Your hospitality is overwhelming. I must go. From here I travel on leave to see my parents."
He did not want to elaborate. He turned to Odile. "Is it possible
that I could purchase a small creation of yours?"

"Why, how nice, Lieutenant. I shall not refuse such an offer. Only it is a gift for you." She returned with a small pile of
tapestry fragments. "Please choose the one you like." Leonard
selected a delicate grey beveled wedge caught between two dark
masses and set on a blue background. In one corner was a green
line and a yellow circle. The wild blue yonder. Odile rolled it up
in a paper bag.

In the foyer Leonard said until-we-meet-again. He put on his overalls, boots, jacket, and cap in the hall. Ratansi insisted on accompanying him to the street.

"So few people know Greek these days," Ratansi said when he saw Leonard's initials in Greek the back of his jacket.

Leonard thought, He is probably genuine. "Greek is not one of my languages," he said. They shook hands, and Leonard stepped into winter.

The snow had stopped falling. The afternoon sun created a latticework of greys and whites. His watch buried under a jacket and glove, Leonard guessed that it was around 2:00 p.m. There was plenty of time before the train departed for New York. He started walking west, retracing the path of his taxi. Across the street the central tower of the French university rose like an enormous phallis with foreskin partially retracted. Sidewalks and road lay under four inches of snow. Leonard was used to the rarified atmosphere and dry climate of winter on the Wyoming plains, where the air felt crisp and snow returned to the sky by sublimation. Here he felt the wet, thick cold settle in his chest. He pushed the white stuff aside as he walked. Ratansi was a bundle of contradictions, but there could be no mistaking the earnestness of Witte's letter.

He attained Côte-des-Neiges, the main artery that led over to the south side of the mountain. It had been plowed. He flagged a cab with the bag holding Odile's tapestry. It would not do, he realized, as a gift for his mother. Her idea of finer things in life centered on porcelain china, silver, and mahogany furniture; choral concerts and Thanksgiving dinners; and books. He asked the driver to deliver him to Montreal's finest jeweler.

Riding around the west side of the mountain confirmed his earlier impression on the way out, that it was the home of Montreal's bourgeoisie. The higher up on the mountain, the finer the houses, constructed from stone, with leaded glass windows, slate roofs, and secluded gardens. The taxi descended to St Catherine Street and made its way past small shops, bars, and strip joints. The driver stopped just before Morgan's department store at a building with a stone façade. An arch, like that over a minor cathedral door, led into Henry Birks and Sons.

Leonard wandered down the aisles of glass cases radiating silver and gold. This was what most people respected, he thought. There was nothing to prove here, nothing to puzzle over. The jeweler certified that the metal and rocks were genuine; the buyer, flashing a diamond ring or gold necklace, received unqualified respect. The objects of admiration were portable and liquid. Leonard went to the porcelain on the second floor. He settled for a blue Wedgwood plate decorated with ivory goddesses and draped bunting. His gift wrapped, he set off for Central Station, a few blocks away.

A building with the severe, modernist lines of the University of Montreal rose on what was still an enormous pit gouged into the center of the city, where the alluvial plain of the St Lawrence met a higher plateau. As he approached the station for the second time, he thought how well it characterized the city that he had toured in the past eight hours. Montreal, railhead for the produce and minerals of a continent and the port where European travelers disembarked, had two train stations. Windsor Station, owned by Canadian Pacific, was a cathedral of Victorian bombast. The other, that of Canadian National, the one toward which he now walked, proclaimed the twentieth century. Smoke and steam and ice fog rose to meet the silent snow. In the grey and fading light, Leonard descended slowly into a construction abyss from which he hoped he would emerge, the following day, in the city of his birth.

5

Sand between the Toes

My work is going well. Joliot-Curie provides me with everything I need, which is not much really. But with the departure of Ratansi there is no one to talk to. We got along so very well. He helped me with German, even though I could do nothing for him in return. He planned to go to Argentina, to the University of the Littoral, some place close to the Andes Mountains, where an old friend of his had been appointed to direct an institute for the history of science. The man, Aldo Mieli, was in Paris for a number of years, and I met him. He actually knew about wasan and Chinese astronomy! They say Argentina is a splendid land. It is getting two fine people. Heisenberg lectured here, and I spoke with him at length. He has been touring Europe. I asked about our Dutch friends. He thought that Witte was suffering from overwork. I so much liked his cosmic-ray publications. I shall try to visit Leiden. Maybe Witte has some suggestions for research at his old Bandung institute, if the topic is not too delicate to raise. Do we have someone there now?

Toshiko Yuasa to Shin-ichi Tomonoga, 10 January 1943,
Tomonoga papers, privately held

Leonard took a window seat in coach. No one claimed the aisle position, and so, as the train wormed out through the staging yards, slums, warehouses, and marshes of Montreal's littoral, Leonard shed his jacket and overalls and boots and laced on his shoes. The fleeced lining of the jacket would be his pillow and blanket for the night. He caught a receding glimpse of Montreal as the train turned toward the long trestles of the Victoria Bridge and across the St Lawrence River. The city lights seemed modest and dim, as if the northern winds had eroded the city's height and glitter. Montreal was the last metropolis before the North Pole, a small jewel on the many thousand-mile ribbon that stretched across a continent and formed the improbable political entity called Canada.

He had been on a variety of trains before, military and civilian, and this trip to Sandy Creek, around twelve hours including stops and a transfer, he calculated, would be neither long nor exhausting. He had become inured to the grime of American railroad cars (he would be riding on American stock into New York) and to the sour smell of cigar smoke, coal exhaust, and body odor that pervaded rail conveyance. He was able to bury his consciousness just above the surface of sleep as the compartment accelerated and rocked on its predestined trajectory.

Leonard inspected his environment of cast-iron and eroded plush seats, linoleum floors, luggage racks, tin ceiling, and plate-glass windows covered by dirty curtains. He thought that one was nowhere closer to mechanical civilization than in motorized transport—planes, ships, automobiles, trucks, trains. The patriarch of metal moving machines, the one with more than a hundred years of tradition and lore, was the train. Nations rose as tens of thousands of rock-hewers and pile-pounders moved the rails outward from administrative hubs in London, Paris, Vienna, Berlin, Moscow, Washington, Chicago, Buenos Aires, Guayaquil, Vera Cruz, Melbourne, Shanghai, Batavia, Calcutta, and Cape Town. Dozens of shiny slugs radiated from a central nest, leaving a gleaming trail behind them. The trains ferried troops, cavalry, and ordnance to distant outposts. They funneled grain, produce, meat, and precious ores to markets and processing centers. They conveyed pilgrims and settlers to the wilderness for success or failure. Railroad magnates amassed extraordinary and unheralded fortunes. Railroad workers pioneered new forms of associations for self-protection. Railroad engineers designed and operated heavy machines that were on the cutting edge of the Second Industrial Revolution. Railroad controllers brought about new standards and conventions for time, while geographical space contracted into new folds and whorls along the rail right-of-way.

The train left the St Lawrence and the small communities clinging precariously, as they had for three centuries, to its south shore. It plunged into the crystalline, white, sub-zero forests and hills of the North Country. Leonard remembered that this was the land fought over, two hundred years previously, by French, English, and Indians, then by Americans, Scots, and Fenians. What difference had these few acres of snow made to the court at Versailles or the residents of Buckingham Palace? How had the rest of humanity been enriched by the tripartite culture of the St Lawrence River Valley? Besides the inventions of Ernest Rutherford and the team sports of American colleges—football, ice hockey, and lacrosse—how would Montreal be evaluated, decades hence, when the giant to the south had effectively colonized its neighbor?

A page announced the first sitting of dinner. Leonard let the message pass. He resisted eating in trains or planes. He liked to be able to get up and move around after meals, and in the metal monsters he imagined himself a goose pinned to a fattening board. In any event, he was drowsy, not hungry. He snuggled into his jacket and closed his eyes as the train slowed to a stop and then started again.

The purpose of the stop became evident within ten minutes. Leonard opened his eyes at the sound of a door slammed shut. Two United States customs and immigration agents appeared at the front of the car and slowly worked their way back. What is your name, where were you born, citizen of what country, where are you going, how long will you be in the United States? The questioners, in military costume with sidearms and carrying heavy winter coats, were larger than nearly all the passengers. It was their duty to protect America's frontiers by watching for illicit goods and undesirable aliens: uncut diamonds and gold bars, unpasteurized milk, uninspected citrus fruit and meat, the diseased and the insane, felons and prostitutes, German spies landed from submarines in Nova Scotia, Japanese-Canadians escaping from concentration camps in British Columbia, known communists and rabble rousers, and displaced people desperate to find a safe haven. Leonard watched as the two men lingered over a Chinese family, speaking to a boy who acted as translator. His own turn passed without incident. A native-born citizen serving his country, he had safely crossed into America.

Leonard thought about the uncertainty felt by his parents when they first set eyes on the new land. His mother arrived in New York in 1912 at the age of sixteen on the *Potsdam* out of Hamburg, after having first traveled with her family from Chashnik in Byelorussia to Riga. She passed through Ellis Island and wound up on the Lower East Side. His father arrived in Seattle after escaping from Siberia.

The sub-zero winter of northern Vermont, Leonard thought, was a climate his father Max would have appreciated. Max Ranov had spent nearly a decade in Siberia, in two installments, for seditious activity. Stimulated by the revolution of 1905, sixteen-year-old Max persuaded others in Chashnik to form a self-defense group. He then sent a photograph of the armed vigilantes to the local police chief, with a letter to the effect that if anyone thought to create an incident to justify a pogrom, these particular Jews would be able to take care of themselves. The authorities sentenced Max to five years in Omsk. There he grew to manhood, learning to hunt and trap and committing large portions of the Cyrillic Bible to heart, it being the only reading material permitted him. Max returned from exile bearded, tough, and a committed communist. He rapidly found himself exiled for a second, ten-year stretch, this time to remote Yakutsk. When the First World War erupted, he managed to walk south to Harbin in Manchuria, and from there he went on to Port Arthur and Shanghai.

Leonard closed his eyes and floated in near sleep. When his father arrived in New York, he met and married his mother, a girl from his hometown. They operated a hand-laundry for six years, raising Leonard and his sister. Max contracted leukemia. In the hope that the country air would put him aright, the family moved to a small farm in Sandy Creek, some sixty miles south of New York on the coast. There, a handful of Jewish immigrants had set down roots and were trying to survive by producing eggs for the city market. Max died three years after the move.

Leonard wondered what his father's parents were like. He had never before thought to ask. Max Ranov was one of four brothers. The other three emigrated before the First World War. Nothing was heard from the one who went to Argentina. An occasional letter arrived from South Africa. The oldest brother, David, however, established a farm in western Massachusetts, and Leonard knew both him and his children, who were his first cousins. David Ranov, the first to arrive in America from Chashnik, chose the spelling for the family name in the Roman alphabet. He spent several years in Riga, studying farming, before setting off for New York. Without David's certificates in German, the immigration agents on Ellis Island could well have given him a name to fit his origin: Goldberg, Steinberg, Rosenberg, Greenberg.

Farming was a clarion call for his father's people. They were Jews, for centuries denied the right to own property in Central and Eastern Europe. Leonard remembered how his father, during his last three years, took pleasure in hunting and fishing around Sandy Creek. Leonard retained his father's love of the big sky, the weather, the pleasant feeling of accomplishment evoked at the end of a day by aching muscles and dirty hands. The death of his father forever denied him, however, a sense of general optimism and a faith in the eventual happy outcome of human endeavor. Leonard perceived that he could master the immutable words on a printed page or the physical laws of the universe, but he approached all human dealings with a form of ultimate resignation, a vague anticipation that they would end in disappointment. He was accordingly hopeless in finance and remote in intimate encounters.

The sense of remoteness, common enough to rural life, was

reinforced when Leonard's mother married her first cousin, Samuel Barrick, soon after she became a widow. Broadly speaking, it was a consanguinity permitted in Jewish law, although the State of New Jersey would not have been able to obtain information to annul the marriage, even if it suspected a transgression of one of its codes. As far as Leonard knew, the union was Platonic: Sam and his mother had separate beds, and there were no more children.

As the man around the house when Leonard grew to maturity, Sam accelerated Leonard's drift toward the world of ideas and away from the farm. Sam was a short man with a round face and a broad smile. He always smiled, Leonard thought. The farm became his heaven. For the preceding ten years he had been a fruit-picker in California, moving with the crops and cultivating a vegetarian, communitarian ethic. This he brought to Sandy Creek, along with a religiosity based more on mysticism than on reason. While not in any way devout, he was able to use prayers as a mantra to achieve temporary transcendence. He was sometimes called to be the tenth man at Friday-night service in the small synagogue just down the road from his farm. Beyond all this, or because of it, he was a man entirely devoid of personal ambition and temperamentally unable to deal with the mechanical and commercial world. Leonard's mother handled all money matters and, Leonard suspected, owned all the property. Sam was a live-in boarder who gave his surname to his first cousin but not to her children. He was not a father, but there was not a mean bone in his body.

Leonard's mother Miriam ruled the family. She lived for her children, righteously according to her lights. She was a communist because that was the way to achieve social justice. She owned property because that was the way to be self-sufficient. She sang in a local chorus because that was the way to socialize. She had a cow to provide milk for the children. She cultivated a large garden and preserved its produce to take the family through much of the winter. She accepted into her home, for years at a time, the children of indigent relatives and acquaintances. Though respecting books, she was illiterate and, as a consequence, knew the ways of bribing American bureaucrats; the price of a driver's license was three new shirts. Her expression of quiet determination remained unchanged through the Depression, when existence was precarious and the family would huddle around the central coal stove on winter evenings.

Miriam Barrick always acted as if she stood in a cold breeze, Leonard's surface-skimming dream told him as he sped through the frozen Vermont countryside. Leonard's dreams not infrequently unrolled as newsreels, with a narrator linking together clips of intense images. Leonard had read about Freud's theory of dreams, but he found no evidence for it in his own experience. He thought that dreams were the mind's entertainment, with the proviso that the humor, drama, and satire thus revealed were more sophisticated than most of what he found in novels. This was the secular truth of the experiments in surrealism and automaticism that he had learned about in college. The modern novel, he concluded, would be like his dreams. And now a dream featured his mother in a black-crocheted shawl, waiting by the back door of the Sandy Creek farmhouse for Sam and him to finish feeding the chickens during a February evening's blizzard and come into the kitchen for the evening meal.

The train rolled to a stop at St Albans. The dream image stayed with Leonard as he shifted his position and peeked behind the curtain to view the station. Thick flakes of snow were falling. The temperature was probably above zero Fahrenheit and the wind could not be more than twenty miles an hour. In snowstorms, the business of the world succumbed to nature's will and became pristine. White-blanketed trees, buildings, roads, and fields. Leonard always thought it remarkable that snow, when it covered the world, really laid the environment bare. After a blizzard, whatever was not buried—things both large and small—stood out in stark relief. Natural histories became crystal clear: the tracks of a small herd of deer, some feathers and drops of blood marking the death agony of a field mouse caught by an owl, raccoon or fox, footprints leading around the chicken coops, the daily trek to the mailbox or the path from house to barn. Snow produced a global effect of integration and averaging. Drifts emphasized the contours of land and wind. With snow, it became possible to contemplate universal laws *in puris naturalibus*.

Satisfying to contemplate, winter was more unforgiving to live through. Leonard, the same as his father before him, had learned how to tolerate desperately long and cold winters, but he never liked them. He much preferred being too hot to being too cold. He enjoyed the heat of physical exertion in the open air, under the summer sun. Labor was easier in the hot season. One needed only heavy boots, shorts, and a bandana against the dust. Civilization arose in temperate climates, those cold enough to discourage the horrors of tropical pestilence but warm enough to banish the fear of frostbite. Wyoming, Montreal, and Vermont, he thought, were too cold for civilization to propagate independently. Leonard fell asleep with the thought of cold. He imagined himself seven years old, curled up inside a tunnel bored into a snowdrift against the side of the feed room. Everything was quiet shades of white. He held still and heard his pulse and then heard nothing more.

*

*   *

Leonard awoke to the dawn in New Haven. His car accelerated, stopped, changed direction, bumped, and came to rest as part of a new train for the coastal run into Manhattan. Most of the other passengers were already fidgeting, preening, and smoking. Some were eating sandwiches. Others prepared for breakfast in the dining car. Leonard went to work on a chocolate bar extracted from a jacket pocket. It would hold him until he arrived in Grand Central Terminal.

He looked out on the New Haven waterfront. It was busy in

the middle of winter. The war, with its production quotas, labor ententes, and lack of consumer goods, had been a godsend to smaller industrial and commercial towns, like this one. Leonard doubted, though, that New Haven had suffered much during the Depression. Its European immigrants would have been able to find work servicing the institution that polished the sons of factory owners, landlords, and shipping magnates. Yale University had thousands of rooms to clean, hundreds of miles of pipes and electrical conduits to repair, myriad pots to scrub and dishes to wash and sheets to launder and trash cans to empty, acres of floors to sweep and polish, tons of mortar to repoint, and a continuous stream of students to clothe, feed, and titillate.

Leonard knew these things because he had visited Yale once for a conference on cosmic rays. The luxury and excessive decoration of the place, so unlike the forthright character of the institutions of higher learning that he was familiar with, made as deep an impression on him as the pretentiousness and quirks of the professorial staff. Leonard thought back to England. There was something of Cambridge in Yale, sanitized, stripped clean of both grime and brilliance. The general level of activity at Cambridge equaled that at New Haven, at least insofar as he could see, but the qualities of action were quite distinct in the two places. At Cambridge there would be masses in the chapels and scholarly tutoring in the colleges. At Yale, the masses would flock to the cathedral-like athletic gymnasium, and residential-college preceptors would attempt to tutor undergraduates in table manners. Cambridge students, expected to be refined, were infused with civilization. Yale students, exemplars of American civilization, were schooled in polite comportment. England was virtuous refinement in search of enlightenment. America was enlightened virtue in search of refinement.

Leonard watched the enlightened and virtuous Yankee seacoast unfold as the train sped toward New York. Here was a centuries-long tradition of clock-making, manufacturing, and seafaring. Yankee mechanical ingenuity lay, he thought, at the base of America's rise to world prominence. He was unsure, however, if the craft tradition would be sufficient to guarantee American domination of the world economy. Germany and Japan would eventually be overpowered by the United States and the Soviet Union, but it would take only a generation for the Axis powers to rise again, in the probable event that the victors enjoined the vanquished from rearming. German and Japanese cultures seemed naturally suited for industrial life. They had place for neither the romantic American notion of individual achievement nor the romantic Soviet notion of personal altruism.

It all boiled down to a question of which culture was best suited to the mechanical age. Whichever was that culture, Leonard concluded long ago, he did not belong to it. From growing up on a farm, he had been forced to learn how to repair mechanical devices, from pumps and generators to electrical motors and internal combustion engines. He had to know about pipefitting, welding, carpentry, and masonry. Mastery of this knowledge, however, resulted in no special sense of pride or accomplishment. Things were fixed and set in working order so that the family could survive. Machines, far from ends in themselves, liberated time for creative thought. Understanding and appreciating general truths required distance from mundane concerns. Leonard took the latter notion to be the essence of Oriental and Hebrew faiths. He thought that this was also why he had decided to devote himself to physics.

As a boy, Leonard found himself caught up in the romance of physics: radioactivity, relativity, quantum theory, and so forth. He was attracted equally to history and literature. He read voraciously and omnivorously. Tolstoy one week, Richard Halliburton the next, William Beebe the next. Leonard grew up with the idea that culture came from beyond the seas, and that the valuable features of American life originated abroad. Education, therefore, became a process of acquiring that which was unfamiliar. Leonard could not imagine how anyone earned a living by reading novels or travel accounts, so he inclined toward physics. The parts of physics related to machines—experimental physics in all its guises—correspondingly held far less interest for Leonard than those related to cosmic phenomena, such as relativity or quantum indeterminacy. In college Leonard suffered classical mechanics, electrical circuitry, and physical chemistry, for he thought that, in the event that he wanted to eat regularly, these subjects would provide him with a job as an engineer. But his love was for the impractical.

The train rumbled into the Bronx and then underground to Grand Central Terminal. The multitudinous pinnacles of New York, supporting millions of pounds of living flesh, surrounded the cornucopia from Montreal, which by this time was ripe. Leonard's car would pass, he knew, not far from where he spent his earliest years. He recalled, now as always, the atmosphere and smells. He remembered their last, small, third-floor apartment on the day the family moved in. His parents considered themselves fortunate to have a kitchen, a common room, and a bathroom. An earlier apartment lacked the last facility, there being a shared toilet in the hall and a bathtub under the kitchen table. Leonard carried out his own inspection of the new place and found a revolver in a cupboard.

The city had pressed in on Leonard from all directions, a constriction that he never felt until he was on the farm. The entire family slept in a single room until moving to the country. Leonard's playground was the sidewalk, with its theatre of passion and depravity. He thought about why that environment had not corrupted him. The intense drive and clear morality of his parents dominated everything. They ran the most menial of trades, but they felt no embarrassment in their station. They were confident that life would be better for their children.

The train slid into its pocket under Grand Central Terminal. Leonard disembarked and walked toward the subway concourse. He had to transfer to Pennsylvania Station for the remainder of his voyage home. He eyed the Oyster Bar, nestled in the terminal not far from where the tracks disgorged passengers. He had time until departing for southern New Jersey. He was hungry. The restaurant was open.

Leonard sat at the counter and ordered a dozen raw cherrystone oysters and grilled bluefish. The smell and taste brought back his experiences with the shore. During the summer he would sometimes dig for clams and oysters in Barnegat Bay and Seaside Heights, some miles from the farm. There were crabs to jig up from under piers and fish to pull in through rolling surf. The Oyster Bar evoked associations of sea breeze, salt air, creosote pilings, blowing sand, dune grass, bees and birds, late-afternoon thunderheads, and hazy impressionist light.

Leonard turned to take in the scotch movies through a bank of plate-glass windows. All humanity flowed through the station. He did not like crowds, although he minded watching them less than he minded belonging to them. The worst part of travel was the crowds. The intolerable part of the army concerned crowds. Even the civilized pleasures—theatre and concerts—were diminished by large audiences, who forever asserted their individuality. Radio and the phonograph had made the audible part of these *spectacles* into command performances, and Leonard looked forward to the day when electricity could project images as well—cinema beamed into a million homes.

He trundled down to the subway connection for Pennsylvania Station. The concourse was Manhattan's busiest, a many-layered confluence of lines. He had been through it often, and he usually relied on passive memory to guide him, but it was the only place he knew where he could not orient himself. He ascribed the confusion not to massive iron pilings and rails, but rather to the raw and slightly sweet smell of dirt and exhaust, to the distractions of subterranean shops, and to the cells of humanity, pumping through these coronary arteries, pushing through turnstiles and adhering briefly to gates. The pulse was quick here, and a greenhorn would be swept along with the flow.

Leonard's shuttle arrived at the platform. He wrestled his duffle inside and then clung to a leather strap for balance. The system was efficient and, considering the millions of users, basically clean. He wondered what half a century would bring. Trains and beltways across the tops of skyscrapers, people flying about with portable rocket packs, high-speed subways linking the world's cities. He smiled because he did not believe the fantasies. Technological progress could not be extrapolated by a straight-line curve. Half a century ago, who could have imagined powered flight in its present form? Did anyone foresee the importance of the internal-combustion engine—that ultimate domestication of firearms, the half-stroke engine of destruction invented by medieval China? Swords into plowshares, bullets into pistons. The major technological issue of the future, Leonard thought, had already been solved. It was the management of large systems, like New York's subways and the US army. What compromised the new management structures was a reliance on paper. Keeping track of the parts of the systems required a phalanx of clerks, who recorded everything. Useful summaries appeared next to mountains of useless data. Civilization would not move along until it experienced an information revolution.

Unless civilization failed. Leonard believed that the war was an Armageddon, a contest between good and evil. If the Allies lost, Leonard imagined an end to civilization. He wondered if science could give the Allies an edge. By this time he had exited at Madison Square Garden and was walking toward the station. He experienced a brief vision of German troops plundering a New York devastated by naval and aerial bombardment. Could they enslave the entire United States? Possibly, Leonard thought, with local help.

He had missed the express stopping within a few miles of Sandy Creek on its way to Atlantic City. He boarded for Asbury Park, a half-hour from home. The engine inched the cars down toward the tunnel under the Hudson River. They then emerged beyond the Palisades in the marshlands of New Jersey. Leonard contemplated the worst prospect of industrial America, starkly revealed against a leaden winter afternoon. It was the twilight of the Second Industrial Revolution, fashioned by Germany from electricity, steel, and chemicals. Leonard saw vast fields of oil refineries and industrial plants of every description. The marsh functioned as a giant cloaca, funneling waste toward the sea. In the distance, an illuminated sign identified Gottfried Krueger's beer. Germans had already conquered this land. Nimitz, Eisenhower. The Anglo-Saxons were fighting for ownership of the world.

The train crossed the Raritan River, and industry evaporated. New Jersey, shaped like a Smith Brothers cough-lozenge, had two distinct cultures separated by a belt compressing the narrow waist between Perth Amboy and Trenton. The northern part was power, profit, and corruption. Capitalists made their money here while they frolicked with their children at bedroom retreats. The climate was temperate and the soil productive. Forests and lakes once graced the land. Here were, in times past, market gardens for New York. Below the belt everything was reversed. It was a land that the economy had passed by. The soil was nutrient-poor sand, and the natural covering was scrub pine, which burned clear every decade or so. The people descended largely from eighteenth-century settlers. There was no manufacturing and almost no agriculture. It was hard to say how most people scratched out a living.

Leonard's mother and step-father lived by producing eggs. It was an exploitive arrangement. They were at the mercy of feed companies and wholesale buyers. But through constant, backbreaking labor, a family could manage 20,000 birds without help. According to the local rule of thumb, in terms of work and income, a thousand chickens corresponded to one cow. Sandy Creek was dotted with small egg producers.

The train steamed into Asbury Park, the fashionable ocean resort of the previous century. The last twenty-five miles were always the most troublesome. There was a bus, but it passed through a number of towns and took several hours. Leonard wanted to be home. He offered a taxi driver with an eye patch ten dollars for the ride.

"Hop in, boychick," the driver waved.

Leonard sat in front. The radio broadcast WQXR. *Così fan tutti* was ending. A happy ending, Leonard thought. His mother would be listening to it, preparing dinner in the large kitchen. Sam would be sorting and packing eggs. His sister was off somewhere in the Women's Army Auxiliary Corps. She had found a fiancé from a nearby town, a captain in the infantry. He was being trained for MacArthur's assault on New Guinea. Leonard should have called ahead.

"Name's Larry. Like it? The music, not the name."

Leonard introduced himself and agreed that it was a fine opera.

"Someday I'll play in the pit. Mine's the stick. Now I mostly play at weddings." Another hopeful musician. Larry changed the subject. "See this eye," he pointed to the patch, "a guy from Sandy Creek gave it to me, no offense. I went to Rutgers for a few years. I was in a chemistry lab when whatdya know the kid across the bench blew up. Everything. He bought it. He came in looking real strange, crazy-like. Doc said I might see again, but that was years ago."

"I knew someone like that," Leonard said. "His girl turned him down. He had a flair for drama. He wanted to go out with a bang. His emotions were greatly exaggerated, like in a Mozart opera." Bernie Tokay was a close friend. Leonard saw the suicide note. Bernie would have made a fine chemist. A young man at twenty cannot see ahead clearly. Leonard hoped that age allowed one to see farther. But the older people he knew who radiated a certain wisdom nevertheless acquired tunnel vision. Maybe it was inevitable. One could not respond to every peripheral contingency. "I'm sorry."

"No use looking back. I wish it hadn't happened. Wish I had something like a broken arm, something that would heal. Who will marry a one-eyed taxi driver? I cudda been dead. I can still play. Better than ever."

The sun had set and snow was dusting the road ahead. Just before Pine Grove three deer flicked into the woods. Pine Grove, twenty minutes from home, was where his sister's beau Joshua came from. His father kept an orthodox house. Joshua had an ambivalent attitude toward ritual. Leonard liked him.

Mozart was over. The soldiers married their sweethearts. The curtains fell on the Met's stage. The driver turned on the familiar road. The farmhouse came into view. Large and rambling, like most farmhouses it began twenty feet from the road. He saw his mother through the kitchen window, absolutely determined to have dinner ready on time. Leonard bolted from the cab and ran to the kitchen door. He rang the bell. His mother answered. She shrieked, and then hugged him as she cried.

"I'm home," Leonard smiled. He fumbled for the Wedgwood plate and Odile Ratansi's tapestry.

"Lev, Lev, why didn't you call?"

*

*   *

Leonard had been given a week to travel back to Washington. Occasionally he thought about Dr Ernest Bit, reading alchemical works in Cambridge. Maybe Ernest would find out more about philosophical mercury, Leonard wondered idly as he helped Sam with the eggs and tuned up the old tractor. Maybe he would clarify whether Witte had discovered uranium on Java. One afternoon he bicycled into town.

Sandy Creek meandered from the Pine Barrens into Barnegat Bay. It was an anchorage for Henry Hudson, who refilled his water casks, bagged a brace of marsh ducks, and then sailed north for the grander sights of Manhattan and the river that bears his name. Ten subsequent generations of visitors had much the same reaction. To hold the sentiment of the outside world at bay, local tradition produced a motto: *Once you had its sand between your toes, you would always return to Sandy Creek.* The relaxed town that sprang up around the mouth of the creek was a county seat. It had the courthouse and the jail, which were ringed with lawyers' offices. Behind the courthouse was the school.

When he saw it again Leonard realized for the first time that, viewed from the perspective of Europe, it was a special institution. In early twentieth-century America, public schools were grand, federal-style brick buildings with neoclassical entrances. Everything was under one roof. Once the monuments to secular knowledge opened, their small, predecessor buildings were razed. The Sandy Creek school, however, resembled a small college campus. There was indeed a grand building dating from the 1920s, which functioned as an elementary school. Nearby was a recently-completed, rambling complex with cedar shingles. Its basement was for manual trades, while the upper floors were devoted to secretarial skills and home-economics. Here was also the kindergarten, with its adjacent, graveled playground. Nearby, the county superintendent of education worked in an old, white house. Behind the elementary school stood a three-storey, nineteenth-century construction, converted into a secondary school; it had wooden floors and narrow stairs and was wainscoted throughout.

Between the vocational complex and the secondary-school was a two-room building, the place Leonard felt most at ease. It was the science laboratory, also dating from the 1920s. Built of brick, it had windows on two sides and a solid back wall. It was covered by a rather sharply pitched roof mounted with a cupola and weathervane. To Leonard's eyes it now appeared like a Quaker meeting house. To enter, one walked up a short bank of stairs. A garderobe, with pegs on the walls, ran the entire width of the building. Then one faced two doors. One led to the chemistry laboratory, one to physics and biology. Through secondary school, Leonard ate lunch in the building, along with his closest friend, Bernard Tokay.

Bernie's father owned a lunch counter across a narrow stream that separated the school from the shops of Sandy Creek. He and

Bernie spent their time pouring over the latest word about radio-activity, cosmic rays, atom smashers, airplanes, plastics, and electronics. They built a radio transmitter and bounced signals off the ionosphere. They manufactured aspirin. They constructed model airplanes and rockets. In the spring they went out for track. Leonard did javelin, discus, and distance running; Bernie ran sprints and hurdles. They joked about ruling the world together.

Bernie Tokay had a girlfriend, the lovely Suzanne. She was tall and athletic. She had brilliant red hair and freckles and a low voice with an easy laugh. Bernie's parents had emigrated from the Banat in southern Hungary; they were nominally Eastern Orthodox, a faith for which no church existed in Sandy Creek. Suzanne's parents were devout Baptists from Maine who campaigned against tobacco, alcohol, and coffee and ran a temperance camp in the Pine Barrens. The easy democracy of Sandy Creek favored a mixing of ideas and genes.

Upon graduation, Bernie went to Rutgers and Suzanne went to the University of Maine, where she lived with her grandparents. Bernie threw himself into chemistry. Suzanne threw herself into partying. Leonard remembered a letter in which she confessed to having been seduced in the back seat of a Studebaker, begging him not to tell Bernie. Then she wrote to report that she had flunked out. She stayed in Maine and married a fraternity lout. When Bernie learned about it, he felt himself pitched head-forward down an endless hole. Bernie was in a well of despair, Leonard thought, when he saw him in Sandy Creek. The situation was entirely unreasonable, but love, or the security of Suzanne's affection, was beyond reason. You have your life and a brilliant future before you, Leonard told him. Half the people in the world are women. No one ever died of a broken heart, he added without conviction. Bernie returned to Rutgers and immolated himself.

Leonard surveyed the stability and clarity of the school grounds at Sandy Creek. Americans have always called their secondary institutions "high schools" (the cognate in Continental Europe referred to institutions of advanced learning only), and during the nineteenth century some of these compared favorably with colleges and universities. Leonard imagined that this was because of rigorous state control over secondary education and weak state standards for tertiary studies. American colleges (the European cognate referred either to professional corporations like the College of Cardinals and the Oxbridge and Pavian colleges, or to secondary schools) were the epitome of anarchy, with dozens of specialists competing for the attention of immature minds. There was an attempt at moral guidance, but in places seeking a reputation in the world of learning, the attempt would always be greeted with derision. Bernie's anguish must have been evident to teachers and students. No one intervened.

Leonard followed the school's small stream (it originated in the gigantic aquifer under the Pine Barrens, and it sprang from the ground behind the school's baseball field) to the small business district, which ended in the large creek that gave its name to the town. The town was situated at the point where the creek widened into an inlet forming part of Barnegat Bay. It pooled up just above the local railroad depot. There the acid, cedar-rinsed water mixed with the salt and mud of the bay. Leonard cycled to the shore. As he approached, a small flock of ducks greeted him. Then he went on to the public library.

Like so many sister institutions in small-town America, the James T. Deacon Memorial Library came into being from a bequeath. It was a rectangular brick, colonial edifice, harmonious and inviting. Inside was one enormous room, with a large loan counter against the long rear wall. There were maple tables with spindle-back chairs, as well as leather couches. Along one of the short walls was a fireplace with Deacon's portrait over the mantle. Books were shelved on all the walls according to the Dewey decimal system. Half of one wall was reserved for children's books. A small annex in the rear contained fiction. The library received a grant from the municipality, but it functioned independently. Leonard had always found it warm and inviting. After school he would often borrow a few books or use an encyclopedia before cycling home. He imagined how pleasant it would have been to spend an entire day there. The farm had never allowed him that privilege. Now he spoke with the middle-aged librarian, who wore her brown braids as a crown. Her goodness warmed the enormous room. The Deacon Memorial Library was an elegant and nurturing space, quite unlike anything else that Leonard knew.

It took twenty minutes to ride home. Leonard found a telegram from Colonel Cratsley. In five days he was to report to Swarthmore College, where he would begin learning Japanese.

*
*   *

From the Media Local tracks, which split the campus in two parts, Leonard surveyed Magill Walk, which led to Swarthmore's Parrish Hall. The oaks lining the long walk seemed larger than he remembered, or perhaps the buildings seemed smaller. Few people were about in the late afternoon. Frank Aydelotte's paradise of the mind was gliding through late winter, heading toward its spectacular rendezvous with spring.

Before he arrived at Swarthmore, Leonard had never known spring. The season does not exist in Sandy Creek. There winter ends and summer begins. There are no fields to be planted, no flowering succession of bulbs, shrubs, and trees. People lay out a vegetable garden and remark on isolated blooms. Then it comes time to set agricultural machinery in working order. But Swarthmore lies in the verdant western suburbs of Philadelphia, which shade off into Amish country. For more than three generations, the college had been cultivated as an ornamental garden.

Nearly every tree on the campus was tagged. Ivy ran wild. Here and there, thick vines of wisteria ascended skyward. When spring arrived, just as Leonard was preparing for examinations, the place exploded in an excess of fragrance and color. Hundreds of ornamental fruit trees bloomed, carpeting the carefully groomed grass with white and pink petals. These were accented by thousands of rhododendrons and azaleas, which cascaded down into the ravine that contained Crum Creek. The show deprived Leonard of reason for a week. He wandered aimlessly, awash in the primitive sense impressions that Ernst Mach identified as the source of all knowledge.

Leonard turned his back on the northern part of the campus and walked south, past the power plant (furnishing steam to all the buildings by way of pipes in subterranean tunnels) and the oval track. He glanced left, toward the cluster of shops spelled and pronounced as the future tense spoken by a German immigrant—"vill." A tall, gangly man loped down the sidewalk pulling a wooden wagon loaded with groceries. Student? Professor? Vagrant? It was hard to tell. Leonard followed a street rimming the Crum until he came to rambling villas known as Mary Lyon—named after the great nineteenth-century educator. A girl's school before the war, it had been transformed into a convalescent home for sailors. Colonel Cratsley had reserved a garret room here for his point man. Leonard dropped off his bag and strolled back to the northern campus by way of the Crum.

The Crum Creek was still in the unimproved state that Leonard had remembered. The east bank, however, showed signs of manicure, as the Arthur Hoyt Scott Horticultural Foundation slowly pruned the late-winter detritus. In the ravine's only meadow, beneath the railroad trestle, Leonard spotted a sailor walking with a young woman. On the road from the meadow to the rail overpass, he saw several more sailors. Then he ran into a platoon of sailors marching and grunting their way to the vill. The college, heritor of a pacifist Quaker tradition, had indeed shed its neutrality. With millions of young men under arms, it had to invite in the military to maintain a credible level of instruction. The compromise, after all, resulted in his present affiliation, whatever precisely that was.

Cratsley's telegram instructed Leonard to report to Dr Shinichiro Sasaki, lodged in one of the older dormitories. Leonard found the door and knocked.

"Enter, please," came a soft voice from within.

Leonard did as asked. "Leonard Ranov, reporting for duty."

He spoke to the back of a bald, robed figure facing the window. After some moments the figure stood up, more quickly than Leonard had thought possible. He faced an Oriental man who seemed barely five feet tall. Leonard could not guess the figure's age.

"Good day, Mr Ranov," the figure said in an incongruous Scottish lilt. "Excuse this spartan cell. I have been expecting you. My name is Sasaki. Please come with me to dinner in the dining commons. Wait for me downstairs while I change into my uniform."

Leonard and Sasaki walked to the dining commons in Parrish Hall. Dinner was a formal occasion at the college. People were seated in groups sufficient to fill a vacant table. One could either wait for a party of congenial spirits, or one could dine at random with whoever happened along. Leonard felt discomfort as he recalled the panic that sometimes welled up while he waited for a table. These feelings were complicated by his present, anomalous situation. Sasaki wore what was clearly the uniform of a naval officer, emblazoned with Chinese characters. Outside the commons he met a number of men dressed like him. After some discussion in an Oriental language, Sasaki turned to Leonard.

"Please join me and my colleagues." Leonard and seven Oriental officers then filled a table.

"You see," Sasaki said when they were seated, "I am something of the warden here. I supervise the moral and intellectual progress of my men, and I make damn'd sure they learn English."

Sasaki explained that he was part of a contingent of officers from the Chinese Navy who had been sent to Swarthmore to learn English. He imagined that Swarthmore was their billet because of its proximity to the Philadelphia naval yards and its ability to deliver dormitory space. Some of his men were taking science courses. He instructed all to strike up conversations with ambient women, who constituted the grand majority of students. Leonard stared at him.

"My dear Lieutenant Ranov. You will be asking yourself, how the hell did this chap learn English? There is no trick to it. My father sent me to Edinburgh to become a surgeon, as he had done in his time. He was professor in the Chinese University of Hong Kong. I am in fact a British subject protected by a Chinese diplomatic passport. But now to work."

The soup had been served. He plunged into it with gusto. His men proceeded more gingerly, a number of them tucking a cloth napkin into their tunic. Knife, peanut butter, bread, salt, pepper, soup, water, none of it came naturally yet. Sasaki chattered effortlessly in English about the men and their food, and Leonard replied to his queries. Leonard offered that he had passed four years at Swarthmore before the war. The rest of dinner was spent comparing impressions.

After dinner Leonard and Sasaki walked down to a sitting room near the dining commons. It was deserted. Students, both in uniform and in mufti, had fled to the library or to their rooms.

"Dr Sasaki," Leonard began, "I wonder if there is a mistake. I am supposed to study Japanese here. Is Chinese the best way to begin?"

"So you shall, laddie, so you shall." Sasaki laughed. He straightened up in the armchair that he had commandeered. "You see, my father was Japanese. Oh yes, there is a large chasm separating the Japanese and Chinese languages. But my grandfather insisted that my father learn Chinese in school. Grandpa was something of a traditionalist. His family were warriors who had been displaced by the end of the shogunate. Most of his relatives turned their back on Chinese and the Confucianist canon, preferring to learn the new religion of Western science and technology. He had a fondness for the old ways, a fondness my father shared and one that I honor. He died before my father completed medical school. I wonder what he would have thought about Edinburgh.

"Sometimes you chaps here do not recall that the Japanese were honorary Westerners during the Great War. When Britain oversaw the expansion of the Hong Kong medical school after Versailles, my father's name came up as a professor. He was happy to teach in an English milieu, and his Chinese improved a great deal over the years. I grew up with Chinese nannies, and nearly all my friends were Chinese. Learning Japanese was the problem. My parents instructed me, and I spent vacations in Japan with relatives. Then I went to high school in Kyoto. I shall lick you into shape, my boy."

Over the next months Sasaki did what he had promised. Leonard reported to Sasaki every morning at five. There were no days off. Sasaki elaborated the day's lesson and then spoke for an hour—in Japanese. Leonard spent the morning trying to make sense of it. At eleven Sasaki had him in for an hour's review. Leonard repaid the instruction by dining with the Chinese officers. From two to four he led them in physical exercises.

Due to the war emergency, Swarthmore ran courses through the summer. By the middle of July Leonard could converse with Sasaki and read simple books. He asked his instructor for something in the line of Japanese scientific texts. Sasaki shook his head sadly. "Not a scrap of Japanese physick here."

The situation changed one evening when Leonard visited Swarthmore's observatory, a 24-inch refractor mounted inside a rectangular stone structure once the home of the college president. Leonard had intentionally avoided it, just as he had as an undergraduate. The director, John A. Miller, vocally opposed Einstein's general relativity, and he spent time trying to find counter-evidence. Late in the summer, Miller's assistant opened the telescope for a lunar eclipse. Leonard turned up, looked through the telescope at the shadow crossing the moon's surface, and then poked around the observatory's corridors. He entered the library. Journal runs were on shelves, and file drawers were dedicated to special themes. Leonard recognized the names of several anti-Einsteinian physicists. One slim drawer bore the word

"Japan."

Inside were several books and reprints dealing with Einstein. Leonard saw at once that they were expository and favorable treatments. From an inscription, it appeared that the author, Ayao Kuwaki, had sent the material to Miller to indicate that, even in Japan, people knew that Einstein was right. There was Kuwaki's treatment of relativity from 1921, a biography of Einstein from 1934, and several articles about the history of science.

Leonard worked his way through Kuwaki's texts, and he prevailed on Sasaki to discuss them during the daily tutoring. For much of the summer, Saski had spoken about Japanese civilization. Leonard was an avid pupil. In the evenings he ransacked Swarthmore's modest library for additional information. Leonard adopted Sasaki's ways. When they talked, they sat on the floor, dressed in simple robes. The war had thrown Swarthmore's sense of propriety to the wind. Students wore all variety of costume. Under the circumstances, there was nothing scandalous about the Zen sessions. Sasaki gave in to the desire of his amanuensis. For the first time in six months, for nearly one hundred and eighty days, Sasaki allowed the syllabus of Japanese tutoring to spill into dinner conversation.

European epistemology fascinated Kuwaki. He believed that it had begun late in the nineteenth century with a profound debate about whether the goal of science was explanation, as traditionalists held, or description, as the younger voice of Ernst Mach proposed. Kuwaki greatly admired Mach, but he could not embrace Mach's Socratic brand of positivism. Hypotheses were necessary, Kuwaki believed. Theoretical constructions could mirror the real world. Max Planck had persuasively criticized Mach on just these grounds. Kuwaki could not believe that Mach, at the end of his life, had finally opposed Einstein's relativity; to be true to his own critical approach to natural law, Mach almost had to embrace Einstein. But Einstein had somehow gone beyond epistemology, or at least Kuwaki was uncertain about the philosophical underpinnings of Einstein's work. Einstein certainly sought to create timelessly true expressions about the physical world. There was apparently no relativism in relativity, and no statistical uncertainty in Einstein's mechanics.

"How could one even begin to believe in the primacy of sense impressions?" Sasaki asked at dinner in his best Scottish voice. "The mere describing of the impression, anchored in the ambiguity of language, requires conventions. Otherwise no one could ever be understood. Imagine placing one of my rice-farmer relatives next to an atom smasher. Whatever would he see as significant? The color of the paint? One must be part of the culture of a particular laboratory to make sense of its data. The knowledge is conventional.

"Ah," said Leonard in American English. "I think you have twisted the case. Are not facts transcendental? Some things may stand indisputably as facts. The fact of the matter is that my father is dead. I spent four years in this place. I hold a spoon in my right hand. Which are the relevant facts to bring to a particular question? Now that is not so easy to answer. Possibly the only rule is that there is no rule. Yet the world works in one way. I do not think that any culture could posit $2 + 2 = 5$."

"Your example proves nothing because it is not of the real world. One really does not know what one is talking about with mathematics. In the real world, propositions are turned on their head all the time, and with good effect. Did not Marx succeed by turning Hegel on his head? Surely this is what Einstein did when he formulated relativity, if I read Kuwaki correctly. Einstein thought, Let us reformulate mechanics and electrodynamics without worrying—as physicists had for generations—about the essence of motion or light. Immediately there was no place for imaginary notions like absolute space and an electromagnetic ether. I admit, there is something Mach-like about this procedure. Later, of course, with the geometry of gravitation and the light-quantum mechanics, transcendental essences reappeared.

"Let us use this procedure to reformulate one of the greatest synthetic achievements, Darwin's theory of natural selection. It is based on the notion of competition. Individuals of one species, who exhibit a certain spread or variation in their traits and attributes, compete for limited resources. Species compete to dominate a set of conditions in an ecosystem. The successful competitors propagate their kind; the losers are destroyed.

"Suppose now we stand Darwin on his head. Imagine that evolution proceeds by coöperation. Successful individuals are those who coöperate effectively with their own kind. Successful species also coöperate with other species to preserve the equilibrium of a habitat. Wolves and caribou coöperate to maintain appropriate numbers so that each species may survive. The same holds for cats and mice, foxes and lemmings, whales and krill, and even humans and viruses."

"Now, wait a minute," Leonard interjected. "How is the equilibrium established? Is there an interspecies council of elders who vote on how many must die each year? And surely the equilibrium is frequently upset. Lemmings run to the sea in mass suicide."

"It is all no more mysterious than your vaunted laws of physics. Newton's third law and Heisenberg's uncertainty principle are general cautions. They are invoked to warn a calculator about fundamental constraints inherent in a particular system or situation. In some measure this also resembles Darwin's principle of natural selection. Taken by themselves, these grand principles predict nothing. They do, however, channel inferences.

"What is interesting about arguments in natural history is the way that they depend on an interaction between animate and inanimate nature. Normally inanimate nature is simply called the 'environment.' This is a tradition extending back beyond Darwin to your eighteenth century." Leonard detected a slight sniff when Sasaki pronounced the word "your," in his oxymoronic Scottish lilt. "But true principles of nature must hold in all situations. Do not your atomic physicists," again the sniff, "pretend that consciousness is not excluded from quantum uncertainty?"

"The question is controversial. It has even received a designation, the 'Schrödinger's cat' paradox. A cat is placed in a box with a cyanide device. There is uncertainty involved in knowing when the device extinguishes the cat's life. But there is no uncertainty for the cat. It all seems to turn on the meaning of life."

"Ah, laddie," Sasaki smiled, "you unwittingly confirm my view. How clever of Herr Professor Dr Schrödinger to have anticipated the mass extermination methods now used by his countrymen. You see, life works with the grand forces of inanimate nature. Fields and forests, streams and marshes, winds and clouds, volcanoes and ocean currents, all enter into an unspoken pact with plankton, seaweed, algae, and the astonishing variety of life in the sea to preserve the optimal oxygen balance in the atmosphere that may permit life on land. There are compensatory and self-correcting mechanisms everywhere. How shall we otherwise explain the continuing breathability of the air when, over 300 million years, the sun has burned inconstantly? Hovering over the earth is a spirit favoring life, and life of our kind, the teleological guide glimpsed by Buffon, elaborated by your Shaw, Bergson, and Teilhard de Chardin. Has your mind been so conditioned that you cannot see it? Kuwaki understands the point. He sees that ultimately Einstein is no Machian—indeed, that Einstein follows none of your epistemologies."

Sasaki rose and walked out on the front porch of Parrish Hall, from which Magill Walk descended to the train station. Leonard followed him. A warm wind flowed around them. A few lamps pushed the night away. An occasional student or sailor walked to the library, with its enormous clock ringing Westminster chimes. There went the Bodes, the studious ones. How very like America, Sasaki rolled out the arrs, to mispronounce the Bodleian Library when appropriating it for a whimsical attribution.

"You know I shall be leaving in a few weeks," Sasaki spoke after some silence. "The government is sending me deep into the interior. I am to organize field hospitals. Ironic, isn't it? A naval surgeon in the mountains. Maybe it is to keep me as far away from the Japanese as possible. They think I can work well with the British liaison, Joseph Needham, an embryologist of great attainments who has Sinological sympathies. My men will be scattered to gunboats, if your people can find any for them." He paused. "You have been a good student. Here is your diploma."

Sasaki pulled a folded vellum paper from his tunic and handed it to Leonard. Lettered in black and gold, in the *kanji* of Japanese calligraphy where (as in a Matisse drawing) an unusual amount of care goes into an apparently spontaneous effort, was a certification of Leonard's proficiency in Japanese. It went further. Sasaki pronounced Leonard an honorary member of the Sasaki clan. At the bottom of the diploma were the Sasaki arms, a diamond with a superimposed X, forming four smaller diamonds each with a small diamond at its center, the whole ringed by a circle.

Leonard saw that Sasaki had given him a name in three Chinese characters—Pei Lu-wen. A rough translation would have been "Learned White Deer." The name came from a T'ang poem by Li Pai about Tianmu Mountain, which, in a rare, idle moment, Sasaki had worked through with Leonard:

> *And so I say goodbye, not knowing for how long.*
> *Let me invoke a white deer*
> *And ride to you, great mountain, when I need you.*
> *Oh! how can I bow to illustrious men*
> *Who would pale before an honest, good-hearted face!*

"Ezra Pound," he sniffed, "seems to have missed this one, when he looked into the great writer whom he called, in Japanese, Rihaku. You became part of my home here, Lu-wen," Sasaki shrugged. "What else could I do?"

Leonard bowed and offered a formal thanks. He and Sasaki sat on white Adirondack chairs and absorbed the evening. A group of women naval officers passed, speaking in hushed but animated tones. During his months at Swarthmore, Leonard had not found himself attracted to the young women everywhere around him.

The students he found amusing but immature and indescribably plain—a legacy of Frank Aydelotte's Quakerly bias against beauty. The radiance that interested Aydelotte shone from within, through flat chests, large noses, and stringy hair. The women from the navy, well, some of them reminded him of women from Wyoming, open and friendly and presenting themselves as quite unable to vocalize anything more than simple emotions, a construction, he imagined, by no means capturing the real person. He just did not want to invest the time to penetrate deeper, and Sasaki-san would not allow him the time. Was Sasaki married? He could not tell, and he never asked.

There was one Wyoming woman he remembered, Alice Throop. The daughter of a rancher from Rawlins, she was vaguely studying literature and psychology. She turned up in the physics laboratory one evening as the friend of a date for one of the graduate students. She and Leonard talked for hours about Melville, Joyce, and Hemingway. A few days later she drove Leonard into the Snowy Range for a walk in the trees. Alice ("We say it 'troop') was short and trim. Leonard found her shape unconventional and amusing when he lay next to her that night in the bed of her basement apartment. Her small breasts sagged, and her abdomen sloped out as it circled down to her hips. They became good friends and occasional lovers.

John Kazantis, a fellow physics instructor, relayed a rumor about Alice's past. "She had a child when she was seventeen." Leonard never got around to asking about the allegation. He did not care.

Leonard stared into the early autumn darkness, taking in the musty spores released by decomposing leaves. A lanky figure walked by, accompanied by one of the Chinese officers. He was the man Leonard had seen on his first day at Swarthmore.

"Who is he?" Leonard asked Sasaki. "I've seen him now and then. Does he work here, in the library or business office?"

"Do you not recognize one of your greatest poets?" Sasaki laughed. "It is Wystan Auden, with his new boyfriend."

6

Uncertainty

Everything into its opposite, that is Hegel's rule. The world is as we make it. The act of perceiving affects the data, the noumena and the phenomena execute a dialectic. But certain things confront us brutally, unalterably. We grow old. The planets move in their regular course. Everything tends toward a state of maximal entropy. And however much dialectical spin is applied, some things are forever excluded. Shall we ever seriously imagine, once more, that the Earth is the center of the universe? It is for us to make sense of the world through clever experimentation. Bohr did not pull his atomic model out of thin air. It was grounded in the observations of spectroscopy and radioactivity.

Jacob Witte, *Contra Hegel* (Amsterdam, 1935), p. 7

"Oh, dear. Létoile." The thin, white-haired man pronounced it Dutch fashion, sounding out the final vowel. He rose from his desk and walked around the room. It was meticulously neat. Journals were bound in rows on shelves. Filing cabinets along one wall held reprints, manuscripts, and correspondence. On another wall hung large photographic prints of stars and nebulae, accompanied by a framed illustration of the zodiac with a commentary in Latin.

"Years ago I corresponded with him, and we co-authored some papers. An unusual man."

Leonard looked at Bartholomew Dijk van der Aa and waited for an explanation. He had taken the train to Princeton following a note from Ernest Bit, who had returned to Washington and was pursuing the Witte file. Ernest found that Létoile and Dijk were scientific collaborators. He wrote that Cratsley wanted Leonard to see Dijk while he was in the neighborhood.

"Létoile was very much a self-made man, more an engineer than an astronomer. Thirty years ago there were many American astronomers like him, but very few Europeans. So he shipped out to the colonies. First to South Africa, where he wasted years trying to work in a private capacity. Then to the Indies, where he had actually been born. There he became director of a grand private observatory, eventually absorbed by the colonial regime. As he told me, he owed nothing to any astronomer, and so he pursued what he liked and received whom he liked in his small kingdom."

"Do you think that his judgments are reliable?" This was really all that Leonard could think to ask.

Dijk walked to a cabinet and after a moment pulled out a thick file.

"I think that Létoile does not improve his observations. That is the great temptation in variable-star work. Measuring luminosity over the years tends to become subjective, if one is not careful. Ah, here it is."

Dijk had opened the folder on his desk and examined a stack of letters.

"Létoile grumbles a lot about his telescopes and his isolation, but he really has a fine set-up. He lives at the observatory with his German wife. Here is a photograph."

Leonard saw a collection of structures viewed from the air. Dijk described the scene. There was a large domed building housing the double photographical refractor—until the war the largest telescope in Dutch hands. A central villa was Létoile's home. Separate installations were for the library, photographical laboratory, and the Schmidt telescope. Outbuildings were reserved for observatory staff and invited guests.

"Létoile invited me to spend a year there, but my wife objected. She has grown accustomed to the cultivated, bourgeois pace here. Actually these photographs probably do not reflect the observatory today. They were taken about twenty years ago. The grounds are pretty much bare. Now I expect that there would be trees everywhere."

Leonard returned the photograph. "Why is Létoile unusual?"

"Well, you know, despite his name, he is Dutch through and through. He is unusually willful. Not arrogant or abrasive, but determined to do what he thinks is necessary. He has a reputation as a loner. At least, the Dutch astronomical community never got on with him." Dijk chuckled. "Well, the reason is that he ran the big telescope and did not humbly offer it to the great savants of the motherland, as they imagine he should have done. Létoile never took a doctorate in astronomy; his advanced degree came *honoris causa* from Germany. I heard that he retired several years ago. But that was on the eve of the German conquest of Holland. I cannot see him returning to Europe. Well, he's still there hanging around the observatory, I imagine. Are you an astronomer, Lieutenant?"

Leonard mumbled that, alas, it was not his privilege, but that he'd been researching cosmic rays when the war broke out.

"Birth cries of the universe," Dijk laughed. "Millikan has persuaded the public that cosmic rays are messages from the time when matter was created. Cosmic rays fund his empire at Caltech. You did not study there? Good. Oh, I overstepped the bounds of polite conversation."

A clock struck a quarter to the hour. There was a moment of silence as an angel passed between Leonard and the Princeton astronomer.

"A real physicist lectures here at Fine Hall in fifteen minutes. Niels Bohr is giving a little talk about quantum philosophy. Shall you come along? It is tea-time."

Fine Hall, Leonard knew, had been for a number of years the seat of the Institute for Advanced Study, an elite club built with Bamberger money. It was the closest modern equivalent to

Alexandria's Museum, of classical Antiquity. The institute was what finally attracted Einstein to America. Dijk led Leonard out of his office (he did not lock the door) and across the campus. He explained that he was merely a professor at the university, not at the institute, and so he had to work for a living. The institute's mathematicians were installed at a new, sylvan campus, but they still turned up for the lectures in Fine Hall.

"I grade papers and smile at new students," Dijk murmured. "And I give the astronomy course for non-scientists—it gets the literary types, the ones who want to know more about 'The Man Who Saw Through Heaven' and John Donne's tribute to Galileo. Well, there is something to it. When I look through the telescope, I see the face of God. Only, I wish there were girls in the class. Back in Holland I could have packed them in. Here they are only a handful allowed to study photogrammetry."

The two men walked toward the salon at Fine Hall. There was a crowd approaching a hundred, and it spilled into the corridor. The young men were all well-dressed, a sartorial condition that deteriorated with increasing age. A few middle-aged men wore ill-fitting suits. Here and there were sweaters and sandals. Leonard wondered about the art of aging with grace. Whatever it took, these men did not have it. By the time that Leonard made his way to the coffee urn and teapots, there was nothing left. The crowd had then begun to jangle toward the big lecture room, compressing and expanding like a garage-door spring.

Leonard found a seat at the back. After a few minutes a bald man took to center stage. Frank Aydelotte, Leonard knew, had moved from Swarthmore to follow Abraham Flexner as director of the institute. Aydelotte explained that Bohr had only recently fled Denmark. Bohr agreed to say a few words about complementarity. The pope of quantum mechanics, Leonard thought, had escaped to tell his tales, while Jacob Witte's tales remained in Leiden.

Bohr, with his drooping eyes and heavy lips, delivered a round-about talk. It was round-about because it was circular, ending up where it began. Along the way he spoke about indeterminacy. We could not know with absolute precision where something was and what it was doing. And by the same token, it made little sense to ask whether an electron was a wave or a particle. We had to be content with calculating the *probabilities* of an object's motion. The probabilities were the object's essence. Nothing more could be known.

Hands flew up when the talk was over. Bohr first recognized a bespectacled man with blondish-white hair sitting next to Leonard.

"Yes, Professor Neugebauer."

"Professor Bohr, what was the probability of your arriving here?" The remark drew scattered laughs. Neugebauer, whose ancestors were Austrian Aryans, had quit a chair at Göttingen in 1933 rather than serve fascist masters. Bohr's Copenhagen had taken him in until, in 1939, Brown University made him an offer he could not refuse. He arrived in New York with kit and caboodle.

A broad smile propped up the speaker's sagging cheeks. "One hundred percent. You remember that I know a bit about sailing, and of course I had a reliable travel agent." Bohr had made it to Sweden on an open boat. He loved the sea, even though a sailing accident had claimed his eldest son. Bohr then called on people he didn't know. Aydelotte stopped the questions after about fifteen minutes. Otto Neugebauer, the master of ancient Babylonian astronomy, scurried to the podium, and the two men chattered in German about Copenhagen.

Leonard filed out with the crowd. He fell in behind an old man in dirty clothes. He was overwhelmed by the smell of body odor, and he was grateful when the man disappeared down the corridor. He hung around the building's entrance for a moment. There was no reason to linger, but the place was Xanadu. He glanced once more at the thinning crowd. The old man was speaking with Dijk. Then the old man's animated face became visible. Einstein. He sat through Bohr's apology for a probabilistic universe, a vision that he rejected, without saying a word.

*

*   *

Leonard had a week before reporting to the naval base at Oakland, there to ship out for the Pacific. He was going to Java, although ways and means had yet to become clear. That was the reason for learning Japanese. There was time to pass by Laramie.

It was nearly two years since he suddenly left Wyoming for the war. He had asked an assistant to finish his courses, ended the lease on his apartment, and shipped his books and papers back to Sandy Creek. For a week, until he could join the army in Denver, he slept in a shed used by the Physics Department to store equipment. He used the time to analyze some of his cosmic-ray data and say goodbyes. He was able to get a publishable note out of the data. After hoping that someone would continue measurements, he reconciled himself to ending the research project.

He anticipated seeing, once more, the open and smiling people who took the natural majesty of the high plains in stride, not with the trace of awe that Leonard still felt. The mountains covered in white, the hundred-mile panorama with half a dozen things happening in the sky at once, the dry washes and scantily-clad pastures, the smell of sage and pine, the sharp exhaustion of breathing deeply with some seventy percent of the oxygen available at sea-level—people took all these things in without reflecting on them.

The way to these memories began at the air base outside Trenton, and Leonard took the bus from Princeton down US 1 to get there. He went to the airfield and looked for flights west. Twenty hours later he was in Denver, having found a crew flying propeller blades into Colorado. They were quite stoned when he met them. It was night, and they took off with oxygen masks. Leonard put on a spare flight suit, spread out his parachute, and went to sleep, knowing that the cockpit would be level sober within an hour.

The only train from Denver to Cheyenne and then to Laramie left late in the afternoon, and Leonard looked into a blazing October morning. It was actually above freezing, and there was no snow on the ground. Leonard decided he would hitchhike.

His first lift took him to Fort Collins. From there it would be anywhere between an hour and two hours, depending on the roads. He stared at the Front Range for the entire trip. Every time he saw the mountains they put him in a reflective mood. The driver, a teenaged Mormon missionary, listened while Leonard tried to express his feelings for the mountains.

"I know them. I've climbed all over them in every season. They are intimate but not commonplace. From a distance, with their plumes and mantles, shadowed in clouds and fringed in brown and green, as the light plays along their angles, their exquisite lines invite worship."

"Not married, I guess," the boy again. "No ring. Family is the way to God, don't you know? Without your family, what are you?"

Leonard didn't know. He got out of the boy's car at the northwest end of Fort Collins. The temperature was dropping rapidly. Leonard hoped for a ride to take him into Laramie before dark. The first possibility, a milk truck, passed him by. Then the wall of snow descended.

Mountains play their cards close to their chest. The weather comes at travelers like a hand of pinochle. Experience helps in playing, but the main parts are beyond understanding. Leonard had placed his back to the wind, a pose that also allowed him to stare into Fort Collins and look for a car, and so he did not see the blizzard that rushed down from the peaks. After a minute, he was lost in a universe of white. The snow clumped in large, wet flakes that adhered to every surface. Two eyes approached slowly. Leonard waved madly, and the action displaced enough snow to make him visible to the driver.

"Howdy, fella."

A truck with five cows, headed for Rawlins.

"Thanks very much," Leonard expelled as he muscled his duffle into the cab. "My toes were beginning to freeze." The first winter in Laramie, Leonard had gone into the Snowy Range with a group of students. They were out all of a weekend. The weather snapped cold overnight. Leonard's toes came close to freezing. He lost sensation for a month, until he felt them tingle and apparently thaw while he was reading in the library. Peripheral circulation returned as minor blood vessels expanded to carry the load of their debilitated compatriots, but ever since then his feet were sensitive to cold.

The driver stared into the blanket of white, a cigarette in his right hand on the wheel. "Smoke?" Leonard declined. "Drink?" The driver reached behind his seat and brought out a bottle of bourbon. Leonard took a sip. The illusion of warmth. Leonard tried to move his boots closer to the heater.

"Going far?" The driver had trouble pronouncing consonants. He was missing many of his front teeth. His face was brown and wrinkled. Irregular black spots disfigured the left side of his forehead. "Laramie? My cousin lived there, worked for the railroad. You from around here? Know Steffie's down over by the station? Best food you'd want. Lest you'd eat Steffie herself." On it went at thirty miles an hour. They glided through a void, marked on occasion by a row of utility poles or bridge railings. At first, Leonard tensed every muscle. Then he decided it was pointless. The cowherd knew every turn in the road. They rose from the bare plains into a finger of the Front Range thrust east. Trees appeared, and the occasional mailbox cantilevered out toward the road. The storm abated as they crossed the finger's divide. After a half hour, down a long curve, the road opened on a long plain. Dusk, and the stars.

At more than seven thousand feet, the stars appeared wanton in their profusion. On a night without atmospheric turbulence, they rained down light. After a few moments, Leonard felt that he could fall up and be enveloped by them. The experience was intensified by the thin air. Leonard took exquisite pleasure in breathing deeply, hyperventilating to feel the sharpness of oxygen deficit. He imagined following cosmic-ray trails back to their celestial origin, pulled up by ineluctable, cosmic attraction.

The cattle truck approached the lights of Laramie. It was a *bague* on the finger of a long ridge. Leonard watched the lights rise in intensity to rival the stars and then surpass them.

There are two kinds of town. First came the organic European *cités*, whether grand like Madrid and Paris or compact, like a village in the Auvergne or in Tuscany. Here space was dear, and where one did not live one had to grow food. In these towns, people arranged themselves by accident and lived by usufruct. Second were the mechanical renaissance towns, laid out according to the artificial laws of perspective and numerology that captured the imagination of Renaissance painters, and which led into the Scientific Revolution. The New World was new by virtue of its towns, where streets sprouted in anticipation of inhabitants, condemning future residents to lie in a Procrustean bed of arbitrary proportions. Each kind of town was a steady-state solution for civilization. Then came the rise of fecundity. The closed towns and the grid towns sent out tendrils and generated monstrous appendages, as industrial and commercial centers grew beyond imagination in oncological metastases. In eastern America, settlements beyond coastal New England grew by grid and faded slowly into the surrounding countryside. In the American West, grid towns ended rather abruptly in fields and pasture. They were paradoxically the American *cités*.

The cowherd crossed a culvert and entered the town. He dropped Leonard at the main intersection and rolled on to his pastoral destination. Leonard looked about. Activity and energy were evident in vigorous pedestrian gait. People were placing packages into automobiles. Men laughed as they strode the streets. Women walked here and there in everything from heels to work boots. In the distance there was a symphony of whistles, thumps, clangs, and squeals. That was where Leonard headed.

The best food was down by the tracks. As Leonard approached, his duffle slung over his shoulder like a giant croissant, he saw that the yards were busier than he had remembered. Here was the source of Laramie's energy. The two-ocean war had supplied people and resources, for much of what flowed across the continent passed through the town. The war had given *élan* to people crushed by the Depression. It also brought new voices and new customs. There were black and brown faces; shouts in Russian and Italian; hats, shoes, and trousers that had nothing to do with Wyoming tradition. Leonard walked past Steffie's. He came to Pipo's, where he occasionally ate before the war. The diner introduced him to Mexican food, and he never found better elsewhere. The place had changed. He recognized no one, and the food, from what he saw on the tables, was perfectly common. He slid on a stool at the counter and ordered the special.

Leonard recognized for the first time that the war had fundamentally changed the temper of America. It was a coming together, a de-regionalization, an imposition of mechanical solidarity for organic collectivity. Was what he saw in Laramie so different now from a street near any war industry? The war had forged a nation where previously there had been only a confederation of regions and races. These new citizens should demand tangible improvement in their lives, he thought optimistically. Or would they simply vote in the generals and admirals who commanded them to cross oceans on wars of retribution and conquest?

He paid for the meal and walked in the direction of his old apartment. Maybe Frank Simms, the owner of the large house that had been partitioned into a warren of rooms, could put him up for the night. It was ten blocks in the general direction of the university. Leonard loped down the center of the streets, dodging an occasional car and shouting to a testy dog. A thin layer of snow blanketed everything, but the sky was clear. He was sweating when he rang Simms's bell.

"Got a berth for an old shipmate?"

Simms greeted Leonard without much interest and showed him to the garage. He could have a bed there for a few days. Simms would bring out a pile of old blankets and some sheets. Five dollars would do. Leonard sank into the sagging bed and closed his eyes. He thought he heard mice. He had pleasant associations with Laramie, and he was glad to be back.

Some parts of the past are best left alone. Unlike the tired formalism of a novel, where the premise and the plot must achieve a measure of unity, life is quantized and incomplete. Premonitions of death lead to a list of last things—here are all the bills to pay and all the letters to keep—an impulse that generates pathos in everyone except the list-maker. Things do end abruptly. It can be unsettling to pick up a strand of the past and give it new life. Imagine receiving back correspondence sent to an acquaintance a quarter-century previously. The principal emotion in the receiver is surely consternation mixed with annoyance. But Laramie seemed bright, warm, and secure.

*

*   *

"Leonard! A general in the army." John Kazantis smiled and embraced the errant physicist. "Tell me everything, and come to dinner tonight. I'll call Jacqueline. She will cook a French feast."

Leonard had walked up to the wing of offices and laboratories used by Laramie's physicists. John was the only one of the assistants Leonard recognized. The permanent staff had undergone mutations: None was visible. Doors were closed. The building, constructed of yellow and brown stones quarried locally, had the air of a castle. Now it seemed immobilized, in suspended animation.

"Research is gone, and many professors, too," John lamented. "We teach army engineers about beam loading and stress. Introductory physics is flooded with girls who want to be nurses and engineers. Remember, you made me read *Moby Dick*? I alone have survived to tell the tale." John added extra emphasis on his consonants, the overcompensation of a foreigner for whom English was a third language. Leonard hoped that everything was well with him and his wife.

"We have a daughter. Greece and France have faded from sight, but she is an American. Her name is Laramie. Soon Jacqueline and I will be Americans, too." Leonard knew that a heart murmur would keep John out of the army. John told him where the assistants and professors had gone. "Micheel died a few months ago."

Richard Micheel had supervised Leonard's master's thesis. He was a solitary and private man, but Leonard came to like him. Micheel was an orphan from Pittsburgh. He put himself through school by working in the steel mills. In his youth, he liked to say, no one was stronger than he. When Leonard knew him, he had a thin and wiry build. He subsisted on beer and steak. Pancreatic cancer cut him down.

John opened a door. "No one has cleared out his office. Want to look around?"

Leonard looked in. It was as he remembered. Bookcases lined three walls. They shelved bound copies of a dozen periodicals, notably the *Physical Review*, *Journal de physique*, and *Zeitschrift für Physik*. There were books and manuals, instrument catalogues, encyclopedias, and dictionaries. Leonard saw pressure gauges, flanges, bottles, and an electrometer. A few weeks' mail, including copies of the New York *Times* and what appeared to be printer's proofs, formed a pile on Micheel's desk. A small table held a chess game.

"I'll just be a few minutes."

It was a mid-game contest. White had knights in the fifth and sixth ranks, protected by a bishop and a rook's pawn. Red had castled early and was pressed by an apparently berserk attack in which the white queen had been sacrificed. Ever since high school Leonard preferred king-side attacks to the predictable monotony of queen-side maneuvering. Throwing everything against the opposing king, it was possible to pull out a victory with few pieces. Of course, if the attack stalled, an opponent would win by the inexorable pressure of superior forces. Leonard became known in local chess circles as an unpredictable and dangerous player. Whether he was winning or losing, it always appeared like he was losing. From the way the board was set up, with red backed into one of the room's corners, Leonard imagined that Micheel was white and that the game proceeded by mail. Now it would be unresolved forever. Where fate with men for pieces plays, Leonard remembered.

The cosmic-ray notebooks occupied two feet of shelf space. They ran from Leonard's arrival at Laramie up through the early part of 1943. Leonard had not known that Micheel continued the work. He looked through the volumes for 1942. Data from high-altitude balloons, background measurements, intensities at various times of the day, all set down in Micheel's precise hand. Micheel believed that research notebooks should reflect all parts of an investigation. Here and there were newspapers clippings about Robert Millikan's views on cosmic rays. Leonard saw memos about repairing instruments. There was also correspondence with suppliers—Micheel paid for research out of his own pocket, and he kept scrupulous accounts. A folded, airmail letter fluttered to the floor. Leonard absently picked it up. He saw Létoile's return address.

Létoile wrote in English. He was responding to Micheel's questions about tropism in cosmic-ray intensity. He explained that because of preparations for war, it was impossible for him to continue observations. For the past two years he had done little except a bit of uranium prospecting. By accident he had found a large deposit. He had mapped its contours and ascertained its purity. After the war it would make him rich. It was most unusual, he wrote, because the deposit seemed to be an intrusion on the side of an active volcano. He knew that there were uranium deposits in the Rocky Mountains. Were any located near dormant or extinct volcanoes? And if Micheel wanted more on cosmic rays, he could write to Létoile's close friend, Reverend McIntyre at Riverview near Sydney.

The letter was dated in March 1942. Leonard looked through the notebooks for other traces of Létoile. He scoured the bookcases and rummaged through Micheel's desk. There was nothing. Who was McIntyre? Leonard knew most of the world's cosmic-ray researchers by reputation, and he had never run across a McIntyre. Why had Micheel kept the letter? Poor Micheel. Leonard resolved to correct his proofs, the final obligation of a student.

*

*   *

On the evening of the following day, Leonard walked to the Kazantis apartment, a small suite in Laramie's most elegant building, built of brick with an occasional Tudor motif. Up to the second floor, a knock, and Jacqueline answered the door. She had lost a bit of her exquisitely petite dimensions, but the radiance was still there.

"Leonard, what a pleasure," she said and offered her cheeks for him to kiss, which he did. "John is with Lara. Come in, please." She shepherded Leonard into the small living room. It was still decorated with her found art: old cans and bottles, a few mailboxes and whirligigs, a door painted to advertise Mail Pouch tobacco, a weathered Spanish trunk. Half a dozen Indian blankets were thrown over the furniture.

Jacqueline was spectacularly refreshing to Leonard. Raised with and trained in Western European art, she gloried in the exuberance of the American West. She wore her long blond hair in a single braid, a concession to practicality which she sometimes intertwined with a scarf. John and she were mildly offbeat in complementary proportions.

John carried Lara in for a viewing. She was almost asleep.

Leonard saw that she had earrings and that she sprouted half an inch of thin, darkish hair. "A Peruvian folklore," John laughed and gently rubbed Lara's head. "Shaving the baby's head stimulates luxurious hair."

With Lara sleeping out of sight, the three moved on to the serious business of dinner. For in these rooms nothing was more important. Dinner, with its costume and courtesy, is where civilization resides, and no culture has done more for dinner than the French. The kitchen table was set with Jacqueline's monogrammed silver and ancient Sèvres china. There were decanters of white and red wine. First came an ox-tail soup, then a liver and spinach terrine, then antelope chasseur, then a slaw of cabbage and tubers. Dinner ended with a sabayon, which John whipped up on the counter. He brought out an Armagnac and filled three tiny leaded *ballons*. Leonard was swimming happily. Jacqueline was falling asleep.

"War brings out the finest in the human spirit," Leonard offered. "De Maistre. I would not have deserved such a splendid dinner if I had not come dressed as a warrior. Do we honor warriors out of pity, or out of fear? Pity, because their exploits are not merely unnecessary, but totally devoid of reason. Fear, because they have the means to extinguish life uncompromisingly and suddenly. The honor invented for professional killers is wergild. The ones we should really honor are not Wellington or Saint Joan but Ossietzky and Barbara Frietchie."

"Garbage," said John. "You signed on for the duration."

"They've fed me and taught me Japanese."

"A lamb to the slaughter. But I am proud of you."

Leonard changed the subject. "Do you remember much about Micheel's last work on cosmic rays? I found this letter in his notebooks."

John accepted the letter and looked it over quickly. "Oh yes, the Dutchman with the French name. The Star. He got interested in radioactivity. There's a fortune in it after the war, if he's right. But there's more. A few days after the letter arrived, Micheel said to me, 'It should be possible to construct a uranium bomb.' And he showed me how, assuming that somehow you could throw enough U^{235} in a heap—or, and this gets tricky, bombard U^{238} with neutrons to make a new radioactive element. But how could that be done? A giant centrifuge? And how to manipulate it without dying from radiation? We looked up the articles from the late '30s."

"Did Micheel write back to Létoile?"

"I think so. It was early May. With the Japanese moving south, he thought the letter would probably be returned. He never said more about it. Did you find a copy of his letter? No? Maybe he described the nutty bomb business. What do you think?"

Leonard shrugged, "Eh. Who knows, maybe." If the letter did arrive, it would have been on the eve of the Japanese invasion. An accessible uranium source would be of great interest to Japanese physicists, who were moving into radioactivity. Suppose they were now mining the stuff. Suppose they were working on a bomb.

Jacqueline had closed her eyes, secure in the achievement of her dinner. Lara gurgled peacefully. It was time to move on. Leonard embraced his two hosts.

"Send us a card when you get where you're going." That would be Los Alamos.

*
*　　*

The train pulled out of Pueblo, the northern gateway to the Sangre de Cristo Range. The wealth of Climax and Leadville near the headwaters of the Arkansas River came downstream to Pueblo, at the dry beginnings of the Great Plains, to be refined. The smoke stacks were now working overtime. Leonard looked out the window and saw his own reflection in the dark. He regretted that the rest of the trip would not follow the Arkansas's canyon into the high meadows. The train would skirt the mountains in a grand arc. Yellows and browns and reds, with occasional whites and greens, would be his companions into Santa Fe, once daylight returned.

He had occasionally thought about Los Alamos, the ornament of the Manhattan Project. That was where the best physicists went to construct an atomic bomb. He knew a number of people who spent time there, but they did not speak about it. Colonel Cratsley had cleared him for war work. He imagined that his clearance would get him through the gates. No one actually forbade him from going there, but no one had invited him. He thought that he might camp for more than a week in Laramie, but he felt uncomfortable after a few days. So he decided to see the New-Mexico highlands.

The history of war in the United States of America is unlike that of any other country. Scores of thousands of young men plucked from domestic complacency and thrust into foreign adventures: the eighteenth-century war against Libya, expeditions against Mexico, Venezuela, Spanish Cuba and the Philippines, Imperial China, Imperial Germany, Red Russia. The regime in Washington expanded its territorial control by conquering a dozen autochthonous North-American civilizations; it reconquered land whose people had decided, by majoritarian voice, to seek their sovereign destiny. Farms and industries powered the bellicose expansion. Ripped from pastoral equanimity, sons left their mothers for the most intense education of all. This expansive brutality formed the competitive, unprincipled, domineering spirit that has guided American fortunes.

The people remaining behind, the laboring women and men who supported the warriors, developed an outlook of skepticism and self-sufficiency. Among visible minorities there was the passive aggression of people constrained by unreasonable domination—what one sees in European peasantry—but this contrasted to the relative lack of radical insurgency in cities, that which fueled European socialism. American collectivism has always been strongest in rural settings, from the religious and utopian sects of the early republic to the progressivist movements of California, Minnesota, and Vermont. The American experience derives from a dialectic between foreign destruction and domestic common-wealth. The common thread is a notion of elitism—an aristoc-racy of ownership. Here is the legacy of Franklin and Jefferson.

In this time of war, following on ten years of very bad luck, intimacy was both heightened and compromised. Intensified as people imagined love and sought oblivion in passion; diminished as people avoided the past, whether their distant origins or the part of their life owed the war machine. It was hard to talk about childhood; it was dangerous to talk about work. Conversation often hovered about the day and the immediate future.

"Name's Joe Schumacher," the round-faced, mustached man announced as he hefted his leather valise into the overhead rack and sank into a seat diagonally opposite Leonard. "Schumacher Foundry. Going far? Smoke?" He fished out a case of fine Havanas. The babbittry revealed that Joe Schumacher had suf-fered no great deprivation in the Depression and was now flour-ishing as a war profiteer.

"Not one of my habits. Lieutenant Leonard Ranov." They shook hands.

"You guys in the army use my shell casings. See, there?" He pointed out into the night. "Those stacks? That's where they're made. What's in the caissons as they keep rolling." He laughed. "Ever shoot a field piece?"

"No," Leonard answered flatly. "But I've dropped bombs. Make those too, do you?"

"Naw, takes special tools, would have cost too much. Dad got into this business with General Pershing. Our shells went into Mexico, pulled by mules the caissons were, after Villa. Pershing bounced me on his knee."

"Going on vacation?"

"Naw, going to San Diego to see the brass about the really big shells. Swell place. You?"

"No vacations for soldiers."

"Yah, sure. You're the heroes, God bless you. Smack those bastards good." Schumacher lit his cigar. It was about eight in the evening. Leonard curled up in his seat and settled under his coat. He woke about midnight. Schumacher had disappeared. Leonard ambled into the bar car. There was Schumacher, scowling into a poker hand. Leonard ordered a soft drink and returned to his seat. He had an intense aversion to gambling. He liked to imagine that, along with Einstein, he rejected a universe of chance encounter. Life was about making things matter.

As it was a commercial run, and not a troop transport, the train had a dining car. Leonard woke with the sun. Untypically, he had breakfast in the first seating. Eggs, toast, juice, coffee. Then he returned to his car and studied the landscape. It seemed more muscular than the high plains of Wyoming. Erosion was more intense, with deep canyons and arroyos. Mesas appeared as the train turned west. Dramatic changes in ground level became apparent. Who could look at all this and not imagine the long ages of the earth? And yet the thought did not come to Brigham Young, who saw something like this scenery in his exploration of the wilderness.

Schumacher regained his seat a half hour before the train was due to arrive in Lamy, as close as it would get to Santa Fe. He gave Leonard two thumbs up. "Me and the boys back there had some fun." He ransacked his bags for a comb and mirror. When Schumacher had finished his toilette, Leonard pulled down his duffle and went to wait in the end of the car, outside the cabin by the doors. The air raced around faulty closings, and the undercarriage noises formed a nearly regular percussion and whine. The train swept around a steep curve and then ran along the flat approach to the town. Leonard set foot in New Mexico and looked back into his car. Schumacher was shouting at a conductor.

Leonard checked the duffle and asked directions for Santa Fe. There was a bus due to depart. He hopped on. Two hours later he was in Santa Fe. Leonard began walking to the center of town, confident that there he could learn about a ride to Los

Alamos. Only then did he look around.

Santa Fe was a lush, metropolitan Laramie. The air was thicker, the mountains were closer, pines were omnipresent. Clouds hung overhead, much lower than in Laramie, threatening to unload. The buildings, packed together in an approximate grid of streets, resembled a collection of wooden blocks that Leonard had played with as a child: planes of light oak accented occasionally by bands of color, as if a giant alphabet letter was struggling to make itself known. He found the center. Leonard recognized it immediately as a transformation of Cambridge's market square.

The imitation of Europe is found not in old New-England and Middle-Atlantic towns, with their frame structures set up around two cross streets, but rather in towns of Spanish and French heritage. The English and the northern Europeans arrived as dissenters. They rejected old forms and erected new harmonies. Latin Americans elaborated designs from home, and principal among these was the plaza. Northern Europeans, swaddled in mists and rain and winter darkness, crave sun. Colonnades and porticos, Mediterranean inventions, take their inspiration from Islamic modifications of Roman vaults. The cloistered academic unit of Cambridge is nothing but an allusion to authentic designs in France and Italy, a Bridge of Sighs from sunnier climes.

Leonard viewed Santa Fe's main plaza with all this in mind. In concept it was a Spanish construction. In detail, however, it was a New-World adaptation. Construction was principally post-and-lintel adobe, and Leonard imagined that some of the buildings really were authentically mud-walled. Arcades faced the central square. A group of Indians caught the sun against a wall of the low adobe Governor's Palace, vacated by the government and converted into a museum.

Erect people—the ones who gave the town its look of studied inattention—walked quietly into various shops. An occasional automobile puttered by. Elegance combines self-confidence and ease. The costumes—tooled boots, heavy silver and stones, feathers and leather—would have appeared *outré* in another setting.

Elegance is defined by contrast. Leonard saw that the square revealed a remarkable mix. Anglo overlords and freeholders, Hispanic tenants and laborers, and Indian tradesmen and retainers. Each moved with a special grace. He detected interlopers. Nasal accented women in severe coats marshaled toddlers and carried babies. Older men in business suits and loud ties straggled up the streets leading from the square. These were visitors out to buy trinkets. Two women scampered out of a shop, arm-in-arm, nuzzling. Bohemians knew Santa Fe from the days of Governor Lew Wallace, whose chariot race in *Ben Hur* drew inspiration from the buggies he saw circling the dusty plaza in the late 1870s.

The ease, diversity, and stark natural beauty of the place had made Santa Fe a destination of choice for generations of intellectuals. The professional killers could have located their bomb project in a barren waste, Leonard suddenly realized, undifferentiated prairie or high, flat desert without notable landmarks for many hundreds of miles, the Texas panhandle or eastern Montana. Instead they chose one of the most visually stunning places on earth. The intellectuals who were concocting the most horrific of weapons received daily reassurance that they labored for the preservation of the world, not its obliteration.

Leonard ducked into a café to consider whether he really wanted to visit the secret installation where thousands of intellectuals hoped to construct a device that would incinerate many orders of magnitude their own number. Ever since Cratsley seconded him to Washington, Leonard had been part of the scheme. They had taught him Japanese and were likely sending him into the jungle to scout out a lode of the bomb's key ingredient. The physicists dreamed up the device, he would provide them with the explosive, and hundreds of thousands of people would abruptly die.

He had ordered chili but did not feel much like eating it. He slid off the counter stool and walked toward the door. In the front corner of the café, seated European-style against the window, was a man with bushy eyebrows who nursed coffee and buñelo. Why not talk to him?

"Professor Bohr, I heard you speak last week in Princeton." Niels Bohr looked up absently. "Lieutenant Leonard Ranov." Bohr looked at him. "Do you mind if I join you?" Bohr nodded.

The biggest dilemma in life is how to begin. First impressions are not everything, but first words are decisive. Their delivery and their tone set the course of a conversation. It is possible to recover from a false start only if there is enough time. A disastrous introduction will not lead anywhere. To become a client, one must hook a patron. And the more prominent patrons have seen all manner of lure.

"Before the war I was a physicist, and I worked on cosmic rays." Not a good beginning, but it had to be said. "Do you mind if I ask your opinion about the ethical implications of indeterminacy?" Leonard decided that it was best to speak English. Bohr studied him. "That is, if quantum mechanics requires a new epistemology, a new way of *knowing* truth, does that imply a new way of *acting* on that knowledge? Is there a probability calculus for right and wrong?"

"That is an interesting question in these times. My brother tells me that, in previous centuries, courts of law used probability to fix innocence or guilt. Testimony was given a probability of truth, depending on the credibility of a witness, and then one simply summed to convict or acquit the accused. My experimentalist colleagues carry out something like this operation today. They assign weights to experimental data. A 'good' run counts for more than a 'bad' run, and they decide on good and bad by appealing to a variety of conditions. That is why we have so many more experimentalists than theoreticians. A calculation is like a painting. Done correctly, it is true forever. But an experiment must be checked many times."

"Does this mean that scientists cannot be inflexibly scrupulous in seeking truth? Does this affect how we ought to act now?"

"Probably," and Bohr laughed. "But let us look at things from the other point of view, a Bayesian retrospective. We know things that are certainly wrong. Fabricating experimental results, mendacity. If science tolerated such action, it would undermine not only its authority, but also its claim to transcendental values. Science appeals to all men by their common faculty of reason. In this, it is a very moral undertaking."

"But science does things in secret. Scientists do not tell the whole truth, especially now."

Bohr paused. "That is so. You must not think that everything a scientist does is science. Do I do science now, having coffee in a restaurant? Is that not like saying a baker bakes when he is on a skiing holiday?"

"Helmholtz reported that he came up with his best ideas while walking up a hill. Kekulé dreamed of the benzene ring. No doubt you have had ideas outside your institute. How do you know where science stops? Is it not all consuming? And if so, it seems to me that the infelicities of so-called private life will have a direct impact on the credibility of scientific results. I have trouble believing the claims of Nazi or fascist scientists."

"Yes, of course. We should be skeptical in all things." Bohr had finished his pastry and made to leave.

"Do you know if there is a bus to Los Alamos?"

"Come with me," Bohr said.

Leonard followed him back to the station, whose clerks had feigned indifference about Los Alamos. An olive green bus waited at the end of the platform. Bohr lumbered on. Leonard scrambled after. The bus was about a third filled, mostly civilians, mostly women. Bohr motioned for him to sit alongside.

"Look what I found." He held out a silver medallion. "It is a Zuni compass rose. I think there are four, non-orthogonal directions." Leonard found the item unsophisticated and uninteresting.

"Did you ever hear of an astronomer named Létoile in the East Indies? Double stars?"

Bohr fingered the medallion. He slowly shook his head from side to side. "Jacob Witte. The professor in Leiden. We corresponded occasionally. I think he spent time on Java."

"His daughter is in England now."

"I thought he deserved a Nobel prize for the cosmic-ray work. But you know that fool Millikan, the *Obertrottel*, he kept the prize back."

The bus took several hours to reach the gates of Los Alamos. It was slow, and the roads were bad. Bohr had pulled out a sheaf of papers and was making notes with a pencil. Leonard gloried in the scenery. The bus stopped by a gate set in the middle of the plains. An MP boarded.

"Have your papers ready for inspection."

The MP made his way toward the back of the bus. Bohr handed him a letter of endorsement. Leonard offered his military ID.

"Got something else, Lieutenant? 'S no good."

"It's a clearance."

The MP kept Leonard's card and finished his inspection. "Follow me, Lieutenant."

"Nice chat we had," Leonard said to Bohr. He disembarked. The bus wobbled through the gate. Bohr looked out the window, right through him.

"You don't get in without an order," the MP explained.

"But I work for the outfit in Washington. Its budget passes over my desk," he lied.

"Then you go back to Washington and get me the right order. A bus'll be through in a few hours."

The MP returned to his small guardhouse. It was cool, but the sun shone brilliantly. Leonard stood for a few minutes. His Trotskyist uncle related how Lev Davidovich, head of the Red Army, had to ask special permission from the Moscow Library to keep an overdue book. Reality was not indeterminate after all. There were absolute laws, and they ruled bureaucracies. Leonard watched the autumn sun play over the land, shading orange into red. A thunderstorm blew across a distant mesa. He would return to the train. It would take him to a ship. He would cross half the planet and walk into a jungle. With good fortune he would live to make a report that might speed the day when the civilians behind this gate unleashed the demons of hell on an unsuspecting world.

Part III

Blue World

Some people think the sea has a spirit. Painters and poets give it a life. I have traveled on it and in it. I can tell you that the sea does not care. What is it, really? Waves, wind, and rain. Large and tiny creatures here and there. Flotsam pushed around by high and low pressures, evaporation, temperature inversions, you name it. All to no purpose. The sea does not know you.

Jack Kerouac, "Blue World," 3 December 1943, Kerouac family papers, Fall River, Massachusetts

The stars of the tropics are so wonderfully intense. The Milky Way spreads out grandly. When we dock, I'll look for Saturn's rings with my binoculars. How did the ancients do it, navigate from one island to another? Polaris sets when the equator is crossed. I guess the height of any fixed star gives latitude, but what about the meridians? Still, I suppose that the Hawaiian chain and especially its grand mountains give a cross-section visible for many miles when coming up from the south. Maybe it is enough for dead reckoning. The Polynesians live close enough to the sea to survive a long voyage. The sea provides, it takes away.

James Michener to Mabel Michener, 4 June 1943, Michener papers, Swarthmore College

7

Southern Cross

I am now where I long to be,
The storied land of memory.
Time to see and time to know,
And time to watch the flowers grow.
If when the wind blows cross the bight,
The stars revealed to light the night,
Think how I loved to hold you tight
Then greet the golden morning.

Robert Louis Stevenson, fragments, Stevenson House, Edinburgh

Two days out of San Francisco, Leonard Ranov felt that unseen creatures were gnawing at his mind and sapping his sanity. He was used to working at close quarters. But in airplanes, fuel reserves imposed a limit on proximity. After twelve hours everyone was on the ground, one way or another. A submarine, however, offered no escape, even in present circumstances when the submarine had a transoceanic escort. The boat was packed to its gills. A sliding shelf allowed Leonard and Ernest Bit to bunk in what seemed to be a broom closet.

"We must consider ourselves fortunate that we are not in an American boat," Ernest observed as Leonard was trying to pike his toes into army skivvies. Ernest sat crosslegged on the opened shelf. Leonard grunted with accomplishment as the shorts wormed their way up his legs. Then he thrust his pelvis forward, allowing him to pull the waist up to the small of his back. He sat up with accomplishment and hit his head hard on the supports of the bunk above.

"Why is that, doc?" Ernest's sabbatical at Cambridge had mellowed him. Or perhaps immersion in Renaissance alchemy had worked a minor transmutation. At first Leonard welcomed him as an anodyne to the boredom and unreasonableness of the voyage, but with time the non-stop encyclopedic commentary became tiresome.

"All the gears would creep and the latches would ricochet. And to stop the noise, there would be grease everywhere. Noise is the foe of all submariners. Creepless gears began with big telescopes, you know, for focusing on a star precisely while the entire instrument tracked the celestial vault from east to west. The Americans have the biggest eyes, but the Germans were able to mass-produce the gears to the highest tolerances. How strange, then, when precision engineering made its appearance at Göttingen about 1905, it was called the *Fakultät Schmieröl*, the division of lubrication."

The appeal to a German precedent was, in the circumstances, normal. They could not turn around without seeing German inscriptions. They were on a German submarine.

The boat had been captured in the Galápagos Islands. It was there to scout out the possibility of establishing a base of operations, just as the Germans had done in 1915. A US destroyer had the good fortune to surprise the boat, and it fell a prize of war. Bled of its secrets, the submarine received a second incarnation with a US commission. Four weeks in the docks at Oakland fitted the boat with tiny cabins for its officers, since American decency rejected the communal German accommodations inspired by the rank intimacy of Portuguese caravels. The sleek, black killer received the eponym *Turtle*, which the Galápagos did have, even though its tortoises have always attracted more comment.

"Quiet, Perfesser."

The voice came from the bunk that Leonard's head had connected with. It belonged to the third inmate of the broom closet.

Leonard found the man relaxed and otherworldly. He went through the motions of living here and now, but he resonated to an exterior beacon. He smiled as he moved, threading his way about the boat with uncanny grace. The voyage was his vacation, he said, and to celebrate it he stopped shaving and slicked his hair straight back. In a matter of days or weeks he would board a merchant-marine steamer. Until then he was prince of infinite space in the walnut-shell of a German submarine.

"Okay, Jack," Leonard offered, tensing the corners of his mouth and lifting his chin in Ernest's direction. "He'll pipe down."

Leonard had an uncomfortable feeling that Jack was clairvoyant. He had an unerring sense of where things would be. After Leonard spent twenty minutes searching his gear for his razor, Jack offered with his face to the wall, "Try the toe of your boot." Or, as they padded to the galley for a meal: "The soup will be uncommonly bad but the custard makes up for it." Again:

"Use the head aft, the one close by is on the fritz."

"Now's the time to grab some air on the top. We've just met a cruiser."

"Keep your left hand in your pocket today, unless you want it skewered on an instrument panel when the sub rolls."

"Why do you think Buzz has a tarantula on a string in the engine room?"

Jack was always right. And these were things he could not know. He spent hours writing in a notebook. Maybe he was casting horoscopes. It was relaxation, he said. He enjoyed setting down words clearly, so he could hear them. Leonard, who fancied himself a bit of a writer from his scientific publishing, asked to hear some of Jack's words.

"Jeez, what for? That long road ended somewhere near Santa Fe. The wind rattled my collar and froze my thumbs. I wish I could take a hot bath. Somewhere in my bag I've got half a bottle of tequila. This calls for a drink."

"No, really. I'm serious."

"But that was it. I just read you some."

Leonard had to agree that there was a certain charm in the aimlessness. Jack's words were apparently devoid of purpose. Lack of pretension, too, which rated high marks. But underneath it all, there had to be sense and order. Words did not put themselves on a page. They occurred in sequence. They had sounds and meanings. They spun shapes, they sported colors and hues, they resonated with overtones of other works and deeds. The automatists had it wrong: Only the greatest discipline could result in pure, aimless narrative.

"It must take concentration to project an image of complete openness and simplicity," he said to Jack.

"Not at all. Why ask an enormous and complex machine to produce something simple and true? Why not just begin and end with simple things?"

He had a point, Leonard thought, but training rebelled at the implications.

"But the universe *is* a complex machine. To begin to understand it, we need to call on sophisticated mathematics. We guess about how certain things work, and sometimes we get lucky." Leonard recalled Bohr's lecture. "And when life is involved, we must act even if we know almost nothing for certain about causes. And so we must bring everything to bear on vital questions. Words come from everywhere. The writer disciplines them, animates them to kick at the reader's eye, to bring life to a page. No random sequence of words or letters can do that."

Jack smiled. "Now you're a smart guy, Leonard. There's plenty around here, around us now, that we don't begin to know about. The waves around this boat. They say people have looked at water flowing by obstacles for a thousand years, and yet we can't cut out the froth. We get orders by radio. How? They're not airwaves 'cause they bounce off electrons and things higher up than air. So how do radio waves move through empty space? We don't have the beginning of a toolbox for understanding these things. So I say, Let's not try. Write flat, if that is what you see."

The conversation had taken a turn for the worse, Leonard felt. Jack apparently knew something about physics—more, probably, than he himself knew about writing. Time to bring in the heavy artillery.

"What you see is the result of what may be constructed," Leonard began. "Look, now, at electricity. You could write about the electrical circuits in this boat as if they existed only by virtue of switches and dials and the men to manipulate them. So many amperes registered on a meter and the lieutenant moves a pointer twenty degrees. He picks up a cup of coffee, and a radio signal is heard. The coffee is irrelevant, of course, but really the thing works because of the will of an electron. It wants to go in a certain path. It and countless others flow through gates and doors until we receive a mechanical vibration in the air, a sound. Without the notion of an electron, it could not have happened."

Jack folded his hand together, a closet priest. "Oh dear, oh dear. One of my Canadian cousins worked for Marconi near St John's on the transatlantic radio beacon. He told me that Marconi knew not a whit about electrons. His competitor Reg Fessenden knew even less. These guys were pillagers and builders. They ransacked the storehouse of the greybeards and heaped things together until something worked. Generally something will result if you work at it long enough. They drank lots of coffee. *Tabarnouche.* I think the coffee is every bit as important as your invisible electrons."

This was a novel thought. Imagine no guiding principle, no scale of values. Watch the world for regularities. It was against every lesson that Leonard had assimilated. He felt the submarine vibrate. The sea was angry. That was a good description. Maybe the astonishing profusion of life, the impossibly complex parameters of weather, maybe all this was best reduced to simple sayings, something his mother would know. This knowledge could be learned, passed on from one mind to another, but it was expressed in simple form. "I love you always." Or, "It is my duty." To state these truths, and then to describe how people follow them, is that not the essence of great writing? But what was that funny word Jack used?

"Oh," he said, "something my mother said when she was exasperated. It's French, or it started out as French. I think it's an expletive that began life as 'tabernacle.' I'm American, you know, but my parents were French Canadian. They came down to work in the mills around Boston, at Lowell. My name is really Jean-Louis," he said softly. "My mother called me Ti-Jean."

"We all come from somewhere," Leonard said. "That's what we're fighting for."

"You will see your sweetheart tomorrow," Jack added as he rolled up in his blanket.

*
* *

Leonard stumbled toward the galley, performing the combination of sideways crabwalk (down a corridor) and forwards launch (through a vertical manhole) that German designers had invented to keep submarine crews in shape. He turned over Jack's last remark, which he took to be facetious. A physics book? A plane? Who was his sweetheart? He didn't think he had one. No one on the farm in New Jersey or at Laramie. He swung his leg around the bench of one of the eating surfaces, coffee and sandwich akimbo. It was a practiced move, something he learned when working over the family Ford on a winter's evening. Ernest beamed.

"Just got word that tomorrow we go over to the cruiser for a briefing."

Leonard had to ask: "Ernest, how much do you know?"

"Leonard. This is obviously very big. It concerns a weapon or weapons factory. Somewhere in the islands. We're going in to wreck it. I hope they have enough quinine. The affliction is endemic everywhere there. Quinine suppresses symptoms, but not the residual effects of the plasmodium. Maybe we'll do the job from the air, though I think this sub will be our taxi. We're headed far south, Australia, mate. We'll know, of course, if the sun rises over our left shoulder." The last few words in Japanese.

"Can you also read?"

"Only about five hundred characters," Ernest replied. "Soon after I landed in America, a prosperous uncle found me a summer job cleaning out at the Peabody Academy in Salem, the one run by the great naturalist and list-maker Edward Sylvester Morse. Stuff was in barrels and boxes, untouched for fifty years. And much of it was Japanese, brought back by sea captains and by Morse himself, who had professed at the University of Tokyo. I taught myself enough to classify the goods. Some haul. The usual trade articles: kimonos, swords, porcelain, lacquer-boxes, netsuke. Also writing desks, murals, books, panels and beams for an entire house, a small boat, children's toys, seeds and herbs, minerals and oils. All squirreled away among the paraphernalia of whaling—the harpoons and ships' parts deeded over the years by owners and captains. The money came from whales and the China trade. When Japan opened up, New England was ready to exploit it. The nineteenth-century American enlightenment—Transcendentalism and Impressionism and lyric poetry raving about special effects in the New World—it is all a pale reflection of Asia."

He might be right, Leonard thought. Sasaki-san had expressed the point at Swarthmore. When the dust settles, the twentieth century will be seen as the time that Buddhism came to America. The truly significant parts of life are the grand combinations. The genius of Umayyad Islam, Elizabethan England, Revolutionary France, and, yes, Leonard thought, the inspiration of his own time, came from aliquots exotic. Large egos, running headlong into each other from all directions, and all displaying such distinct auras. Was this the social statistics dreamed of by Quetelet and latterly elaborated by Mussolini's professor Pareto? A statistical thermodynamics of culture.

Leonard looked into his coffee. The cream had mostly mixed

in, but traces of fat swirled to a central node, whitish arms flung out by centrifugal force and then sucked by capillarity to the mug's rim, which represented all the remaining mass of the universe. A hundred million stars mirrored on this tan surface. Were cultural currents like that? If comparisons arose through analogue, rather than through digital expression, maybe chemistry provided the appropriate frame of mind. Reactions and reaction-rates, grand dilutions and titrations. Or, and here he was on shakier ground, perhaps cultural evolution followed Darwinian precepts.

Leonard looked up at Ernest. There he was, with a broad grin, waiting for any kind of response.

"Yes, well, look at it the other way, Ernest. The Japanese were good at assimilating Western notions. Telescopes, uniforms, dreadnoughts, and now the notion of racial stereotype. Some of the assimilation had rather nice effects." He thought about Sasaki-san and Kuwaki's books. "It's a mistake to think that the Japanese can only copy what we do."

"Exactly." The grin hardly changed its aspect. "So we must expect to see innovations from the Japanese. Maybe a monstrous new weapon. A new literary form. New theories about the universe. I have mostly thought that we would see a new interpretation of life." Ernest paused. "All this stuff about Darwinian struggle for existence. It's pretty irrelevant for understanding intraspecies conflict. And it's entirely opposed to the idea of an ecological system, what the *philosophes* called economy of nature. In natural economy, diverse species work together for mutual benefit. Ants mine rotten trees; woodpeckers eat ants and scour out rot—all species gain. Now, you will ask, What is the law that binds an individual to perish for the good of another species? Not to worry. We see general laws of this kind in Darwin. But with Darwin, everything is keyed to the marginal gains of superior adaptability for any one species. All species compete against each other. Nature, to paraphrase Huxley, red in tooth and claw. What we really need is a general principle where species survival is based on successful interspecies collaboration. It would be as if a spirit guided the apparently selfless action of plants and animals."

Ernest paused, and for the first time Leonard saw in his face a pensive attitude. "The answer lies in the East Indies. There is the key facilitation, after all, for the transmission of knowledge from Hellenistic civilization to China. Oh, yes. The seventh-century Buddhist monk I-Hsing traveled from China to a grand monastery in Sumatra, and from there to the university at Nalanda in India. He worked up all the science he learned, apparently everything from Galen to Euclid to Archimedes to Ptolemy before eventually returning to China. And then through the East Indies came the great Eastern gifts of the compass, the sternpost rudder, the printing press, mechanical clocks, and firearms. Or I imagine so, for it was so much easier to travel by sea than over land on the silk route. And in recent times the East Indies have given us dramatic insight into the ways of life. Robert Mayer's conservation of energy arose from his observations as an East Indian physician; Christiaan Eijkman's vitamins came from hospital observations in Batavia; and we have seen that the essence of cosmic rays came from Jacob Witte's observations in Bandung. The very notion of a life force, what Bernard Shaw lectured us about in his *Superman* and his *Methuselah*, was formulated rather precisely by the naturalist Baas Becking from his time on Java. He called it 'Gaia.'"

"How long have you known about this mission, Ernest?"

"In war, Dame Fortune must eventually show her hand. The posting to San Francisco was suggestive, but I knew definitively when we boarded the *Turtle*. The Dutch girl in England, your quick course in Japanese, what else could fit?" His eyes narrowed. "We'll know more tomorrow, when we go over to the cruiser."

*

* *

Leonard was on the boat deck with Ernest. He had bolted down breakfast and was watching the rigging of a line that would haul both of them to the *Dewey Rattie*, the escort cruiser. The *Turtle* was about a hundred feet from the *Rat*. Both had slowed to five knots, just enough to keep an even keel in the gentle swells. Leonard studied the line strung from the cruiser to the conning tower. He was then manhandled into a harness and dragged into the gap between the two ships. About like some of the maneuvers he pulled on rock faces in the Snowy Range back at Laramie, Leonard thought. Just slide on a cable between two points. But here the points were moving. Leonard's heart flipped as the *Rat*'s crew grappled him onto their deck. Then he watched while Ernest submitted to the same operation.

He and Ernest were army air corps, rare birds on a naval ship. Whom to salute? His orders were cut only for Sydney. He absently studied the seamen coiling the hawser that had kept him high and dry.

"Lieutenant Ranov and Corporal Bit, I am Lieutenant Hansabout." An energetic naval officer with reddish-blond hair everywhere extended his hand. Men at sea from earliest times did not shave or cut their hair. We know wily Odysseus as a hirsute confidence man sporting a liberty cap, bow in hand, and nothing much round the loins. Hansabout's grip, Leonard decided, had Odyssean overtones. It crushed his fingers.

"Please follow me. Colonel Cratsley is waiting."

They padded over the deck, Leonard and Ernest somewhat wobbly from submarine confinement. Around a funnel vent and through a door, down a stairwell and along a corridor, down once again to where the heart of the ship should be. Hansabout knocked at a door and then entered. He held it open for his retinue, whom he announced.

Leonard saw a small room with a rectangular table that nearly filled it. At the far end was John Cratsley, a diminutive air-corps officer, balding with a beetling brow, who sat in a relaxed posture with an intent look. To his left was a rating poised near a film projector. It would be show and tell.

"Come in, gentlemen. Please take a seat." Leonard saluted and, almost hypnotized by Cratsley's gaze, dropped into the first chair that came to hand, placing his back to the door. Ernest could only take the chair on his left. Out of the corner of his eye, Leonard caught a fleeting image to Ernest's left, tan and shimmering. He could not break contact with Cratsley. Hansabout had exited and closed the door.

"We all should be flying, but it's easier to float across the Pacific." Cratsley paused. "I called you over to summarize what we are about to do. First, we have a name. Operation Electra. It's not my doing." He laughed. "Actually, it's pompous and alarmingly suggestive. Doghouse or Rodeo would have been much better. The Greek allusion, doubling as a scientific metaphor, was nevertheless useful for arguing our case. It took a great deal of talking to authorize sending you into Java.

"Let me summarize. We are looking for a mountain of uranium. You will know that uranium can be used to produce a weapon of extraordinary force, something that could end the war in a matter of days. Presently MacArthur is inclined to island-hop north toward the Philippines, but if we verify the uranium deposit, he is prepared to divert his resources to the East Indies."

Cratsley motioned to the rating. The projector came on as the lights went out. The film strip began with Dutch footage of Java. There Leonard saw the untidy abundance of the wet tropics. Dutch supervisors towered over Javans—laborers and policemen. He saw Dutch colonial homes, Javan buildings with sweeping roofs, hillsides terraced for thousands of vertical feet, railway trestles constructed precariously over gaping ravines.

"It is here," Cratsley commented. A hill appeared on screen. "On the slopes of a volcano."

The film ended and the lights came on. Cratsley studied Leonard. "We can get you in and out. Your job is to tell us about the mountain. What do you think?"

He would be going in on the ground, Leonard thought, and

the realization brought an adrenaline rush. How would he get there? How would he get back? How would he speak to the locals? Why couldn't it be done from the air? What if the ore deposit is deep underground? How do you survive in a jungle—if that is what covered Java?

"Oh, I think you know your partner." The shimmering mass to Leonard's left stirred. He turned.

"Hello, Lieutenant," Anneke Witte smiled.

*

*   *

Leonard had thought about the physicist's daughter from time to time. He wondered what she was like, whether she had adjusted to England. Since returning to America he had not had much occasion to meet women—or, rather, he had not taken the initiative to do so. There would be no point to it, he concluded. Ridiculous position, exorbitant price, fleeting pleasure. Now in the *Rat*'s briefing room, she wore an olive jumpsuit, and a leather flight jacket draped her chair. She seemed relaxed and radiant. Her fine hair was cut short, and it circled her head like the halo of a Byzantine saint. Her carriage, however, was lithe and easy, no resemblance to the slope-shouldered, anemic patriarchs on icons in the *krasnyi ugol* of home or chapel.

"Dr Witte—Anneke—will fill you in on how we think to proceed."

Leonard followed Anneke through the door and along corridors. He ducked into the officers' mess behind her. She folded into a chair near a corner.

"Drink?"

"Genever they don't have, only what the English call gin. But scotch would do." Leonard ordered two scotches, neat.

Anneke laughed. "I know what you have done over the past months. Your Japanese shall be useful. You see, they found me irresistible. I know the terrain. I speak the local languages, enough of them anyway, and on Java there is usually someone around who knows a bit of Dutch. I have good will in Bandung. It would please my father."

Drinks arrived. Leonard took a big sip. "Been wearing those long?"

"Actually I'm not in your army. They sent me to San Francisco several weeks ago. I knew for a long time that I would return to Bandung, but I held back for months in Cambridge. I had my patients in the hospital, and father's colleagues were there, some of them Dutch. I suppose that I did not want to go so far from Holland. But my formative years were on Java. It is my second home. It called me. And soon I could not resist the call."

Leonard slouched down. "Know much about tropical diseases, Dr Witte?"

"I have had many of them," she smiled. "Professionally, I am a psychiatrist."

Leonard felt the corners of his mouth drop. "Now correct me if I'm wrong. A captured German submarine will drop us somewhere off the coast of Java. We find our way to the interior. There we take some data. We walk back to the sea. Then we swim to Australia."

Anneke's blue eyes completely dominated his field of vision. "Well, there are alternatives, but walking is safest. Your spies suggest no significant Japanese patrols. Javans are uncertain about the new conquerors. We should be able to talk our way out of any chance meeting. The bush is not unsafe—much of it has been turned into agricultural land—although we shall have to cross the central mountain range. We can do it in ten days. We shall return the way we came. Three weeks from landing, we shall be back on the submarine."

"Nuts," Leonard pronounced. He was not sure what he expected, but a month in the jungle was not it. "The scheme is nuts. Why can't we parachute in?"

"Too dangerous. All clear land in Java is densely populated. A parachute would certain to be spotted by hundreds of people.

And to drop in the forest would be to risk injury. Nor can your people spare a carrier for staging such a drop."

My people, Leonard thought.

"Do not be concerned," Anneke offered. "I am not concerned. I know the people of Java. They will help us."

They are people like all other people, Leonard thought. He studied Anneke. She sat erect and certain. The plan drew strength from her unreasonable conviction. She heard voices. The army gave her a suit of armor. His own people wanted to be on good terms with the Dutch, who commanded a number of ships and planes that had fled the Japanese conquest of Java. The Indies were a rich prize in which America would like to share.

Leonard was part of a war machine, but he did not have experience with war. He had joined as an officer with the expectation of fighting. He had a vague idea of the battlefield, colored by Homer and Scott and Tolstoy. He could picture himself leading a platoon to capture a bridge or farmhouse. The sounds and smells, the emotions and intensities, might be like free fall. An electric sensation from elbow to elbow. Sneaking through the underbrush hardly resonated with his expectations. After all, he was in the air corps.

"Anneke, don't you find this whole thing unrealistic?"

"What is real? It is all ephemeral. What is real about my father? Does he still live? Is this vessel real? It transports us, as in a dream, from one state to another. When we leave it, it will fade to uncertain memory. The self is nothing. It ends in the absolute certainty of death. Reality can only be dedicating one's life to others, and most of all one's family. My family, you see, is Holland, and by this trip I affirm that bond. What else can I do? I have no children." Leonard thought her eyes advanced several hues on the color wheel.

Anneke stood up and walked to the piano. A Steinway grand, made in Hamburg. She opened it and began a song from Hoffmann von Fallersleben. Leonard sang the words: "Alle Vögel sind schon da, alle Vögel, alle." All the birds are already there, all of them. They announce spring. And *sumer is icumen in.*

*

* *

Leonard reckoned that it would be a quick slide down the hawser from the *Rat* to the *Turtle*. But as he descended the submarine caught a swell. The hawser's arc dropped into the sea. Leonard flopped helplessly in his harness until the *Turtle*'s deckhands cranked him up to the conning-tower rail. The water was cold enough to bring shivers, and he stumbled down the hatch toward his broom closet. Jack was relaxing on the top bunk.

"She didn't hose you down, did she?"

"What the hell is it to you?" Leonard snarled as he began peeling off the layers of his uniform. "Anyway, how did you know I would meet the woman?"

"Hard to explain. When I try to understand things, I just screw up. But if I clear my mind, associations force themselves on me. It was that way in school. I did well on exams because I could imagine the pages of my books and I could feel what the teacher wanted as an answer. So I never studied, because if I did I would fail. You know, I don't believe in magic. Some of this is just a good memory coupled with unconscious, close attention to small gestures. I kicked around a bit before the navy. You seemed preoccupied in a personal way. I guessed that it was a girl."

"Well, there was nothing to it," Leonard grumbled as he pulled on dry shorts. The door opened, and Ernest Bit bounced in, dry as a bone.

"I was wondering where we would meet up with the Dutch girl. She holds the essential parts to the puzzle." He fingered his toothbrush.

"I like puzzles," said Jack.

"No way." Leonard laced on a pair of boots and headed for the mess. It was the only destination on the boat. He had looked around when he boarded in Oakland. Really no place for quiet reflection.

The discipline required of submariners was, he thought, unusual. Living for months inside a tin can, the smell of sweat and fuel everywhere, another man never more than a few feet away. He recalled his short tour of the *Rat*. Pretty tight there, too. Maybe this is a condition of sailors from the beginning. Ships never had room to spare. Leif Eriksson, Columbus, Shackleton. His parents knew. They crossed continents and oceans. He imagined that they were on deck for the crossings. He wondered where the money had come from. In Sandy Creek, they were simply poor farmers to the locals, but suddenly he was struck with the pain of admiration. The least he could do was not to grumble about accommodations.

He nursed a coffee in the mess. Anneke. She was well put together on the outside, but her demeanor and gestures were definitely masculine. Some of that might be the language problem. Things came out too abruptly, as they did when the Jewish farmers in Sandy Creek spoke English. The overtones were missing, even when the speech was certifiably brilliant. Einstein appeared ridiculous to the American press because he spoke to them in uninflected, uncomplicated, high-pitched English. But it was possible for foreigners to master the language. He and Jack had both learned English in school. Leonard thought back to Bohr's epistemological discourse at Santa Fe. The Danish and the Dutch learned English as a matter of course. Anneke had done so. The directness of her speech and gestures, then, could be typical of Dutch temperament. Fancy speech and multiple meanings were the enemy of a civilization built on the brink of inundation. What mattered was whether something held water.

This practicality would be a strong asset for the Javan operation. Cratsley, evidently his controller, would have seen it, too. It was the general concept that he resisted. Leonard had imagined that he was being trained to analyze intelligence about the uranium mountain. But he would also obtain the data. A walk through the jungles of Java. Snakes, bugs, and worse.

Ernest drifted in. "Borobudur," he announced. "It is the opportunity of a lifetime."

"Grüss Gott," and Leonard continued with half a dozen more salutations.

"Not a greeting," Ernest took his schoolmaster's pose. "Borobudur is the great Buddhist temple in south-central Java. Scores of stone stupas ring a small mountain. Built in the wave of Buddhist zeal that swept the Indies during the seventh century. A spectacular failure. Brahman syncretism extinguished Buddhist simplicity in the East Indies, just as it did in South Asia. And then Muslim conquest imposed new norms and values. How remarkable that the traces of Buddhism are strongest in Tibet, Japan, and Korea, where they were appropriated and modified by autochthonous traditions. Borobudur exhibits the synthesis. The images are Javan, not Indian. One would have less angst about dying after having seen this temple. Depends where they land us."

Us? Who exactly would take this walk in the jungle? Leonard imagined four people split into pairs. Ernest had some of the skills required and could be taught the rest, but did he have the reactive capability? Faced with a new situation, his natural inclination was to trot out an obscure fact or propose a bizarre analogy. He had sown the field of genius, all right, but he'd neglected to take care of it. Among the rows of corn there was every variety of weed and wildflower. His place was as a corresponding secretary. Leonard pictured him listening on the *Turtle*'s radio somewhere off Java, sometime in the not-too-distant future.

*

*   *

John Cratsley filled a tin mug with bourbon. He was a trim man of thirty-five. He drank alone, and seldom something he liked.

These were times when he reflected on his calling in the army. His father had been with Gorgas in the Canal Zone, where

John was born. He had grown up with military engineering. Only when he went to Caltech did he see another side to life. What captivated him was science, and the part of it he loved concerned big machines. The biggest, noisiest machine at Caltech was Theodore von Kármán's wind tunnel. Kármán arrived at Caltech when Cratsley was a junior. Bought from Aachen with Guggenheim money, Kármán continued his research into airplane design. Cratsley became a laboratory assistant. A doctorate seemed pointless in 1932. The army was interested in aviation. Lacking alternatives, he signed on when he graduated. His father arranged for him to become an officer. Over the next five years he put in time at nearly every military airfield in the country. It became clear that he had talent as an administrator. His manner was direct but non-confrontational. He radiated confidence, and he persuaded people to do his bidding.

Emergencies accelerate careers. Cratsley made major late in 1941, the promotion required because he had been called to Washington as air-attaché and technical liaison. His wife Miranda, who had suffered quietly at a string of ramshackle army bungalows set up in cornfields, was ecstatic at the prospect.

"John, dear," she said as she carried dinner to the table. "Washington must be so exciting. Oh, yes, the parks and museums, the elegant receptions. I shall need new clothes. Oh, John." She turned to face him. John watched the maneuver. Polio, which she contracted in their first year of marriage, had left Miranda's left leg thin and recalcitrant. "It will be a splendid setting," she reiterated as she turned to survey the fields of Akron.

Miranda died suddenly several days later. John came home to find her sprawled on the kitchen floor. The doctors called it a coronary thrombosis. It should not have happened to her, they said, but it did. Cratsley threw himself into the Washington work, and the war rewarded his diligence. He met Leslie Groves, builder of dams and commander of men, and Groves bought out his contract to place him in the Washington office of the Uranium Committee, later known as the Manhattan Project. Cratsley's first task was to exclude British and French physicists who were working on their own bomb in Montreal. He knew enough French to keep everyone confused without being overly resentful. Groves, a good engineer and a better judge of character, saw that Cratsley would be able to keep in mind all parts of the project—the Hanford reactor and Oak Ridge uranium-separation plant, the Chicago plutonium laboratory, and the Los Alamos colony of longhairs.

While in London on one of his diplomatic missions, Cratsley, promoted to colonel, met a friend from his Caltech days who was teaching calculus to British army recruits for £3 per day. They talked about European émigrés. The friend, Arne Ulfson, who had a fellowship at Cambridge, brought up Anneke Witte. Ulfson thought she was swell. Her father had a crazy idea for a new particle accelerator. A very big machine. Might be looked into. Cratsley put his man, Leonard Ranov, onto it.

Cratsley had met Leonard when, crossing the continent, he was grounded in a thunderstorm at Omaha. He went up to the control tower for a better view. "Here it comes," Leonard announced, "following on the biggest low of the year. Lookit that spitzenbanger!" He was the airport weatherman, and he liked to use local lingo. Cratsley and Leonard talked for three hours. Weather, physics, American education, Brahms, Hemingway, Miranda. As soon as he returned to Washington, Cratsley commandeered the grounded airman. He saw Leonard only once more before he sent him to Cambridge.

Cratsley remembered when he first read the translation of Witte's Dutch material, made in Washington from photographs taken by Ernest Bit. He nearly fell from his chair. An astronomer reported about taking atmospheric measurements on the side of a volcano. His electrometers would not work. He came back several days later with different ones. Same outcome. He determined that the inoperative area stretched over a square kilometer. When he developed photographs that he had taken, he knew the reason: The film was exposed. The astronomer wrote, "It would be worth looking into. It appears to be a deposit of high-grade radioactive ore. Some laboratory tests in Bandung reveal uranium." Cratsley imagined what the astronomer wrote in a missing letter: "It is hopeless to do anything about this now, my dear Jacob. When the fighting is over, I rather imagine that it could lead to a profitable enterprise."

Suppose there was a mountain of uranium on central Java. Jacob Witte had thought that the letter and measurements were important to send with his daughter. How many other people knew? The girl spoke about it to anyone, if asked, although to judge from Ulfson she only talked in general terms. Whom else had the astronomer alerted? Probably no German, but could one be sure? Did the Japanese have time to make anything of it? Were they building a uranium bomb?

Cratsley put the questions to Groves during a short meeting. Groves was prepared to take the matter seriously.

"We need our own report," he said, "Find out." Cratsley then became head of Mission Electra.

The Mission had a budget and an office, but not much of either. Cratsley promptly set Leonard to learning Japanese. Ernest Bit was a first-rate clerk for the Washington office. It was the German submarine that brought his plans to a head. The navy hoped to use it to prowl around the Pacific. Cratsley obtained a commitment to have it ferry his operatives to and from Java. Groves drew the line at sending one team into the jungle.

"Two people," Groves said flatly. "Make good choices."

While Leonard was sitting at the feet of Sasaki-san, Cratsley had visited Anneke Witte in her Cambridge hospital.

"I think that it must hold water," Anneke said earnestly. "I am not a scientist. Fifteen years ago my father discovered the nature of cosmic rays. The Americans would not believe him, especially that horrible Millikan. Real physicists know his worth." Cratsley remembered seeing Millikan set off from Caltech on his cosmic-ray expeditions. In a sense Millikan had made Caltech. He never wasted an opportunity for publicity.

"Would you like to have a look for youself?" Cratsley asked.

"You have the languages, you know the terrain and the people."

"Except the Japanese," Anneke laughed. "I do not imagine that they would pose a serious obstacle." She looked Cratsley straight in the eyes. "My country is conquered. How do you propose to send me to Bandung?"

Cratsley didn't know until the *Turtle* docked in Oakland. By then Anneke was ready to trade wartime England for her memory of the tropics. She was a nice girl, Cratsley concluded. He liked her offbeat intensity. It reminded him of the theatre. Anneke was a successful performer. She dressed carefully, but with a dissonant edge. How different from Miranda. No dissonance there. Just elegance, bearing, and cheerfulness. She could project excitement to a dinner of spaghetti carbonara.

The bottle of bourbon was a third gone when Cratsley opened the door to Anneke. "Come in," he said. "I wish I could offer you something decent. I didn't know I would be entertaining."

Anneke closed the door and stood by it. "Ranov is unsure. There are many imponderables."

"Think how dull life would be if everything were predictable. No margin for negotiation and strategy. No opportunity for fortune and heroism. Why, it's just a walk in the sun. We bring you to the beach. We meet you there a few weeks later. Not exactly, perhaps, but close enough."

"That's why I brought this." Anneke pulled out her kris from a leg scabbard. "It is alive, they say in the Indies. It moves of its own accord. It flies at the heart of evil. This I received from the nationalist Soekarno. It speaks to the people of Java."

Cratsley took the kris from Anneke. It gleamed in blues, purples, and silvers, and it bore a terrible scar. Meteoric iron, beaten and annealed countless times, folded and refolded until it took the characteristic shape of a serpent. The handle, curved like an elegant steak knife, had no guard. Eminently impractical, it was a symbol of rank. He smiled and handed it back. Anneke pointed it at him.

"Be sure that you get us out," she said. "I should not want

my kris to find your heart, which it will certainly do if I die."

"Give your knife a drink. Won't you have a seat?" He gestured to the chair and the bed.

Anneke installed herself crosslegged on the bed. "Don't get ideas," she said. "But who can resist a colonel's invitation to drink?"

*

*   *

When the flotilla docked at Pago Pago in American Samoa, Leonard had his first experience with the tropics. Everything about it seemed outlandish. It was too much. The hillsides were too lush and green, the trees and vines grew in almost ridiculous abandon, the buildings seemed too flimsy, the insects were brazen and persistent, the sky was too blue, the fish and fruit flooded the town, the sights and smells of corruption were everywhere.

"My kind of place. What do you think they smoke here?" Jack Ti-Jean Kerouac waved at Leonard and Ernest as he trotted off in the direction of the local action, who were already waving at him.

Leonard surveyed the harbor. It was a narrow inlet with hills rising steeply on two sides. Both the *Turtle* and the *Dewey Rattie* were tied up at dock. They were at the center of a jumble of hoists and trucks. Pallets of every description were loaded on and off. Ants, Leonard thought, beginning to take apart two large beetles. In the distance, a tanker was fueling a destroyer. It would be a prize for any Japanese raiding party. The harbor had gun emplacements and remote sensing equipment. Leonard wondered if a Japanese carrier would risk coming this far for a harvest that changed from day to day. He thought not. The prize would have to be guaranteed—something like the Panama Canal.

"How quickly the locals have adapted to lucre and violence," Ernest said softly. It was an unusual, somber tone. "The anthropologists are wrong to imagine that the Samoans live in uncomplicated harmony with nature. Margaret Mead projected her own lascivious awakening on her subjects. Samoans indeed grew up with sex as a normal part of life. But the norm produced no heightened sensibility. That, as the Indian yogis emphasized, must be learned. In some measure the data is flawed. Before she arrived there were five or six generations of contact with Westerners. The British, Germans, and Americans meddled in Samoan civil wars later in the nineteenth century, even threatening to fight each other over who would control the islands. The Germans and the Americans split the property. Then, in 1914, New Zealand conquered the German part. Nearly a hundred years of traders, exploiters, and adventurers. It is hard to imagine no impact on Samoan morality."

They walked slowly toward Pago Pago, a muddy prospect peppered with decaying wooden buildings. During the night it had rained. The air filled with the humidity of evaporation. Leonard remembered "The Family."

He found it accidentally when he was thirteen. He had set out to read the nineteenth-century British classics at Sandy Creek's Deacon Library. The adventure novels came first, and then, after Scott, he began Stevenson. He returned *Kidnapped*, with the full-color illustrations by Wyeth, and found next to it a small volume of poetry. Here was a different Stevenson. Leonard let himself be carried off by the rhythm of the words. They were Stevenson's last poems, about homesteading in the South Pacific. Leonard, while having seen death, did not know it as a companion (that usually comes in middle age), and he was mightily confused by Stevenson's "Requiem." Who would gladly die, willingly go down into a final home in the cold earth? He read more poetry— Hardy, the Rossetti family, the Brownings—to see how to accommodate death.

The naming of beauty, Leonard concluded, made the prospect of death bearable. It was not sufficient to experience beauty, for the experience made sense only if it could be talked about. There could be no raw, unanalyzed experience, for all sensations were relayed by words, or by implicit speech. For he imagined that when a cat purred to express contentment, the vocable formed a notion in its language. Later, in college, his views were compromised by the latest psychological theories. But Leonard firmly believed that words held the key to the human condition. Philosophy's aim might be to teach acceptance of death, but it did so with words. Leonard suspected that many deep philosophical problems were nothing other than confusions about language.

Leonard wanted to visit Robert Louis Stevenson's grave. It was at Vailima, near Apia in Western Samoa, some twenty miles distant.

"Sorry, Ernest," he said, "There are some things I must do."

Leonard learned that the *Turtle* would be docked for three days. He badgered the harbor-master for the schedule of local shipping, and he found a daily supply run leaving at noon. Then he boarded the *Rat* and made a nuisance of himself until he found Anneke's cabin. She answered his knock. She was dressed in army fatigues. He guessed that she was about to take in the sights.

"Come with me to see the grave of the greatest nineteenth-century poet," he implored.

An hour later they slipped out of the harbor on a stripped-down PT boat. A few clouds puffed over the island. The sky was deep blue overhead. Light was everywhere. Leonard and Anneke had dark glasses. The wind led them to sit aft, in the boat's well. It was not possible to talk. Leonard imagined himself on a long pleasure yacht. He had seen them in Sandy Creek, owned by lawyers and bankers. He felt the freedom of the ocean. One could go anywhere, do anything. Until, he thought, the engine failed.

The boat slapped the gentle waves. After land disappeared, Leonard realized that he had tensed all his muscles. The boat's vibration made him shake. He felt more at ease standing next to the pilot, a short, uncommunicative boy with white hair. One of the crew passed around coconut, dry biscuits, and a white paste.

When asked, he pronounced it cheese.

Anneke let the experience flow around her. The sun and the spray felt like the sea around Java. She closed her eyes. The vibration and methodical rocking of the boat brought to mind a visit of the governor general to Bandung. Anneke was eight or nine. There was a celebration to mark the opening of the new telescope at nearby Lembang. It was the most powerful telescope anywhere in Dutch realms, and it had been endowed by rich planters and merchants. For the occasion, some of the royal family had come from the *kraton* in Yogyakarta. The governor general stood two meters tall. He walked in full regalia next to a royal, who barely came up to his chest. Both were protected by umbrellas as they walked to the library of the institute of technology. Under the stone arcade that surrounded the library was a small *gamelan* orchestra. The daughter of a professor, Anneke watched from a corner of the library as the pair entered and took their seats to the rhythmic upbeats of a Javan symphony.

They sighted Upolu's Mt Vaea around mid-afternoon. They watched as it grew larger and eventually gave way to a vista of Apia. The harbor was a gentle crescent that did not allow deep-drafted ships to dock. No craft were visible except for a few beached sailboats. The white-haired pilot guided the boat to a dock that extended about a hundred feet into the harbor. He cut the engines. At the foot of the dock Leonard and Anneke met a barefooted man in a sailor's cap.

"You Yanks?" he asked. "Got to know. I'm the checker." Leonard nodded and the checker was satisfied. He and Anneke walked into town.

Apia reminded Leonard of sleepy mountain towns in Colorado. There was one unpaved street with a jumble of wooden buildings on either side. Everything wanted paint and attention. Nearly a generation of New Zealand administration had not been kind. Western Samoa was a burden for New Zealand, which kept the islands as an assertion of independence from Britain. The New Zealand flag fluttered over Apia's general store, Kesselgiest

Provisions. It seemed the only trace of what had been, early in the century, a bilingual English-German culture. In 1921 New Zealand had transported most of the German colonists to Hamburg.

From Kesselgiest Leonard bought biscuits, jam, and a tin of something that may or may not have been meat. A chat resulted in directions for Vailima and the poet's grave. It was a short walk into the forest. Leonard was assaulted by rank untidiness. It seemed as if decaying garbage, covered by insects, lay everywhere. A rat crawled out from under a broken crate. Not what he had expected from Robert Louis Stevenson. The road wound up a hill. It gave way to a large wooden house.

Stevenson had fled to Samoa in an attempt to recover his precarious health. There, surrounded by a coterie of women, he built Vailima, a multistoried villa. He wrote tirelessly, for by then he had become a popular author. While dictating one of his novels, he died suddenly of a stroke at age forty-four. He collapsed under the strain of wandering, building a new home, laboring in the garden, and writing. The villa, with gables and verandah, bore traces of blue and crimson paint. Shutters were lacking and the grounds were untended. Until 1914 it had been the residence of the German governor, after that the New Zealand administrator. Leonard imagined Stevenson, pale and filthy alongside his women, grubbing in the earth, quite unlike the reveries of "The Family."

At a bit more than one thousand feet, the high point of Upolu was the summit of an extinct volcano, Mt Vaea. Leonard and Anneke passed by the disintegrating villa and continued on the road. After a half hour it became a track. They were climbing, but they could still not see the ocean. Trees grew larger with the altitude, Leonard observed. Farther from human hands, he thought. The woods were quiet. Only an occasional flutter or twitter, provoked by their footfall, broke the natural silence. There is a profusion of life in the tropics, but the habitat does not sustain profligate activity. Actions are deadly serious. Creatures move with an economy of effort. It did indeed seem like what Stevenson described, a "devil-haunted wood."

The trees broke off a short way from the summit. Leonard and Anneke were breathing hard, the result of maritime inactivity. A warm sea breeze dried their soaking clothes. They found Stevenson's grave about an hour before sunset. His requiem was carved on the stone. Leonard read it aloud. "Gladly I lived," he repeated. It was the only phrase that made sense to him. Stevenson was neither hunter nor sailor, at least not professionally. He had wandered far from Edinburgh, but Scotland remained on his mind. Who could want to sleep in this volcanic ground? On a rock ledge he set out the food that he had brought.

"This is not unlike Java," Anneke said through a mouthful of biscuit and jam. "It is warm and familiar." She turned to Leonard. "I came for this, to feel at home. It is no picnic, I know. There is a war. But I am beginning to feel whole again." She looked at the setting sun, brilliantly reflected off the water. A gibbous moon beamed in the east. "We should go back. We are fortunate for the moon."

They loped down to Apia. Light enough to see the path, but not to avoid tripping over rocks and roots. Apia had several hotels. The largest one took them immediately, offering two rooms opening to a common walkway.

"Bath?" Leonard asked the clerk.

"Two dollars extra."

"Dinner?"

"Whatever you want, from whatever we got."

Leonard and Anneke opted for food first. It was a large, bony fish cooked with fruit, which they ate silently in the nearly deserted bar. Wrong to ask her for the night, Leonard thought. They were partners for the Javan mission, and their relationship had to remain collegial. But he also sensed that he had always introduced distance into his relations with women. It came from the romantic, nineteenth-century novels—Scott and Stevenson. He wanted to be natural and smooth. He thought it would be possible if Anneke were not so idiosyncratic.

Leonard ordered the baths. They took place in a room at the end of the walkway. The clerk filled a tub halfway with hot water.

"That's all for tonight," he said, disappearing down a stairwell.

Leonard insisted that Anneke use the water first, which she was glad to do. She came out after five minutes, wrapped in a towel, and padded into her room carrying her clothes. Leonard sank into the suds and emerged a bit cleaner than when he started. The clothes, unfortunately, would have to serve for the trip back to Tutuila. He entered his room. Anneke sat on his bed, a towel round her middle.

"I enjoyed today," she said. "It allowed me to relax, to sense my surroundings and feel part of them. It's been many years since I felt this way."

"It's all quite new to me," Leonard answered, trying mightily to control his surprise and depress his heart-rate. "But I liked it, too. The forest is not so bad." He paused. "Anneke, we should be careful. I mean, about sleeping together."

"Silly boy. I am a tough nut."

*

* *

Before the PT boat left, at 8:00 a.m., Leonard persuaded Anneke to walk around the harbor crescent. One point ended in a spit of rock and sand. On it stood a two-storey clapboard building with a concrete foundation. Around it were a number of small structures, including the ubiquitous kitchen. The compound seemed abandoned. To one side there was a scaffold dwarfing the building, and from it hung various instruments and wires. Leonard knocked at the building's entrance. Then he pushed open the door.

The inside was surprisingly dry and unpleasantly hot. Dust

and dirt showed where large objects had once rested quietly for many years. In a corner of the front room was a plaster bust, of the kind that graced grand pianos. Leonard studied it. The name was H. Wagner. Not the composer. A scientist? A cupboard in another room had various mechanical contrivances, or parts of them. In a cardboard box, nearly disintegrated by rot and bugs, there were scores of glass negatives. Leonard held up a few to the light. They were photographs of waves inscribed on a graph. The dates were all before 1914. One bore the signature, "G. Angenheister."

Leonard thought for several minutes and then remembered why it seemed familiar. When he and Cratsley had met in Omaha, conversation turned from weather to geophysics. Cratsley described the geophysicists at Caltech. They were mostly concerned with earthquakes. The sharpest man among them, Beno Gutenberg, came from Göttingen in the 1920s. Gutenberg's pioneering studies of the earth's interior structure, Cratsley said with glee, originated from data taken in a tropical paradise, an observatory in Samoa. What Leonard saw was all that remained of what had once been the finest geophysical operation beyond Europe.

He and Anneke walked up the beach toward the waiting boat. Thus the glories of the world. People live a precarious existence, threatened by events over which they have no control. The institutions and associations people construct may be abandoned at any moment. What remains, Leonard thought, is the word. That alone, published in thousands of copies, has permanence. Apia lives through the words of Stevenson and Angenheister. Once set down, words have their own destiny. Leonard reflected that his impending introduction to Javan culture originated in a water-stained manuscript written years ago, a text that threatened to animate millions of men under arms.

8

The Antipode

The Jesuits have a good observatory at Riverview. They are quite helpful and friendly. I worship in a separate church, but I share their approach to science. No secrets between observers of nature, no rank or privilege, only dedication and invention. How different the history of the Indies if the Jesuits had set up a college. Why did the Portuguese Jesuits set down roots at Macau and Japan and in India but nothing in between? We have done everything ourselves in the Indies, everything from scratch.

Joan Létoile to Jacob Witte, 14 April 1931, Witte papers,
Boerhaave Museum, Leiden

Magnificent harbors produce great cities, each of them unique, and Sydney has one of the finest anchorages on the Pacific rim. The commercial center of the South Pacific since the nineteenth century, it radiates cosmopolitan sophistication. The war provided a tremendous stimulus to every part of Australia, but most of all to Sydney. It became a safe haven for vessels fleeing the Asian colonies of France, Britain, and the Netherlands. It serviced neutral tonnage. And it received the apparently endless number of ships launched from American yards. The war did more than break the domination of Mother England. It provided a climate of prosperity and an air of gaiety.

Leonard took in the foreign presence when the *Turtle's* belly expelled him on the docks of Middle Head. He saw an Allied flotilla. The *Dewey Rattie* was joined by two American destroyers and an aircraft carrier. There was a British submarine tender and a number of Australian shore-patrol vessels. A Dutch submarine rounded out the picture. Sydney was nowhere to be seen.

The sea air and land smells washed over him. The green hills shimmered, as narrow leaves fluttered in the breeze. Sea birds called, and their land cousins, a kookaburra and a flock of brilliant lorikeets, replied. He stood for several minutes in the spring morning. Then he struggled to regain his composure as he sensed the sun arcing overhead toward the left. Do the astrologers in Australia predict fates as they would in Mediterranean cultures? Were Australians antipodal in sentiment and temperament? In the next few days he intended to find out by getting to know two of them, his distant relations.

Leonard's step-father Sam Barrick had four brothers. The oldest four of the five left Russia before 1917. Itzhak stayed behind. He dodged the draft for eighteen months and then got out by way of Crimea, with the White Russian fleet that finally dropped anchor at Bizerte. He was allowed to become an orderly for two Australian doctors who were studying plague in Tunis with the great Charles Nicolle. When they returned to Australia, he accompanied them. Sydney offered unlimited opportunities for someone who lived by his wits. Itzhak assembled a small fortune in scrap metal. He invested in land on the North Shore, and when the Harbour Bridge opened, his investment grew by an order of magnitude. He married, but no children arrived. So he adopted an infant son. David Barrick, according to a letter that Sam received, had qualified as an optometrist. He landed a contract for supplying eyeglasses to the Australian navy, no doubt at the very base where Leonard was now lost in reverie.

Leonard regretted not taking Anneke to bed in Apia—or not trying to. They would be trained, he imagined, in jungle warfare. Theory and practice of the blowgun, rigging a sleeping hammock, the art of cooking poisonous reptiles. He would see whether Joseph Conrad and Richard Halliburton were right about the emotional impact of tropics. Or was it all in the telling. Could Arctic ice and desert heat inspire similar passions?

Leonard walked to the harbormaster's office and looked for David Barrick in a naval phone book. He called. No answer. He then found him in a greater Sydney directory.

"Gdye," a woman's voice.

"Hello." Leonard knew enough about things antipodal for his greeting to signify a foreign presence. He explained that he was Sam Barrick's step-son and that he would like to speak with David Barrick. There was a pause, which Leonard took to be Australian recapitulation of what had been conveyed in an unfamiliar accent. The woman then asked him to hold.

"Leonard," came the strong male voice. "Where are you calling from? Well I'll be. Don't move. I'll meet you in half an hour." Business, Leonard figured, must be good for the optometrist to drop everything on a moment's notice.

About forty minutes later a red-haired giant walked into the office and asked for Leonard Ranov.

"David, you look like a Viking."

"A junior officer," David Barrick grimaced at Leonard's bars. "Aren't they the ones who lead hopeless charges? So tell me about things in Sandy Creek." And Leonard chattered away about home, feeling at ease in the presence of his cousin. "Come back with me for dinner. I live a few miles up the coast. These days we walk. Petrol is impossible to find, and horses are trouble."

David Barrick and Leonard Ranov walked along a gravel road winding up into the cliffs dominating Middle Head, one of the grand fingers that the smallest continent thrust into the ocean at Sydney. The landscape seemed wild, or at least not recently cultivated. Salt and sea breezes, Leonard imagined, kept the vegetation down to a height of twenty feet. The brush twinkled in the wind as the native leaves presented alternating colors of green. David pointed out birds, which were everywhere, and the occasional insect. He took Leonard on a short ramble into the bush to show him aboriginal rock carvings.

"I imagine all this will change in my lifetime," David mused.

"They say soot is killing trees and eating away stone. But this concerns me more." He pointed to a seedling. "A broad-leaved invader, sycamore I think. The seed came here from the streets of Sydney by wind or water, carried up by birds or animals." He looked down at the naval yard with its complement of floating, grey forms. "Every one of those boats carries worms, snails, and weeds that sooner or later will infect these estuaries. Don't get me wrong. We need trade and agriculture, and we must have the navy. But I love this pristine place."

The road circled a knoll. A dirt path branched out and down. They descended rapidly for five minutes and then opened into a small cove. A frame house of unpainted clapboard nestled against the cliff. Smoke came from its chimney. Leonard made out a vegetable garden and several outbuildings. The cove had a dock with a sailboat tied up against it. It was David's paradise.

"Home. Before the war I used an outboard to travel to the yard, but now I mostly walk. You see, it takes me only three or four days a month to fit sailors with spectacles. Much of the spectacle-making can be done here—and before the war it was. The navy operates by contracts. I fulfill my end of the bargain with lots of time to spare." His hand swept out an arc. "I call it Spinoza Cove."

They walked into the house. Downstairs was one enormous room. A corner held things optical. Leonard saw an electrical kiln and a collection of polishing wheels. In another corner, the kitchen, stood a small, stocky woman. She was poking a piece of driftwood into the stove.

"Mandy, let me present Leonard Ranov."

"Welcome to Australia," she smiled. "I hope you like vegetarian fare."

"Mandy is not above throwing anything cold-blooded into the pot, but for years we've drawn the line at fowl. We harvest much of what we eat. Dad tells me that Sam was a vegetarian in his California days. Wine?" He walked to a sideboard on which sat a large barrel with a spout. "Our own pressing. Varies with

what comes our way. Last year we bought a truckload of grapes."
He poured out three large bells.

Leonard reflected on the scene. Unfamiliarity with material
want—good fortune from the time of infancy—underlay what he
saw. It was manufactured by the Australian taxpayer, who footed
David's salary. It was sustained by optimism and the absence of
children—nothing in the house suggested their presence. It en-
dured because David provided an essential civilian service, and
so could flex his large frame in mufti. The Barricks had retired to
Walden Pond, but like Thoreau they turned up for tea in conventional drawing rooms. The circumstance did not make their life a
counterfeit.

Mandy served an eel on a bed of rice and vegetables. Leonard
found it unexpectedly flavorful.

"How long are you in Sydney?" Mandy asked.

"A few days. Soon I begin training for the tropics." The
abbreviated explanation was all that people expected during the
war. He changed the subject. "There is one place near here I
want to visit. Riverview Observatory. Do you know it?"

David thought. "You mean the Jesuit college, St Ignatius?
At Riverview?" He said slowly, "Yes, they study earthquakes.
Not much earthshaking here, though." Leonard nodded. "Come
with me," David urged. "We can sail there in a few hours. We'll
make a holiday of it."

David bussed the dinner plates to the kitchen sink, leaving
Leonard to wonder about their source of fresh water. Mandy
smiled as David scooped up an armful of fruit and a thermos of
water and then led his cousin down to the dock.

As a boy, Leonard had sailed several times on Sandy Creek
in small boats owned by school friends, but the romance of it all
escaped him. Now he saw something that could fire emotions. It
was a twenty-eight-footer, rigged with one mast. The varnished
deck and hull gleamed as the boat rocked at its berth. Leonard
saw that it had a large, low cabin. Across the stern was emblazoned: *al-Kindi,* Spinoza Cove.

"The sea breeze will blow us in," David shouted after he had shoved off. "Pull up the mainsail," he said to Leonard, who had parked himself near the tiller. "I'll make it fast. But mind the boom as it comes round." Within a minute *al-Kindi* was speeding up Port Jackson. They were traveling with the wind and hardly felt it, while the shore and distant points continually changed their aspect. Relativity, Galileo's relativity, was founded on just such an apparent paradox. They rounded a point and Sydney came into view. The tops of a few buildings and, spanning the narrows from the Rocks to North Sydney, the Harbour Bridge. They quickly passed Fort Denison, the improbable island guardian of the harbor, and swooped under the bridge. The whole thing—city, bridge, ships, and semi-tropical foliage—recalled a smaller, more intimate San Francisco. Behind the bridge were industrial anchorages, foul loading docks for a hundred years. Everything changed when David steered *al-Kindi* up Lane Cove River. There were fields and woods, the playground of Sydney's elite. The Jesuit college grounds came down to the water. The two sailors tied up their boat and stepped down their sail.

St Ignatius College was a secondary school. It owed its title to French tradition, where religious orders ran *collèges* to educate children beyond the clutches of secular wisdom. True to Jesuit tradition from Shanghai to Montreal, the college—a large building with rooms for classes and dormitories—was attached to a church and a residence for the Jesuits who ran the show. There were outbuildings. Leonard made out a small hut with a moveable roof that might have sheltered a telescope. The Riverview Observatory. At the college office, Leonard asked an attractive secretary for Father McIntyre.

"Down in the Chinese tomb, he is. Down the hill. The building with the cylindrical roof."

Leonard and David returned in the direction of the boat. Leonard had noticed the building and wondered if it was a root cellar or mausoleum. Apparently it was the latter. They knocked and entered through a double set of doors. They saw a scientific laboratory. Shelves held rows of journals, dictionaries, hand-books, and instrument catalogues. Desks were covered with pa-pers and calculations.

"It would have been better to ring. But no harm done." A tall, thin man emerged from a door in a wall that closed off most of the half-cylinder's volume. "My name is McIntyre. How can I help you?"

"Lieutenant Leonard Ranov, United States Army Air Corps. I came to find out about Joan Létoile." Leonard pronounced the name Dutch fashion.

"Well, that is a story." With an easy gesture, McIntyre mo-tioned his intruders to take chairs. Then he told things as he knew them to be. "Létoile is to thank for our double-star pro-gram. Outside, in a hut, we have an astrographic telescope that Létoile and his mechanic built for us more than a decade ago. The idea was for us both to scan the southern skies with identical equipment, looking for double stars. The way to do it is with a blink comparer. We photograph the skies at various intervals. Looking through the comparer, we see a rapidly alternating pic-ture of both photographs. The eye is generally attracted to any change in relative stellar positions. We've published some of our discoveries in our observatory's bulletin. Anyway, Létoile is the architect of our astronomical work. Before I met him at a conference in Tokyo in 1924, we had only a small and not very serviceable refractor. Until Létoile took an interest in us, we were really only a geophysical institute restricted largely to seismol-ogy and effectively *sous la tutelle* of the French Jesuit observa-tory at Shanghai. My predecessor received his training there. Would you like to see our seismographs? They are among Australia's finest."

McIntyre led Leonard and David into the seismological vault. The floor was six feet underground, the better to guard the instru-ments against temperature fluctuations.

"There are the old Wiecherts, now out of service. We record with a Galitzin and a Mainka. We've connected them to our master clock, and the recordings are done automatically on photographical film. We change reels only every fifth day, although for a big event we may need to reset the needles." Leonard saw that the master clock, a Riefler pendulum, connected to a second, slave clock; the Riefler kept time, every so often correcting the slave with an almost imperceptible touch, while the slave clock marked out time for the instruments. A bit behind the times, but still servicable. "You know, we used to pick out the time ball at the Parramatta Observatory, but trees now obscure the view from our church. Presently we shoot the sun ourselves, just like in the old days."

"Did you visit Létoile at Lembang?" Leonard took in the circulation of knowledge on the Western shores of the Pacific. Here was a story quite unknown to the pompous toads who managed grand research operations in the North Atlantic World. How many discoveries, he wondered, had been passed over by old men who declined to look beyond the corridors of their own, élite institution?

"He came here briefly in 1931, and I spent three weeks with him later that year while his mechanic built a mounting for the astrograph. It was a remarkable experience. I never would have believed that such fine workmanship could come from Java. The mechanic showed his Javan workmen a picture of the parts for the mounting—not a blueprint—and they machined everything to perfection. I stayed in a small guest house. Létoile was a gracious host. He showed me around. I remember one excursion to the nearby, active volcano. It is called the Overturned Boat, and there is quite a mythological story behind it. Several years ago our seismographs picked up what I took to be an eruption, and Létoile confirmed my conclusion." McIntyre paused and raised his eyebrows at Leonard. "Do you have business with Létoile?"

"In a manner of speaking. A physicist friend of his suggested that I look into his publications."

"He kept to himself at Lembang, you know. The nearby TH

left him alone. That was the way he wanted things. We've just published some of his observations in our local bulletin. He sent them along right before Java fell to the Japanese. It's rather difficult now to find paper and printers. Would you like a copy?"

Leonard accepted the offering. Létoile had met Japanese on their home territory. Was there something more? "Did you and Létoile learn Japanese for that conference?" Leonard posed the question in Japanese.

"I speak only a little Japanese," McIntyre pronounced slowly in the voice of a traveler. "Please repeat your question."

"You have been very kind, McIntyre-san."

"Will you stay for tea? It is rather good by Australian standards."

Leonard looked at David, who had been standing for the technical discussion. David's eyes darted to the door.

"I think my captain has obligations."

At river's edge, McIntyre bade them Godspeed. "I would say come back to visit if you are ever in town, but I won't be here to greet you." He looked down shyly. "I've been appointed director of the Vatican Observatory." It was a signal honor. McIntyre was the man to rehabilitate Galileo, whose importunate arrogance had brought down the wrath of serious Jesuit thinkers at the Collegio Romano—they appreciated his telescope and its revelations, and they even admitted (in their publications emanating from the Chinese imperial court) the utility of the Copernican point of view. Papal condemnation, of a piece with Martin Luther's disregard of the new astronomy, was an error brought about by political intrigue.

Standing by the river, they sensed that the sea breeze had picked up. The sailors set off. *Al-Kindi* zigzagged across the harbor for ninety minutes until David caught sight of Spinoza Cove. "Mind if I drop you off at the yards?" he asked Leonard, who nodded. David took a long leg out toward the ocean and then ran straight for the naval moorings. No one challenged his entry. Either his boat was familiar, or the threat of armed attack was minuscule.

Leonard thanked his cousin. "Regards to your family."

"I enjoyed meeting you."

"They will probably find things to keep me busy from now on."

"Take care. They tell me water is the big problem in the tropics. It's everywhere, but you can drink none of it." With that he cast off and saluted Leonard palm-in, like a tar.

Leonard watched him disappear around the docks. Some people spend their entire life without dislocation, catastrophic illness, or financial worries, Leonard reflected. Perhaps David Barrick would live out his days in the pleasant air of Spinoza Cove.

*
* *

The *Turtle* was taking on supplies. Its deck plates were off. Leonard saw a torpedo disappearing into the aft compartment. Were torpedoes standard size the world around, Leonard wondered? Or did this international port stock weapons of every caliber? He dropped down into his cabin. Ernest and Jack were out. There were no messages. He felt slight disappointment that Anneke had not looked him up. He bounded up, passing the dock workers who had begun to screw down the deck. He boarded the *Dewey Rattie*. His sense of direction brought him directly to Anneke's cabin. He knocked. There was no answer.

Leonard walked slowly toward the docks. Anyone's first reaction after a sea voyage is to take in the land. He imagined that she had gone into Sydney. Leonard knew that he could not expect her affection. There had been little enough sign of it. Anneke was independent and strong willed. She would decide what suited her best. The thought made Leonard desire her more.

"Where do I get coffee?" he asked a sailor, stripped to the waist, who was dragging a chain to a truck.

"Officer's mess for you, Yank. Serve you up proper." He gestured vaguely in the distance. The sun was nearing the end of its left-handed arc, but the temperature had not dropped. Leonard gained on a cluster of buildings identified by the sailor. There were a number of two-storey barracks. Several had wide verandahs—the signal affectation of Australian architecture. All were painted white. Leonard had seen scores of military bases. They shared many features.

The military lacks humor. Wars are not won with grace and subtlety. Commands are devoid of literary allusions and harmonics. Ornament is direct and obvious. Everything must be recognized at a glance. Redundancy exists at every level because it has positive survival value: Even with his uniform in tatters, one can recognize an officer. The principles carry over to military architecture. In the army, military bases have an air of impermanence. They are temporary inventions, and they hang on the changing demands of strategy. They are installations where soldiers improve their wind and steady their trigger finger. They are the seat of continual discipline and practice. For the navy, however, bases signal safe havens and peaceful abodes. Naval practice takes place on ships at sea—that which the French called naval *bâtiments*, or buildings. Naval warfare is largely a matter of positioning, that is, seamanship, which depends less on raw muscle than on spirit and knowledge of water and weather. The navy, then, has been able to deck itself more easily than the army with the appearances of learning. Costume suggests the different rôles of soldier and sailor: Army uniforms are made in the image of dust and mud, while the navy takes its colors from salt and sky.

An enormous anchor lay before the officer's club. Leonard knew it to be a symbol of hope, and he took it as a favorable omen. He entered, found a table in the bar, and ordered a coffee.

"Sir, we regret to be out of that substance," a waiter replied. "May I suggest tea?" Leonard nodded, and felt for his billfold. His hand ran over the reprint that McIntyre had given him.

The publication, Leonard saw quickly, was typical of observatory bulletins. The typesetting was a bit clumsy and unimaginative. There was a cover of stiff paper, which he had to crease back to read Létoile's title page: "Double Stars, War Series." In creditable English, Létoile described his small astrograph and his large double-refracting telescope, and he provided the location of his observatory. Then came four pages of celestial coordinates, with various comments. It was the intermittent record of only a few months' observing, Leonard saw. He turned to the last page, a verso. He read:

> *Note: These records, taken from September 1939 to April 1942, constitute a continuation of a systematic survey of the southern skies down to the thirteenth magnitude. For assistance over the past year especially I thank Ing. Mehmet Mafugi. I do not know whether there will be an opportunity to complete this work. Fortune has nevertheless presented an unusual research opportunity in another direction. I hope soon to be able to communicate the preliminary results of this new project. J.G.E.G.L.*

Leonard recognized the strategy. Létoile had left a trace of the uranium deposit in print. Later he would be able to point to this trace as priority of discovery.

How little is conveyed by a scientific paper, Leonard thought. Uncertainties and misgivings seldom receive airing. The results appear as immutable facts. Leonard knew them as guesses. The most remarkable thing about science, he felt, was that measurements were repeatable and reliable. Agreement transcended almost every feature of the material world: Religious persuasion, sexual orientation, and annual income were irrelevant when the physicist studied meters and dials.

Or were they? Ideological doctrine certainly pervaded medicine, the most inexact and unreliable of the sciences, where there was only the grossest agreement about the meaning of vital signs. Traditionally, astronomers did not falsify data, for any shepherd with a good eye could verify the relative motion of a planet, although in medieval Japan—where the new Buddhist astronomy was a state secret—there apparently was such imaginative interpolation (sacred writings referred to nine planetary lords). And today, Leonard thought, we have Robert Andrews Millikan, whose speculations about cosmic rays had been disproved decisively by Jacob Witte—and yet, Millikan succeeded in denying Witte his well-deserved encomium.

Létoile's remark was really too cryptic to aid him in any priority dispute. It might, however, preserve his life. Létoile could not have known that it would take more than a year to publish his paper. He might have wanted to show it to the invading Japanese army, which he and many others expected to overrun Java. He might have imagined that the Japanese would provide him with resources to exploit his new discovery. Could he claim German nationality through his wife? Leonard imagined stranger claims.

Tea arrived, which Leonard recognized as a small supper: sandwiches spread with a mysterious concoction, cold beets and apple sauce, anemic bread, and a pot of strong, Indian tea. David was right to reject this fare. Leonard nursed his teacup for a long time. He felt that he was coming to know Létoile, but he could not yet imagine how the Dutch astronomer acted. Nor was Leonard sure what motivated him, unless, true for most people, it was flattery and money.

He paid in Yankee currency, which the waiter readily accepted, and strolled back to the *Turtle*. He had nowhere else to go. A crumpled form perched on an oil drum near the submarine.

"They are sending us north of Brisbane to train with the Royal Marines," Anneke said. "In the mangrove swamps. It is their idea of preparing us for the tropics."

"I would go to the gates of hell with you," Leonard said gallantly.

"Let us hope it does not come to that."

"There is something I want to show you," Leonard said tentatively. He took Anneke's hand. He thought that she would pull back, or at least stiffen. Not a trace of reticence.

Leonard led her out the gate and into the nearby hills to the rock carvings. They did not sign out—antipodal regulations were relaxed. The sun had moved beyond sight to the west. A crystalline stillness descended over the hills. Pastel flowers and leaves took on an iridescence, bleeding light from the indigo-washed sky. Birds darted to nests. In the shadows, insects began to buzz and chirp.

They stared at the aboriginal design. An enormous, toothy maw, with superimposed bulging eyes, ended in a sinuous and attenuated body sprouting six appendages. It ran twelve feet from stem to stern.

"There is a resemblance to Javan totems," Anneke offered. "The beast seems friendly and benevolent, like the comic heads of *wayang purwa*. Does it not resemble Disney's Goofy?" Leonard smiled at the analogy, which warmed Anneke's tongue. "The West imagines that it alone commands caricature and satire, that the subtle juxtaposition of deep philosophy and exaggerated buffoonery are its unique possession. If that were so, how could any other people laugh? They certainly do laugh at Javan *wayang*. If only you could see." She dropped her head in the luminous dusk.

"Enough philosophy," he said. He sat on the rock, which radiated warm comfort. "Anneke, will you sit next to me?"

"I suppose so," she smiled.

Leonard kissed her hand. She let her fingers stay on his lips. Then she threw his shoulders to the rock. She tugged at his belt until his swollen penis saluted through military buttons. She took it in her mouth, tasting the thin seminal fluid. Leonard grabbed at her crotch and fumbled until he caught her labia with his tongue.

Anneke whispered in his ear, "No, please. Stop. I can't now."

"Why not?"

"Because I have never let a man into me. My only intimate friends have been women."

Leonard held her. He thought back to meeting Anneke in Cambridge, where she had lived with a companion. Dusk magnified the trees against the fading sky. They contracted as the stars came out. Nothing moved.

"I don't care," Leonard said. "I believe love is where you find it."

They lay on the tattooed rock, watching the constellations rotate westward through a lattice of still branches, imagining that they were falling through heaven.

*
* *

The crocodile clamped its jaws on an ammunition case. It pulled for the water. The case connected by a thick rope to two sets of arms, which resisted the reptile's invitation. If they held firm, the crocodile would have to give up or charge for a better grip. For thirty seconds neither party budged. It was the worst sort of isometric exercise, guaranteed to force a mitral-valve prolapse, or worse. Suddenly the tension collapsed as the crocodile opened its jaws. The bodies attached to the arms fell back on the shore. The crocodile flashed up the bank for his prize, which the drillmaster had coated in bacon fat. The bodies scrambled back as the rope snaked into the lagoon.

"Lucky," the drillmaster said in Dutch. "Next time it will be your ass."

Leonard needed no translation. For three weeks he had been presented with a continuing series of tropical conundrums. How to make a fire with wet wood, how to dress, how to avoid predators and parasites. He memorized hundreds of botanicals—most of these from books—and fried up dozens of slithering, crawling, and buzzing creatures. On occasion he faced salivating obstacles.

Anneke was there with him, and he concluded that she gave a better account of herself. She had an unfair advantage in her knowledge of the tropics. She was not as strong as he was. She could neither shoot nor handle a knife. But she had good balance and remarkable recovery. She was much quicker than Leonard, even if she did not always practice economy of movement. Her resting pulse was 42 beats per minute. She attributed it to years of meditation.

Intimacy does not by itself stimulate libido. Leonard had much opportunity to verify this proposition. There was nothing particularly sexual about collapsing on a riverbank after having grappled with the maw of a crocodile. Anneke, at least, was not aroused. Leonard and Anneke developed their relationship along the lines of friendship.

The drillmaster, Wim van de Sande, was one of the first Dutch alumni of the American Marines' training camp at Camp Lejeune. The idea was to create a Dutch force capable of spearheading the invasion of Java. Tens of thousands of men would be required. Ten were not yet ready. Van de Sande did not mind being assigned to an airstrip in Queensland. He took pleasure in watching planes of the Dutch air corps take off and land, secure in the notion that his feet were on the ground. He enjoyed making Leonard and Anneke jump through hoops. He laughed frequently, which his pupils interpreted as an encouraging sign.

There was relatively little attention devoted to the art of killing. Van de Sande coached Anneke in pistol and rifle shooting, and he showed both prospective commandos how to dispose of an opponent armed with a knife. All in all, however, he was a professional killer little interested in demonstrating his talents. The army existed for the purpose of murder, and yet in its parades, uniforms, medals, monuments, and its patronage of science and art, it sought to create the illusion of performing a polite social function. Van de Sande spent no time on an eventual Javan landfall.

"Maybe now we can be dropped from a plane," Anneke mused during a meal of swamp tuber and iguana tail. Overhead a B-17 with Dutch markings climbed toward the ocean.

"Too far, they say. The plane would have to be a large one, weighed down with fuel drums. A fighter escort is out of the question. An easy target for land-based interceptors. The *Turtle* is our taxi. Cheer up. Remember Stonewall Jackson. The only real danger will be from friendly fire."

"I trust we will practice navigating the rubber raft."

The three-week bivouac put Leonard and Anneke in a relaxed mood, and both were grateful for an opportunity to spend time in the Australian sun. Anneke pointed out that, though Java was closer to the equator, the days were hazy more often than not. Indeed, Javans were not an especially dark-complexioned people. Nothing could prepare them, it seemed, for tropical humidity.

When they boarded the *Turtle* at the Brisbane docks, Ernest Bit intoned, "They've taught you circus tricks. Now the real work begins."

Ernest was fretting. He had the qualities of a middle-manager: encyclopedic recall, obsessive organization, and a voice that disallowed emotional engagement. He stood on the submarine's deck leafing through a wad of papers attached to a clipboard. Like science, the military was a world on paper.

"I've requisitioned all your gear. Do go over it before we leave. That gives you about eight hours. And make sure your boots fit." He passed the clipboard to Leonard. "It's my idea. I wanted to come for the ride. They decided that I could be useful language-wise, if the sub got into trouble."

"How prescient. Have you arranged for separate staterooms?"

"Her, not you. No space. This boat is armed to the teeth. Our little game is a sideshow for the captain. He wants to bag tonnage."

Leonard looked through the papers. They would be traveling light. Weapons and ammunition took twenty pounds apiece. Dehydrated food, medicine, maps, a change of clothes, and a tarp made up another twenty pounds. There were ten Mexican silver dollars and one hundred Dutch guilders. They were expected to live off the land. Listed separately were the rubber raft with its waterproof bags, life jackets, radio transmitter, and compressed-air cylinder. Leonard looked at Ernest. There was something else.

"Like them captain's bars? Cratsley's idea. Seems to help requisitioning material in the field. The military does not respond to reason, only to hierarchical command." The new responsibility fell naturally on Ernest's unassuming shoulders. He glowed as Leonard saluted.

"Simple," Ernest continued while Leonard and Anneke stood on the *Turtle's* deck. "In a few days we drop you off on the coast. You hide the raft and radio. You walk to Lembang, check out the uranium deposit, and walk back to the coast. We will be waiting in three weeks' time. Leonard, on the way out it would be helpful to brush up on Japanese. I suggest listening on the boat's radio."

Time, the river we measure ourselves against, flows before our life begins and continues after it is done, but the river's composition changes continually. Here are the parameters: volume, velocity, sediment, and temperature. Leonard remembered the engineers at Laramie, who trained students to dip milk bottles in mountain streams for establishing particle transport, to measure stream cross-section, to calculate drainage basins, all this to determine the height of fifty-year floods—the standard for bridges. Life, too, ran along quickly or not, overflowed with events large and small or with nothing but feelings. It washed away the tenuous thread that connected people to each other, or it meandered under the highest bridge of years. How tranquil it had been to study Japanese with Sasaki-san. Now events hurtled forward too quickly to internalize. Let them pass, he thought, and preserve yourself. He smiled to the seabirds, took a deep breath, and dropped down to inspect his quarters.

*
*   *

Captain Emmanuel Merlin's notion was to shake down the *Turtle* on its way to Darwin. He had commanded boats in the North Atlantic, but the tropics were new to him. So was the German submarine. On the run from Sydney to Brisbane he had concluded that the deck gun was useful only as a close-range cudgel, for it lacked sophisticated stabilizers. After Brisbane dropped from sight he set the boat into an emergency dive.

The crew and the supercargo sought handholds where they found themselves. As Merlin suspected, with the nose at thirty degrees a variety of objects fell from their racks or hooks: books and bananas, charts and cantaloupe, pots and pasta. At a depth of three hundred feet there were groans and sizzles. Merlin leveled off and cruised for five minutes before taking the boat to the surface.

"Please tell the men to secure their loot," he commented to his exec.

Leonard was walking to the head when the dive began. It was nothing compared to rolls in the air or on the surface of the sea, and it did not bother him. Still, he held his water until the all-clear signaled. In a confrontation with hostiles there would be depth charges, the subsurface analogue of flak. The boat would shake. Bolts would pop and pipes would burst. If the hull were breached, the bulkheads would be dogged. There were a dozen ways of dying, and a dozen ways of cheating death. In the depths, just as at the heights, life hung on machinery for pumping air, generating thrust, finding the way. Enveloped in a metal skin, the *voyageurs* were born again upon reaching home.

He returned to an alcove containing his gear, including the deflated raft, and Captain Bit.

"Nice maneuver," Ernest Bit commented. "These really are built solid."

Emmanuel Merlin made sure that his boat was responsive.

He took five days to shadow the shore between Brisbane and Darwin. Respectful of his fearsome profile, he broadcast continually on a number of bands. He brought a record player on board for just that purpose. He limited transmissions to Grofé's "Grand Canyon Suite," a medley from the Red Army Chorus, and the "Rosenkavalier." There was some audacity in the latter, but Leonard thought that it lent a playful, slightly wistful air to the metal tube that contained thirty-odd lives. He enjoyed pouring over the maps of Java in Anneke's cabin, the two of them relaxed, cheerful, and dressed, listening to the Marschallin's regrets. They had become, he realized, good friends.

Anneke saw everything, most recently the swamp bivouac and the map lessons, as a means to an end. That end, recovering the tranquillity and abundance of the tropics, was entirely irrational, but it provided motivation just as intense as Leonard's abstract curiosity about Létoile's uranium. She inverted the loss of her brother to feel that she had failed him by remaining alive. Java became the goal of her flight from reality. She gave no thought to the aim of her mission. The mission itself was what she keenly anticipated. She allowed herself to imagine fading into the Javan countryside, a slave to the seasons, the diverse festivals, and the complex Javan calendar.

Battle brings out three kinds of emotion: the instinct of self-preservation, the reflex to obey orders, and the bond of camaraderie. Each emotion contributes to survival and to success, and each balances the other two. Self-preservation, the most primitive of the three, is also the most rational, for nothing is more of an artificial horror than a field of combat. When self-preservation gains the upper hand, the result is cowardice and desertion. The second emotion is the desideratum of military training: Soldiers must obey orders without thinking, for if they did think, they would never perform the task demanded of them. Following orders unthinkingly deprives men and women of humanity. To mask this savage principle, armies and navies patronize art and learning. They pay for scientific research and dinner parties to hide the unshaven, ulcerated, drooling face of war. Camaraderie, finally, is what produces heroism. Bonds of immediate affection are what nations transform into motivation by the imposition of transcendental ideas. Without the sanction of orders, however, camaraderie results in polemarchy and banditry. Leonard and Anneke, never having fought on a battlefield, did not appreciate the benefits of Strauss's arias.

Ernest Bit saw the benefits and approved of them, although he much preferred the precision of Baroque counterpoint to wistful, if lyric, Romanticism. He called Romantic music "Marfluggio," and he identified Puccini and Sibelius and, oddly enough, Stravinsky as the worst of the Marfluggiacs. But he was prepared to admit that the music could charm disingenuous uncouths like Leonard and deliberate regressives like Anneke. He began to imagine that the pair would actually walk through the jungle and return to tell the tale. He sensed that the sorest hour would come at the final rendezvous. Even with adequate communication, the odds went against sighting and then docking a small craft at sea.

He had asked the expeditionaries to come up with a landfall. Bandung, in the center of the Preanger Regency, was a mere fifty miles from the Indian Ocean to the south, but that side was ringed by mountains, and at least five of the peaks were active volcanoes. This was the reason for allowing a week to walk to Bandung's satellite town, Lembang. Anywhere along the southwestern coast of Java might make a logical point to begin the journey. Borobudur seemed too distant for his team to visit. Much depended on roads and paths, and the map exercise might bring Anneke to recall something about them.

The three settled on Sindangbaran. Anneke had visited it once, and she preserved a mental picture of the road from Bandung. When she tried to draw a map, however, or even to conflate her memory with the Dutch topographical maps strewn about her cabin, she came up dry.

"Passive memory," Ernest observed. "It will come to you

when you are in the middle of the stimuli that generated it. For this, smells are most important."

Darwin greeted Merlin's *Turtle* with silence, the anticipated welcome. It was dominated by the various Allied air corps, and following the Japanese raid of 1942, its defenses were highly strung. An Australian patrol boat followed the submarine into port. The city shimmered in morning heat. An emissary of gulls broke the silence, crying out, "Walk, walk, walk," advice that the crew vowed dutifully to follow, perhaps for the last time on dry land.

*

* *

Leonard had taken a break from listening on the radio, so he missed picking up the Japanese pilot before the watch on the conning tower spotted the plane as a flyspeck on the horizon. Merlin sent the boat down to forty feet, executed a half-mile corkscrew, and then surfaced to periscope and radio depth. By good fortune the plane flew across his field of vision. It seemed like a flimsy copy of the *Spirit of St Louis*. Merlin raced through his silhouette manuals. The flyer might be a Yokosuka. The shape of a tiny scout, with its wings removed it could be stored in a hangar on the deck of a giant submarine. Leonard confirmed that the plane was returning, having exhausted its fuel. It announced the sighting of a German submarine. Merlin floated the *Turtle* and determined the direction of the fleeing scout. Anywhere from two to four hours away might be a Japanese submarine—or perhaps a flotilla. Merlin plotted a prudent course at right angles to the scout's apparent destination, a heading toward Bali, one hundred miles distant.

The passage out from Darwin had been uneventful. They were far off the shipping lanes. Friendly bombers kept them in sight until they cleared Australian waters. Leonard sat with the radio. Anneke kept to herself, in a reverie of maps and memories. Ernest calculated and fretted. By the third day on Java, Leonard and Anneke would run out of dry food. Infection, the principal medical concern, would be kept at bay by alcohol, iodine, and the new penicillin. He had included a surgical kit for Anneke. Was it sufficient? Had he supplied enough oil for the guns? Why had he not thought about silencers? Would their rubber-soled boots shred on volcanic rock? Could Leonard and Anneke launch their raft through surf? Would they have the strength to fight waves and currents? If they foundered, could he persuade Merlin to risk the *Turtle* for them? For the first time in his life, Ernest Bit experienced the anxieties of an administrator.

Merlin ran west, staying 70 miles off Java's southern coast. It was just close enough to pick up the odd commercial vessel, and also just within the range of coastal air patrols. The Japanese kept most of their large warships out of the Indian Ocean, but Merlin felt that one could never discount the enterprise of a maverick raider. Merlin had enough oil to drop off his supercargo and return to Darwin. It was poor form to radio for a high-seas refueling.

When he passed the Tji Tanduwi, the only large river in West Java that flowed south, Merlin edged the boat toward land. At ten in the morning he found the prize he sought. It was a Japanese freighter escorted by a corvette. Leonard, on the radio, experienced the cold precision of a submarine attack. Orders were given and repeated back as Merlin lined up the *Turtle's* nose with its prey. Four torpedoes spread out in a fan.

Only in form do torpedoes, self-propelled explosives with the name of lethargy, resemble the remoras that slowed the ships of Antiquity. The explosive projectiles recall, rather, the paralyzing effect of slowly moving electric rays, the *Torpediniformes*. Torpedoes proceed by internal, self-contained logic, swayed by currents, winds, and waves. Merlin's second torpedo hit the freighter's bow, his third the corvette's stern. Leonard picked up the frantic radio messages. The freighter took water quickly, and it was quickly abandoned. The corvette had lost its rudder. Merlin sent two more torpedoes at the corvette and ran west along the coast. The *Turtle* echoed a thud as one torpedo hit its mark. With the night Merlin surfaced and made to the point where his military intelligence-gatherers could be set ashore.

The lives probably taken by Merlin's orders weighed on Ernest Bit. Whoever thinks war has been depersonalized over the past one hundred years does well to cast a longer glance into the past. As far back as records extend, we see the field of battle strewn with spent arrows and stones. Then come chariots and cavalry, siege engines, giant slings for hurling Greek fire, torched ships and burning mirrors, and, a gift from the Middle Kingdom, firearms. The absurdity of hand-to-hand combat has continued into the present, but irrational and unpredictable death was always a part of war. Javans gave consciousness to this irrationality by infusing life into the kris, which was held to seek and punish evil of its own accord.

For people schooled in Western rationality, there was something comforting in this attribution. The most rational of cultures cannot do without such fictional allusions. Ernest knew that imperial German troops had carried Nietzsche's *Zarathustra,* Goethe's *Faust,* and the *St John* gospel into battle. Anneke, a medical doctor, surely took comfort from the feel of her kris, which she strapped to her right calf. But would its presence engender the state of mind that favored courage?

Courage, Ernest thought, had little to do with bravado. Courage was intentional and deliberate. It was a quality that could be measured only against relative obstacles. There was no greater courage than that displayed by a terminally ill man who laughed with his family, who stumbled about a room while conducting a breathless conversation. Courage was *for* others. There was courage in starting out on a perilous adventure. When the real test occurred, would Leonard and Anneke succeed? The thought came to him and then, like Mozart's second oboe concerto, disappeared without a trace.

The night after Merlin's naval engagement, Leonard and

Anneke brought their gear on deck. Low in the sky, a full moon, which no one had thought to avoid, illuminated the action. Ernest handled the raft. He inflated it with a compressed air cylinder, which he then strapped to the rubber bottom. The rifles, flare gun, and radio were similarly stowed. The two packs went into a waterproof bag.

"Good hunting," Merlin smiled at the two and shook their hands. "You will be met here in precisely twenty-two days, unless, of course, we receive word from you. Remember the wave bands for broadcasting. Land is to the north, three miles."

"Think of it as an intimation of paradise," Ernest smiled in a faint imitation of Merlin. He added, "Come back to tell the story," and he immediately regretted the codicil.

Two crew held the raft while Leonard and Anneke boarded. The sea was quiet, with swells of several feet. They began paddling, guided by a luminescent compass strapped to Leonard's wrist. After five minutes, Leonard looked back. The *Turtle* had vanished. After a half hour, his and Anneke's arms ached. They settled on a rhythm of paddling for fifteen minutes and resting for five. They watched the moon's image dance off the gentle waves.

"Dewi Ratih," Anneke said. "Moon goddess, enchantress. Her powers are slow, continual, and victorious. She continually triumphs over Raksassa, the monstrous node that swallows her during lunar eclipses. Létoile recounted the myth. He was amused because the monster was nothing other than a projection of the earth's shadow. The story originated in South-Asian epics, but the adaptation is so bright that it can be studied in its own right." Leonard hoped that the moon's nemesis would not swallow them on the sea.

Live long enough and the world will honor you, Leonard remembered a saying of Sasaki-san's. Travel far enough in one direction and things will change. When the moon was two hours short of zenith, they heard waves breaking. From his summers on the New Jersey surf, Leonard estimated that they were within a quarter mile of shore. He wanted to see land before he fell on it. As the swells marshaled themselves for an orderly assault on the beach, the raft edged forward. A swell brought it down on a rocky outcropping. For a moment Leonard and Anneke, sitting on a fixed fulcrum, experienced the sensation of streaming through the sea, seeking to rejoin their departed compatriots. A second, smaller swell rotated the raft off the rock. The strain ripped open one of the raft's inflatable compartments. The radio, strapped to the deflated side, plunged toward the bottom at the end of a rubber membrane.

Leonard and Anneke floated in their life vests. Leonard gripped the wrecked raft, Anneke the bag with their packs, which held air. They found that the raft was completely unmanageable. It could not be coaxed in any direction. The radio was the culprit. Leonard could not haul it in. He pulled a knife from his boot and, slicing the rubber membrane, cut the radio free, in the process losing the knife. The remaining part of the raft, holding up the rifles, resembled an inflatable surf mat. Leonard climbed astride it and began paddling, with his arms, to the shore. Anneke used her time constructively by shedding her boots, taking care to string them around her neck. She quickly powered herself ahead of Leonard's clumsy bazooka. Twenty minutes put the pair of swimmers on top of the crashing surf. To Leonard's great relief, the sound indicated a beach, rather than a wall of rocks. He prepared to ride a wave to its end. The keel of his surf mat, the rifles, caught on a rock. He turned a semicircle and pitched forward into a confusion of froth, sand, and water. He struggled against the undertow and, pushed by a succeeding wave, stumbled on the beach. Anneke was standing next to the bag containing their packs. There was no sign of the surf mat or its cargo.

Leonard smiled at his impassive companion, took a last glance at the sea, and turned to face the land. They had what was necessary for the task ahead. The two walked gingerly to the forest's edge. They heard nothing. Anneke laced on her boots. They shouldered their packs and walked north by Leonard's compass, hoping to place miles between the shore and their first camp on the world's most densely populated island.

Part IV

Green World

My student years brought me into contact not only with European values but also with people from across Indonesia. I grew to feel that there could not be a single, unchanging prescription for what was true, just as beauty also took many forms. This is not to say that everything is relative and that there are no criteria for righteous living. Practice is the great sifter, winnowing grains of wisdom from a random harvest of experience. There must be something right about the laws of electricity, for we enjoy electrical lighting and telephones. Standards of physical beauty in Europe are actually not completely different from those we know here.

Soekarno, "Notes for an Autobiography," in *Political Writings*,
ed. R. Andaro (Bandung, 1979), p. 43

You must know, my dear children, how much I love you. We moved to the Indies for you, and I think that the experience gave you something special. The night is very dark as I write. No moon, and storm clouds obscure the stars. I hope that I live to see the dawn breaking and to look on you once more, smiling, with the optimism of youth. Keats is only partly right. Fame is indeed nothing, but there is some merit to honor and duty, for they give structure to a life that otherwise would be chaos. Love is honor's internal complement. It is not enough, but without it, nothing matters. Love well, and love intensely.

Jacob Witte, "Notes for an Autobiography," 1943, Witte papers,
Boerhaave Museum, Leiden

9

The Batavian Hospital

We felt an earthquake yesterday. The observatory says that it relates to the eruption of a volcano near Bandung. Reagents fell from the hospital shelves and smashed against the floor. I had to resterilise my surgical kit. But no windows broke, and no one was hurt. The Javans are not perturbed in the least. Perhaps there is something about our Western scientific outlook that makes us want to hold nature in abeyance, rather than follow its rhythms.

Christiaan Eijkman to William Osler, 23 January 1893. Osler Library, McGill University, Montreal

The clip-tailed cat deposited a small lizard under Fatah's nose, meowed, and rubbed up against his ear. Fatah had been dreaming about his first day in school as a small boy. He had walked seven kilometers over hill and valley to the gate of the school compound. He entered with the other children who seemed to know where to go and what to do. Many of them spoke languages he did not know; most had elegant clothes. Eight-year-old Fatah found a quiet corner of the garden and decided he would wait there until noon, eat his rice cake and banana, and then return home. After everything was quiet, the groundskeeper found him and led him to class.

"Hello," said Mevrouw Verwoern in Dutch, "please tell us who you are and take a place on the bench. This morning we shall hear from the Queen about the peace in Europe."

Whenever Fatah was under stress he would dream about the confusions of that day. Normally these dreams were not compounded with a wet lizard.

He got up, purring cat in one hand and rubbery lizard in the other, and shuffled into the courtyard. He found the remnants of a fish for the cat and flung the lizard over the wall into the street. The cook had just begun to stir. Fatah sat, waiting for the tub of hot water that would constitute his *mandi*, and tried to imagine what would happen in fewer than four hours.

The Japanese commandant of his hospital told him the previous evening about two Europeans who had been captured north of Tasikmalaya. One had a wound or a fever, and he would be passed to Fatah, as the resident expert in tropical diseases, after preliminary questioning.

Which kind of European? Fatah was fluent in Dutch and could get by in German. His German was improving, in fact, as he treated the occasional German submarine crew who docked at Batavia for repairs. Over the past week he had grown to like Lieutenant Schroeder, the number-one of a boat that had barely limped into harbor. He and Schroeder had spent several afternoons trying to revive a twenty-year-old X-ray machine. The Europeans Fatah had to see this morning, however, were certainly not German. Nor, he thought, could they be Dutch. The Japanese had succeeded in rounding up the former colonials.

Fatah's languages were not especially useful in dealing with the Japanese military command, who tried to communicate in Malay interspersed with English. The Japanese had installed themselves at the top of the Dutch bureaucracy, but they were unable to make sense of it. Nearly a hundred years of files and case studies at the hospital lay untouched. The expensive equipment—centrifuges, autoclaves, X-ray machines—had in the first week of occupation been shipped to Japan; the Dutch staff had been interned. Fatah, as the senior autochtone, had been named hospital regent. The promotion meant that he would be responsible for the quotidian operation of a hospital stripped of resources.

From time to time he received a bag of rice or a chicken from the new masters.

The cook placed a steaming tub in the tile bathroom next to a large cistern of cold water. Fatah showered himself with hot and cold dippers, toweled dry, and walked to the dining room where the cook had set out a bowl of soup and some fruit. As he ate, Fatah heard the city's pulse quicken. Bicycles and pushcarts began moving down his unpaved street; various kinds of waste water splashed into the open sewers. Fatah walked back to his bedroom and dressed in his uniform of white cotton. As a lecturer in tropical epidemiology, he had worn the uniform for more than a decade. The privilege was enjoyed by only a handful of Javans, and most of those who received it in other capacities—as customs officer, policeman, or meteorologist—sported Dutch jacket and cap with traditional sarung and sandals. The hospital uniform had become second nature to Fatah. Until the Japanese conquest, it identified him as the lowest of medical professionals in the Dutch institution. Since the conquest it signaled his new position of authority.

Fatah's wife had already left their bedroom to prepare the children for school. Education had continued since the conquest, although Fatah imagined that it would soon cease under the desperate measures instituted by the Japanese to increase commodity exports. His son Bambang was twelve, and Fatah hoped that he would be too young to be drafted into a labor gang. If it came to that, he would send Bambang to cousins in the countryside. Bambang possessed the elements of Arabic and Dutch, knowledge enough for whatever he would turn his hand to.

Pocketing a banana and a sesame rice-cake, Fatah set off for the hospital. As he splashed through the streets, wet from a pre-dawn thunderstorm, he heard the Islamic faithful called to morning prayer. Fatah's roots were Muslim, but he had never followed Islamic regime. His father, as head of his village, had embraced the Ethical Policy of the colonial regime, where resources were turned to local needs. Fatah remembered when running water came to the village square, and when a new steam-train line was cut into a nearby hillside. Fatah, the youngest son, had been sent to school by his father to discover how pumps and locomotives worked. He did learn something of technology, but he decided for a career in medicine when, as a boy of fifteen, he saw his father die from a sudden fever. The impotence of the village mullah in the face of disease led him directly into the Doctor-Djawa School, the forerunner of Batavia's medical school in which he now lectured. Fatah knew Quranic verses by heart, but he believed few of their injunctions. When he sought solace for confusing realities, he preferred morality plays of the Javan shadow-puppet theatre, *wayang purwa*.

Water vapor rose from the streets, as if the city had been placed in a steam oven. The sun, large and orange, rose abruptly on its predestined path. After five minutes Fatah was soaked by run-off, splash, and sweat. Sandals were his one concession to tradition. He could not understand why Europeans wore shoes. He threaded his way past merchants setting up awnings. He was almost pinned between a cart of firewood and a cage containing a few emaciated dogs. Then he stopped at the Japanese roadblock.

Four soldiers armed with rifles and bayonets stood inside a wicker barrier. When a gate opened, people passed through and submitted to an inspection. Normally the procedure deprived Fatah of a quarter hour. He waited behind the ripening cart of a refuse carrier. When his turn came, Fatah bowed before and after crossing the barrier. It was the formal bow he had learned ten years earlier when he attended a medical conference in Tokyo. He presented his hospital laissez-passer, which gave him entry virtually everywhere in the city. The sergeant, a bespeckled and reflective man in his early twenties, blinked his eyes for Fatah to pass. Sergeant Tsukahira could speak some Malay, but he generally chose not to talk at all. Just having allowed past a fish monger, he was thinking about *ayu* and *tamari-zuke*, the trout and pickles that his family served at Lake Chuzenji high in the mountains.

The roadblock restricted access to a central square. There was a loudspeaker, which generally played military music, flanked by two machine-gun emplacements. Fatah set off across the open area and on to his hospital. He was halfway across the square when he heard shouting. An agitated man tried to explain in Malay that he was late in delivering firewood. Tsukahira, barely audible, repeatedly asked him for his destination and his papers. Fatah thought it best not to look at the scene. He heard a load of sticks clatter to the ground. The delivery man had dropped the leads of his cart and fled. Tsukahira shouted what Fatah imagined was "stop" in Japanese. A rifle shot rang out. When Fatah had cleared the square, he turned to survey the roadblock.

Tsukahira was berating one of the three soldiers, who stood at attention, a thin trail of smoke rising from the muzzle of his rifle. The other two soldiers slouched nervously. The crowd at the barrier had evaporated. A man lay on the ground, moaning, twenty paces across the square.

The reflex of Dutch medical training brought Fatah to the man's side. He walked quickly, oblivious of the machine-gun crew that, he knew, was ready to shoot.

"Do not be afraid," he said to the man, "I am a doctor." The man's thigh was bleeding profusely.

"I must get to my boss or he will beat me," the man cried, "and I have nothing to eat."

"If you are quiet, I will help you. What is your name?"

"My legs are my life," the man sobbed. "Who cannot walk will starve."

Perhaps the man did not know what a doctor was. Fatah looked more closely at the wound. The bullet had cut a clean hole through the thigh muscle, and the bone had been spared. Infection would claim the man if the wound was not dressed properly. He opened the small medical case that he always carried in his uniform. He quickly bound the wound in gauze, tying off the dressing in the shadow of Tsukahira. Fatah scrambled to his feet and bowed.

"Greetings, soldier, sir," he said in Japanese. Then in Malay: "The man is hurt. I will take him to my hospital."

Tsukahira bent down and recovered Fatah's medical case. He turned over the scalpel and fingered the clamps. They were nickel-plated Solingen, acquired at great expense. He closed the case and handed it to Fatah.

"I apologize for the incident," Tsukahira began in Malay and switched to Japanese. "One of my soldiers fired without waiting for my order." Tsukahira paused, thinking about his certain censure for lack of leadership. Then he brightened. "Take care of the poor man."

Fatah understood only the apology. Tsukahira led him to the upended cart, placed the leads in Fatah's hands, and followed him back to the fallen *pengantar*, who, though not gravely wounded, lay moaning with closed eyes. Tsukahira motioned for Fatah to place the man in the cart. Fatah did so as best he could, for he was not strong and the man weighed more than he did. Tsukahira led Fatah to the front of the cart and waved him away. The senior autochthonous medical officer in the Malay Archipelago trotted off to his hospital, a brancardier pulling a moaning laborer on a makeshift gurney.

*

*   *

When he received word to report to Fatah's office in a matter of extreme urgency, Naval Lieutenant Rainald Uwe Schroeder was up to his elbows in dirt and grease, surrounded by a nest of wires, pipes, and tubes, and accompanied by two Javan assistants with whom he had, he told himself, occasional rapport.

"Where is your tape?" Schroeder muttered in German to his helpers as he tried to wrap a copper wire about a screw post. "Tép," he repeated hopefully in what he took to be Malay.

"Pléstér?" asked Harry Joyo, who held the metal cowling for the rusting pump motor that Schroeder was attempting to repair.

"He wants a bandage," Joyo spoke in Sundanese to Rusli Thalib, who sat quietly on the floor in the corridor outside the room where Schroeder poked at the innards of an obsolete French radiograph. "Must have cut himself. Better bring some alcohol, too."

How far the German had come since arriving at the hospital two weeks previously complaining of pain in his hand! After Dr Fatah set his left wrist in a cast, the German put away his pistol. Eventually, he did the same with tunic and boots. Dr Fatah was the agent of this transformation. He had taken the German to the market, to the Dutch museum of antiquities, to the botanical gardens at nearby Bogor. Joyo was glad that his boss had persuaded the foreigner to renovate an X-ray apparatus. All their best equipment had disappeared within days of the Japanese occupation. The German was learning true language and eating proper food, too. Did Germany have banana trees?

Schroeder looked up in time to see Thalib at the threshold of the small room, carrying a wad of gauze and a bottle of alcohol. He could think of no reason for the appearance of the alcohol, but he used it along with the gauze to swab the contacts of the circuit he had completed. He wanted the tape to insulate a wire where the rubber had long since cracked away. His words were close, but *tép* and *pléstér* were not *tape* or *plaster*, as they would have been in Shanghai, where he had grown up. He sighed. Speaking Malay based on his knowledge of Pidgin was like using English to fathom French nouns and verbs. Maybe he could use gauze and plaster as insulation. At least the material would keep moisture away from the leads.

"Gips," Schroder said in German, pointing to his wrist cast.

"Gips," Joyo and Thalib concurred in Malay, and Thalib ran off for a box of plaster and a mixing bowl.

Schroeder had been working in the room for two hours. He stood up and stretched. It was not yet mid-morning and still relatively comfortable, but he was soaking with sweat. The room was three meters square but it rose four meters high, and it was open at the top. Cool air flowed in the door as hot air rose up and out through a vent by the strutted collar beam in the peaked roof. He thought that the Dutch had done an admirable job of wedding modern building techniques with Javan forms—much better than the pretentious monstrosities of stone and brick erected by Europeans on their properties in Shanghai. From the Dutch presence he sensed optimistic adaptability, a genuine desire to construct a new Eurasian culture. He liked Javans, whom he found gracious and enterprising. He felt at home for the first time in more than a decade.

He mixed the plaster. Joyo and Thalib watched, wondering why the German was doctoring himself. He drenched gauze in the stuff and wrapped it around various wires. He hoped that he would be able to generate enough voltage for a discharge to produce X rays. Fatah had told him that a few photographic plates remained.

Schroeder wiped his hands on an old tunic he had used as a pillow. Then he brushed them against his trousers, already stiff with grease, dust, and insect carapace. He reached for one of three glasses of tea, which Thalib had set on the floor outside the room. He removed the metal cover and sipped without wondering about drinking hot liquid in the tropics. He had learned the rule as a boy: Tea and beer could be consumed safely anywhere. And the tea here was served European style, without the stems and leaves that he remembered from Shanghai. He smiled at his helpers.

"Soon it works," he announced in Malay.

Schroeder touched his cast. His wrist no longer hurt, and he had been working for days with both hands on the X-ray machine, ever since Fatah had shown it to him. Fatah had suspected a small fracture, but he could not be sure without an X-ray picture; fixing the machine was a way for Schroeder to diagnose his own infirmity. The project appealed to the interests of both physician and mariner. Fatah, Schroeder quickly learned, while not adverse to using machines, nevertheless had no affinity for mechanical reality. Fatah radiated a sensibility attuned to vital forces. In his view, disease flowed through an entire organism, and it could in principle be mastered by meditation.

"Look at the great storm coming our way," Fatah had pointed from the hills of Bogor toward Batavia and the sea. "It is a vast engine for cooling the earth and making it fruitful. Water falls in the hills, cascades down terraced fields, returns to the sea. Rice and fruit, fish and ducks grow in this eternal cycle. The ocean knows our needs." This was how Schroeder reconstructed Fatah's reverie, for though Fatah began and ended in German, in the middle he lapsed into Dutch. Schroeder knew this style of conversation, often used in Shanghai. With the reflex of being able to move quickly between languages and with his knowledge of English, he found that he could understand most of what Fatah said.

"Surely the atmosphere does not act for the sake of humanity," Schroeder answered. He was the atheist son of a Lutheran surgeon. He had been trained in independent thinking. He felt no affinity for the atavistic return to racial purity retailed by the political authorities in Germany. "How can it? Where are the decisions made for more rain or less rain? Do the winds speak to the ocean currents? Do the fish and the trees cast parliamentary votes for feeding us?" Schroeder paused after evoking the congress of nature, with its subversive connotation.

The irony was lost on Fatah, who, while raised with a model of consensual democracy in village affairs, was entirely innocent of the vicissitudes of republican politics in Europe. He had learned about chemistry and electricity, but he understood physical processes in terms of volition. Metallic sodium elected to combine with gases; electrons wanted to move from anode to cathode. Mechanics, however, he could not fathom. An arrow sought its target by following a trajectory that depended on any number of imponderables. How could one predict its course? That would be only for God to say if, and here Fatah interpolated his own heresy, if there was a God. For Fatah's favorite image of the world came from the Hindu mythology of the *wayang purwa*, with gods as avatars of moral qualities, with heroes facing dilemmas, and with consciousness given the kris.

"Why not?" he replied, not sure what a parliament was. "Mountains wake up and snort. The earth shakes herself. Why can't the sea also decide to intervene in our lives?"

Schroeder thought it best to test, if possible, the diagnoses of the physician for whom mountains breathed fire. The X-ray apparatus still needed attention. He sighed and set off down the corridor to see Fatah. Schroeder was, in more ways than appeared, an engineer.

In 1913 his father had shipped out with his bride to become professor at Shanghai's Paulun Hospital and coincidentally professor at the Tung-Chi University, which gave courses in German at a campus in the French Concession. Germany's smallest university ran under federal Chinese protection until 1917, when French gendarmes shut it down and transported the staff—physicians excluded—to a concentration camp. Dr Emil Wilhelm Schroeder continued to treat patients at his hospital, under French management, until the Peace sent him and his pregnant wife to the camp as well. There Rainald was born in 1919. Within a year the German professors continued their vocation at a new campus in the Shanghai suburb of Woosung. After a decade they were in charge of Shanghai's finest institution of higher learning. Rainald Schroeder grew up in Woosung. By age twelve, when he went to school in Germany, he was comfortable with German, English, and Chinese. His passion was machinery. He haunted the laboratories with giant engines, which German steamship companies had given to the university. He learned how each of them worked—their tolerances, their capabilities, their pulse. For to a trained mechanic, the sound of an engine signals its health. Rainald's father did not discourage this inclination, since he was a confirmed biological materialist. If only they had more biological lubricants and finer needles, he told his son.

In Berlin Schroeder boarded with a maiden aunt while he attended the Französisches Gymnasium, a bilingual French-German bastion of democratic values that had been founded for Hugenot refugees. He graduated in 1938 and went on to the local university, studying (as he had known he would study for many years) physics. His first lecture course was taught by a pompous abomination who elaborated *Deutsche Physik*, which dealt with the reputed virtues of politically correct thinkers. He accordingly spent most of his time at the TH, or institute of technology, in the suburb of Charlottenburg, where he audited courses on electrotechnology. Electrons might ask if their conceiver were Jewish. Machines needed only to work, and it was rumored that Himmler had personally allowed certain Jews to work in vital engineering posts. There was an absolute measure for the efficiency of a power train and the speed of an airplane. By 1939 it had become extremely difficult for Schroeder to avoid serving in the military. He wanted nothing to do with armies of goose-stepping zombies. He volunteered for the navy.

By virtue of his education, Schroeder became a communications officer. He was posted to Kiel and assigned to a desk monitoring British broadcasts. He thought that he could ride out the war there. But in September 1943 he was transferred to U-137, a pre-war submarine that had been refitted for transoceanic activity. In principle he might have declined the new posting. In practice such insubordination would have resulted in immediate exile to the Baltic front.

U-137 left Kiel with first officer Schroeder on board. It avoided the shipping lanes, traveling to Lisbon without incident. Schroeder felt comfortable in the boat. The machinery seemed admirable and reliable, much more so than the crew, to whom he relayed commands. The men did not dislike him, as he was neither unreasonable nor arrogant. They called him *der junge Seher*, the young seer, for the way he listened to the sound of the engines and the radio. When the boat left Lisbon and the captain informed them of their destination, Schroeder understood the reason for his presence on board.

"We have the honor to constitute our nation's squadron in China," the captain said.

They were lucky to have reached Batavia, Schroeder concluded. They had circled Africa, robbing food and oil along the way. When they were picked up by a Japanese destroyer, they had been drifting for four days south of Sumatra, out of fuel, short on rations, and unable to control the boat's rudder. The Japanese sent over a bag of rice and towed them to port. When he disembarked, Schroeder slipped on the dock, landing on his left wrist. He watched the crew and the Javan dockhands trying to reëstablish communication between rudder and helm until pain drove him to Fatah's hospital, down the corridors of which he now strode in filthy undress, followed by two correctly attired Javan assistants.

*

* *

Leonard Ranov stood in a small room. He contemplated the iron bed and straw mattress, where he had slept, and the washstand with metal bowl, whose water he had drunk. There was nothing to do, and he had been awake for several hours. He found consolation in reviewing his progress.

Since his and Anneke's capture, two days previously, the two had been in transit to Batavia, or as it was called by indigenes and by the new Asian masters, Jakarta. The first day by foot to a narrow-gauge railway, then on a succession of slow trains over the mountains and finally down to the port city. He stuck to his line: shipwrecked and befriended by a colonial girl. His dog tags pointed to the US army, but his ability in Japanese gave pause to an ascending hierarchy of inquisitors, from the corporal who discovered the bivouac to the colonel who finally sent the two on to the general command. The Japanese had separated him from Anneke at the Jakarta station.

The present is dark, the future is uncertain, only the past is uncomplicated, Leonard thought. Turning away from dwelling on how much of the past he would be able to complicate, Leonard pressed all his attention toward his surroundings. His person stank. His clothes were stiff with sweat. He was contemplating the door when Fatah walked in.

Fatah scanned Leonard's face, focusing on a gash that ran from his forehead across his nose to his right jaw. The result of a wake-up call on one of the train legs, the wound was inflamed, and dried blood clung to hair and skin everywhere. The prisoner would be in trouble soon unless he received medical attention. Was that why the Japanese had brought him here?

Leonard considered the spry Javan physician. He smiled faintly and said hello in Japanese, English, French, and German.

"You are at the hospital of the Batavia medical school," Fatah announced in halting German—pointedly using the Dutch name for his institution. "I am the director." He called through the door for alcohol, gauze, and soup. "You are hurt. I will help you."

Leonard looked past Fatah at the open door. Two Japanese guards were visible. "Thank you," he said, and then added, "Are those your soldiers?"

Fatah did not reply immediately. Through a Dutch translator, the Japanese commandant had explained the situation of the two European prisoners as soon as Fatah arrived. Fatah stood at attention; he had had no time to change his tunic, stained with the blood and sweat of the morning's exertions. Why so much fuss about two Europeans who had avoided detection until now? Perhaps the American officer had survived the sinking of his ship. Perhaps he was a spy, as his medical kit and shoes suggested. Why involve the hospital?

"He carried this." Commandant Katsuro Omori pointed to a lead tube on his desk. "It is a medicine against infection." Omori looked down at a report in Japanese. "Tell us how it works and make more of it."

In his office, Fatah translated the tube's instructions into Dutch. The substance was called penicillin. It was an experimental drug to be applied on open wounds. He went to the library, whose state of disarray of two years—between the fall of the Netherlands and the Japanese invasion—had been preserved by the hospital's new owners. To economize on freight costs, medical journals turned up in annual or semi-annual shipments, and the last shipments to arrive—those for 1940—lay under a pile of dust in a corner. Fatah looked through the index to *Lancet* and found Chain and Florey's description of penicillin as a "chemotherapeutic agent." Fatah realized that it would take him days to translate the article, and even then he could not be sure of obtaining a correct understanding. He had to ask Schroeder, and he needed to see the prisoner.

The prisoner. Fatah eyed Leonard. "My staff do not have guns," he finally replied. "The soldiers belong to the new owners."

Fatah's assistants returned with alcohol and gauze. Leonard did not object as Fatah cleaned his wound, which had become infected, but he winced when he saw Schroeder appear at the doorway. Schroeder wore a relatively clean tunic, unbuttoned over filthy undershirt and trousers. There was no mistaking the swastikas.

"Entschuldigung," Fatah offered, mistaking Leonard's reaction for pain, which there was plenty of in any case.

Schroeder considered the patient. He knew that there were German colonists in Indonesia, but their allegiances were even more questionable than his own. Perhaps here was someone who could help him with Dutch and Malay.

Fatah finished working on the sepsis. No dressing would hold up to animated discussion, which would surely transpire during interrogations to come.

"Infection is a danger," he explained to Leonard as he handed the gauze and alcohol to an assistant. "Your wound must be cleaned every four hours." He paused and took the tube of penicillin from his breast pocket. "Shall I apply this?"

Three men dressed in impossible clothes considered their situation. Schroeder sensed an unusual circumstance in the patient's military-style clothes and in Fatah's peculiar question. Fatah realized that he should have spoken longer with Schroeder beforehand—he had intended to ask for his help in translating the *Lancet* article, although now perhaps he could ask the prisoner directly about the ointment in German. Leonard knew that penicillin was a strategic product, and its present form as a topical ointment could be of great importance. Nothing would be gained in denying its utility, especially since the Javan doctor knew something about it. He nodded, and then recalled that gestures were insufficient. Body language is culture-specific. On Java, people did not shake their head to indicate assent or disagreement. He remembered one of Anneke's first lessons. He must never place his hands on his hips or wave—the first gesture was defiant, the second vulgar.

"Bitte."

Fatah took a small amount of ointment and applied it along Leonard's wound. Schroeder's sudden appearance eliminated all possibility of strategy. It made no difference to Fatah if Europeans who spoke a common language were killing each other in a distant corner of the world. He simply needed to find out about the medicine, and he saw no reason why the prisoner would not respond to the questions of another European. Fatah turned to Schroeder.

"Lieutenant, please ask the prisoner about this medicine." And then he added, "Commandant Omori wants to know."

Schroeder took the tube from Fatah. He neither liked nor understood Omori.

"In my father's time your wound would have guaranteed a brilliant military career," he offered to Leonard in German. "But I think that you are not a German officer."

Leonard recited his name and rank. "The Japanese gave me this," he pointed to his face. Schroeder's wrist-cast, hair, and trousers smelled of oil, glistened with spots of flux and solder, and exuded plaster dust. It was not usual for an officer to fix machines. The German was doing something that could not be confided to Japanese or Javans, or to a technician. Leonard guessed that there might be a temporary advantage in appealing to the man's sense of superiority.

Schroeder, however, did not feel at all superior to those around him. He was engaged in a recreation, rebuilding the X-ray machine. He did not understand the Japanese, whose reserve was entirely foreign to the rich expansiveness of the Chinese he had known in Shanghai. He was intrigued by the prisoner's reply in German, which he took as a touch of arrogance.

"What is this stuff?" Schroeder studied the label.

"Medicine to kill bacteria. It comes from bread mold."

It was possible, Schroeder thought. He remembered his father's treatment of syphilitics with Salvarsan. Diseases could be cured by chemical means, as Paracelsus had dreamed. Was the new ointment standard issue for American soldiers, along with iodine and condoms? Perhaps, assuming that there was any therapeutic value in it.

"Yes, certainly." He added, "You may relax. I have no authority over you. How do you come by your German?"

"School," Leonard made an extra effort not to lapse into Yiddish accent and cadence. "One cannot study physics without knowing German." This time Leonard's effort at establishing rapport brought raised eyebrows from Schroeder.

"Perhaps we will have the opportunity to discuss things of mutual interest," Schroeder added flatly. But here was something unexpected.

In Fatah's office, Schroeder read the article from *Lancet* and then explained it to Fatah. It was more than interesting. He urged Fatah to conduct a clinical trial on the prisoner's wound and to analyze, as best he could, the ointment.

"Why bread mold, and what kind of bread?" Fatah asked him.

"Probably wheat, and possibly related to ergot, a traditional European hallucinogenic."

"There is no wheat here, but I will see if spoiled rice cakes can kill bacteria." Fatah remembered the high regard of his teachers for Christiaan Eijkman's research, near these rooms, on beriberi. He could begin a research program like Eijkman's.

A physicist might help with the X-ray machine, Schroeder thought. He wondered what an American physicist was doing on Java.

*

* *

Commandant Omori did not relish taking charge of the two prisoners. Why could the soldier not be sent to a military prison? Why bother with the woman? He had orders to prepare the soldier for interrogation—that meant repairing his horrible-looking facial wound. The woman would be kept here, just in case her testimony was required. He posted two guards at Leonard's room and sent Anneke to the laundry.

"The woman is your responsibility," he told Iti Besar, the matron in charge of washing, through a translator. "You will be shot if she leaves the hospital." In this way Omori passed his unhappiness to a subordinate. The Japanese were worse than the Dutch, Besar concluded. The Dutch were open to negotiation. The Japanese indicated conditions.

Anneke followed Besar into a large room on the ground floor. It opened into the back courtyard of the hospital. There stood a shed that served everywhere on Java as a kitchen. The laundry was cooked clean in an enormous pot. Nearby stones served to scrub out stubborn stains. A network of lines dried the result. Anneke labored at washing and scrubbing along with other Javan women, from six in the morning until one in the afternoon. She dined with them on rice, soup (with whatever might be in the pot, whether fish, fowl, or reptile), and fruit or vegetables; it was a good meal, she concluded, for they ate what the Japanese ate. But it was her only meal, and she learned to eat as much of it as she could. Hot tea was freely available throughout the day—a practical necessity to prevent dehydration. After the midday meal Anneke washed the hospital floors until dusk. Then Besar locked her for the night in a closet filled with the day's dirty laundry.

Anneke thought that she might escape from her laundry cell. It was built of beams and stucco with a ventillation window too narrow to accept a person. She climbed up to the ceiling on the first night, only to find a perimeter of solid construction. With a metal tool something might be possible, but she did not know how much time she had to chip away.

She had an advantage in language. She understood much of the continual chatter and gossip that provided rhythm for the day's laundry. Nothing broke it, for Muslim women did not have an excuse to abandon temporal concerns, five times daily, for prayers. Since she could speak Malay and carried out the least desirable tasks—risking serious burns by extracting the laundry before tipping the soiled water—the women saw no reason not to treat her correctly. After a few days she learned that Leonard was being held in isolation under orders of Director Fatah. The director had coincidentally begun to act strangely. He had placed various kinds of baked cakes in a laboratory, a banquet for insects; these he inspected several times a day, sometimes sampling one or another moldering plate with a fine knife. He and a German officer spent increasing amounts of time together, sometimes entire afternoons; they talked incessantly.

Anneke liked Leonard—a month can be a year in the land of affection—but she tried to push that feeling away. On the eighth day of captivity, one of her co-workers reported having seen Leonard—a European with a pink scar cutting diagonally across his face—talking with the German in a corridor; the two men spent several hours working on an old medical machine. Anneke could learn only that the machine was located not far from the laundry area. She adjusted her afternoon floor mopping to finish up there (the Japanese guards seemed to have no interest in her routine, although they were careful to supervise her nightly incarceration), but she saw no Europeans. She could not understand why no one had interrogated her.

"Do you miss your husband?" Iti Besar asked her one morning. Whether from politeness or insouciance, she spoke as if Anneke were married. "He is now healthy and works with the German officer."

"Yes, thank you. It is so cruel to be apart. We have done nothing wrong."

"The Japanese say that they have liberated us from you. I see only that I must work harder and have less to eat. Many who have done nothing wrong have been imprisoned; others have been detained and deported. Where are you from?"

"Bandung. My family needs me there." It was an attempt to gain sympathy, and, if she had to, Anneke could talk for days about Bandung. But as soon as she pronounced the half-truth, she felt it to be a mistake. The Japanese, if they found out, would expose the lie. "But I worry that they will be hurt if this is known to the Japanese."

Besar smiled, "It is not right to keep husband and wife apart." She brought her hands together in a gesture of thanks and then turned away to begin another conversation.

*
*   *

"Hand me that wrench."

Schroeder placed the tool in Leonard's outstretched hand. He was flat on his back, wedged under the X-ray machine. He finished bolting the Gaede molecular-diffusion vacuum pump to its vibration-absorbing base. He slid free and stood up. The exertion channeled sweat down the rivulet of his swollen facial scar, by now partly obscured by nearly a fortnight's reddish-blond beard. He drained a glass of lukewarm tea.

"Let's see how hard it is."

Schroeder turned on a small generator. The pump was considerably quieter than it had been before the German stripped it under Leonard's supervision. The Pirani gauge read less than 10^{-6} mm of mercury, three orders of magnitude better than when they had started and more than sufficient for generating useful X rays. Benefitting from Leonard's knowledge of vacuum-pump technology, Schroeder hoped to be able to produce X-ray pictures of great clarity.

"All modern physics depends on motors and plumbing conduits," Leonard had offered to his German companion in English, "but it is not merely that. Without mechanical technology we could carry out no experiments, but something larger tells us which instrument to build. The same is true of observations, although maybe less so. The point is that the hardware acts as a sobering counterweight to idle speculation. Experiment chastens theory. The problem with the Americans is that they think experiment replaces theory. They imagine that science is nothing but applied technology."

Sometimes the two men spoke English, sometimes German. There was everything to be gained by this kind of conversation. Both speakers enjoyed working together on the X-ray machine; their talents were complementary. Both believed that scientific activity could not proceed without a set of values, an ethical predisposition. This affinity, coupled with Schroeder's detached approach to the Japanese, led Leonard to suspect that the German was ambivalent about the state whose uniform he wore. He would need support for passage to a prisoner-of-war camp, instead of being shot as a spy. Leonard had noticed right away that Schroeder was unarmed.

Schroeder had recovered from the shock of Leonard's German. After all, it was indeed impossible to know modern physics without German. Furthermore, and most interesting, the American ascribed American theoretical poverty to an inability to ponder publications by Einstein, Bohr, Pauli, and Heisenberg.

Schroeder suspected that Leonard had spoken German at home (he remembered reading once about the Saint Louis Hegelians—German émigrés who became America's first serious philosophers in nineteenth-century Missouri). Leonard's English was entirely fluent, in what Schroeder mistook to be flat, full-mouthed American twang; in fact Leonard's English delivery had slowed as a result of learning Japanese and speaking with Anneke. Schroeder thought it improbable that Leonard had left Germany after 1933, for such a trajectory seemed excluded by Leonard's apparent openness.

"Theory is all grey, friend," Schroeder repeated his favorite nineteenth-century epigram. "Machines are the only certainty. The theoreticians may speculate about this or that, and the laboratory notebook may record thus and such numbers to the best of the human eye, but only the machines know if nature is being sounded out in the right way. We have given life to them, and by this act we assert, as a species, our uniqueness in the universe. Machines have a spirit of their own. And their spirit defines what we know."

"Yet are there not revolutions in thinking?" Leonard asked his co-worker. "Think about Copernicus—despite current propaganda, he was certainly not German—whose new synthesis emerged from observations made by instruments that had been available for hundreds of years. Think about electromagnetism and radio waves, the light quantum." And before he had a chance to reflect: "What about the artificial disintegration of the atom? All these developments depended less on new instruments than on theoretical insight."

"Not quite." In secondary school Schroeder had read a great deal about history of science, above all the writings of Karl Sudhoff, a brilliant professor who, as a fading octogenarian, joined the Nazi party. "Throughout the medieval period there was a slow evolution in the design and precision of astronomical instruments. Islamic technicians invented a universal astrolabe, useful for all latitudes. A Provençal Jew invented the cross-staff.

A Portuguese navigator discovered how to interpolate between the markings of a dial, an instrumental development leading directly to Tycho Brahe's zig-zag scale on his mural quadrant and then to the Vernier. The Ottomans produced the torquetum. Perhaps there are sudden changes with new instruments—the telescope, the electrical machine—but most of our knowledge of nature derives from slow, continual improvements in mechanics. Here is true scientific progress. And from this perspective there was no medieval decline in learning: Islamic astronomers substantially improved on Ptolemy's instruments.

"The fact of an instrument gives life to new ideas. That is what happened when Galileo pointed the telescope skyward. Yes, that is how absolute space and time disappeared. It was not Einstein's genius, but rather Michelson's interferometer. The light quantum came directly out of men building better light bulbs in a laboratory for industrial physics; the X-ray tube now before us came from the tinkerings of an obscure, middle-aged physicist; electron diffraction was shown in an American industrial laboratory. The splitting of the atom has nothing to do with theory. It came about because men with dirty fingernails played around with particle accelerators."

Leonard did not know why Schroeder had a good command of English, nor why indeed he was in Batavia. Could he, too, be seeking the mountain of uranium? Leonard remembered that Joliot-Curie's reports of artificial nuclear disintegration appeared in print in 1939; he had read the English summaries in 1940, when the University of Wyoming finally received its semiannual shipment of *Nature*. The notion of an atomic bomb was not secret. There was nothing to lose by continuing the conversation.

"Do you think that the splitting energies can be tamed?"

It had begun to rain, the beginning of a short but intense storm. The two lieutenants could hear a barrage of drops pounding the outside wall.

"Perhaps with time," Schroeder answered. "I rather imagine that the effect will be used for an explosive device first. The general staff is possibly now considering how to place an atomic bomb on a rocket aimed at New York." He saw Leonard's shocked expression. "And why not? The machine has always seized war as a means of evolving more rapidly. But if the reports I read in school are accurate, this time the machine's pride will be its undoing. Radiation from the apparatus before us is a minor nuisance; radiation from an atomic bomb—not to mention all the artificial, disintegrating isotopes produced as trash—could make the survivors of an atomic explosion envy the dead. What is the point of victory if New York and Berlin are luminous graveyards?"

What was the point of it all? It would not take long before the bomb was constructed and used. The bomb mounted on rockets, aimed in ballistic trajectories. True rockets, carrying their own propellant and oxidizer. A rain of terror. Here was the end of the project that Leonard worked for. He thought about Niels Bohr disappearing through the gate at Los Alamos. Did the pope of physics abandon all hope as he passed through those portals?

"Let us direct a bit of radiation against my wrist."

This had been the point of the exercise in repairing the X-ray machine. Before Leonard's arrival, Schroeder had wired the machine into the hospital's main generator. He now closed the circuit, dimming lights in the corridors and in the main yard. To the sound of *qui vives* and soldierly activity on the part of the Japanese guards, he produced a glass plate that he had prepared with silver emulsion earlier in the day. He inserted it in a wall box. He placed his hand between the box and the old Coolidge X-ray tube. Unable to move behind a lead screen (and without warning Leonard), he tapped a switch for an X-ray pulse. Then he shut off the generator link. The room's electric light bulb blazed once more.

"Come with me to develop the plate."

Leonard trotted after Schroeder through the kitchen and the old interns' mess, by a machine shop, to another wing of the hospital. They passed two men, whether orderlies or surgeons Leonard could not say, who showed no interest in the Europeans.

Leonard followed the German into a small darkroom furnished with running water. In the red glow of a low-wattage bulb, he watched as the plate went through developer and fixer. Schroeder's skeletal wrist shone white, the color of uranium metal.

"An accessible source of high-grade uranium would result in Armageddon," Leonard said softly in English.

Schroeder had turned on the yellow incandescent light and was scrutinizing the photograph of his wrist. He counted five weeks from his fall. There was no sign of a fracture. He would show the picture to Fatah, but he resolved to cut off the cast whatever medical advice he received.

"The machine works well," Schroeder said in English. "We work well together." He looked at Leonard, studying his pink scar. "We are both healing. Health cannot be taken for granted in the tropics. Yes, it is always the problem of refinement, obtaining pure chemical elements. Civilization is built around them—iron, copper, nickel, silver, gold, platinum, aluminum. Machines and commerce are unthinkable without them. It shall be the death of us. Humanity's future lies here, in Asia."

"But if Asia provides the uranium, we would all live under a *pax japonica*—Japan would expand to fill the vacuum left by the crippled nations of Europe and America." Leonard paused. "I know where there is a great supply of uranium on Java."

"Very interesting," Schroeder said to Leonard. "Now I must return you to your quarters."

On the way back to his guarded room, Leonard saw Anneke bent over on hands and knees, at the far end of the corridor, scrubbing the floor with slow, methodical strokes. He had thought of her often, during his captivity. If the German swallowed the uranium line, would he also take charge of her?

*

* *

Penicillin killed bacteria. Of that Fatah was sure. The ointment put an end to bacterial colonies in petri dishes, and it substantially sped the healing of the prisoner's wound. Fatah was having less success with attempts to grow the mold. Rice cakes in the tropics would not replicate what leavened wheat bread produced in England. He plunged into mycology with enthusiasm. The hospital library had a good collection of publications about molds, acquired before the war through the benevolence of the great Dutch mycologists. He finished entering the latest of his analyses in a notebook. He would have to travel to Bogor and consult with the botanists there. Antibacterial toxins must surely be secreted by one of the molds or slimes that afflicted tropical agriculture.

"Hello, Doctor."

Schroeder entered Fatah's office. He shared Fatah's interest in the penicillin project, reading him German summaries of English publications and listening as Fatah described his experimental results. Penicillin confirmed Schroeder's faith in a mechanical explanation for biological processes. Here was the clearest kind of cause and effect, like a steam engine or a pendulum clock. Whereas the German naïvely assimilated the remarkable result, Fatah's organicist predilection led him to ask for an explanation. The world was a theatre for struggles between good and evil forces, a gigantic *wayang purwa*, with an essentially harmonious story line. Fatah found his worldview confirmed by the alliance between humankind and such a low form of life. The mold carried a kris with magical, curative powers. Leonard's ointment provided the German and the Javan with hours of discussion, after which each man felt vindicated. The most significant scientific results may be understood in many ways.

The American prisoner was the key to the penicillin question. Fatah had kept him from Japanese inquisition on medical grounds. Coherent with the political fiction of freeing Javans from Dutch rule, the Japanese had invested Fatah with responsibility for medical decisions. The authority had seemed innocuous enough. Once granted, however, it could not easily be revoked. Commandant Omori found himself caught between the almost daily requests for information about the prisoner's health from superiors in intelligence and Fatah's firm insistence that the prisoner's wound would not allow him to put up with an interrogation. Now that the prisoner was moving freely about the hospital, the charade would soon be over.

"Here is my X ray. The machine works fine." Fatah held the photograph up to the window.

"Pretty good," Fatah announced. "It has healed as if it was never broken." Which it might never really have been, Fatah thought. "Let me remove the plaster." Schroeder placed his cast on Fatah's table. Fatah split it open with a scalpel from his medical case.

"The prisoner knows something of great importance," Schroeder began, flexing his wrist. Fatah nodded. "Not medical. There is a strategic reserve on Java that would interest the Japanese. It is in our interest—yours and mine—for my people to find it first." Fatah waited for an explanation. "It is a metal that is the source of great energy, much greater than coal. It is a radioactive cousin of radium."

Fatah knew about radium. From his student days he saw Dutch physicians treat various cancers with radium needles. These were inserted into or near tumors, sometimes kept in place for days by monstrous collars. The hospital possessed about a milligram of radium in all. The Japanese had commandeered it along with other desirable equipment. Fatah was not clear where radium came from and how it was refined, but his attention focused on the possibility of a local substitute.

"The Japanese will enslave Javans to mine the metal," Schroeder continued. "None of it will remain here. If Germans have a say in the matter, however, it will be otherwise. A large German presence here would serve as a counterweight to Japanese autocracy." It was a feeble argument, Schroeder knew, yet he believed it.

Before he left Germany, Schroeder had spoken with an old

physics professor of his, who had been seconded to work in something called the U-Association; he mentioned that he would be looking into an extraordinary new energy source. Schroeder had thought of it as an appropriate title for a club of aging university scientists. He realized now that the U-Association had to be a uranium research group. A mountain of uranium would bring the scientists to Java, and there would be jurisdictional disputes with the Japanese over mining the ore. Uncertainty would benefit an oppressed nation. The last thing a conquered people wanted was an efficient bureaucracy.

Fatah wondered about autocracy, a word he had never heard. Schroeder was his only contact with Germany. If all Germans were like him, things could only improve with their arrival. He liked and trusted the naval officer. He smiled.

"Suppose we go off with the prisoner to find this deposit."

Fatah did not question Schroeder's proposition. The two Europeans spoke fluent German. Perhaps the American was really in sympathy with Germany. Perhaps the German wanted to help the American escape. Perhaps the American was lying. None of that was his concern.

"They will not allow it," Fatah said after several moments of reflection.

"The Japanese will respect the proposal of a German officer," Schroeder said flatly, "especially if you counter-certify it." Fatah frowned. "Let me try," Schroeder added quickly. "There is nothing to lose if you and I probe the limits of our prestige and authority." He stretched his fingers and made a fist with his liberated arm.

*

*   *

Leonard Ranov and Rainald Uwe Schroeder walked out the main doors of the hospital. It was the hottest part of the day. Water, evaporating from a morning thundershower, hung in the air. There

was almost no ambient activity. The hospital exuded postpran-
dial torpor, and other residents in the city who could afford it
were also resting after their main meal.

Schroeder had chosen this time to conduct Leonard out of
the city. The Japanese guards would be less inclined to question
the action after a big meal. He had arranged for a truck from the
dock area to wait for him beyond the central checkpoint. Bringing a vehicle closer to the hospital would call attention to the
operation. The hospital was not, after all, a place of involuntary
confinement. It seemed likely that the prisoner could walk to
freedom.

The plan was entirely without risk, Schroeder had concluded.
What could go wrong? If they were refused permission to exit,
the American would return to Japanese custody and he would be
banished to his submarine. If they did succeed in finding the
uranium deposit, Schroeder's career would be made.

From his office window, Fatah watched the two Europeans
set out. He thought that the ruse could not work, but he had
signed a discharge paper for the American. Because it had not
been counterstamped by Omori, Fatah imagined that the Japanese guards would turn the pair back at the compound gate. He
did not know that Leonard had added a line in Japanese, to the
effect that he was placed in the German's charge. Leonard ended
the vertical sentence with Omori's name, copied from a stamp on
one of Schroeder's transfer orders.

At this moment, too, Anneke paused in a doorway. She saw
the two officers. After several seconds she recognized Leonard's
gait. It was a dramatic scene, but to what end? What were Germans doing in Batavia? Why had Leonard gone over to them?
And what would become of her?

Leonard walked half a pace behind Schroeder. He composed his face in what he hoped was a neutral, submissive stare,
even though he knew that the Japanese did not understand Western body language. He had shaved his beard for the occasion,
hoping that a visible expression would make him seem less re-

markable. But now the pink line of his scar stood out even more.

The pair stopped before the sentry. Schroeder saluted and presented the release form. Leonard bowed deeply. In a moment of panic he remembered that he had not instructed his companion in disarming etiquette. Then he thought that perhaps it was best for Schroeder to behave as a foreign boor. Authority radiated from self-assured actions. Nervous inattention signaled trouble in any language.

The sentry scanned the paper and bowed. He said, "I consult."

Schroeder, who understood no Japanese, took that for free passage and set off. Leonard followed in his slipstream. He knew that their progress could be challenged in a moment, but hesitation was certainly fatal. Confusion on the part of the guard detail, if it lasted several minutes, would allow them to reach the far side of the plaza and the safety of the German crew.

Leonard was sweating profusely as they traced a chord across the plaza—close to the machine-gun emplacement there. His eyes stung, but he thought not to wipe them. Dark stains spread from under Schroeder's arms across the back of his wool tunic. The German had chosen to wear his pistol—he possessed no baton, a recognized symbol of authority in Asia. The pistol-belt and shoulder-strap turned his torso into a sea of salt and water. How could he have been sent to the tropics without suitable clothes? Schroeder looked straight ahead. He caught sight of a small truck, besides which four crewmen were standing. They had rifles. He calculated that it would take two minutes to reach them. He walked faster. Leonard followed.

Loud and animated discussion emanated from the hospital's sentry post. The duty officer demanded to know why the men had been allowed to leave without verbal confirmation from the commandant's office. He sent a soldier into the hospital compound and shouted after the departing Europeans to halt pending verification. Schroeder continued on his course. Leonard kept walking.

"Halt, or I shoot," the officer shouted across the plaza. Leonard understood and stopped. Schroeder did not. Fatah and Anneke saw Leonard standing as if he were an ornament of the plaza.

"Stop, now," Leonard spoke out. Schroeder continued on his preconceived trajectory.

The order to fire came moments later. Leonard dropped to the ground as Sergeant Tsukahira, perched under the plaza's fountain, found the receding Schroeder in his rifle's sights. Leonard heard a single shot and looked ahead to see Schroeder crumple forward. The German crew witnessed his forehead arcing out in a red and white geyser. Boots clattered across one of Jakarta's main squares to watch blood form a batik on the ground.

10

Star-Gazer

Do you remember the time we all had a picnic at the observatory? We drove there in an automobile. The Létoiles met us, and we sat in their rose garden. Anneke ran after butterflies. Mother played the harpsichord. I droned on about cosmic rays. The memory of these things is what remains. My children, when you read this, remember. I love you.

Jacob Witte, "Notes for an Autobiography," 1943, Witte papers,
Boerhaave Museum, Leiden

The train yawed gently as it started across the trestle, the first of a score of trestles on the line from Jakarta to Bandung. Fatah's wife enveloped her two children in a large batik shawl. She and they were asleep. Fatah, sitting on the same bench, also slept fitfully, his hand cradled around the kris protruding awkwardly from his belt. A large, European-style valise was on the seat facing them.

Leonard was awake and alert in the dark. He sat several rows behind the Fatahs, Anneke at his side, also wrapped in batik, also asleep. Leonard squirmed uncomfortably in Schroeder's grease-stained tunic. The temperature had fallen as they climbed into central Java's mountainous spine, but he continued to sweat. Although he and Schroeder had looked each other in the eye levelly, the German's upper body had been thinner. Leonard thought that if he moved suddenly, he might split out the tunic's seams. A holstered Luger completed his costume.

From time to time Leonard carefully stroked Anneke's hair,

which was longer now than he remembered. Apart from a two-day walk in the Javan forest, they had spent little time alone. People were particles suspended in a vast plenum, pushed this way and that by Brownian movement. He and she had been brought together by chance, separated by misfortune, and installed here by the Javan benefactor who just then woke with a start at the train's new nose-to-tail jangle.

Fatah was going home. He savored his good fortune for a few seconds before reflecting on the circumstances that led him to it. When Schroeder died on the plaza, the tether binding him to his hospital stretched and broke. The Japanese administration was a grotesque parody of Dutch rule. The Dutch would not have visited arbitrary violence on Javan and European alike. The Japanese, he thought, were pirates, stealing anything of apparent value in the name of a war against European masters. The freedom heralded by the Japanese occupation was slavery. Why had he not seen this before? The daily degradation of deep bows to Japanese soldiers, the short supply of food, the restricted personal mobility—all these signs pointed in one direction.

A *dalang* spoke when Fatah witnessed Schroeder's death: *You will no longer serve the Japanese.* As two guards trooped the American back to his hospital room, Fatah sent an orderly home with a message for his wife and children to meet him at the train station in three hours; they were going to his brother's house near Bandung—a possibility they had discussed intermittently over the preceding months. Fatah would take the American with him. Together they would look for the mountain of uranium.

Commandant Omori had summoned Fatah soon after Leonard arrived back in safekeeping. Omori was in an awkward position. His guards had given the command to fire on the German, but the fatal shot came from the city's military police. He had not authorized the American's release. Fatah blamed it on Schroeder. The two Europeans had become friends—Omori had surely seen signs of their friendship—and the German planned the escape. The Germans were allies of the Japanese. How could a simple Javan physician refuse the wish of a German officer?

"You are no longer associated with this hospital," Omori told Fatah through an interpreter. "Leave by dark. Before you go, clean up the German's body." Tomorrow he would deliver the American prisoner to the general command, and the episode would be closed. He had completely forgotten about Anneke Witte.

In his office, Fatah considered what to take with him on his journey. Into a large bag he placed a Dutch anatomy, the German translation of Osler's *Principles and Practice of Medicine*, a Dutch-English dictionary, and a Dutch road map of Java. He added his collection of surgical clamps and retractors, his supply of morphine, bottles of iodine and alcohol. He had barely finished when a Japanese soldier entered without ceremony and led him by the arm to the room where Schroeder's body lay.

Fatah removed the corpse's pistol and tunic. He sponged the face and upper torso. The bullet had entered about an inch below the crown of the skull. The exit hole in the forehead, about three inches in diameter, had drained the entire frontal lobe. Apart from that horrible wound, Schroeder seemed to be asleep. Two flies entered the cranial cavity. For a moment Fatah watched them. Then he wrapped the pistol in the bloody tunic and set off down the corridor toward his office. He made an unscheduled stop in the X-ray room, where Schroeder had spent a good part of his last days. There Fatah found a grease-stained tunic with German insignias that, worn with the pistol, would transform the American into a German.

Sitting in his office, Fatah considered his future. In his brother's village, he would be a prestigious healer, a *dokter djawa*, as colonial medical graduates had been known since the time of his grandfather; his family would live better. The immediate future was less clear. He could get the American on the train to Bandung with Schroeder's identity card—to a Javan or a Japanese soldier, one clean-shaven Westerner looked pretty much like another. He hoped that the scar would be understood as a war wound. By the time of their arrival in Bandung, however, the Japanese would have alerted all train stations of the American's escape. The American would have to jump off the train before it pulled into the station.

Fatah had to accompany his family to their place of refuge. How would the American—knowing neither Dutch nor any local language—be able to join him? If the American were arrested, the Japanese would begin looking nearby for the sacked physician. There was no way around it: He would take along the Dutch woman.

At 5:00 Fatah filled three drinking glasses and carried them on a salver to Leonard's cell. The Japanese guards squirmed uncomfortably. They stood straighter when Fatah arrived. With a deep bow, Fatah offered them the drinks. They did not accept immediately, as Fatah suspected. He placed the salver on the floor and picked up a glass, inviting them to join him. They looked at each other and accepted the remaining two glasses.

"Kampei," Fatah proclaimed, and drained his glass of water. The guards drained theirs of grain alcohol. They smiled. Fatah collected the glasses and returned to his office. In fifteen minutes the guards would be unconscious, drugged with arsenic.

Leonard followed Fatah's instructions for assuming Schroeder's persona. Fatah conducted him to the laundry room. The two collected Anneke, near the end of her *ménage*. Fatah placed both foreigners in a cart under a heap of clean linen. He wheeled the cart to a side gate, which he unlocked. Down the street, around a corner, and the three renegades headed for the railway station. There, outside the Japanese cordon, Fatah met his wife and daughters. Throwing on a *kain kebaya*, Anneke quickly became the Fatah family governess. The party passed to the sentry, where Leonard waved their identity papers and explained that they were traveling to Solo. Fatah realized that Leonard could speak intelligible Japanese.

"Pass on," the guard responded to Leonard's explanation. Hearing a German speak Japanese, he was prepared to believe any explanation offered, especially since he had just questioned a self-important Javan official.

Fatah had not allowed much time between drugging the guards and the train's departure. It was an express, and once it departed they would be safe. Purchasing tickets, which Fatah did, and gaining the platform took fifteen minutes. There Fatah passed Ali Utomo, the man who had preceded him through the checkpoint. Utomo had been placed at the head of Jakarta's police force, although like Fatah he took orders from a Japanese controller. Fatah had known him slightly in his pre-war incarnation as a customs clerk. Fatah, hoping to avoid a conversation, placed his hands together and nodded as the two men passed. Utomo did not acknowledge him.

*

*   *

As the train inched around a hilltop before crossing a final, long trestle into Bandung, Leonard and Anneke jumped off into the night. They watched the last car recede across a deep valley. A machine gun pointed vacantly in the train's wake as two Japanese guards discussed Bandung's night life. The hegira had been made in isolation. The *réfugiés* were alone in their car, and no one had checked their tickets or papers. There was no need to patrol an express train.

Fatah's plan was uncomplicated. He would settle his family, and in three days he would meet Leonard and Anneke at the Bosscha Observatory, located on a hilltop about fifteen kilometers outside Bandung. Fatah would bring a Geiger counter, assuming that he could find one at the Bandung TH. They would then set off to prospect for uranium on Tangkuban Perahu, the mountain in the shape of an overturned boat. Fortune would preserve the Europeans until he encountered them again.

Anneke guessed that Lembang was about thirty kilometers from where she and Leonard stood. She had looked through

Fatah's maps on the train. They might make half the distance by dawn. She looked down at the main constraint. Fatah had not thought to provide her with sandals. Weeks of hospital drudgery had thickened her skin, but it would be folly to attempt a long journey unshod.

"We must get to the road in the valley," she looked earnestly at Leonard.

"Relax," he smiled. "I'll carry you down." The army had trained him to carry a hundred-pound pack, and before the war in Wyoming he had managed that weight during winter mountaineering. He stripped to the waist. Anneke climbed aboard piggyback and held tunic and pistol above his neck.

Leonard's boots found relatively secure purchase, and his trousers allowed him to ignore low brush. The hillside, like everything else on Java, was in a state of continual erosion. Ravines of exposed earth were everywhere. Leonard found that Anneke's weight caused him to slide. After thirty feet it was apparent that she would do better on her own. Leonard took back his costume. After a hundred feet he and it were covered in mud. Anneke was an intaglio of orange and brown from the waist down. Leonard was tracking down a gulley when he slipped and found himself in free fall. He knew the sensation from flying. He waited to die.

Was death wet, he wondered? Was it like embracing a giant fish? He found himself under water and swam to the surface. He was breathless, but uninjured. About ten feet away the water spattered incessantly. He paddled away from the spatter until he felt bottom. He waded into a marsh and up an embankment. There was enough light from the waning moon, intermittently showing through low clouds, to reveal a large pool opening to a terraced hillside.

"Anneke," he shouted. "It's deep water. Jump."

Water was not deep in the Netherlands, except where it had been dredged for shipping. Anneke doubted the wisdom of jumping into the void to plunge toward an unknown destiny dozens of feet below. The doubt transformed into fear as she approached the cliff from which Leonard had fallen. Peering into the dark, she could make out the reflection of rice paddies. A primary catch-basin lay below. Leonard had survived the fall. She leaped. As she fell, her wrap flew up around her face. With the shock of entering the water, she struggled to the surface and clawed at the smothering envelope.

"Over here." Anneke towed the heavy fabrics toward Leonard's voice. He waded in to help her to the bank and then surrounded her nakedness with an embrace. She was crying softly.

"Stay by me," she spoke into his chest. "Don't leave." They were alone together for the first time in nearly a month.

After a time they dressed and loped through and around the terraces, descending with the flow of water. Anneke scrambled over the dikes easily. Leonard followed, weighed down with soggen boots and trousers. The water would contain nasty parasites. Anneke had seen the course of various afflictions, and she worried about worms and protozoans. But it was impossible to avoid splashing in ditch and marsh, and in any event they both had been soaked head to toe. Leonard, less aware of tropical disease, felt relief at having escaped the malarial littoral; malaria did not affect higher altitudes. Presently they came to a path. Anneke struck off in the direction away from the pool, and Leonard followed. After thirty minutes their clothes had dried in the cool night air.

The path approached a village engaged in a celebration. Drums and cymbals, at first indistinct, grew louder, and they were supplemented by gongs, flutes, and singing. The path took a sharp turn. Leonard and Anneke found themselves several hundred yards from a brightly lit extravaganza. Leonard's reaction was to circle around it and continue making progress toward the observatory.

"Come," Anneke buttoned up Leonard's tunic. "I will show you something quite extraordinary." She redeployed her batik shawl and took his hand. "It is Javan theatre, the *wayang*."

"This is nuts. Assuming that we won't be turned in. We have three or four more hours of darkness. That can put us half-way to Lembang."

"Silly boy. In the first place, we will need local help even after making contact with Létoile, and it is unclear if he will be of any use in that. All this assumes that Létoile is even at the observatory. Maybe Fatah will meet us, maybe not. It will not hurt to see the theatre. It starts at about 11:00 and runs until dawn. People from the countryside attend. You have papers. I can pretend to be half Javan—Bandung has a great many Eurasians. Anyway, the Japanese will not be here."

"No," Leonard said flatly. "Fatah will provide. We need distance now. It is crazy to walk into public view." Leonard's agoraphobia rose above the surface of anxiety.

"It's not exactly public," Anneke continued. "Only the stage is lit, or rather backlit. The audience is in darkness. It is a classical Javan drama, narrated by the *dalang* who manipulates puppets behind a screen. Several women will sing as *pesinden*, and there will be an orchestra, the *gamelan*. No one will remark on us. And we will come away with the true feelings of Sundanese, who live here. The songs are in classical Javan, which almost no one understands, but the puppets speak in modern Javan and Sundanese, and the *dalang* sometimes explains the action in Malay. The mythological drama, largely a battle of virtue—not goodness—against evil, is usually given a modern overlay. It is Java's forum for political commentary. We will see how people here view the Japanese."

They walked past the burning torches into the darkened pit in front of the large screen, which was filled with shadows of grotesque faces and emaciated limbs manipulated by the invisible *dalang*. The great light they had seen was an oil lamp that provided the shadow source, placed behind the *dalang*. Around the lamp clustered the orchestra and singers, some of whom were visible at the sides of the screen. The puppets underwent magnifications and distortions, as the *dalang* placed them at various angles and distances from the light. It was as Anneke said. No one noticed them. All attention was riveted on the screen. At one point the *dalang* compared the new rulers of the world with the old ones. The new ones were pint-sized and mean-spirited, whereas the old ones were merely tall and slow-witted. The audience laughed occasionally. From time to time there were interruptions from a heckler behind the screen. After an hour, Anneke pulled on Leonard's sleeve.

As they left the pit a middle-aged man said something softly to Leonard. It was Dutch. He kept walking. Anneke, however, stopped and began speaking with the man in Malay; Leonard turned when he heard her voice. After five minutes the conversation continued in Dutch. Leonard stood silent, his face as impassive as he could manage. Anneke motioned him to follow the man. After several minutes they were inside the man's home. He offered them tea and *krupuk*.

"Our host is named Soedjoeno. Until the invasion he worked as a clerk on Malabar, one of the largest tea plantations in the region. The Japanese have no interest in Indies tea. They imprisoned the owners, installed a general in the principal mansion, and stopped paying the workers. Soedjoeno returned here, to his sister's home. Three weeks ago his nephews were conscripted for labor in Eastern Java. He thinks you are German, but to him all Europeans are cousins. We may rest here."

After rice and soup, Leonard and Anneke slept on mats in the back of Soedjoeno's hut. Leonard awoke around midday with a start. Anneke slept quietly next to him, a tiny rivulet of saliva streaming down her cheek. Suppose we were in paradise, he allowed. We would live out our lives in simple and sublime harmony with nature. No snow. No electricity. Only love and ritual. And noise.

He heard the sound of low-flying aircraft, which he did not recognize. A number of propellers. The sound rose in pitch and crescendo and then diminished in a Doppler fade. Not surprising. Bandung was an administrative seat. He removed the Luger from its holster for the first time.

Since his landing on Java, Schroeder had worn it only for a day. The side-arm had not projected authority. What use could it be against a Japanese platoon or (Leonard reflected on his immediate situation) a hostile village? Pistols were effective only at short range against one or two unarmed opponents. Officers wore them to threaten recalcitrant soldiers. Leonard examined the pistol. The magazine had five charges. He removed them and checked the mechanism. Everything was in order. It had been well-oiled and was unaffected by the previous evening's swim.

Anneke watched him as he placed the gun in its holster. She had been awakened by the planes. "Hold me," she said.

*

* *

At dusk Leonard and Anneke set off for Lembang. Soedjoeno came along as their guide. Leonard's clothes had been cleaned. Anneke had new ones, along with sturdy sandals. They brought along a basket with fruit and rice. Leonard rubbed his face. He had carefully tried to shave with Soedjoeno's kris. The blade was certainly sharp enough, but its curves produced cuts and scrapes everywhere.

Their presence was not remarked on by the village adults, a sense of invisibility that grew as they passed occasional travelers. It did not derive from fear or servility, Leonard concluded after some thought. People were for the most part even-tempered and cheerful. Perhaps it was their intentional rejection of an intrusive anomaly, a phenomenon quite outside their cosmology. Leonard offered his speculation to Anneke. She laughed.

"What you see around you is a civilization as old as Europe's, and a good deal more complex. The Javans have traditionally accommodated foreign invaders, eclectically borrowing from them whatever seemed of greatest value. After assimilating South-Asian Buddhism, the Javans experimented with the Taoism of

Chinese traders. Muslims then arrived in the towns. When the Portuguese took over the Muslim forts and pushed the Arab traders into the countryside, they brought about the wholesale conversion of Java to Islam. Then the Dutch displaced the Portuguese. Each civilization left behind concepts and traditions. They interpenetrate each other. It is not at all like those concatenated Russian dolls, for there each figure stands on its own. Here everything is woven tight. When my father's students spoke among themselves about physics, they used words with Arabic, Portuguese, Dutch, and Javan roots. You see, they know that they will assimilate you. You are not a problem."

Leonard peered into the rice fields, by then quite obscure. It seemed like an enormous garden. Again he relayed the observation to Anneke. They spoke English freely. Anneke had assured him that Soedjoeno could not distinguish it from German.

"Yes, I was always struck by that, too. It is largely an unforeseen outcome of Dutch rule. Everything here works by water. As a drop of water flows from the mountains to the sea, it performs hundreds of tasks. It nurtures rice and provides a home for fish and ducks. It turns mills. It purifies waste. It flows in and out of dozens of human bodies. The notion of cyclical use and purification is indigenous, as far as I know. But it resonated with Dutch attention to agriculture and the domestication of water. When the Netherlands lost its industrial base during the nineteenth century as a result of Belgium's secession, Java was transformed into a giant plantation. Paddies replaced slash-and-burn agriculture. Hillsides sprouted tea and coffee and, what brought Bandung to world attention, quinine. Java's population exploded."

"Why was that?" Leonard asked absently.

"Nutrition," Anneke said brightly. It was her country, and she would instruct Leonard in its past. "Calorie intake increased dramatically as sugar and rice became abundant. And in addition to the carbohydrates, protein became available when fish and fowl were raised on the side. Infant mortality declined. Geometric growth took over. It is the obverse of the West, where improved diet correlated with a decline in fertility over the past four generations. You see, there has been no birth control in the Indies. Wealth is measured in children."

Possibly, Leonard thought, but Fatah had only two children. Following Anneke, that was the surest measure of Fatah's Western sensibility and reason enough to trust his resolve. Could history be understood in terms of frustrated libido?

Anneke chatted in Dutch with Soedjoeno. Clouds and a fresh wind rolled over the valley. They were drenched by a curtain of rain, which lasted only a minute. After two hours the path swung in a wide arc to the right. They crossed a footbridge and came to a dirt road. Anneke explained, after talking with Soedjoeno, that they had to follow the road for about two hours. It was a major artery, and for that reason caution suggested that they split up. Soedjoeno and Anneke would walk about a hundred feet in front of Leonard. They could talk their way out of a difficult situation. That would give Leonard time to seek cover. They would all be able to hide from a vehicle overtaking them. The plan had a certain logic, Leonard thought. He did not mind watching Anneke's hips swaying darkly in the distance.

And the stars had come out. They swarmed into Leonard's field of vision. Not as crystalline clear as in Wyoming, but looming and fecund. He saw the Milky Way, what an uncle had called, in Ladino, the Path of Santiago de Compostela—the road of Saint James of the Starry Fields. He located the ecliptic, and then his eyes turned right, toward the south, where he saw unfamiliar constellations. The stars comforted him. They shone for him on the farm in Sandy Creek, when on a winter's night he went out to check the heat in the chicken coops. In Laramie, walking home after working late in a basement laboratory, the sky showered him with accolades—even though he had accomplished nothing. He learned to navigate by the stars, flying over the Appalachians at 20,000 feet, seeking Polaris through scratched and streaked windows. He abandoned himself to celestial reverie until he sensed that the sources of his fantasy were going out. A quarter moon, amplified by intense gegenschein, softened the heavenly signs. In imitation of the moon, two headlights appeared on the road ahead.

Leonard found an embankment and made himself part of the landscape. He drew the Luger. If there were only one vehicle, it might be useful. The headlights stopped, and then continued in his direction. It was a heavy truck. Leonard heard laughing inside. He watched it go, its recessional marked by the red glow of a fading cigar end. He rose to his feet, scrambled up to the road, and stepped on a soft rubber tube. The tube recoiled and hammered his ankle. Leonard was so shocked that he dropped his pistol and skipped ten feet toward his traveling companions. The snake disappeared into the ditch where Leonard had lain.

The pistol went back in its holster and Leonard ran to join Soedjoeno and Anneke. His ankle hurt, but he felt no loss of mobility. After an interpretation from Anneke, Soedjoeno inspected the bite without removing Leonard's boot. Feet were, after all, the lowliest part of the body.

"Kala," he pronounced. Evil. The bite had landed on Leonard's steel eyelets. A thin white tooth fragment decorated the laces. The attack had failed to draw blood, Allah be praised. It was a good omen. Their voyage would be protected.

"What if the snake had broken my skin?"

"Then, my dear, you would now be drawing your last breath. We were both lucky. If the soldiers had seen my face I might have been raped then and there."

Leonard insisted that they walk together from then on. Soedjoeno stopped at a place where the road swung north and west.

"From here the observatory is less than an hour's walk, up this path," Anneke said. "I know the way." Soedjoeno brought his hands together in a gesture of thanks and began the trek back to his village. All so abrupt. Situations were sized up, alliances and friendships struck, and action undertaken quickly. The page turned as soon as the ink dried. It occurred to Leonard that the ability to judge character and intentions had value for survival in multilingual cultures. Action substituted for small talk among people who spoke many languages but had no sophistication in any of them. He had lived with this condition from the time of his youth. In addition to Yiddish and English, his mother could speak Russian and, from her time in New York, Italian.

The moon had fallen from its zenith, scattering light across the heavens and the fields of Java. A short way up the path, Leonard and Anneke ate Soedjoeno's bananas and rice by a stone fence of European inspiration. Leonard wondered how Létoile would receive them. Would he show them where to go?

"He is a difficult man," Anneke reflected, "but an entirely honorable one. He directed the observatory from its inception more than twenty years ago. His wife is German. I remember the visit of a German astronomer, just before we left for Leiden. He lectured at the TH with lantern slides. I did not understand a thing. Then Létoile gave a Dutch summary. It was about moon-light."

Anneke guessed that the observatory might not be guarded, or at least not guarded carefully. Whatever it had of value would surely have been sent to Japan. The observatory had no strategic importance; it surveyed neither rail lines nor airfield. The director's residence was unpretentiously spacious, but for the rest there were only small sheds, outbuildings, and telescope housings. Of what possible military use were the large telescopes?

"Mirrors and lenses," Leonard suggested, "could serve industrial needs, calibrating and testing bomb sights, range finders, and the like. The barrels could be stripped of their micrometers, and the drive motors might be used elsewhere, too. How devastating for an astronomer to live in the empty shell of his life's work."

The main obstacle between them and the observatory was a private club. Anneke remembered it as the place where she had met Soekarno. They passed the club, filing down a ditch on the opposite side of the path. As he watched across the path, Leonard tried to feel the ground before he stepped. Against the main buildings, fifty feet away, were a number of military vehicles. There were no guards. A few rooms were lit, and the structures radiated several grunts and squeals. They regained the path and hurried along a gentle upward slope. Then they saw the cupola of the observatory's large double refractor. Like the club, the observatory compound was unguarded. Leonard drew the Luger.

A crushed stone road led down toward the director's residence. Closer to them was a complex that, Leonard knew, housed the library, darkroom, and machine shop. Off to the left, on a knoll in a semi-cylindrical hut, was the Schmidt reflector. The large silo for the double refractor dominated the east side of the compound. Beyond it were small structures for the servants, assistants, and visitors. Apart from the concrete telescope housings, the buildings were understated and well-proportioned. Walls were half-timbered stucco on stone foundations. All had grand sloping roofs of wooden shingles, an architectural concession to the tropics. Improbably, a light burned in the library. The night was clear but too bright for observing much except the moon. Leonard and Anneke approached the building and peered in a window. Seated with his back to the window, a grey-haired man scribbled attentively at a table. A brown-and-white cat, huddled on a nearby bench, stared directly at them. It meowed and bounded for the window. The interlopers ducked below the outside sill. Now was the time to introduce themselves. Leonard went to the door, knocked once, and opened. He and Anneke entered. The scribbler pushed back his chair, stood up, and turned around. Professor Shinichi Nakamura stared in disbelief at the two European faces.

*

* *

Joannes Gijsbertus Erasmus Gerardus Létoile was born in Cirebon, the son of a sugar-plantation owner. When his father died, ten-year-old Létoile was sent to board with his mother's family in The Hague. From secondary school he went on to the Delft TH, where he took a civil-engineering diploma. Then his mother died in Cirebon, and he inherited property that provided a substantial income. Létoile liked working with mechanical things, but he disdained useful endeavor. Civil engineering had been an easy trade to learn. In 1903, at age twenty-three, he no longer needed it. He wanted to study the stars. He went to Leiden's astronomical observatory, where he took courses and helped with odd jobs until, in 1908, he received an appointment as the third assistant. He continued on for four more years, happy to carry out tasks assigned by the astronomers. Létoile should have been devoting all his spare time to a doctoral dissertation. He never got around to it, or, indeed, to writing up publications of any sort. He watched as younger men blazed through the observatory and up the professional ladder. That was not his way.

In 1912 Létoile married Henrietta du Pleissix, a young woman with relatives in South Africa. He liquidated his Cirebon assets and decided to relocate near his in-laws as a private astronomer. The Dutch had no Southern-Hemisphere observatory. He could present Leiden with a *fait-accompli* and in this way become a peer of his academic masters. The Létoiles established themselves at Stellenbosch. Joan began to catalogue double stars with an eight-inch reflector. Henrietta found the enterprise uninteresting and the conditions appalling. Joan fell to the snare of another bored matron. He divorced, leaving much of his fortune with Henrietta, and remarried. The second Mrs Létoile lasted eighteen months before she ran off with a local playboy. Létoile came to the end of the line in 1918. He sold his telescopes and tried to persuade the new University of Stellenbosch to hire him as an astronomer. He implored his former superiors at Leiden to sign him on as their South-African agent or, failing that, their junior metropolitan assistant. And he wrote to the Batavian geophysical observatory—the center of weather prediction in the Indies—to see whether they needed a star-gazer.

At just that time, one of Java's richest planters sought to become a patron of learning. In the 1880s Dirk Bosscha had been caught cheating at Delft, where his father was a physics professor. He exiled himself to the Indies, where he made a fortune in tea, quinine, and coffee. He decided that he would endow a monument to the incorruptible harmonies of the stars. He organized the local oligarchy to contribute to a new astronomical observatory, the biggest one in Dutch territory. He needed to appoint a technical director whose primary allegiance would be to the benefactor, not to the metropolitan academics who had embarrassed him.

The Batavian geophysicists, worried that their preëminent position in colonial society would be compromised by Bosscha's energies, were only too glad to bring a renegade astronomer to the oligarch's attention. They wired passage to the Indies for Létoile, offering him a minor post. Much to their dismay, Létoile and Bosscha became fast friends. Bosscha commissioned him to plan and then direct the observatory, located on land that he had purchased near Bandung. In 1923 Létoile took up residence at Lembang with a new German wife. For the next seventeen years he guided the observatory to world prominence by carefully avoiding coöperation with the astronomers in the Netherlands who had treated him with such contempt—no small matter, since Dutch astronomers were then setting research agendas in the discipline.

Létoile announced that he would retire at age sixty, in 1940. Dutch astronomers scrambled to find a replacement. They settled on the astronomer son of Leiden's grey astronomical eminence. Since the observatory had been absorbed by the colony's general secretariat in the 1920s, Bosscha's league of oligarchs thought not to dispute the choice. The new man arrived early in 1940. After four months he, along with every other able-bodied Dutchman, was mobilized in the colonial army. The government asked Létoile if he would return from retirement to take charge of the observatory, where he was in any event working as a volunteer on projects of his own. The fall of Java did not disturb the stars in their course, nor Létoile in his work. One day a Japanese captain deported him to a concentration camp. Two months later he was returned to the observatory. There he met Professor Nakamura.

Nakamura had visited Lembang during the meeting of the Pan-Pacific Science Congress of 1928, hosted at the Bandung TH. Too old for active service during the war, he volunteered as a member of the Japanese general staff's scientific advisory bureau. He toured the Taihoku Imperial University at Taipei, which the Japanese had built, and then looked into the Zô-Sè Observatory near Shanghai, which the Japanese had recently surrounded. Zô-Sè, managed by French Jesuits, was under the protection of both Vichy and Rome, and the French saw no need for Japanese supervision. Tokyo then sent Nakamura to Lembang. He would take charge of the finest astronomical campus in the overseas Japanese Empire.

When Nakamura arrived at Lembang, a military detachment had just completed boxing most of its equipment. Nakamura asserted his authority and saved the double refractor. Strenuous negotiation resulted in the return of darkroom supplies and some machine tools, but the army would not release the smaller lenses. Nakamura had seen Zô-Sè's double refractor, but it was thirty years older and much smaller than Lembang's. He spent four weeks familiarizing himself with the telescope before concluding that he needed expert help. Whereupon he reclaimed Létoile from hard labor.

"Dr Létoile," Nakamura spoke in English when an emaciated Létoile stepped off the truck, "please help me run the observatory. If you refuse, you will perish and I will be disgraced."

Létoile thought for a moment. He had already made peace with death. "I will conduct the research. You will assist me." He stood erect.

Nakamura bowed slightly. Létoile's German wife, who had sought refuge in one of the servant's huts, would make Létoile a Japanese sympathizer, so long as no one looked into the matter closely.

Létoile spent every clear night on the refractor, taking photographs whenever Nakamura could obtain silver salts and developer. These he compared with an archive of many thousands of glass exposures by means of a blink plate—he looked at one exposure of a portion of the sky and then flipped to stare at a second image taken months or years later. His practiced eye caught any small change in configuration that signaled a double-star system. When there were no chemicals for developing plates, he observed known double stars and, if they were at conjunction, estimated their period. He had enough to eat and no administrative cares.

Nakamura serviced the telescope according to Létoile's instructions. He admired the Zeiss configuration and mounting, which allowed the telescope to turn in any direction and to focus at all altitudes. Since the image emerged from the bottom end of the barrel, most large refractors employed cumbersome scaffolding to accommodate the astronomer. The base of Létoile's telescope, however, was a mechanical floor that could be raised or lowered by an electrical motor. The system allowed an astronomer to observe in comfort and safety. Nakamura played for hours with the floor, the telescope drive, and the cupola blinds. Sometimes Létoile would remove the camera from the second barrel, and the two astronomers would observe side-by-side, each through his own, 60-centimeter lens, discussing one or another technical point. Nakamura concluded that Létoile was heaven-sent, and he resolved to make the most of the opportunity.

He contrived to work evenings. An astronomer was supposed to work at night, and in any case there were fewer interruptions that way. The observatory's servants carried on as before. From time to time the army looked in. Nakamura lived in the director's residence, poking into the personal effects of the previous residents. He could not get accustomed to the enormous rooms and grand ceilings. He much preferred the closeness of the library. He spent spare moments there reading about double stars. He would sit in the library, fortified against the evening chill, while Létoile generated a mass of data. His favorite wrap was an academic gown left in the director's residence. He did not know that it was the Leiden rector's mantle belonging to the father of Létoile's younger replacement, who was then slowly dying in the tin mines of Taiwan.

*

*   *

"Excuse me," said Leonard in Japanese, "we are looking for Professor Létoile." He let the Luger drop to his side. He remembered too late that he represented an ally. The pistol at first did not register with Nakamura. The sudden appearance of two Europeans, one of them speaking Japanese, produced a crisis of cognitive dissonance, which Nakamura struggled, mouth gaping, to master. Anneke then greeted him in Malay and Dutch. She had seen more faces from the Indies than Leonard, and she thought that the man before them might be Javan.

"Are you Professor Létoile?" Leonard asked in Japanese.

"My name is Nakamura. Létoile is asleep." It had not been a good night for observing.

"Lieutenant Schroeder. It is essential that we see him at once."

Nakamura had recovered and was furiously weighing his options. The situation was irregular but not outlandish. The man was German and spoke Japanese. Perhaps he had a claim on the Dutch astronomer. And he had a gun.

"Follow me."

Nakamura led Leonard and Anneke to a small cabin and pounded on the door. "Létoile, Létoile, wake up. Lieutenant Schroeder is here to see you." There was muttering in German as the Létoiles stumbled about. The astronomer opened the door. He was about six feet tall, with watery blue eyes, crooked yellow teeth, and a droopy white moustache. He had not shaven for several days. Dressed only in a sarung, he looked every inch Quixote.

"Who asks for me?"

"My name is Lieutenant Schroeder. I must speak with you about a vital matter."

Like every good astronomer, Létoile had mastered the night. He was used to catnapping while clouds passed overhead. He could emerge suddenly from sleep and reason effectively in the dark. That was no German officer who stood before him. The uniform was wrong. The accent betrayed its full-mouthed New-York origin. But there was no mistaking the earnest tone.

"I shall be with you in a minute, Lieutenant."

Létoile reappeared in white trousers and jacket, the sarung over his shoulders. "Thank you Professor Nakamura. Will you see to tea for our guests?" Nakamura padded to the cooking shed and lit the fire. He placed water in a pot and assembled cups. It was so much easier to do things himself than to prod the resentful cook to break rituals kept by the kitchen for nearly twenty years. He often made tea for himself and Létoile late at night.

"We have a few minutes alone now," Létoile observed in German as smoke rose fifty feet away. "How did you ever come into possession of such a lovely American accent?"

Anneke pulled a face. "He is American, of course," she blurted in Dutch. "I am Professor Witte's daughter. You must show us to the mountain of uranium." Her delivery was too fast. By Létoile's raised eyebrows and oh-ed mouth, Leonard knew that she had been too assertive. Létoile evidently commanded his Japanese master, and he would not be told how to behave.

"You young people should know that my hosts play for keeps. But you have the drop on me. Do not hurt my wife or the Japanese astronomer. I will do my best to tell you what you need to know. Please repeat the question." Létoile spoke deliberately in English and weighed the situation. If the refugees from a costume ball were genuine, they could help him only if they succeeded in leaving the Indies, and he did not see how that was possible now. But if they were German agents, they knew about his discovery, and his chances of living out the night were slim, indeed, whatever his response. The only clear course was honesty. Leonard repeated the identifications and the question in German.

"Professor Nakamura does not understand German," Létoile began. "If you are who you claim to be, you know that several years ago I sent Professor Witte my hypothesis about a mountain of uranium. I never received an unqualified reply. I assumed until now that my notion was dismissed out of hand." He frowned. It would be in keeping with the feeling that Leiden had about his operation. "Now I must know if the young lady is indeed Mejuffrouw Witte. May I ask her to tell me about her family."

"Doctor Witte. My mother has been dead for many years. My father remained behind when we sailed to England during the invasion. My brother Hendrik Diderik died crossing the Channel. Is this enough? Your discovery came with me to England. The Americans know. The outcome of the war depends on it." Anneke continued, switching to German, "Oh, you know me. I remember your wife joked about my father, 'That Professor Witze, he is the True Jakob, and I would know him anywhere.'"

Deprivation and suffering anneal emotion. They impede communication of sadness in large matters. For people who have experienced too much, just as for people who know too much, small things have the greatest impact. This is why incidental courtesies lie at the base of sharing. They keep isolation at bay. They are the principal antidote for alienation. They define the essential features of civilization. France, the nation that invented the civilizing mission, based its militant, proselytizing vision on the diffusion of French manners—from the meeting room to the dining room to the bedroom.

Létoile's emotional well was dry. He had erected his observatory by challenging the authority of the astronomical establishment in the Netherlands, and he had scars to show for his willful insubordination. He had seen a good measure of horror over the past two years. Before him stood a beautiful young woman who was trying not to cry. It brought to mind the last image of his mother, holding back tears on the dock when he shipped out to *gymnasium* in The Hague. Létoile knew that Anneke was Jacob's daughter, but his emotions were so depressed that he gave himself over to his hard, analytical side, which, he rationalized, had preserved him during the Japanese occupation.

"How are you sure that I will not turn you in to the authorities here?" Létoile was a Baconian observer of nature. To ask 'why' was to begin engaging in verbal abuse right out of Wagner's *Rheingold*. Scientists were the lucky few in the world who reduced 'why' to 'how.' The grounds of knowledge were paved in stones of how.

If Leonard had followed the conversation, which except for the brief sentences in German he did not, he would have placed his hand on the holster. He looked toward Nakamura, who, dressed in the improbable robe of a Dutch rector, was now bringing tea.

"Let us continue this conversation after tea. You will like Nakamura."

*

*   *

When dawn's soft light extinguished the higher-magnitude stars, Létoile led Leonard and Anneke to the double refractor. It was constructed like a Martello tower, Leonard thought. Ribbed and monolithic, no windows and one door, the suggestion of a balcony around the copper dome. They entered and headed toward the cellar. It smelled of mold and machine oil. Chains and wires ran everywhere. Leonard made out a motor surrounded by gear trains and a massive set of weights. This would be their abode for the next two days.

When they were drinking tea on Létoile's verandah, Leonard had calculated how to secure the Japanese astronomer's silence until Fatah arrived. He could kill him or hold him prisoner and hope that no Japanese soldier came round. He watched Nakamura refill the cups. Nakamura apparently enjoyed low-grade Indonesian tea. He continually deferred to Létoile. And he was a civilian.

"Yes, very lucky to be here," Nakamura answered a polite question from Leonard in Japanese. "The research is going well, thanks to Dr Létoile. In Japan it is rare to have such facilities, and only the emperor could live in such a lovely estate. Fruit trees, water, and lovely English roses." Leonard saw nothing in the dark, but he was impressed by Nakamura's earnestness. "Before the war I spent most of my time lecturing on basic science at the Tokyo Kogyo Daigaku, an engineering school. Here I do astronomy."

Science is the very opposite of a direct apprehension of reality, it occurred to Leonard. Reality means coming to grips with vice, horror, and death. The scientist escaped to transcendental realms, formulating and testing ideal propositions where moral judgment could be suspended. The harmonies of natural law did not necessarily reflect the socioeconomic baggage of their formulator. Where was Copernicus's Catholicism in his heliocentric system? Did he not consort freely with Protestant colleagues at a time when such contact entailed practical difficulties? Did Lavoisier's exploitation of the French peasantry, as a tax collector, find any echo in the chemistry of weights and immutable elements—beyond the reduction of human misery to a column of accounts received? Where was the evil in Fritz Haber's chemical synthesis? Could it not be distinguished clearly from his abhorrent production of poison gas?

The scientists working toward an atomic bomb, locked up in secret laboratories across America, could quite reasonably suspend moral judgment about their work—to the extent that they knew about the end to which their labor would be put. There they were by the thousands, applying their skills to construct a marvelous new toy. What they were doing was easier than science. Liberated from the uncertainty of formulating new knowledge, enjoying unlimited resources and inviolate personal security, they had the run of God's junkyard, welding and wiring together an enormous mechanical egg. Engineers had always to think about social consequences: Will the bridge hold under heavy traffic? Will the dam withstand a fifty-year flood? Will the landing-gear lock in place? People figured nowhere in the calculations of scientists. That was Lavoisier's achievement in chemistry. Lavoisier and his ilk were ideally suited to become cogs in a military machine.

Or at least the American scientists were, the ones whose childish optimism and theoretical naïveté projected them to prominence as common-sense philosophers. And then there was Einstein, the exquisite incarnation of European theory who struggled to pick a path through the moral minefield of the past decade. Leonard remembered him in the halls of Princeton's greystoned splendor, turning to speak and then pausing to hitch up his pants. Somewhere Einstein wrote that the world may really be governed by avarice and stupidity. "But I would not choose to live in such a world," he concluded, leaving Leonard to imagine that scientists were the architects of the world's images and illusions.

Science had enveloped Nakamura, Leonard thought as the Japanese astronomer described the distribution of double stars in the southern skies, just as it had enveloped Fatah. Keeping track of a hundred bacterial colonies did not differ greatly from observing a hundred double stars. Science must have bound Fatah to the German whose uniform Leonard now wore. Poets spoke of the Muse who brings inspiration. Science has also had a female spirit, but Athena appears in full battle gear. The militant scientific spirit demands obedience. Scientists are rightly perceived as idiots in the grip of grand mal. Their vocation continually courts disaster. How many scientists sense destruction by sword or fire, the fate of Archimedes and Bruno? Scientists imagine that they pursue truth, but truth really pursues them. It waits around the corner to club them over the head.

"I understand," Leonard addressed Nakamura. "Before the war I was a physicist. Not a very good one, however. I never gave myself completely over to the numbers and the apparatus. I always looked beyond the part of the universe that I had to work with. Scientific revelation was for me always mixed up with morality. I tried to divide nature according to human categories. But sometimes I caught a glimpse of the great harmonies."

They fell silent. Létoile held Anneke's attention. Nakamura stared absently at Leonard's boots. Night had passed.

"You have things to discuss," Nakamura said and excused himself. He retreated to the director's residence.

"I cannot be sure, but I believe he will say nothing," Létoile said in Dutch. "He is in love with this place. He will do nothing to jeopardize his position here, and informing on you would certainly put an end to his idyllic existence. He will probably not inquire about you. He will not challenge you."

Létoile looked toward the lightening horizon. "My mother told me about the early Dutch visitors to Bali. Their ship was entirely ignored by people along the shore. The Balinese universe would not accommodate a European vessel. I remember reading in the newspapers about the final battle on Bali. The royal family dressed in white and left their *kraton*. They walked unarmed toward the Dutch line, which cut them to pieces."

11

The Overturned Boat

Chronicles of the past are preserved in the kraton's library, but it is no easy matter to establish their age. Everything depends on a dynastic history, which we have only to a certain extent. Kings and battles interest me less than comets and novas. I would like to see how Halley's comet was recorded before Europeans arrived, and how the nova that led to the Crab Nebula was observed. Did the Javans use Chinese or Greek frames of reference, astrolabes or torquetums?

Joan Létoile to Jacob Witte, 4 March 1936, Witte papers,
Boerhaave Museum, Leiden

The children squeaked and cooed as they ran after the duck. At the end of the first day in the village, they had figured out how to catch it. Because its wings had been clipped, it could only waddle. But it was good at evasion, frequently changing direction. Brother and sister had to work together to drive it toward a wall and then converge at 45° angles. Depending on the bird's mood, it wound up in one or the other's arms.

Fatah was about to leave for Bandung. What a pleasure to be here, he reflected. His wife and children were radiant. He felt relaxed. He was finding his way into harmony with the world. What a fuss people made over him here. Yes, civilization. The faintly sweet smell of decomposing vegetation and sewage, the spicy-oily smoke of cooking fires, unlocked his past. It was as if he had stepped back thirty years to the time before he went away to school.

But he returned not quite as he had left. He brought stainless-steel surgical instruments, bottles, and books. He would work on the penicillin notebook. Molds grew everywhere in the village, and some of them were undoubtedly fatal to the organisms that caused human disease. He would proceed at his own pace. No supervisor, no clock, no foreigners. Once, that is, he sped the American on his way. Fatah sighed, causing the cat in his lap to purr louder. He would conduct the American to the volcano. The two foreigners would walk off toward the sea. He would then take care of his people and study mold. He had promised to bring the American a radiation counter. It would require a detour by the TH. On that point his reverie evaporated. He displaced the cat and walked to Bandung.

Fatah reached Bandung in the middle of the afternoon. The trip in was as uneventful as his trip out had been, several days before, except that on the way out he had rented a cart for his family. He ate lunch as he walked. He crossed the town to the TH campus, hoping to borrow a radiation counter from the physics institute.

Like other cities, Bandung had been cleansed racially. European men had been interned in labor camps; women and children had been segregated and set to work as slaves in garment shops. Young Sundanese patrolled the streets as paramilitary police. Fatah had always found Bandung stimulating. Now he recognized that the interest derived from richness and diversity. Wealth, channeling through administrative power, attracted people from across Java, who produced cuisines, costumes, theatre, and endless chatter. New ideas from abroad had circulated. There were new ideas now, Fatah reflected. Japan had certainly not freed Java from colonial domination, but the Japanese regime had begun to galvanize a nation. For the first time, people everywhere in the Indies felt themselves united by destiny into a common political unit. The state was the father of the nation.

Fatah viewed the new state with detachment. He saw the

shadows and traces of the Dutch regime everywhere, transformed in a bizarre and dissonant tableau. The Japanese army looked and behaved much as the Dutch army had, but the soldiers were smaller and walked differently. The Japanese issued direct commands, ignoring the consensual and mediative tradition of the *priyagi*, the autochthonous administrator class. The Japanese were infidels like the Dutch, and they also followed the faith and directives of an overseas monarch. But the new masters had added little to what Fatah found most interesting in life—drama and unexpected revelation. They had done nothing so far for science or art.

The city had developed as an amalgam of local traditions and Western learning. In the late teens, the Dutch planned to transfer their colonial administration to Bandung, located in the salubrious mountains near their richest plantations. To this end they endowed it with a Mining Bureau, a law faculty, and the TH. The colony's commercial hub, Batavia, retained its corps of administrators, the governor general continued to live in his palace at nearby Buitenzorg, the Dutch *sans souci* known to Javans as Bogor, and Bandung flourished as a retreat for intellectuals and vacationers. The institutions of higher learning attracted scientists like Anneke's father, who had set the physics institute on its feet and whose research into cosmic rays there made him a serious contender for a Nobel prize. While at Bandung, Witte discovered that cosmic-ray intensity varied with geographical latitude, a phenomenon that verified the corpuscular (rather than wave) nature of the extra-terrestrial radiation. The research succeeded through Witte's talent in constructing ionization counters that functioned in tropical heat and humidity. Even if the Europeans had been deported, Fatah imagined that one of the Javan staff would be able to lend him a suitable instrument.

The city slept in the hottest part of the day. An occasional soldier or administrator shuffled away at a distance. Fatah crossed the center and walked up the northern slope toward the TH campus. He approached the main gate. He had long held that the TH was one of the most beautiful things that the Dutch gave to his people. Its design followed the drawings of a Dutch architect with the unlikely family name of Maclaine Pont. All the buildings had half-timbered walls surmounted by sweeping ship-prowed roofs in the Minangkabau style. Along the buildings and across the campus were rough, stone-pillared arbors. The towering roofs were supported by exposed, dark-stained timbers. It was a delight to spend time in the science laboratories.

Fatah's papers had been found in order when he disembarked from the train. He bowed to the Japanese guard at the TH entrance, presented his identity document, and was motioned inside. At a small building, the groundskeeper's house, he asked for directions to the physics institute; he knew the way, but thought it better to be accompanied. The bald head who looked out had been there from the school's inception. Now bent and frail, he was glad to speak Dutch. The groundskeeper was not sure if Fatah would find the instrument he wanted. The Japanese had removed much of their equipment, even shovels and trowels, but some things remained. There were plans to turn the TH over to the collaborationist regime of Soekarno and Hatta. He was the only "Dutchman" left.

The main room of the physics institute was covered in dust. Instrument cases lined the walls. The Japanese had been selective in what they claimed as tribute. Fatah saw that the optical equipment was gone. Not a telescope, theodolite, spectroscope, or optical bench remained. Yet a pendulum clock hung silently on one wall next to a thermometer and barometer. In another glass case there were a few small electrometers and batteries, along with stray resistors and capacitors. A German periodical chart of the chemical elements hung over the entrance door. Reference books remained on a shelf in one corner. The groundskeeper motioned to a narrow staircase. Fatah followed him up to a gallery that ran around the perimeter of the room under the roof. Against the timbers were storage cabinets. The groundskeeper opened a corner cabinet and removed a false panel.

In the dim light it revealed a treasure of glassware, tubes and alembics of all shapes and sizes. He then went to a cabinet on another wall and removed another panel. Here was the institute's stock of precious metals—a platinum crucible, gold foil, a large roll of fine copper wire, and a lead box that surely contained radioactive material.

They searched all the cabinets. Most were filled with papers or photographic plates. There was nothing resembling a Geiger counter. Fatah announced simply: "I will build an ionization chamber."

While the groundskeeper watched, Fatah selected a thin cathode-ray tube and connected it to battery, resistor, and electrometer. The electrometer jumped when he opened the top of the lead box. Fatah performed the experiment quickly, in semidarkness. He did not hope for success or worry about failure. Any of the components might have been inadequate—he had no way of knowing which gas the tube contained, and whether the resistance and voltage would produce a measurable effect. A merciful God satisfied his desire.

The tube had been designed for demonstration experiments. It was mounted securely on cork rings which were attached to a wooden frame, and it came with a velvet-lined case featuring a complementary storage compartment that would hold Fatah's electrical components. He asked the groundskeeper if he could borrow the apparatus for several days.

"Yes, yes," the groundskeeper said brightly without asking for an explanation. Fatah was on the staff of a cognate institution and spoke good Dutch. "But I have a problem. Look here." He fumbled in the precious-metals cabinet. Fatah stared at an enormous rifle. The groundskeeper hefted it, a forty-year-old Mauser. He explained that it was used to demonstrate ballistics. Hung by wires from the ceiling, the rifle fired into blocks of wood. Students measured action and reaction, verifying Newton's third law. Outside, students had traced the trajectories of bullets. "And once they shot a snake, in there," he pointed toward a sink. He pulled out two boxes of cartridges. "Take this stuff with you and don't bring it back. It will go badly for me if they find it."

Day was fast ending. Fatah contemplated the four-kilogram monstrosity in the fading light.

"Don't worry," the groundskeeper insisted. "I will let you out the back way. No one will know."

Fatah knew the value of back doors at imposing institutions, but the prospect of shouldering a firearm provoked a minor convulsion. Village gossip had it that there were armed freedom fighters in the mountains, men whom the Dutch had at the last minute equipped to fight against the Japanese. Now they fought for *Indonesia*, the neologism for the East Indies which had been popularized by a German anthropologist late in the nineteenth century. Mohammed Hatta and Soekarno, whom Fatah admired for his elegance and technical imagery, had decided to collaborate with the Japanese, but some nationalists, under the inspiration of Sutan Sjahrir, had not. Fatah had long suspected an underground resistance movement. To pick up the weapon would be to support the guerrillas.

In leaving Jakarta, Fatah had not thought of armed struggle at all. He did what was necessary to free the American and the Dutch girl (the Japanese guards would no doubt revive), and he was now accompanying them in their quest, but he did these things mostly out of loyalty to his dead German friend. In a few days, they would be gone from his life forever. When the German fell to the pavement, Fatah concluded that the inner tranquility he sought would come only among his own people. He wished to be above it all. The rifle was an unwanted intrusion.

"I cannot carry it, and anyway I don't know how to use it."

The groundskeeper shook his head and slowly returned the weapon to its hiding place. He thought, Fatah was the very embodiment of three centuries of Dutch rule. He spoke Dutch. He knew about science. He could undertake independent projects. But he could not relate these skills to abstract values. Javans would not fight the Japanese, even if the new regime proved much harsher than the old one. The Dutch had produced a Eurasian culture among the administrator elite, but the elite would not assert their individuality. The tribe was still everything.

Family responsibilities would not allow Fatah to remain in a state of insurrection. There was a far-fetched rationale about his present activity. The power arrayed against him could be dissipated only by spirit, the collective will of his people. One rifle was worse than useless. He could not imagine a circumstance under which it would save his life or anyone's life. A rifle would not have saved Schroeder. It would not have helped the American. It would not have preserved the leg of the poor Javan laborer whose shooting he had witnessed a few weeks ago. Fatah was not a religious man, but, in dealing with the forces of nature and humankind, he found comfort in a certain fatalism. His kris would protect him.

As the groundskeeper unthinkingly accompanied him back to the main gate with the contrived radiation counter, Fatah concentrated on the kris that rode under his belt in the small of his back. It had been in his family for generations. He called it to mind. The blade's cutting edge undulated about fifteen centimeters toward a point. The handle, dark wood with inlaid silver, curved in a pistol grip. The blade exhibited marvelous contours and colors, calling to mind the rainbow of an oil film on a puddle. It had been forged from meteoric iron, stretched and folded dozens of times. Trace elements made it hard and resilient. He knew that the kris possessed a soul.

They reached the gatehouse, and Fatah realized too late that he was in trouble. Why had they not gone out the back way? He could not communicate with the Japanese guard. The groundskeeper's explanation in Dutch—lending an instrument to a colleague—produced nothing but an intense stare. Fatah took a step toward the street. The guard twitched and shouted, "Stop, you have no permission to take that thing away." Fatah turned and felt the sheath of the kris against his buttock.

"What is the problem?" The voice, speaking in a language

he did not know, came from the street behind him. Fatah turned and saw the rotund face of Police Chief Ali Utomo.

Apart from what people usually remember about war—death, injury, destruction, starvation, terror, and boredom—we know that it mixes things up. People rise to positions for which they have little training and less affection. A school drop-out and a clerk in a dry-goods store become commanders of an American Civil-War army. A civil engineer is placed in charge of ten thousand civilians building an atomic bomb. Royalty go to work on dairy farms, prisons are opened up and then refilled, thousands of women conceive children by men whom they know nothing about. So it was that because Ali Utomo bowed when a Japanese officer entered the customs building, he became a *collaborateur*.

First he went to work in the Office of Islamic Affairs, the army's attempt to control Java by way of religious discipline. He graduated into the paramilitary corps of spies and messengers orbiting the general staff in Jakarta. Utomo had an unusually good ear for language. Within six months he was comfortable with spoken Japanese, and he could pick his way through official documents. When the Japanese commander, Lieutenant-General Markies Maeda, died in a plane crash, his replacement Lieuten-ant-General Masataka Yamawaki, in an unusual but significant gesture, named Utomo to head the Jakarta police. Utomo de-ployed his men about the city as if he were filling in a customs chart. They were highly visible and quite ineffectual, armed with sticks and uncertain whether they had the authority to issue sum-monses or make arrests. The result met Japanese expectations.

The police chief without cases to solve, without firearms, and without even a motor car visited his homologues in other cities. At conferences they discussed how best to be useful to their people while satisfying their conquerors. Utomo had just finished attending one of these gatherings in the Savoy Homann. Fired up with the Japanese civilizing mission, he was heading to blow off steam at a local brothel when he passed Fatah at the TH.

"Leave this man to me," Utomo intoned with authority in

Japanese. "He is known to me." If Fatah had understood, he probably would have let the remark pass, given his circumstances. The men exchanged greetings. Fatah explained that he had borrowed the X-ray tube to treat a man in his village, down there to the south, and that he would return it shortly. Utomo wondered how things were going at the hospital. Fatah offered, Not too bad. A glorious future for us, glowed Utomo. Sure. Never felt so good. The position does honor to your physique, Fatah thought. Must go now, patient waiting. Regards to wife and kids. And Utomo watched Fatah trot off. Here was an interesting diversion for a police chief on holiday. Let's tail the physician, just for practice. Utomo gave Fatah a decent lead and then followed as silently as he could.

Fatah hurried to the intersection and on to the Lembang road. Lucky so far, but now he wanted the adventure to be over. He walked quickly under the trees and past the villas perched on a panoramic cliff. These were mostly silent now, although some seemed inhabited by Japanese. The most palatial of all the homes, built by an Italian planter, fairly buzzed with activity. That man's star would clearly rise in the coming months. Fatah shifted the box to his left hand. He was unaccustomed to the exertion, and his smooth palms did not accept the carrying handle easily.

Utomo puffed along after Fatah for twenty minutes and then stopped. He was falling behind, and the game would have to be abandoned in any case. It was a fact, however, that Fatah moved away from where he said he was going. Who was running his hospital? What was really in his box? Why was he traveling alone into the hills as night fell? These are the questions a good detective would ask. Utomo resolved that he would answer them. He turned back toward Bandung. He would requisition a squad from his Bandung counterpart and pursue the matter.

*

*   *

Leonard knew about basements. In Sandy Creek he had spent a good deal of time in the egg cellar, next to the chicken coops. There he washed, graded, packed, and stored the day's collection. His mother's house, which dated back to the early part of the ninteenth century, sat above a basement that had been excavated early in the twentieth century, and there were stored preserves enough to feed the family during the winter. It had narrow plank stairs that descended too quickly beneath the floor's hand-hewn beams.

The basement where he and Anneke spent their days at Lembang was cleaner than the ones he remembered. At an elevation of 4300 feet, the air was cool and crisp, even in the absence of windows. The basement was a thirty-five-foot circle of concrete, above which perched a moveable steel roof. At the center of the circle, pushing upward through a doughnut-hole in the roof, was a concrete pillar on which stood the double refractor. The basement held both the floor motor and a separate motor for driving the telescope, allowing it to track a portion of the celestial sphere as it circled across the night sky. There were also weights for turning the telescope without electricity. The floor's elevation was controlled by three great chains. Létoile assured them that the lowest position of the floor was still three feet above the ground, as indeed it had to be to avoid the motors, but the general sensation in the building's basement remained one of sitting at the bottom of a cylinder waiting for a downward expansion stroke.

Létoile brought their noonday meal, and he supplied an enamel chamber pot. On the first evening they sat with Létoile on his verandah. It was clear. Nakamura was on the telescope, hoping to take double-star plates. Under other circumstances Leonard could imagine working here in splendor and tranquility.

"Now I must tell you about Tangkuban Perahu," Létoile began in English after many minutes of silence. "As Dr Witte will attest, it is a volcano. The Sundanese say that it was formed when a legendary queen, discovering that she had married her disinherited son, assigned him the impossible task of damming the Citarum River and building a boat to cross the resulting lake—all in one night. The son-husband had nearly succeeded when the mother-wife called on the sun to rise several minutes early. The Javan Hercules destroyed his dam and kicked over his boat. He has fumed ever since. The cauldron is seething in sulphurous emissions, and on occasion there are lava flows. It is, however, a most interesting volcano. It may be a unique case of a volcano bisecting a granite intrusion.

"Now I am not a volcanologist, you understand. When I went into Bandung, I was in the habit of playing chess with a mineralogist of about my age who worked at the Mining Bureau. More than five years ago we began a game in the usual way, but it was apparent that he had his mind on other things. When I bore down on his uncastled king, he conceded cheerfully, reached into his pocket, and placed a strange object on the board. It was a velvet-black crystal, a cube with the corners knocked off, the size of a tennis ball. 'What do you think it is?' he said smiling. Imagining it a lump of high-grade coal, I reached out. At first I could not pick it up. I thought it was iron, held to the table by an unseen magnet. 'It is a pure crystal of uraninite,' my friend exclaimed. He said that it would make his fortune, that he had found an enormous vein on the east side of Tangkuban Perahu. He grabbed my arm, asking me to write to an academic in the Netherlands, a physicist, who could tell him about the purity of crystals then known in Europe. 'My rock ticks uncontrollably,' he laughed, meaning that a Geiger counter buzzed when placed near it. 'My crystalline timepiece.' I eventually spoke with your father, Dr Witte, when he visited here. With the Dutch *débâcle* in Europe and mobilization here, all thought of commercial gain ended. My friend was sent to a labor camp. He is not well, and I cannot think that he will survive it."

"Do you have the crystal?" Leonard asked.

"No, no. Maybe it is somewhere in a closet in the Mining Bureau."

"How big is the east slope, where he said it came from?"

Létoile thought. "The rim of the main cauldron is two kilo-meters wide. On the east side there is a large ravine, and one side has a cliff. In one place I saw a thin, dark, horizontal band. The main deposit might be there." He paused. "Now humor an old man for whom there must be no more surprises. Why are you so interested in this radioactive mineral?"

"The American war machine is gearing up for large-scale invasions," Leonard said. Nothing was gained now by introduc-ing an atomic bomb. "Not tomorrow, maybe not next year, but soon. Strategy is everything in this war, and once decided on, it cannot be changed easily. Please don't be offended if I say that the East Indies are not a high priority for the United States Navy. But if the deposit of this stuff is large enough, I think the Ameri-cans will turn west and strike here first."

They sat up until midnight, talking, and when Létoile led them back to their basement, Nakamura was still on the telescope. Even though the moon had by then washed away the stars, he walked above Anneke and Leonard for the rest of the night, fid-dling with the finest instrument he had ever played.

*

* *

They entered the pine forest soon after the crescent moon had passed over the volcano's rim. Here the road began a thousand-foot climb. The trees were apparently cultivated. All about a foot in in diameter, they formed a dense picket crowding out ev-erything else. To Fatah, who had been to the volcano many years earlier, the pines seemed to protect the privacy of the prince who still grumbled at the base of the cauldron. To Leonard the wonderlandish trees hid vaguely menacing, silent watchers. Anneke, too, had been here before as a girl. Perhaps she and Fatah had visited the rim on the same day. If she were reincar-nated, she wanted to be a tree.

Fatah walked first, in his white suit, rice cakes and fruit in a basket slung over his shoulder. Leonard carried the box with the radiation counter. He had a shoulder basket with presents from Létoile: blankets, matches, a pot, a notebook and pencils, and a small copper plate. Anneke dressed in sarung and sandals, carrying nothing and listening to everything.

Fatah had appeared at the observatory after 10 p.m., on the second night of Leonard and Anneke's stay there. His pace had slowed on the long climb into Lembang. His hands were raw from carrying the makeshift radiation counter. In the darkness he made out villagers and farmers inspecting their fishponds and vegetable plots. The rhythm of rural life continued from one colonial regime to another. What was the impact of foreign kings here? These people, who organized their life so effectively on a local level, certainly merited the opportunity of determining their destiny.

On this point Fatah entered a domain where, though his feelings were clear, his thoughts were obscure. If foreign kings were swept aside, what about the various sultans and princes who still held court across Java and beyond? Maybe make one of them ruler of all the Indies. Fatah thought that this was a bad idea. None of the traditional powers knew how to govern. Maybe a democracy, with representatives from each community. Fatah imagined a national meeting, where a dozen peoples spoke in their own interest. Fatah's head swam, as it usually did when he reflected on applying grand principles from abroad to Javan reality. Somehow we will transform the new ideas into an authentic expression, he thought.

He passed the club and reached the unguarded observatory gate. He called out in Sundanese, Malay, and Dutch. Létoile brought him to the verandah where he greeted Leonard and Anneke. They seemed healthy and rested—an uneventful few days.

"Dr Fatah brought us here from Batavia," Leonard explained to Létoile in German. "We owe him our lives."

"I bring a radiation counter," Fatah said in German, "something I constructed." Leonard smiled with admiration. While Létoile assembled a meal for the new visitor, the uranium seekers discussed their plans.

It was an easy walk to the volcano. They could survey the eastern granite escarpment in one or two days. Then Leonard and Anneke would hike north toward the coast, which they would gain in a week. From there they would try to find a sailing ship that could deliver them to Dili in East Timor—a 3000 kilometer voyage. Fatah's eyes widened when he learned about the final destination.

"Before the war such a trip would take about twenty days, counting stops. But now there are restrictions on coastal transport," Fatah offered. He wanted to ask how a boat would be contracted and paid for, and how they would avoid the Japanese navy. Returning with rice and soup, Létoile spoke Fatah's thoughts.

"No chance. Without help you will never find a boat. And even if you do find someone to take you, it will be hard to avoid the navy's cordon." He thought. "Go to my nephew's house in Cirebon. The servants there will help you if you show this." He went into his hut and returned with a copper plate the size of a small envelope. Leonard looked at it. A coat of arms with a telescope and a motto. Létoile laughed, "It is my bookplate. The *devise* is *foi et bonté céleste*, a play on my name. 'Létoile' means 'the star' in the French of my ancestors, although they pronounced it 'Lay-twol.' You see, I was destined to watch the stars here, and I am destined to help you." He drew a map indicating the address of his nephew, which Anneke and Leonard memorized. Fatah listened and thought, no chance at all. He would be rid of them in at most two days.

Climbing up the volcano's slope, nearing the end of the pine forest, Fatah concentrated on the task at hand. "Here we must skirt the edge of the forest and walk until we meet the large ravine. Higher up the trees are small."

The smell of sulphur dioxide had permeated the last part of their walk through the forest, contributing to Leonard's discomfort. He thought back to Milton's vision of hell, brimstone lakes and flying fiends. The smell grew stronger as they left the road behind, and Leonard detected what could not be: snow. The trees and rocks ahead glimmered faintly in the moonlight with white confection. As they walked into the whiteness, Leonard saw that it was precipitated sulphur. Farther along trees and scrub were denuded. They had died with their outstretched branches imploring the gods to deliver them from Lucifer's poisonous cloud.

The ravine was three miles long, and it stretched down the volcano's entire flank. The granite cliff formed its north wall. They would climb to its high point, just below the rim, and then descend, taking radiation measurements every hundred feet. If there were a massive uranium vein in the exposed granite cliff, crystals like the one Létoile described would have washed down into the stream bed on the floor of the ravine. If they were lucky, Fatah's electrometer would reveal what they could not see.

After studying their edge of the ravine, Leonard found a spot where they could begin descending. He thought it best not to follow the edge to its apex near the volcano's cauldron. The ground was a stark moonscape. They risked discovery by the Japanese, who surely manned a pre-war observation post at the summit. After five minutes of slipping and fumbling in roots and vines, with great concern about the box holding Fatah's counter, Leonard thought the better of it. He proposed that they rest just below the cliffs, waiting until dawn to make their descent. The green vegetation inside the ravine would hide their movements from inquiring eyes. Fatah and Anneke were glad to stop. Leonard found a narrow ledge formed by an enormous root. He passed out the blankets. They ate and then huddled, waiting for the light, serenaded by the whistles of a hundred thousand bats, eager to feast on fruit and insects.

*

* *

"So, Bung Ali," the Bandung police chief began with familiarity, "you think that there is something wrong with the medical doctor's story."

Koiso Minami had been in the military police for many years, serving both in Korea and on Taiwan. He knew that it was best to hear out the tale of a *collaborateur*. In the past he had even acted on collaborationist suspicions, not because of evidence or compelling reason, but rather for the indigene in question to experience the exercise of power. He always tried to avoid unpleasant consequences, but in the end the allegiance of a supporter was worth more than the agony of an innocent victim.

"It is like this," Utomo began slowly. "What is a medical doctor from Jakarta doing at the TH? He is carrying a strange box. I see him walking away from the direction he pointed at first. So I think maybe something is wrong in Jakarta," he used the new name.

"How can I help you?"

"Please, I want to telephone my office and ask about this man."

Minami sighed and pushed the telephone to Utomo. Slowly a case is built up. This one said something. That one said something else. The man came home late one evening. A radio was heard near his home. He is seen with strangers. Maybe he has a mistress. Perhaps he is experimenting with a new religion. Nothing in itself unusual, but a dossier grows, and the man is called in for interrogation. Minami twisted uncomfortably in his chair. Other matters called for his attention. Just that morning he learned that the general staff in Tokyo was sending a man to Bandung to look into the records of the Mining Bureau. Minami was asked to spruce the place up. Whenever the military did not know how to proceed, it called on the police chief.

Utomo put down the receiver. "My associates will ask at

the doctor's hospital. Did you hear about the shooting of a European in Jakarta? They say he was a German. It happened right in front of the hospital. They will call me here tomorrow with news."

Minami greeted Utomo with intensity when they met the following afternoon. A doctor had been dismissed from the medical-school hospital. The doctor had spent much time with the dead German. He and his family had disappeared. And more, two prisoners in the doctor's hospital had escaped. They were Europeans. Utomo looked pleased. The dismissed doctor was Fatah.

"Yes, yes, I saw the doctor with two Europeans at the Jakarta train station," Utomo said quickly. "He helped them escape. I know it. He betrays the great goals of the Triple-A Movement."

Minami smiled. Here was a native who might actually believe the movement's propaganda. Minami believed that Japan was the leader, protector, and light of Asia—the three A's—but he knew that the slogan could not possibly form the basis of a mass organization.

"We must bring him in." Conviction rang in Utomo's voice.

Maybe so, Minami thought. There would be no harm in it. He would be complimented in the unlikely event that Utomo did find the renegade doctor.

"Let us assume the worst case," Minami began, "that the doctor and his European associates want to meet with the terrorists in the mountains. We have thought for some time that there was a terrorist cell in the lava caves on the Overturned Boat." He could get Utomo off his back by sending him on a quest. It would not hurt to tweak the army commander under whose control the volcano fell. "I will send you out with some of my men." He rose and walked with Utomo into a neighboring office where he instructed the adjutant to have a truck crew conduct the Jakarta chief around the volcano.

"Good hunting," he bowed stiffly to Utomo.

Utomo left the next morning. Three hours later, he and his detail were passing through the volcano's pine forest. The night's mists dissolved in the day, walls of fog becoming wispy trails and then in an instant evaporating. The detail were Japanese military police. They drove the truck and they shouldered rifles. Utomo was along for the ride. They reached the rim and piled into a watchtower. It had been erected by the Dutch as a tourist attraction on the site of a volcanological observatory. It was three stories of stone, with a large room for a restaurant. The scientific instruments, unmanned since the fall of the Netherlands, had been shipped to Japan. The edifice had radiated Dutch culture—scientific, architectural, and gastronomical; now it was simply a military observation post. Curses and banter greeted the new arrivals.

Utomo crossed the stone terrace that opened out on a panoramic view of the cauldron. The mist, extending tendrils toward the rim, had settled into the crater. It mixed with a creamier miasma exuded by an enormous sulphur pit. Dark brown gas or smoke spewed near the cauldron's center. Sulphurous clouds vented outside the rim, and, pushed by the wind, flowed over the top and down along the inside slopes. Peering into a vision of hell, Utomo felt the ground shake. He imagined that the god beneath the volcano turned over in his sleep. Walking into the volcano would be a terrifying prospect. Utomo wondered if the terrorists chose it as their abode with this thought in mind.

He turned to scan the valley. It was his land. The Japanese had promised independence after the Europeans had been defeated. They were human, after all. Utomo imagined what a great and rich country Japan must be to have defeated the Dutch. Banana trees and motorcars everywhere. How proud Japanese mothers must be of their sons. He wondered what Japanese women were like. His eyes dropped and followed a ravine that sliced up the slope to the left of where he stood, about two hundred meters distant. Mists trailed languorously from vents in its dark recesses.

Ali Utomo saw what appeared to be an enormous grey bird floating down from the ravine's far side and into the chasm's

night. It could have been a giant eagle. Or, maybe, the legendary firebird, Garuda. He walked forward for a closer look. There
was a man clinging to the cliff, slowly edging his way down a
dark band of rock.

*

*   *

Fatah and Anneke could not see Utomo. They were hidden in the
ravine's shadows by a bubbling hot spring. Leonard was on the
rock face about a hundred feet above them, completely exposed
in the morning sun. He swung on handholds and ledges until he
found a vertical crack that served as his ladder. In five minutes
he scrambled to the floor. Anneke held the blanket, which showed
scrapings from large uraninite crystals.

With first light they had descended to the hot, salty stream
that occupied the ravine's base. The slope's white moonscape
gave way to luxuriant verdancy on the way down, large trees and
vines anchored into the sides, reaching out into the chasm. Roots
and branches, which would have sent the threesome to their death
in the dark, offered secure purchase early in the morning. They
negotiated a grand and irregularly spaced staircase. At the bottom, the water flowed around fallen boulders and tree limbs. They
tramped their way upstream. Mosses and ferns covered the
ravine's sides. Between major obstacles the path forward was
uncomplicated. Sulphur dioxide hung in the air, but not as intensely as on the slope. They faced into a light wind, which
Leonard found disorienting. He concluded that it was a pressure
effect, originating lower down on the slope where the ravine no
doubt ended abruptly.

On the walls of the ravine were garlands of flowers. Anneke
had seen the gardens at Buitenzorg—built as part of the governor
general's residence—but here were things quite unfamiliar to her.
Varieties of orchids, rooted in decomposing trees, sought the light
of open air, their convoluted petals so many upturned skirts and

disheveled counterpanes. Succulents extended six-foot tongues ending in brilliant red blossoms. Cousins to rhododendrons massed buds ready to explode. The profusion of color took place in an atmosphere of decay. The overwhelming smell belonged to decomposing vegetation. Anneke recoiled at what she took to be a disembodied animal and then recognized its festering purpleness as the fruit of a small vine. She watched a lizard contemplating the flies that hovered above it.

By mid-morning they had reached the head of the ravine. Leonard passed round *tempe* cakes and cucumbers. Noxious water bubbled up from a large pool. Anneke waded out and then, for half a minute, sat in it up to her neck. As she walked to shore, smiling, Leonard imagined her as Aphrodite. Then he remembered that goddesses did not appreciate private scrutiny. He opened Fatah's box. The sealed tube was a French manufacture, dating from 1921. Its glass had fogged slightly, victim of silica-hungry fungi. The German electrometer probably also dated from the founding of the TH. The battery had to be at least three years old. He passed the apparatus to Fatah, who connected the circuit and threw the switch. The electrometer jumped halfway up its scale.

"Background radiation?" Leonard mumbled absently, and then he recalled that background radiation was precisely what they sought. "How accurate is that thing?" he asked Fatah.

"Radium needles at the TH pushed the pointer to its limit," Fatah explained, "but I do not know the source characteristics. I did not have time to calibrate the counter." He looked apologetic. The wonder was that the instrument worked at all. Fatah carried the box around the hot spring.

"It is stronger on the other side," he announced. Granite would reasonably radiate more intensely than lava and ash, the constituents of the wall they had scrambled down. Leonard studied the granite face, the top part of which gleamed in the morning sun. For the most part it was grey, but about a hundred feet from the top there was a dark band running the entire length of their ravine. Easier to inspect the band than to prospect for crystals in the stream.

Leonard scrambled up the granite face, a blanket in his shoulder basket. He climbed on roots and trees for twenty feet, where the granite face relegated vegetation to cracks and ledges. Up a chimney for forty feet, then over to a broad but denuded ledge. He was still thirty feet from the dark band and sweating profusely in the bright sunlight. The face relented to a 60° slope. He loped toward the band and then followed a crack until he was upon it. The crack sliced into the band, allowing it to weather. He beheld an array of octahedral black crystals. With his left hand wedged in the crack, he took the Luger, which he had forgotten to leave at the bottom, and chipped at the formation with the handle. He dislodged several fist-sized crystals and flipped them into his basket. He scraped out a handful of smaller material for a trousers pocket. As he turned to descend he caught a metallic glint on the far rim of the ravine. It belonged to Ali Utomo's buttons.

With that visual stimulus, Leonard lost his balance and grasped for a purchase. Rules of comportment vary wildly from place to place, but laws of physics are the same everywhere. The basket pitched forward and back, discharging its hard and soft contents. Leonard watched in horror as the blanket fluttered into the ravine's shadow.

*

*   *

Ali Utomo scrutinized the ravine bottom. At least two figures scrambled downstream. He did not know what the large object had been, but he was sure that the people down there had no legitimate business. "Terrorists," he cried as he ran into the observatory's mess. Lieutenant Noboru Hashimoto looked up from a novel. The soldiers and the policemen continued joking. "I saw them in the ravine. Two of them. We can capture them."

"Occasionally local people hunt lizards and birds' eggs,"

Hashimoto observed.

"I saw the terrorists," Utomo insisted. "They had guns."

Nothing receives attention quicker than a rod. The Japanese army wanted eventually to arm natives in a militia for use against possible invasion by the Europeans, but firearms had remained in the hands of the conquerors, except for the terrorists in the mountains, whom the army was trying to infiltrate, or at least isolate. Hashimoto looked at his watch. Ten o'clock. There might be some sport in it—birders or murderers. He put down the book and rose to his feet. "Well, men, what do you say we catch these fleeting spirits?"

The plan was the simplest one that Hashimoto could devise. He had three of Utomo's men walk down each side of the ravine, occasionally shooting into the stream. He drove Utomo's truck near the ravine's outlet, where it joined a broader valley, and strung out his own men in a picket across the 200-meter mouth. He returned to the truck, parked by a bluff that served as the mouth's first incisor, and waited for results from his beaters.

The three prospectors had a ten-minute advantage. Leonard's big crystals had gone to the bottom of the hot spring, but the scrapings in his pocket pinned the needle on Fatah's electrometer. Leonard was prescient enough to rip off his trousers and signal to his companions that they had best flee downstream. They ran along on moss, over and around boulders and fallen trees, sliding down cataracts and wading through crystalline fantasies of sublimated salts. Their progress, painfully slow, still kept them ahead of the beaters, for while the men at the top had a relatively clear path, they were frequently obliged to undertake long detours around and occasionally across secondary ravines. After two hours Fatah, who had carefully dropped his ionization counter in the hot spring, pointed to the end of the ravine's cliffs.

They could run down the stream, which issued more or less in the center of the ravine's mouth, and hope to avoid shooters on the cliffs, but Leonard decided to hug the ravine's right side. If they gained the larger valley, they would be exposed to full view and suffer withering fire. For whatever was in store, it would be best to eat. Standing in his shorts, Leonard handed Anneke and Fatah some rice and fruit. Higher up the ravine came rifle shots. He led the way to the ravine's right bank. The three filed along the crease where the cliff met the valley. The crease turned suddenly and Leonard saw, a hundred feet away, Hashimoto leaning on the hood of a truck, absorbed in a small book. A dirt track stretched toward the left. The Japanese officer raised his hand in protest against an insect's lunch. Then the ground shook violently and, with an elephantine roar, the sun went out.

Increasing microseismic activity, had it been monitored, might have foretold a volcanic eruption. The slowly rising lava dome in one quadrant of the cauldron should have been detected. The soldiers on the rim, however, were uninterested in chronicling natural wonders, and for them a smoldering volcano was less exotic than the women of Bandung. Ground tremors are familiar to all residents of Japan, and many Japanese live under a volcano. Having no control over acts of nature, one simply reacts to them. Divine retribution is risked, in any case, by preparing for future calamity. Tax auditors and traffic police derive from a citizen's pact with the state, but insurance agents, who earn their living from intangible fear, are as bats—demons from hell.

Leonard threw himself to the ground. His companions stood quaking. Their survival depended on the intensity of the eruption, the direction of the plume and its asphyxiating gases, the possibility of mudslides and lava flows. Later in the century, Indonesian geologists wrote this about what happened. The event produced only one dislocation: Half the mountain's massive granite intrusion crumbled into a ravine, there to be buried by a hundred meters of lava. The plume drifted east and cleared within a week. The sides of the Overturned Boat realigned themselves, like the collapsing walls of a sand castle by the sea. No one recorded the demise of Ali Utomo and his platoon of Japanese policemen.

A soldier came running from the left. Noboru Hashimoto tried to assess the situation. He saw the soldier crumple to the ground. Several seconds later, when he tried to shout, nothing came out but a torrent of blood. He gagged on the hot, sweet liqueur, involuntarily fell to his knees, and pitched forward. He heard footsteps and words before his field of vision swam in a brilliant flame and then ended forever.

Afterwards Leonard reflected on this, his first experience in taking human lives. It was like nothing. That is, there was nothing to it. He simply aimed and squeezed, as he had done in games of cops and robbers, and, more recently, on a military firing range. About the lives extinguished in front of him, Leonard would never know much. He could not remember either man's face. The officer had a booklet with printed characters. Did their family learn about their last moments, that they were killed by a pistol instead of by a volcano? Might there have been another way—a truce, say, after which everyone sat down to a large meal? Why couldn't everyone smile, shake hands, and go home?

Still grasping the smoking Luger, Leonard took the soldier's rifle and motioned Fatah and Anneke toward the truck. It was of all things a Ford, no doubt stolen from one of the local plantations. He was about to drive in a direction he vaguely took to be toward the valley below when he saw half a dozen men standing on the path about fifty feet away.

The men were certainly not Japanese army regulars, although some sported articles of military issue. All had long, black hair. They were armed with an odd assortment of firearms and knives. Leonard had some sense of the unusual image that greeted these men. He stood in boots and underwear. The men he faced wore sandals, wraparound skirts, and turbans. There was no doubt that he had just killed the Japanese. He placed his weapons on the ground and bowed to the intruders.

"Congratulations," a man at the center of the group said flatly in Dutch. "You have killed Japanese invaders. We have taken care of the other four men. My name is Sjarifuddin."

Poised at the center of his followers, Amir Sjarifuddin might have passed for Japanese. His skin was light. It had been years since he worked in the sun, and over the past months he took cover under mountain foliage and in caves. A compact man, he stood erect, arms at his side. Leonard imagined that he moved like a cat.

"They would not let us pass," Fatah said hurriedly in Malay. He knew, as Leonard and Anneke did not know, that the man, although a partisan, was entirely capable of killing them.

"There is no time now for polite conversation," Sjarifuddin returned. "We have also killed Japanese this day, but now the mountain speaks louder than any of us. I shall take this vehicle. You may come along."

Anneke spoke in Malay: "We have been sent by the American army to inspect the mountain. Our information is vital for their landing. Give us your message, and we will transmit it without fail."

Amir Sjarifuddin coughed. Day was turning to night. The woman might be telling the truth. And what would he do with a truck, anyway.

"We must leave before we cannot breathe," Anneke insisted.

"Yes, we will move to the valley together."

Sjarifuddin's second-in-command started the truck. The rebel chief climbed in the cab and the men jumped in the back. The occasion presented itself, Anneke realized, for them to leave Java.

"Do you know the way to the airfield?" she asked Sjarifuddin. "Now is the time to steal a plane. It is our way home. No one will expect it. You would find interesting things there, too."

"Crazy woman, get in here with me and we will talk as we travel."

Anneke told as much as she thought believable, moving between Dutch and Malay. She explained her pre-war life in Bandung, her father, and their mission as heralds of the Americans. Sjarifuddin said nothing as the truck careened around curves and snaked down the volcanic slope. Ash was now falling, blanketing the countryside in white. The driver had switched on the truck's lights, although that did not help him see. Leonard remembered the only joke in Hegel's *Phenomenology of Mind*: that dark night in which all cows are black.

12

Karma

We kept a pig at your grandparents' farm. His name was Adolf. A clever
animal, and not fussy about his dinner. After about ten months it became
too risky. So we slaughtered him. Every part was used, as in the old days.
Adolf helped us get through last winter, Adolf and tulip bulbs. The coming
winter might not be so kind. I miss you, children. I do my best to calcu-
late, every day, but I think sometimes that I have failed everyone. I hope
you have found the volcano, the holy grail of Dutch physics.

Jacob Witte, "Notes for an Autobiography," 1943, Witte papers,
Boerhaave Museum, Leiden

After peering out the fenestrated nose of the Mitsubishi for more
than an hour, Keizaburo Mishima had to rest his eyes. He had
boarded the plane that morning in Singapore. Four hours later he
was in Jakarta. There the plane refueled and set off immediately
for Bandung. Mishima had spent his life as a commercial translator for an importer from Java. He felt gratified to see the land
that he had written to for more than thirty years. He looked out
again. Most of the ground was obscured in clouds. The plane
skirted an ominous thunderhead.

The navigator swung down from the cockpit to inform
Mishima that they had begun the descent into Bandung. Mishima
scurried back into the central part of the fuselage and wedged
himself in a seat facing a heterogeneous pile of boxes and parcels. In place of bombs, the plane held cargo. Mishima had
never been in an airplane before. It was a privilege for him, as a
civilian, to fly, rather than to travel by ship and train. He owed it

to his flawless knowledge of Dutch, which he had acquired as a youth while his father was a cook at the Japanese embassy in The Hague. He was being sent to Bandung to unravel the administrative records of the Mining Bureau and especially to identify deposits of strategically important minerals throughout the Malay Archipelago.

For the most part his mission concerned things directly useful for the war industries: tin and coal in Borneo, oil around Java and Sumatra. He had a list drawn up by a consortium of major manufacturers. One of the minerals was in a separate category. The file came to him from a university physicist. He was to look for traces of a rare oxide, pitchblende. It was possible that the Mining Bureau had crystals of the oxide somewhere. The physicist provided a photograph of what to look for: a dark cube with rounded corners. Mishima would know he had the right crystal by its high specific gravity.

Mishima knew a bit about science and industry, but he had never heard of this mineral. The crystal's technical term was uraninite. Mishima knew about a distant planet named Uranus. Maybe there was some subtle connection between the stars and what lay beneath the earth. He had always suspected that the stars played a rôle in the affairs of humankind. Why else would the government construct enormous astronomical telescopes? Maybe the stars interacted, too, with machines.

Inside his windowless cabin, Mishima wondered how the airplane stayed aloft. He concluded that the machine was like a giant kite, blown in a wind created by the propellers. Early planes, he had heard, were built like kites, with wings of stiff paper or cloth. He did not understand why planes could change direction without changes in tension from a string fixed on the ground, but he felt sure that if the wind failed, the plane would fall.

The plane fell, although at first Mishima did not perceive it. The new state of heavier-than-air flight revealed itself by a change of sound inside the cabin. The proximate cause of the new sound was evident to the crew: The propeller on the right side of the plane was spinning rather differently from the one on the left. Had he known that there was a malfunction, Mishima would have thought then, as he did on every occasion when he felt mortal danger, that he was prepared to join his dead father. The pilot, however, kept the plane on a steady course. A minute before landing the disabled engine started up. They set down without incident at the Bandung airfield.

As he disembarked, Mishima noticed two mechanics poking at the faulty engine. Dust, they said, jammed the cooling system and caused the engine to shut off. In the time it took to walk from the plane to the gate, Mishima felt a thin grit on his face and in his nose. It was, he knew from experience in Japan, volcanic ash. As he left he saw the plane heading for Bandung's hangar. People going on to Solo and Den Pasar would have to wait while one of the engines was inspected.

The East Indies air corps evacuated to Australia during the last days of the Japanese invasion. It had received some machines from America, but with the fall of the Netherlands most of its activity had gone toward familiarizing volunteer pilots with small, slow trainers. Aviation at Bandung, in particular, had the character of a temporary camp. Sheds and one large hangar clustered on the margin of a large grass field chosen for its favorable winds and clear view.

Anneke Witte remembered her father's experiments there, launching high-altitude balloons carrying radiation counters. Each launching was a festive event, attracting a large crowd of onlookers. The balloon would be rolled out of its large bag and staked to the ground. Hydrogen would be let into it from large metal tanks. The payload was relatively small, weighing only fifty kilograms. An altimeter brought the balloon down after it reached a specified height, although only chance determined whether the instrument basket found its way back to the physics laboratory. Dissatisfied with this inefficiency, Jacob Witte once took his apparatus aloft in a two-seater. When he returned, he told his daughter that he had seen the entire breadth of Java. But he did not repeat the experiment.

Bandung lay between the volcano and the airport. Riding in Sjarifuddin's newly acquired truck, Anneke proposed to circle the north side of the city. Through the haze, people seemed unconcerned about an impending natural disaster. Children played, adults washed and prepared for their noon meal. Confronted with a cataclysm, a person's natural reaction is to continue carrying out routine tasks. Routine becomes a mantra to keep disaster at bay. Mice, pursued by a predator, have been observed to stop and groom themselves. Heart-attack survivors seek to reënter stressful occupations.

Bouncing in the back of the truck, Leonard rubbed shoulders with Fatah. The Javan physician, had he chosen to do so, could have jumped from the truck at any point. His intentions were, however, ambivalent. His fate was linked with the American's fate, although he could not say exactly how this came to be. Was it best to let the American act for him as well? Fatah did not know. The American had done well so far. The path of least resistance was to remain seated and silent.

The American considered options. They could try to sneak through the perimeter of the airfield, but the chances were good that it had been mined—or at least that it was watched. All things equal, it was always best to knock on the front door. In their favor would be the volcanic eruption. Against it was the certainty that word had been issued for him and Anneke. There were no other possibilities. He explained to Anneke through the rear vent of the cab that Sjarifuddin would have to do all the talking while she and he buried their head in a straw hat.

Sjarifuddin was unperturbed when Anneke relayed the plan. "Comrades," he said in Malay, "be prepared to shoot on my command."

Anneke questioned him and received answers. "He means to deliver us to any airplane you name. There will not be much time to choose. There will be less time to get the machine into the air." Leonard borrowed a hat from one of Sjarifuddin's troops and slid his bare legs under a mat.

Sjarifuddin drove the truck quickly to the airfield's main gate, where a Javan guard motioned him to stop.

"The Office for Emergency Preparedness requires a plane immediately to survey the Overturned Boat," he said in Sundanese. The guard walked back into his command post and conferred with a Japanese soldier. Leonard overheard, from the soldier, "Papers... office... verification...." The guard motioned Sjarifuddin to wait. The Japanese soldier was cranking his telephone. Sjarifuddin shot them both and careened forward through the gate.

Leonard stood up to assess his prospects. Along one side of the runway were three Nakajima "Nates," slow but maneuverable fighters used primarily for training. Leonard guessed that none of them was prepared for flight. He needed time and good fortune. He shouted to Anneke for Sjarifuddin to make for the large hangar, where, unknown to them, Ryushi Honjo just closed the cowling on the right engine of the Mitsubishi that had conveyed Keizaburo Mishima to Bandung.

*
*   *

Ryushi Honjo unbent his lanky fame to its 1.7-meter height as the Mitsubishi bomber taxied slowly toward the hangar. With its long, round fuselage and its transparent, protruding nose, the plane seemed like a cigar with wings. Honjo recognized it as one that his uncle Kiro Honjo had designed.

Kiro Honjo was the family success, an engineer at Mitsubishi Jukogyo. Ryushi held his uncle in awe and wanted to follow in his footsteps. But Ryushi had no talent for academic exercises, particularly mathematics. At age sixteen he began working in a factory producing diesel engines. By twenty-two he was supervising a production line of aircraft engines. When the Pacific war rose to a crescendo, he joined the Imperial Army Air Force. His talents kept him on the ground, supervising repair crews.

"I am essentially a lazy man," he wrote to his mother before he left for Southeast Asia. "I know engines, and the knowledge gives me a certain authority. It is all without strain. I have time for contemplation. Someday I may become a priest." Ryushi Honjo felt that servicing planes on Java gave him a better life than he had ever imagined in Japan. He enjoyed fine food and drink, and he had women companions. On the airfield even the commandant deferred to his judgment.

A gang of men towed the Mitsubishi into the hangar. The field mechanics wanted Honjo to look over the engines before the plane continued its voyage, and with ash falling everywhere the hangar offered the possibility of a clean viewing. Honjo admired the plane's lines. It was an efficient, strategic bomber originally designed to pound Chinese lines from a base in Japan. The specimen he saw lacked the heavy complement of weapons added when military command realized that no fighters had the range to accompany it on missions. The men unloaded a few parcels and brought ladders. Honjo climbed up to the right engine. A fine grit covered the air intake. The volcano was to blame. It would be best to wait until the skies cleared. A few minutes in the ash plume would invite calamity.

The men melted away, just as the crew and passengers had disappeared minutes previously. Honjo walked around the plane. Its design, simple and elegant, was rather impractical. Long-range bombers required defensive features like armor and self-sealing fuel tanks—neither of which was standard with the Mitsubishi. No one would mind, he thought, if he looked around the cockpit. He hopped in through the open bomb bay and threaded his way to the pilot's seat. He looked out the window to see a truck speeding into the hangar.

Leonard Ranov could hardly believe the Mitsubishi. "Secure the building," he shouted to Anneke in the truck's front seat. He sprang to the floor of the hangar and bolted for the plane's open bomb bay. He vaulted into the belly, Luger in hand, and stumbled over the crates and bundles until he stood at the door to the cockpit, confronting Ryushi Honjo, who had risen to a gentle crouch and was dangling a wrench in his right hand.

"I take command of this machine. You are my prisoner." Leonard spoke in Japanese, hoping that Honjo was Japanese rather than Javan.

"There is no need for that, Lieutenant. We are friends." Honjo recognized the German markings on Leonard's tunic, but then his eyes fell to Leonard's shorts. Honjo's confusion registered in Leonard's face.

"Drop the wrench and move to the cabin." Then Leonard thought again. "Are you a mechanic? Will this machine fly?"

"It did fly in here less than an hour ago." Honjo immediately regretted his honest answer. "I cannot say if it will fly in this, this dust."

Leonard motioned Honjo aside. He opened the side window on the cockpit's canopy of glass. "Anneke," he shouted, "we take the plane now. Have the men open the hangar doors wide. Take care. There will be shooting. Room for everyone in here."

Anneke relayed the message to Sjarifuddin. The Javan fighters slowly pulled back the huge doors. Their action attracted no fire. They and Anneke then mounted into the plane. Anneke found Leonard in the cockpit.

"Watch this guy," Leonard said as he passed her his Luger. He sat in the pilot's seat and studied the plane's gauges. As far as he could determine, the fuel tanks were nearly full.

"Sit here." He motioned Honjo to the copilot's seat. "You will assist me. Do not fail if you wish to live."

The man was not friendly, Honjo realized with a falling heart. A German renegade who just committed a crime of passion? Honjo looked back into the cabin as he swiveled into the designated seat. Sjarifuddin grinned broadly. Leonard was flipping switches and manipulating handles.

"Tell Sjarifuddin to dump the cargo." Leonard wanted to be in the air as quickly as possible. Boxes and parcels rained out the bomb bay and side door. Heavier objects descended in fragments.

As he stood by a bank of shelves near the hangar wall, Fatah watched the operation. What action should he take? The question paralyzed him. If his fate was linked with the American's fate, did he need to help the American? Or was it enough to be pulled along in the current generated by the American, as if Fatah were an intravenous infusion carried into a body by suction? Would his family be honored by a courageous decision? And if so, which one? He could board the plane and leave for points unknown. He could flee to the Japanese and hope to reinstate himself in their favor. He could disable the plane to speed his rehabilitation.

Fatah was of two minds—Javan and Dutch—and although his reflexes were formed in youth, European analysis had become a convenient tool, at least where Europeans were concerned. Analysis produced the conclusion that the Japanese military would not reward action against the American. Fatah had observed that they expected fealty and obedience; deviance was punished, but devotion was observed in silence. Material deprivation, and there was plenty of that on Java, had to be internalized and transcended through contemplation. The Dutch, however, honored devotion to duty. They handed out medals and privileges. The Japanese were robbing his country. The Dutch were robbers too, but they had worked in collusion with Javan regents to erect an infrastructure of dams, roads, and railways. And the Dutch ran schools, staffed by caring instructors like Mevrouw Verwoern. What would she have advised?

"The Queen is pleased with your work," Mevrouw Verwoern said a lifetime away. "She wants you to think for yourself and improve the world around you." Europeans often spoke about improvement. It determined their existence. Improvement meant questioning tradition, imagining different surroundings and acting to bring them into being. Action created new objects. It transformed the natural world.

The Japanese had succeeded in building and transforming,

as the airplane before Fatah's eyes demonstrated. Were the Japanese really Europeans in disguise? Not exactly, although they readily formed alliances with European powers. Fatah looked through the cockpit's glass at the American. What was he? He spoke German and Japanese. What, indeed, was America? Maybe it resembled the Archipelago—an assembly of many tribes that might one day become a nation.

Fatah watched as the airplane's engines began turning. The noise brought a hail of bullets. The Japanese airport staff, still unseen, had trained a machine gun on the hangar and were firing indiscriminately at whatever was inside. Fatah lay flat on the dirt floor. He saw the plane bob, as if it strained to leave through the open door. A man dropped out the door and scurried to pull the blocks from the front wheels. There was forward progress as he hopped back in. Again the plane stopped. Fatah saw the problem. The jettisoned cargo had formed a thrombus in front of the plane's rear wheel. Fatah ran to dissolve the clot.

Bullets were flying everywhere inside the hangar. Sometimes they hit the plane and the jetsam. Fatah actually felt secure surrounded by boxes and crates, as he pushed wood and canvas aside to create a channel for the wheel. It was a geometric puzzle, like arranging reagents and cultures on a laboratory bench, or making sense of numbers in a notebook. Arabic numbers, Fatah thought. Dutch digits were close to the numbers in the Quran, but not quite. Once, years ago, he had seen a stele from the Buddhist time bearing Arabic numbers. Why was that, he wondered? The crates he muscled this way and that were stenciled with Japanese characters; he knew that some of those were numbers. All this mixing up of languages and peoples. He thought about his pleasure at living again in his village. What he knew there as a simple and harmonious experience might really be a distillation of traditions having widely separated points of origin. The idea made his head spin.

The plane crept forward as Fatah worked on his knees, absorbed in matters ethnographical. When the plane was free, Fatah tapped on the belly doors. The plane accelerated. Fatah scrambled alongside it, waving to whoever might see. The plane's nose cleared the doors and Fatah, following the plane, came into the line of fire. He took a bullet through his neck, and he expired as he fell toward the hangar in a gentle arc, pushed by the engines' wash.

When he started the Mitsubishi's engines, Leonard had Anneke send Sjarifuddin's men to the gun ports. Shouts revealed that the machine guns and the canon had been stripped out. "Use them as loopholes," Leonard shouted, "I mean as windows. Use your rifles." Anneke relayed the instructions. Sjarifuddin dropped into the nose cupola and excised the empty turret, smashing his rifle barrel through the plug where a machine gun once protruded. After the chocks had been pulled out, the plane moved forward. Then it stopped. Leonard provided more power. The plane jerked toward the door in quantized leaps as, unknown to the people inside, Fatah cleared a path for the rear wheel. Then they emerged into a haze that entirely obscured the midday sun.

The Japanese had set up the machine gun on the back of a truck. They did not have time to anchor it properly, and as a result it was capable only of spraying bullets in the general direction of the advancing Mitsubishi. Encouraged by having sent a bullet into Fatah's neck, the Japanese soldiers placed their trust in the heavy gun. None thought to use a rifle. The result was that the plane's tires remained intact, and the cockpit glass sustained only one hit, while the fuselage and wings took a random scatter of bullets. The plane was moving slowly enough to give Sjarifuddin a chance to fix the machine gunners in his sights. He unloaded his magazine at the truck. Fortune that had killed Fatah allowed Sjarifuddin to jam the machine gun's firing mechanism.

Ryushi Honjo watched silently as Leonard took the Mitsubishi down the field and into the air. The German desperado handled the controls competently. The left engine sputtered.

"Which way do the winds blow here?" Leonard shouted to

Anneke. She had never given it much thought. She remembered the balloons her father launched from the airfield. They blew away from the volcano.

"From the southwest."

Leonard thought about Létoile's relative in Cirebon, to the northeast. To get there he would court disaster by flying in the volcano's plume. He swung the plane in a wide arc to the south, hoping to arrive in clear skies before his engines were hopelessly clogged with ash.

*
*   *

Poets and artists who have no experience with the substantiality of wind may imagine that heavier-than-air flight is a miracle. The Dutch, on whom the wind conferred an empire in the Far East and for whom the wind powered mills at home, know better. Anneke Witte had flown a number of times in different machines. She thought the experience did not differ much from riding in a train, except that it was much less pleasant. In both cases the world came effortlessly to her field of vision. It was all so matter-of-fact. Distant objects obscurely seen might be imagined as one thing or another. Either they disappeared from sight and from mind, or they gradually became clearer. Only at their peril did aviators project fantasies of castles in the clouds or angels in heaven. In flying, there was nothing like the imagination required for reading a book and inventing pictures for words. Air travel in some respects resembled watching cinema, which Anneke did not like. Maybe someday films would be restricted to airplane cabins.

Anneke sat in the navigator's chair and studied the impassive Ryushi Honjo while Leonard manipulated switches and levers. "This will be a pretty vacation," she said idly in Dutch. Then she asked Leonard, "Where are we going?"

Leonard wondered. After flying south by the compass for

five minutes, they had emerged into sunlight. The terrain rose and the plane with it. Leonard skimmed tall peaks that were rimmed with clouds, green-brown islands in a sea of mist. Where were they going? First, how were they doing so far?

"We need a status report, Anneke. How many people, who is hurt, what has happened to the plane."

They were nine. Sjarifuddin and five men, plus the three in the cockpit. The left side of Sjarifuddin's face was gored by a fragment of metal. The plane had a number of bullet holes. Anneke had Sjarifuddin watch Honjo while she rummaged for a medical kit. Then she bandaged the wound. Wherever they were going, Leonard decided, they would be there shortly. The fuel gauge revealed that a bullet had penetrated the fuel tank. Leonard knew that the Mitsubishi's tank had been designed without a self-sealing skin.

Had they been on Java for twenty-one days? If they had, would captains Bit and Merlin be waiting for a radio call? Could he pilot the Mitsubishi to their rendezvous? If the plane carried inflatable rafts, he could ditch it in the sea. Leonard asked Anneke to take the yoke. He backed into the cabin and surveyed what was left of the cargo. A few lengths of rope and some canvas sheets were scattered about. Large machines, bolted to the floor, had escaped Sjarifuddin's wrecking crew. A dozen drums of what he took to be aviation fuel were piled against the tail section. Nothing resembled a raft, although life vests were stowed against the roof.

Leonard began looking for an internal connection to the fuel tanks, which was suggested by the fuel drums. Using the inboard fuel would give them extra hours of flying time, provided that the leak did not grow larger. Five minutes of intense searching yielded nothing. Leonard stormed back into the cockpit.

"Show me the fuel connection," he said to Honjo. The Japanese mechanic sat impassively. Leonard took the Luger from Sjarifuddin. "I will kill you now if you do not show it to me."

Ryushi Honjo concluded that his life had come to an end.

The outlaws would not get far—he had read the instrument gauges. His proper aim was to impede their progress. He rose slowly and shuffled into the cabin. There he removed a side panel and pointed to the alimentary orifice.

"You will refuel." Leonard passed the Luger back to Sjarifuddin.

"Do you like piloting?" he asked Anneke in the cockpit.

Anneke smiled and nodded. Now that she was in command, she actually enjoyed how the plane swayed as she moved the yoke. The hum of the engines were a white noise enveloping her in a sense of well-being, like the garden conversation of her parents, regular in its timbre and pitch, as it filtered into an upstairs bedroom where she dozed off to sleep. The instrument panel, which she could not read, resembled a meadow brushed by a gentle breeze as dials and pointers moved from one setting to another. The clouds covered the green island and opened to the bright blue of the Indian Ocean. Serenity washed over her, until the hum changed tone.

Honjo had chosen one of the drums and rolled it to the intake cap. He carefully siphoned its contents down the pipe. He made sure not to spill a drop. Red printer's ink, urgently requested by a propaganda office in Solo. Take an active rôle in the Asian Co-Prosperity Sphere under Japanese leadership. Work harder. Sacrifice more. Bow low. Honor the sixteen-rayed, red chrysanthemum. Honjo waited for the engines to freeze.

The engines sputtered and stopped within seconds of each other. The new silence heralded disaster. Leonard took the yoke from Anneke's hands. Everything else responded, but the engines were cold. The plane was at 3000 meters and falling. Leonard had from two to five minutes, depending on winds and his skill as a pilot, to bring the plane down. He guessed that they were fewer than ten miles from the ocean.

"I'm setting down in water," Leonard warned Anneke. "Make sure people are braced for a rough landing. Life vests are against the ceiling." He looked back and smiled. "You will tell your grandchildren about this trip." Anneke returned with two life vests and strapped herself into the copilot's seat.

It is easy to land a plane. The trick is to live to tell how it was done. Leonard had first belly-flopped a B-17 on a runway. It was March, and he wanted to spend a few weeks on the beach in Mobile. It was a perfect landing. He simply neglected to lower the wheels. The result was a crushed fuselage, bent propellers, and an aborted promotion to first lieutenant. It should be easier on water, Leonard thought, provided the water was smooth.

At a thousand meters it was evident that the plane would not make the sea. An estuary presented itself, and Leonard guided the plane toward it. The water would not be deep, he knew, for there was only one large harbor on the south shore of western Java. Leonard imagined landing in Sandy Creek, floating down on the cedar-scented water. His mother and Sam would be watching. The volunteer fire department would be ready to celebrate with Fourth-of-July rockets. He would dive from the cockpit and swim, easily mastering the weight of army cottons. The high-school band would play as he walked up the riverbank.

Anneke pictured the day her brother died. She imagined the German pilot who strafed their small boat in the Channel. It had been, for the pilot, effortless. There was no opposition in the skies, no need to escort the waves of bombers that leveled Rotterdam. He was free to pick out targets on the ground—trains, trucks, ships. He had made a run over Haarlem and headed out to sea on the chance that the British sent over fighters. After five minutes he circled back. He saw the white sail directly on his line of return. He put ten bullets through its sails and made for the IJsselmeer. Arterial blood washed over the boat's horizon.

Ryushi Honjo sat with his back to a strut at the front of the cabin. It would offer the most protection, he thought. He had seen the wreckage of a Mitsubishi where the fuselage remained intact. Possibly only he would survive the crash. That would bring great honor to his family, perhaps even a brevet promotion. The chances were good, in any event, that the Javan with a pistol would have his head smashed by the impact.

Leonard eased the Mitsubishi toward the middle of the inlet, which opened into a large bay. He wanted the touch-down force to be taken first by the front wheels, which would skid over the water as if it was concrete, and then by the fuselage and the engines. He felt the wheels touch and then snap as the plane's weight and lack of lift drove them under the surface. The fuselage bounced several times. The low-slung engines then touched. The plane slowed and pirouetted as the right wing dipped into the water. With an enormous squeal the tail rose from the water and flipped over the nose.

Leonard found himself hanging upside down, unable to breath or see. He released his harness, and he struggled to find Anneke. Her seat was empty. He floundered up for air and found some near the foot pedals. He half walked, half swam through the cabin door. Sun streamed in through the distended bomb bay. Bodies floated in the cabin. Leonard pulled himself into the light. He felt sticky and faint. He lay down on the upturned belly and closed his eyes.

*

*   *

Leonard was rocking gently in the semi-darkness, cradled in cotton sheets. He smelled the salty, fishy, rotten-sweet sea. He looked around, moving his head until it hurt. He lay amidst piles of cloth and barrels of various sizes. Overhead he heard creaks and snaps and the occasional pad of bare feet. He rose on his elbows. Anneke, sitting in the sun, smiled.

"Glad you could make it. You were unconscious for two days. I guessed about the Japanese medicines, mostly by taste. The kit contained morphine and alcohol, at least. The worst was the red dye. When we emerged from the plane we were completely covered by it. I've been scrubbing us since then. Most of it is gone. We appeared like demons to the locals who came out in boats to see what happened."

"What?"

"We are sailing on a coastal trader. I sold the plane to the owner for passage to our rendezvous. This ship is slow. We have two hundred kilometers to travel. Relax. Sleep."

From the length of his beard (he had not shaved since they left Lembang) Leonard guessed at the time spent in the boat. Over the next days he learned that everyone else on the Mitsubishi, except the canny Sjarifuddin, had perished. Sjarifuddin and Anneke had helped Leonard out of the wreck, something he had no memory of, and then he collapsed. A boat brought the most important figure from a nearby village, the Chinese merchant. Anneke effected the trade. The merchant's people immediately began pulling apart the plane. Little would be left for a Japanese investigator.

Leonard had suffered a concussion. He carried a large gash on his forehead. After two days Leonard could care for it himself, changing bandages frequently to prevent infection. Anneke used salt-water compresses, which caused Leonard discomfort but which retarded bacterial growth. She decided against stitching the wound. It would complement the diagonal scar across his face; together, the scars projected an Arabic seven. Age, Leonard thought, was a hand that passed over a person every seven years, leaving wrinkles and infirmities. It was unavoidable. He abandoned himself to the rhythm of sail.

When Europe contained little beyond the embers of the Roman Empire and the peregrinations of illiterate tribes, the Malay Archipelago was alive with scholars of Sanskrit, Arabic, and Chinese, people who sailed in ships much like the one that carried Leonard and Anneke. The form had changed little in more than a thousand years. Planks were butted, not overlapped, and bent around ribs attached to a keel. Hemp was hammered into the cracks and the hull covered in pitch. One mast, on which hung a lateen sail, propelled the ship through the sea. A stern sweep, doubling as a scull, provided direction.

Their ship was about thirty feet long. Four men worked under a captain, who also served as the owner's commercial representative. The deck and the hold, where Leonard had been bedded among rolls of batik, were crammed with goods. The pattern of movement was uncomplicated. They sailed by day from one landing to another. At night the crew left the ship at anchor and slept on shore. Leonard and Anneke shared their noon meal but stayed behind in the evening. The captain knew that they were unable to navigate the ship by themselves.

Does love, like character, emerge under adversity? Does it grow through the knowledge that it may so easily be lost, by the apperception that life may be over in a flash? Or does one's biological clock strike ten, signaling the abrupt arrival of a nesting impulse, never mind how or with whom? We are not given much time for such contemplation, and most of that is wasted in pettiness as, inexorably, the synapses slow and the arteries clog. Leonard watched Anneke from day to day, and sometimes she looked at him. He thought: She is the one, and now is the moment.

"Did you ever think of marriage," he asked her on the fourth day.

"Sometimes. But my parents always stood so high over me. No, I mean, the weight of their station and their personalities always frightened me. My father in middle age was already bald and round, my mother I knew as a large woman. I saw pictures of them when they were young, and I even imagine I remember them young, but their growing old confused me. I worried about growing old with my husband."

Anneke had wrapped herself in batik. Over his boxer shorts, Leonard fashioned a square of cloth as a poncho.

"It is not the fact of growing old," Leonard said. "It is how we bear aging. How devastating it must be to suffer the reversals of middle age without knowing that you will live again through your children. They will make their own mistakes. But they give wisdom to their parents. Or so it seems now. All this stupidity about rocks on the side of a volcano. We have nothing to show for it. The truth your father seeks resides here, with us. Love and the family it brings, there is importance."

"You are a transcendentalist. You imagine that love is the foundation for everything. Surely it is the reverse. Life is grounded in accident, and we can hardly escape the consequences. The accident of birth, of schooling, of the particular junctures in the world economy that produce changes in the price of bread and cheese, the accident of freezing rain, of declining health, of a conversation on a train, in view of all these contingencies we have almost no control over our life. Love gives meaning where none is to be had. And for all that we still love."

Leonard believed in the importance of ideas. There were standards, he thought, even if he could not articulate many of them. "We think in one way, you and I."

A rainstorm caught the ship on the fifth day of the voyage. The crew had fifteen minutes to prepare for it. They lowered the sail and used it to cover the goods on deck. The captain dropped a sea anchor and pulled in the sweep. Everyone huddled close to the deck. Leonard and Anneke wedged themselves in the bow. They hugged each other against the rain and wind, young bodies only hinting at the sags and hollows of experience. The storm ended, and the couple separated as the crew resumed their voyage.

The next day they reached the point where, barely three weeks earlier, they had landed on Java. They had seen nothing of the Japanese, although military posts undoubtedly dotted towns on the south shore. At dusk they joined the crew on the beach. One man had caught a large fish. They waded ashore from their anchorage in a shallow bay. The crew joked about having a woman sailor, but Anneke rebuked them. The ambiance was smooth and gentle. The beach rose toward the forest. Pushed against the rocks was driftwood, which they used to light a fire. The fish was cleaned and wrapped in banana leaves. Rice was set boiling.

At dusk the brightest southern constellations appeared. Then the Milky Way streaked across the sky, undeterred by a half moon. Leonard had never seen it so bright. The fires of his own galaxy, silently glowing, lit the road to the shrine of James the Apostle. A crewman returned from the nearby village with news that a *wayang* performance would begin shortly. The captain had spread a large cloth on the beach. The crew bolted down large parts of fish, rice, and bananas and scampered off to the village in search of amusement and companionship. The captain, Anneke, and Leonard remained in the glow of the fire.

Leonard felt more relaxed than at any time since he had first turned up in Washington at Cratsley's command. He let himself imagine that Java could grant happiness, a notion that he had usually associated with the absence of human constraints. He sensed, looking into the fire, that the constraints were inescapable, whether of a family, an employer, or a state. What mattered was how one dealt with them. One could try to elude death on Java as one might try elsewhere. Anneke and he could crew for a coastal trader, or they could fade into the mountains in search of Sjarifuddin's comrades. Were the chances of survival worse here than in the air over Germany?

They were a few miles from the *Turtle*, which this very hour waited for their signal. But there was no way to alert the submarine of their presence. Ernest Bit would be listening at the radio. Emmanuel Merlin would scan the horizon from his conning tower. They would conclude, after a day or so, that the mission had been a failure. Leonard and Anneke would be listed as missing. Ernest would return to the Washington office, there to shuffle paper and reflect on Renaissance alchemy. The war would follow its course. An atomic bomb would be dropped on Germany, or perhaps on Japan. Native Javans would receive the surrender of the Japanese expeditionary force. Thousands of people like Dr Fatah could run the machinery of state at least as well as the Dutch bureaucracy had run it. Perhaps, when the ashes had settled, Joan Létoile would go uranium prospecting once more on the slopes of his volcano.

"There is no way to leave, I suppose," Anneke said absently.

"Afraid not. They expect radio contact and then a flare."

"Any chance that you could bring us out to our ship?" Anneke asked the captain in Malay. "It is a submarine. Ever seen one?"

"Interesting. But it will cost you."

"My ship will pay you."

"Fine. How do I know your captain would not steal my cargo?"

"Think. Your cargo is of no use on a warship."

"How do I know that your captain would not kill me?"

"What would be his interest in killing a benefactor?"

"Your position is difficult. Appreciate my position. I have obligations and responsibilities. It is risk enough for me to have carried you for seven days. I cannot place everything in jeopardy for the possibility of a reward. I could not take you out even if your ship carried the weight of a king in gold, which I think it does not."

A few of the crew drifted back to the fire, being lovers of women and drink, not of *wayang* and *gamelan*, and having found little in the Islamic village to satisfy their appetites. If she had more time, Anneke thought, she might turn the captain's mind. She stared past the fire into the sea. The *Turtle* waited quietly. If it approached to visual range of the coast, their fire could be seen. Anneke turned to Leonard.

"Let us light a beacon for your countrymen."

She and Leonard collected armloads of wood. The fire slowly grew. In an hour it was an intense column of yellow with a blue-white core. Sparks, small intimations of the legendary Garuda, leaped toward their cousins in the sky.

"A signal, a sign of life is what they must see," shouted Leonard. He seized the dinner cloth.

"Anneke, help me signal in front of the fire."

By raising and lowering the cloth they repeatedly sent the letters A and L. The system was crude. Leonard wondered that the intensity of the fire would have varied at all, when seen from a long distance. He drew Anneke close to him and led her away from the fire. The pair scanned the ink-black sea, barely illuminated by the wraith Dewi Ratih. Whatever happened, Leonard felt, his life had achieved a purpose. Nothing could deprive him of the feeling that he had won something, and nothing could erode his certain knowledge that each day was a gift.

Joanneke Witte thought about the last time she saw her father, before putting out to sea. The sea had boundless energy, but it lacked spirit. It could not evoke a personal outcome. One looked at it, and at nature generally, as the Javans of her childhood had viewed the stars. Personal fate was not written in the skies. The gods were too unpredictable and unreliable for that. The planets could portend the future, nevertheless. There were favorable days, and there were unfavorable days. One had to live with them all. The past week had been good to her, Anneke thought, as she searched for a signal from the sea. It would be foolish to ask for more.

Epilogue

Waterfall

I make this application to obtain documents under the provisions of the Freedom of Information Act in the name of my brother, who was listed as missing in action in the Indian Ocean late in 1943. It has always confused my mother and me that Leonard, an air-corps officer, disappeared over water far from any field of action involving United States personnel. My parents are dead, but I want to know what happened to him.

Dina Ranov Robertson to the US Department of Justice, 20 May 1976, Federal Bureau of Investigation, Internal Subversive, VIII/C/5

Find enclosed a copy of the service record of Lt Leonard Ranov. You will see that he was assigned to classified work in the United States. He was authorized to make one trip to England. At the time of his disappearance he was assigned to an intelligence-gathering mission in the South Pacific. It has not been possible to determine the objective of the mission. It is possible that the private papers of Lt-Gen. (Ret'd) Ernest Bit contained some reference to the matter. His library near Sacramento was destroyed by fire several years ago. You will be notified if further information comes to light.

Amanda Bulnes to Dina Robertson, 26 November 1976, Federal Bureau of Investigation, Internal Subversive, VIII/C/5

Anne van de Sande walked from the Eindhoven station, under large spreading trees that had just leafed out, to the continuing-care facility. The physicists at Leiden had given him clear directions and warned him not to expect much. A light rain peppered the hood of his anorak. He asked the receptionist for Jacob Witte's room. The woman spoke on the phone.

"Please wait here." She then excused herself.

*

* *

Van de Sande had returned several weeks previously from Jakarta. He traveled a good deal by jet. The more he traveled, the less he liked it. Jet travel made his head buzz, and his skin sang for days afterwards with the white noise of engine turbines.

He worked for the Royal Library in The Hague. He had recently upgraded the library's cataloguing system. At a conference in Tokyo, he explained how he did it. His plane ticket allowed him to circle the world in one direction. Jakarta had technically been a stop on the way home.

His father Wim, a colonel in the Royal Dutch Marines, had served in Indonesia during the troubles leading up to independence in 1949. Anne had grown up with a soldier's tales about Java and its peoples. Wim believed that the ultimate and complete break between Indonesia and the Netherlands resulted in substantial deprivation and misery, and that it created a lost generation.

The taxi ride from the airport to the hotel suggested to Anne that Indonesia was still unsure of its destiny. He had seen squalid slums in Shanghai, struggling to house its industrial workforce, and he had toured agricultural districts in the Chinese countryside, where every commodity and material found a station on the wheel of life. Indonesia seemed to depart from the Chinese demographical pyramid by adding a wealthy five percent to the pinnacle and a destitute twenty percent on the base. Both tycoons and beggars were much in evidence.

Anne had gone to Jakarta on a mission of filial piety, a promise made during the last days of his father's fatal illness. Waiting for the Eindhoven receptionist, he recalled how he had walked past the floorboard announcing the latest Philippine rock band, past the bevy of secretaries readying themselves in the lobby to run errands for foreign businessmen, past the French manager conversing earnestly with his *chef de cuisine*, past the safe room where he deposited his valuables, past the elevator banks. He had prepared for the day's outing by covering his exposed skin with concentrated DEET. He donned a light rain jacket with hood. He took with him a small briefcase, which contained a matter that he hoped to clarify.

Wim had told the story to his son many times. The Dutch Marines, a corps extending back many centuries, were given new life by the Americans during the Second World War. The fall of the Netherlands found Wim van de Sande on a Dutch freighter off Cape Hatteras. The ship put in at Norfolk, pending instructions from the Dutch embassy. Wim promptly enlisted in the US army, and when the Dutch Marines were reconstituted for an eventual invasion of Java, Wim was first in line to volunteer. From the swamps of North Carolina, he went to the swamps of Queensland. After the Japanese surrender, he shipped out to reclaim the East Indies.

The Dutch did not understand that the Japanese occupation had completely changed the political landscape. The Japanese had cultivated an independence movement which, once asserted, would not be suppressed. Strategists in The Hague turned a blind eye to the reality of Dutch colonial rule, which proceeded only with the active support of local regents—and this support had simply evaporated. Like their British and French counterparts, the Dutch viewed the world in the light of the recent war. They imagined that a blitzkrieg would bring Indonesian nationalists into line. Wim van de Sande was one of the tens of thousands of Dutch soldiers instructed to secure Java's major cities.

One day he found himself driving a jeep at the head of a platoon on a patrol through Soerabaya. Near the edge of town they fell into an ambush. He sped into the front garden of a large house—apparently abandoned—that had belonged to one of the pre-war Dutch traders. He and his corporal, who was bleeding profusely from the left arm, ran into the foyer. They looked back in horror as two trucks were completely destroyed. No captives were taken.

"Shall we kill them?" It was a high, soft voice, possibly a woman's. The question was posed in English.

Wim van de Sande turned from the open door to face two Europeans on the grand staircase. The larger of the two was extremely dark and wore an incongruous light red beard partially covering a white scar that cut diagonally across his face. He had olive shorts and a military shirt, leather boots, and held a pistol pointed vaguely in the direction of his involuntary guests. The smaller figure, a woman, dressed Indonesian style, with sarung and sandals, but she carried a kris in a belt sash. Her bobbed hair had the aspect of tow.

"No," the man said in English. He looked at Wim. "You are dead men if you do not immediately drop your weapons." The woman repeated the injunction in Dutch.

Following the instruction, Wim thought quickly. "There is a confusion," he countered in English. "We are on your side. We are here to protect you."

His hosts laughed in unison. "You presume a great deal," the woman continued in Dutch. "If you were truly on the side of Indonesia, then you would leave this land today. But if you do not choose to leave, then we will force you into the sea. The Indonesian people have their own destiny." She paused. "Return and tell your chief this. We have hundreds of thousands of people under arms. We are in every town and village, in every rice field. We will no longer take instruction from the Dutch queen. Your mission is completely hopeless."

The man walked out the door and waved his hands. Fighters materialized in the street. He spoke briefly in Bahasa and then turned to Wim.

"You are safe to go. Return to your barracks."

"You see, I knew them," Wim told his son years afterwards,

"although they did not recognize me. They had to be the Dutch woman and American I trained near Brisbane in '43. It was for a mission to Java." He shook his head. "They went native. The woman, her name was Anneke, became known as Harimau Putih, the White Tigress. But, you know, I owe my life to them."

Wim van de Sande took early retirement from the Marines. He began a second career with a Rotterdam shipping firm. His job was surveying Asian opportunities, and to this end he read a large variety of newsletters and trade journals. Late in the 1960s he was glancing through a forest-products magazine when his eyes caught a two-paragraph interview with the public relations director of an Indonesian timber conglomerate. Her name was Airterjun—or Waterfall. She outlined a program of reforestation and conservation. The interviewer emphasized that the woman enjoyed a special connection with the West. She had a Dutch mother and an American father, both of whom died fighting for Indonesian independence.

"They had to be the ones," Wim spoke excitedly to his son Anne. "Waterfall's parents were the ones I trained." He wrote to the woman in care of her company. Six months passed without an answer. "If you ever get to Jakarta," Wim implored Anne, "Please do look for her."

Anne van de Sande left the air-conditioned coolness of his hotel's massive lobby and drew a Mercedes. He gave the street address of Sulawesi Export where, the hotel's secretaries assured him, he would meet Vice-President Airterjun.

A knock on her door preceded the entrance of her secretary. "A genuine Netherlander wishes to speak with you," the secretary announced in Bahasa. He used the word *belanda*, meaning both foreigner in general and Netherlander in particular. Airte assumed that the visitor had arranged to come in relation to one of her company's projects, and she was cross with her secretary for omitting to brief her. She did not imagine, and she never learned, that Anne van de Sande paid the secretary a week's salary for the audience.

"I am Vice-President Airterjun," she said in English while crossing the room to meet Anne at the door. "Please sit down and tell me how I may be of service."

From a chair facing Airte's desk and looking out across the sea of low-rise buildings that formed Jakarta, Anne studied his host. He saw a thin woman with a roundish face crowned by short-cropped hair. Airte wore an elegant batik sarung, diamond-stud earrings, and a Chinese dragon bracelet.

"I am here on a commission from my late father, Colonel Wim van de Sande. My name is Anne, and I am employed by the Royal Library in The Hague. My father learned about your work from this." Anne passed Airte the journal with her interview. "He believed that your parents may have saved his life in 1947. If it is true, he asked me to thank them through their daughter."

Airte had completely mastered the art of recovery from surprise. She gave her face over to a relaxed smile while she assessed the unexpected situation. A man with a woman's name claimed to have knowledge of her parents. He would offer what he knew. She, however, possessed nothing of reciprocal interest—beyond, that is, herself. She would have to tell the stranger something about her early years.

"Smoke?" Airte offered Anne a canister of clove cigarettes. He mumbled thanks-no. "Do you mind if I smoke? It is a vice that finds increasingly little sanction in Europe, I am told, but here it is something of a pleasurable interlude." She lit up a cigarette and inhaled exquisitely as she continued to assess her visitor. The cigarette was God's gift to the administrator.

"How fascinating that our parents may have known each other. Will you tell me the circumstances?" Airte listened while Anne described how his father trained a Dutch woman and an American officer in Australia, and then how he met them again in Soerabaya.

"They called the woman Harimau Putih. The man with the terrible scar may have been the American—his voice sounded familiar to my father." Anne ended his story and waited for a response.

"Now I will tell you what little I know about my parents. My mother was Dutch, although she spent much of her youth on Java. My father was an American airman. They came to Java during the war. Theirs was a mission somehow related to the volcano near Bandung—no one has been able to explain it to me plausibly. I prefer to imagine that they merely invented an excuse to be sent to this most splendid place in the world. I was born in the year you call 1944. My parents lived in the mountains, where they fought the Japanese. They were ardent nationalists. With the Japanese surrender, they fought the Dutch. They placed me with a childless couple near Bogor—the circumstance was unusual but not singular. When I was four years old I remember my guardians telling me that my parents would never return. They had perished in the cause of freedom. I learned later that they were captured and executed. Does this help you?"

Anne nodded agreement. "I think so. I don't know precisely when the Soerabaya incident occurred, but your parents might have been taken shortly after it. You know, if the identification is certain, you may be a citizen of both the Netherlands and the United States. But I do not know their names."

"Does this help?" Airte took off the dragon bracelet and passed it to Van de Sande. He read an engraving on the inside: "Leonard to Anneke, Love."

"It is all that I have from my parents. Those are their names. Oh, their given names—you people of Europe bear appellations whose meaning is of philological interest. I have only one name. It means waterfall. My mother told my guardians that I was conceived under a waterfall. There is more. My mother's dynastic name—her father's name—was Witte, the Dutch word for white. Oh, excuse me, you know that. The name is common enough. But it was Witte, as much as her nearly white hair, that provided her chosen name, White Tigress. Audacity itself, although I rather think that Dutch intelligence never made the proper identification. About my father I am less sure. His dynastic name may have been Runaway or Rainoff—it is hard to know. He spoke Japanese, German, and English, and he mastered Bahasa. They say he was a man of prodigious strength and great learning."

Airte recalled a line by her friend Chairil Anwar: "Time passes. And I don't know where, or why, or when."

"Please excuse me now," she said. "I am wanted for a business meeting. May we continue this conversation later. Shall you visit my home for dinner tonight? Seven o'clock?" Airte extended her card. Anne accepted the card with two hands, vigorously nodding his assent.

At sunset in a taxi bouncing along a dirt road in a suburb of Jakarta, Anne van de Sande could make out new, four-storey structures, shacks of discarded construction material and banana leaves, and the occasional pre-war villa. A billboard advertised Ricoh office machines. Kentucky Fried Chicken attracted the children of Jakarta's bourgeoisie, parking their BMW and Mercedes sedans in a jumble along the road. There were power and telephone lines and an occasional traffic light. Open sewers were much in evidence.

Anne had lost his sense of direction. The taxi turned into a warren of side streets with larger ruts. The smell of rot and cooking fires permeated into his air-conditioned cocoon. They reached a collection of new homes. Each one, surrounded by a large fence, sat on about a half acre of land. The driver came to a stop at one gate and spoke to the guard. The gates swung in, and he nosed the taxi toward the house.

It was a cottage inspired by a century of colonial design, and it would not have been out of place in any tropical setting—from Costa Rica through Tanganyika to Colombo and Kuala Lumpur. A stone, mortar, and half-timbered ground floor was crowned by a steeply pitched tile roof. A few windows looked out on the immaculately kept grounds. A dog barked out of sight.

Anne paid the driver, picked up a small parcel from the seat, and walked to the front door, a massive construction of wood and iron. A grey, clip-tailed cat rubbed up against his leg. A white-

haired man dressed in vaguely military apparel opened the door
and in Bahasa invited Anne to enter. He stood on a cool stone
floor in a large entrance hall. To his left was an enormous carving of Ganeça, the wise elephant god. In this representation
Ganeça's trunk sucked contentedly on a small pot of honey. Inside the house he could see a large pool with a fountain, decorated in a complex geometric design.

As Anne strained to see into the distance, Airterjun materialized before him. She shimmered in the soft light. She wore a
loose sarung in swirls of blue and magenta, a gold necklace with
an enormous emerald at its center, and jeweled sandals. Her short
hair framed her face in an aura. Here was, Anne thought, the
white tigress.

"Welcome," Airte smiled. "Did you have trouble finding
the address?"

"Hard to say. The driver made all the decisions. This is for
you." He extended a small parcel. Airte opened it.

"How lovely, chocolate from the Continental. They are fa-
mous for it." She passed the box to the valet. "Please come this
way. Tonight the weather is deliciously cool." Airte led her guest
past the Moorish fountain and toward a terrace on which there
was a large table supporting an array of fruit and confections.
"You've come during *Lebaran*, the end of fasting. It is traditional to offer gifts of food to friends and family."

The terrace gave way into an ornamental garden. Torches
blazed at strategic points, creating a flickering panorama of angles,
shades, and colors. Airte motioned Anne toward two wicker
chairs.

"May I offer you a drink? I take no alcohol, but Umo will
provide anything you like."

"Something typically Indonesian."

"Splendid." Airte asked Umo, the valet, to bring a coconut-
mango cocktail. She sat in one of the chairs and motioned for
Anne to imitate her.

"I have thought more about what you say," Airte began carefully. "Several years ago I looked through the archives of the Algemeen Secretariaat at Bogor, the files of the Dutch governor general. Bogor, oh, you may know it as Buitenzorg, was an administrative center, not a military office. Here and there I found reports on counterinsurgency. One report mentioned the White Tigress, which it discounted as either an exaggeration or a fiction. But my mother was real enough. I am the proof."

"Your parents became very close in Australia," Anne offered. "My father remembered your mother as radiant and strong-willed, your father as direct and forceful. He sensed that both had ambiguous feelings about serving the interests of the US army. But maybe that is just rationalization."

"Whatever sent my parents to Indonesia, they left it unresolved. I like to think that they had their own mission, which was me." Airte laughed, and Van de Sande smiled. The fruit cocktail arrived. Airte guided the conversation to her guest. Van de Sande described his profession as an information technologist. He sprawled in the chair, rumpling a loose-fitting seersucker suit.

A folding table appeared before them, and dinner was served where they sat. It bore some resemblance to the *rijsttafel* that Anne knew from the Netherlands. The presentation was Asian— large bowls—with flatware from Taiwan.

"Do you mind if I smoke?"

"I have learned to be charitable toward the world's vices," Anne answered. "My sense of piety has not resulted in worldly success. My ancestors would have said that I am not one of those chosen by God. I ask myself, 'What is right?' The answer seems to be 'small courtesies.' The archangels may dispense retributive justice, but we will never know about last things and ultimate causes."

"But are not small courtesies just means to a particular goal?" Airte asked. She then explained her business, which was planning to harvest trees on farms. Her life was close to the land, like that of her adoptive parents in Bogor.

Her talent was an ability to move people. From the time

that she was a girl in Bogor she knew how to have her way. Her sandy hair and blue eyes, coupled with an entirely unaccented command of Sundanese and Bahasa, gave unusual cachet to her pronouncements. And when reason failed, she knew how to fight. Schoolyard altercations inspired children to give her wide berth. Airte had matured confident and lonely. At the height of Soekarno's power, she took the opportunity to study organic chemistry at Hanover. She spent six months in Germany—enough to learn German and English. Then Soekarno fell to Suharto, support for scholarship dried up, and Airte returned to become a clerk at Bogor's botanical gardens. After an oppressive year there she moved to Jakarta and worked for a succession of companies. She had been with Sulawesi Export for eight years. It rewarded languages and managerial skill. Airte had no desire for children and no interest whatever in taking care of the biggest child of all, a husband. She wanted to command.

*
* *

Anne van de Sande, waiting to see Jacob Witte, thought about Witte's granddaughter Airterjun. The receptionist returned.

"You may go to room 114. Prof. dr Witte will see you."

Anne walked up a flight of stairs and into the room. It was colorful and cheerful. Jacob Witte sat in an armchair, covered with a blanket. Nearby was a hospital bed. Witte motioned to another chair.

"Heer Van de Sande," Jacob said, "I am glad to make your acquaintance"

"How are you?"

"I don't know. The doctors have not told me today."

"Did you receive my letter?"

"Yes, yes. It seems I have a granddaughter."

Anne described his meeting with Airterjun. Jacob wore a broad smile.

"Anneke. She has a class at the medical school, but she'll be by later. My wife would have been so proud. The war." He paused.

Henk Cohen, child of twelve, hiding in Jacob's study until ferried one evening to the country estate of Felix Andries Vening Meinesz, the Utrecht geophysicist, aristocratic, French-acculturated, with a burning hatred of the Nazis, who collected Jewish children and kept them from harm.

"One more for the ark," Vening Meinesz greeted him. Jacob knew Vening Meinesz from the Java days. The geophysicist had a gravimeter of his own design fitted in a Dutch submarine, and with it he took measurements all around the Archipelago. Jacob met him at the harbor in Batavia. Not much fun to spend months on a submarine.

"Yes, well, I hope the waters recede soon." Vening Meinesz sent him off with eggs and ham. It was a most precious gift in the starvation winter of 1944.

The Gestapo arrived several days later. Jacob was interrogated for nearly a week. His house was looted, his papers burned. Speechless, he was taken in by a colleague. His more remote memory eventually recovered, but the war years remained a complete void.

"Let's have coffee." Jacob rang for a nurse. He loved coffee, even in the afternoon, when tradition called for tea. "Do you know what life was like for us in Indonesia?"

"I've read and heard."

"It was an idyll, or rather, *Schlaraffenland* for adults. We lived in a villa, filled with furnishings like here, all made by local workmen. Servants for everything, too many, in fact. They tended to trip over each other. The most wonderful fruit and cakes, with all manner of fish and fowl. It was something that no professor in the Netherlands could have aspired to, unless he had an independent fortune, like Vening Meinesz. No wonder they kicked us out."

Anne raised his eyebrows.

"Yes, yes, the evils of colonialism." Jacob paused. "But the local regents were hardly anchorites. They lived in palatial splendor. And it was hardly our duty to transform the place against the will of the people there. The regents showed no interest in setting up schools—not to say universities—on their own, and they had the means for it. They collaborated with us to secure their rule. From a certain point of view—I don't mean to be patronizing—we were the firmest guarantors of traditional Javan culture."

Jacob laughed. "Someone has to be on top. Anyway, the Javans found their way to technology without our schools, especially the radio and the telephone. Don't forget that we invented Indonesia. Before our administrative structure and the modest efforts at training officials and physicians, people gave their first allegiance to their *kampung* or language-group. Without our encouragement of Bahasa Indonesia, there would have been no nation."

A nurse entered with a tray of coffee and confections. Anne poured for Jacob, who held cup and saucer firmly. Anne sipped and surveyed the room. It did not contain much in the way of personal effects. A silken rug, a small desk. Against one wall was a large bookcase with glass doors. It was filled with physics books and reprints. On the top was an ionization counter (or so Anne imagined, for he knew about Jacob's cosmic-ray research) and several wooden carvings. One was a painfully thin woman standing in the mouth of a monster. The other was Ganeça.

Jacob saw his gaze. "Do you know Dewi Ratih, the goddess of the moon escaping from the monster of the lunar eclipse? And wise Ganeça, the mascot of the old Bandung TH? How marvelous, that Hindu myths and Hindu astronomy find an enduring presence in an Islamic country. I always wondered why there was no sequel to the great Buddhist centers of learning more than a thousand years ago, on Java and Sumatra. Chinese traders could have set up schools at their *fondachi*, just as Arab traders could have set up madrasas and observatories. But, somehow, it was the culture of the Gujeratis and Tamils that seized the imagination of the Archipelago. Maybe it was their arrival in a great sailing fleet, around 700 AD, that provided evidence of authority and knowledge. I wonder if our own fleet made a local impression—it could not have been our army."

Jacob paused. "Tell me again about my granddaughter."

"She is beautiful, rich, and strong-willed."

"How does she think?"

"She is careful in speech. I think that she has the gift of command."

Jacob's brow knit closer.

"So like her mother. When she ponders something, a book maybe, I watch, dazzled. Whatever she comes up with then, it always seems right to me. What do you say, Snoopsje?" he gestured to a corner by the window, where an old grey cat curled on an afghan. "Anneke moves continually, poking here and there, turning a thought this way and that. When she speaks, the room glows."

Anne had not noticed the cat before. Anneke likely resembled Airterjun, he thought, but Anneke became a killer. War is about killing. There is no justice in it. What happens is for a distant end. Liberation, freedom, fatherland, generations unborn; slogans shouted in defiance of the firing squad, during hopeless bayonet charges, before the furious rape of a defenseless countryside. Where are the seeds of the White Tigress in the kindly, reasonable man who, wrapped in a blanket, was taking coffee?

Or is it usually this way? Anne studied Snoopsje, who was grooming herself. The cat stood into an acrobatic stretch. Anne saw that a hind leg was missing. Snoopsje posted to the side of Jacob's chair and half-hopped, half clawed her way up into Jacob's lap, a study in warmth and affection. How many birds and mice had the cat beaten to a pulp?

Stroking Snoopsje, Jacob wagged his head from side to side, as if following an unheard rhythm.

What would Airterjun make of her grandfather? It would be as if Kipling's Kim traveled to England to find his grandfather in Sir Arthur Conan Doyle. A filiation of sorts—Conan Doyle and Kipling spun out splendid tales—but there would be little enough to talk about. Perhaps talk did not matter. Perhaps genes were stronger than talk. Perhaps Airterjun and Jacob would laugh in the same way. They would hug and beam in each other's presence, invisible radiation reaching across the silence of a generation.

"I almost forgot. I brought this." Anne handed Jacob a small parcel. "The physicists at Leiden asked me to bring it."

Jacob untied the string. Inside the wrapping was a small box. He opened it. A broad smile illuminated his face.

"Me," he said. "A few more copies of me." He handed a small disk to Anne. "Earlier this year they struck a medal of me, an anniversary of something. They said that they'd send me a few more." The disk was brass or bronze—Anne couldn't tell which one—with Jacob's profile. The reverse described a celebration in honor of one of his discoveries.

Without changing expression, Jacob continued: "I'll give one to Anneke for my granddaughter. You take one, too."

"Sure," said Anne.

"Oh, I want to dream now. Once that was what I sought most to control, first through Hegel and Bolland, then in the spontaneous epistemology of quantum physics. But there were two of me. The one generated philosophical thoughts in an office, while the other delighted in his family. Truth is such a stern mistress. She exists for herself alone, her own reason for being. Truth admits no compromise, but it is not enough. Truth needs love to give direction and sense. Not the love of abstract things, but the love of real people." Jacob stroked the cat absently.

"I should really see you to the door, but these days it is a victory if I can get to the washroom." Jacob smiled.

Anne thought that he seemed oddly relaxed, his face beaming, his eyes far away. He had just caught a few more cosmic rays, the children were buzzing on the quarter deck of a P & O steamer, his wife was reading in the shade. The ship had left Aden for Bombay and beyond, a family set to land in the Archipelago just as, centuries before, people from the West had sought the Indies. As Anne let himself out of the room, he wondered if the old man would throw off the blanket and skip down the hall, seeking the light and the trees and the spirits beyond, singing to himself or holding a tune in his head, a cadence for eternity.

End